AQUA

By Katherine Armstrong Walters

First edition was released August 2014

Cover and interior design by Deborah Bradseth
Edited by Heather Godfrey

ISBN: 978-1-942298-23-6
Library of Congress Control Number: 2016937898

www.snowypeaksmedia.com

ONE

The California Oceanic Alliance of Science and Technology, commonly known as COAST

Marin perched at the edge of the pool trying not to panic. Her feet already hung in the water; it would only take one quick movement to drop in, but she hesitated, heart hammering in her chest and her scuba regulator hissing like Darth Vader in her ears.

How could anyone be afraid of water?

That question had plagued Marin throughout all seventeen years of her life. The best therapists in Los Angeles had never found an answer for her or stopped the nightmares lurking in her mind as she slept. She was seeking her own answers now. Her application to be a summer intern at COAST had been accepted; she was living in a dorm room spending her days researching marine life, and all that she needed now was to pass her dive test, the one impossible hurdle.

In a moment of reckless defiance, Marin let go and tried not to scream as she sank below the water. The weight of her equipment dragged her down, disrupting the clear water and obscuring her vision with a blizzard of bubbles. She fought down her terror, concentrating on keeping her pulse and breaths even, but irrational thoughts broke through.

Vague outlines of the other divers slowly drifted down near her. She turned away, hoping they wouldn't see her face. Fighting to stay calm, she slowly let out her breath, remembering to use the regulator plugging her mouth. She sucked in a lungful of oxygen and shot it out again, shaking against panic that was simmering almost beyond her control. Another breath in, a hiss as it released.

She could do this. Her ears began to ache with building pressure. She kept sinking until the ache blossomed into pain and suddenly she couldn't remember how to clear them. Pain was increasing every centimeter she fell.

NO! She told herself. *Stay calm! Breathe …breathe …* Her body stopped listening to her mind. It hurt too much. It wasn't natural to breathe underwater. This was insane. She started thrashing, kicking, hyperventilating, her regulator sounding off each quick breath, barely more than a gasp. She couldn't fight it; the panic surrounded her and took control. She had to get out! Black spots swam in front of her eyes. The throbbing in her ears was unbearable, crushing all thought but escape out of her aching head.

She clawed at the mask on her face, catching the hose and dragging the mouthpiece out of her mouth. She choked back the chlorinated water as it forced its way inside, biting the back of her throat. She was completely disoriented, flailing, and desperate for air. She hit something solid, and hands caught her, pulling her upward. Still she thrashed, instinct fighting everything that touched her. The last of her breath was stuttering out of her lungs when her head broke the surface. She struggled for air, vomiting up water and most of her last meal all around her in the pool.

Her Uncle Paul dragged her to the cement and helped her onto the deck while her co-workers, Megan and Natalee, came to the top, slipping off their masks. They would both pass their dive test today.

"What happened?" Paul asked, his face full of worry. Behind him she could see Dr. Gilbert, the director of her internship at COAST, watching everything with a frown of disappointment.

Tears of frustration and humiliation slid out of her eyes. There were no answers. All that mattered was she had failed.

* * *

Marin lay with her eyes closed, curled up in a hammock, rocking gently as the waves lapped the houseboat. Gulls cried overhead in the early morning light. Humming came from somewhere above on deck, where her mother was cooking breakfast outside. Safety and comfort wrapped her up like a cocoon. All felt right with the world. If only it would stay that way.

Suddenly her dream turned dark. Her pulse quickened and she tried to wake up but the sun, wind and waves had cast their spell and she couldn't grasp the edge of sleep to pull herself out. It was going to happen any minute. The sun was hot and the wind was blowing. She tensed, anticipating the scream of her mother and the bone jarring crash that would follow.

A freezing shot of water doused her, and she sat up, shrieking and disoriented. Jaycen stood above her in his wetsuit, emptying his fins over her head and laughing.

"Give me that!" she yelled, snatching one of his fins out of his hand and beating him with it.

"Whoa, hold on! I was only joking!" he yelped, dodging her blows. "You looked so peaceful, snoring away there. I just couldn't help myself, Maren." He snickered, easily jumping out of her reach and mispronouncing her name.

She'd given everyone this lecture. "It isn't 'Maren' like rhymes with 'Karen.' It's Mar*in*, like rhymes with violin, emphasis on the second syllable. You know, like Marin County California?"

She threw a lifejacket at his face, still angry from her shocked awakening.

He threw his hands up too late to block it and it bounced off his head. "Ow! Cut that out!" he yelled, suddenly defensive. "You should be thanking me that I got back before Dr. Gilbert did. Did you want *him* to catch you sleeping on watch?"

Marin let her hands drop and glanced guiltily toward the dive deck.

An orange buoy floated to the top of the water, followed by the shiny black swim hoods of the diving group. She ground her teeth, angry that he was right and he knew it.

"Yeah, thanks a lot," she muttered and stalked to the bow, pulling on the anchor to swing the boat closer to the divers.

Her senior year of high school was over and she was already a week into her summer internship. She was finally making a new and different life for herself, but her nightmares resurfaced like a persistent shark. Dr. Barton, her latest therapist, told her the nightmares she had were symbolic of some trauma she'd had as a child, not true memories. Somehow it didn't make her feel any better to think there was something even more horrible than her nightmares lurking somewhere in her forgotten memories.

She looked around, hoping nobody would notice how angry and shaken up she felt, but luckily she was surrounded by strangers and she had work to do.

Until she passed her scuba test, she had the lucky job of watching the boat while everyone else explored underwater, then helping sort through fish brought up by the divers, keeping the ones they'd never seen before and tossing back the rest. Most interns fought for the opportunity to dive, but she was in no hurry to be buried alive in water, despite knowing it was a bridge she had to cross. Lowering the ladder into the water, she helped pull six divers up onto the dive deck before grabbing the net hook to snag the buoys with their cargo of specimens and hauling them on board.

Though average in height and slender, Marin was surprisingly strong. The wind caught her golden brown hair and blew it into her emerald eyes.

"Hey, pull the boat around before I lose this one!" she shouted to Natalee, the girl closest to the helm. Natalee nodded and started up the engine, pulling into a circle closer to the nets.

"Need a hand?" Jaycen asked apologetically, rubbing the water out of his sun-bleached blonde hair.

She shook her head as she shifted the hook, dragging the heavy net onto the deck. Jaycen laughed and snagged a handful of net anyway, making it considerably easier.

"I'm really ok. Go ahead and get your gear off."

Jaycen ignored her and finished pulling the net in before unclipping his tank and hoses. "So, Marin, how old are you?" he asked, trying to spark a conversation.

"Eighteen," she said, not looking the least bit interested in conversing with him.

"Wow, I thought you were older, like nineteen or twenty," he mused.

"How old are you?" she finally asked.

"Just turned twenty this month," he replied, obviously pleased that she was asking.

"Really? I thought you were much younger. Like twelve," she said smugly, walking away from him.

A large, white plastic reservoir sat at the bottom of the boat where the interns dumped the contents of the net and their bags for sorting and tagging. As divers took their gear off, they helped each other unhook and gather up the clumsy orange buoys and store them in the hull. The sun almost compensated for the cool wind, but drops of water flying off everyone made Marin shiver.

"Hey, check out that one! That's the one I grabbed!" Nick said, pointing at a small, greenish opaleye swimming in the mass of fish.

"Yeah, check out the scorpionfish I bagged!" Danny said, poking around inside the water. With a gloved hand, he carefully pulled out a prickly orange fish, mouth working furiously, gasping for oxygen. Marin rolled her eyes. "What, you don't like him?" Danny asked. "If we were selling these things on eBay, I'd get a hundred bucks!"

"That's not a scorpionfish," Marin scoffed. "Look at the rounded nose and white spots."

Danny tossed it back into the pot in disgust. "Stupid rockfish," he muttered.

Dr. Gilbert pulled off his diving hood, sprinkling more water everywhere. He was tall and muscular, with an old time flat top haircut that made his silver temples stand out against the rest of his dark hair. He had a thin scar at his hairline that, combined with his haircut, made him look a little like Frankenstein's bride, a joke not helped by the fact that his name really was Frank.

Still, his steely blue eyes were quick and he knew his marine life like nobody else. Where the others held back a little, he plunged his bare hand into the tank and pulled out the biggest fish, a long, brownish thing, with a row of tiny spikes down his back and a large, flat head. It looked like a weird mix between a shark body and a manta ray head. It hung about as long as Frank's arm, and thrashed angrily at being disturbed. Frank smiled proudly as he dangled it in front of the interns.

"So, can anyone identify this animal?" he asked expectantly. The other interns glanced at each other, mentally flipping pages of their past biology books and still coming up with nothing. "Oh, come on, this is quite a common creature off the California coast, one you should be at least somewhat familiar with!" He shook the animal a little and dipped its head briefly into the water, giving it a short moment to breathe before jerking it back up again.

Marin cleared her throat uncomfortably. She really hated knowing the answers to things like this because she thought it made her look like a kiss-up. But she also hated awkward silences and couldn't help but fidget, drawing hated attention to herself.

Frank turned to her expectantly. "Marin, I bet you remember what our friend is." He raised his eyes to the other interns, making them feel inferior. Marin ground her teeth together, angry at him for putting her in this position. She bit her cheek, not answering.

"Mares?" he repeated. She bristled at being called "Mares" by him, like they were old friends or something. He had no idea how awkward he made things between herself and her fellow interns on this program by his obvious favoritism. She never wanted to be the star of the show. It wasn't her fault she had a great memory for weird things or that her Uncle Paul and Frank Gilbert were old friends. What she really wanted was for someone else to pipe up and save her, or to just once not remember every stupid thing she ever read. It would serve him right if she just shrugged and claimed ignorance.

The silence was itching at her; she had to answer. She met Jaycen's eyes for a moment and he smiled encouragingly at her. Ugh! That only made it worse. Why wouldn't he answer? He knew marine species as well as she did, maybe better. Of course, he also didn't care how awkward anyone felt. He probably enjoyed it. The fish's gills opened and closed futilely, struggling to breathe while Frank and everyone else waited for her to show off her knowledge.

She sighed. "It's a shovelnose guitarfish."

Frank beamed. "Brilliant! Yes, you can tell by its uniquely shaped head, very similar to the end of a shovel. And of course, guitarfish because …" At this, he flopped the animal's head onto his knee and started playing air guitar in front of it. Most everyone laughed. Marin was relieved when he put the creature back into the holding tank.

"This guy will come back to the institute with us. I'd like you to keep the jacksmelts and the perch so we can test them for PCB's back at the dock. Jaycen, you and Erika stow the gear, the rest of you please sort our catch." He started up the engine again and pointed the boat toward the brown sand of the coast.

Marin sat cross legged next to the tank and put on a diving glove, which afforded her protection as well as a better grip on some of the more slippery animals. This was the part of the job she enjoyed—sitting next to the water, not in it, and pulling out amazing animals to look at closely and mostly set free. It reminded her of going to the rocky shore with Uncle Paul, sitting by the tide pools with the tide safely far away, picking up starfish and urchins, tiny crabs and bulbs of seaweed.

The others laughed, tossing fish overboard like expert newspaper boys, and splashing each other. There were ten interns in all. A few were still in high school, and several of them were recent high school graduates like she was, but most of them were very immature in Marin's opinion. Two had actually come last summer and were back with a little more experience—Jaycen and a large Tongan boy named Tui.

Tui looked like he could be twenty-three with his tall, muscular build and easy strength, until he smiled that innocent, boyish grin of his. He didn't talk much, but he laughed a lot, especially at Jaycen, who was always trying to give people a reason to laugh. Jaycen had sun-bleached sandy hair, was tan, well-built, and by far the cutest guy in the program. Marin could easily picture Jaycen being at the back of a fifth grade class-room, making oddball comments and getting everyone in trouble, yet somehow staying out of it himself by using his disarming smile like a weapon. As if summoned by her thoughts, he intentionally walked past her and carried an armload of dripping nets over her head, drenching her once again, this time in smelly fish water.

"What is your problem?" Marin asked, pushing the soggy mesh away from her head.

"You need to lighten up, *Mares!*" he said, mockingly. She scooped up a handful of water and threw it at him, missing him completely, but nailing Dr. Gilbert in the face.

TWO

The COAST building looked deceptively small from the front, but it was actually four stories tall, built up against a cliff and dropping to the beach below.

The huge L-shaped building roughly followed the coastline. The longer arm contained the student dorms, cafeteria, several labs and most of the business operations for COAST. Balconies lined each floor, overlooking the curving bay and the open ocean beyond. The shorter, boxier arm was a huge warehouse containing an impressive array of corporation watercraft, from Jet Skis to the company yacht. The warehouse made up the corner of the bay, extending into the water to shelter Star Chaser, the largest ship, sporting a thick crane designed to carry submersibles out to sea for launch. It had two other oversized doors that could be opened to allow boats to be brought in for maintenance. The warehouse itself was basically a laboratory with banks of computers, tables and tanks surrounding the three open bays of water inside the building.

Three long piers jutted into the water from the warehouse, where boats could be tied up for loading and unloading.

Secluded, beautiful, and functional, the COAST building was an oceanographer's dream, of which Dr. Frank Gilbert was the creator, designer and owner. It was his family and friend, his work and play.

Essentially, Dr. Gilbert was COAST. His empire had been built by his father, now dead, but was now financed with generous government subsidies, supplemented by funding from his private fortunes gleaned from generations of Gilbert business ventures and investments.

He spared no expense in his great mission; the best equipment and the brightest minds were to be found at COAST, and he took a keen interest in students that had the potential to become the next generation of boundary pushers. It was for this reason that he created the internship program, to nurture and expose those minds to the frontier he was exploring, and to keep them close in order to woo their attention as future employees.

Frank Gilbert had been watching Marin ever since his dive instructor, Paul Donnegan, had taken her in from foster care as a child. He knew Paul was an accomplished Search and Rescue Diver as well as a retired Navy Seal and a good man, and he had personally written to the foster care facility to recommend Paul as a guardian for Marin.

Gilbert was especially interested in the fact that Marin had such a great fear of water. He felt it terribly wrong that a child who had entered a family that obviously had a great love for the ocean was terrified of water, and had quietly encouraged Paul to take her to the best psychologist money could buy, which he was more than happy to personally, albeit anonymously, pay. While Paul spent much of his time with Search and Rescue, he taught regular dive classes at COAST, affording Gilbert an indirect channel of observation that was satisfying to his curiosity.

It was always in his plans to bring Marin into the program, playing his hunch that if she could overcome her fears, she could become a very gifted oceanographer. So far his hunch had been correct. She was brilliant in the classroom, had a phenomenal memory, and a genuine concern for marine life. The final test would be getting her underwater. If she couldn't do that, everything else was academic. There were dozens of scientists that could sit at a desk and analyze data, run tests on specimens, or design new equipment. What was truly rare was someone who could get in a submersible and get out there and see, discovering and deciding in the field.

He wanted her to get under the mirror of the water and see the world hidden beneath it, become one with it and embrace it as he had.

If she didn't have what it would take to clear that final hurdle, his silent interference in her life would end. But if she did, it would all be paid in full for the satisfaction of winning the bet he had waged against himself concerning her future.

* * *

The digital clock by her bedside read 2:00 a.m. Marin put her pillow over her head and tried to think of calculus problems, moon phases, or the hunting habits of falcons, but all her thoughts eventually spiraled into one terrifying moment: making it through the second open water dive test. And the dive test was just the beginning.

All interns were given assignments on programs after they finished training. Everything from nutrient analysis to unmanned camera programming could be part of the experience. The most coveted assignment, however, was DeepWater, Dr. Gilbert's pet project, which was researching the possibility of human habitats underwater. Dr. Gilbert had hand-picked her to start in DeepWater once she could dive, supposedly a great honor. To her it seemed like it would be a trial by fire.

Just when she'd decided to calm her pounding heart by quitting this internship, she thought of Uncle Paul, teaching her patiently to swim despite her constant crying, helping her put her face underwater with a snorkel to see the pretty fishies, trying to share with her the world he loved so dearly. Uncle Paul, so proud of her accomplishments despite her fears. Uncle Paul, who would be devastated as she turned in her resignation and applied for college in Nebraska.

She punched her pillow and rolled over again. Erika broke into a round of high-pitched snores accentuated by an earsplitting wheeze that shook Marin's fillings. At least that would be one bonus of going onto the DeepWater program—she'd get her own room as of tomorrow night. She couldn't wait to move out and actually sleep in peace and quiet.

The room felt like it was 102 degrees. She grabbed her pillow and blanket and headed for the door. The dark hallway outside felt much cooler, and stepping away from Erika's cacophony made her feel better almost instantly. She padded out into the main hallway and headed toward the common room, deciding which couch to sleep on. Strictly speaking, students weren't supposed to leave their dorm rooms after lights out, but the cool air coming in from an open screened patio in the common room lured her on.

The room was lit by a full moon washing in through balcony windows, making the balcony itself look like it was made from polished marble instead of concrete. Dropping her bedding on a giant beanbag, she crept reverently outside and leaned on the railing. The air was much cooler out here, with a brisk wind that took her long hair in living strands and danced with them behind her back.

The ocean stretched out in a line of silver below her, reflecting the moon in long broken streaks. She tried to reach inside herself to find the missing parts that would make her whole. People all over the world sought out the refuge of the sea for its calming balm; some paid thousands to stand in thought on a balcony not nearly as beautiful as this one, to watch their problems magically wash away with the tide.

She looked at the water below her and saw beyond the beauty to the terror hidden below. Sailors knew the ocean. They understood that it is as temperamental as a child and as powerful as a tsunami, evenly passing out bliss and torment with indifference. She mused how in all the pictures of the sea, it's always the wives and girlfriends standing wistfully gazing out to the ocean, never the sailors. They were always looking toward the land.

Why was she fighting her phobia so hard? Would it really be that bad to live in Albuquerque, or North Dakota, or Oklahoma and never set foot near an ocean again? There are people who spend their lives learning the ways of the Choctaw Indians. Some fill their minds with laws, or dangling participles, or business ethics. There were infinite options out there! Why did she always have to beat herself against the wall of her fear? What kind of strange person was she?

She pictured herself starting a life far from moving water, meeting people who knew nothing of phytoplasms and cared even less. For a moment, she felt a wave of calm possibilities.

But the truth would not let her go. If she walked away, she would always know she had a limit. If she gave her fears *that* kind of power, would she one day be so ruled by them that she couldn't take a bath again? Drink a glass of water? She had heard about hydrophobics that would go hysterical even if someone sprayed them with mist. She didn't want to spend the rest of her life like that. The wind whipped her hair around her face, blinding her for a moment. She absently gathered it up and tied it in a knot above her head, sighing. Albuquerque seemed so sane.

"I hope you're not planning on jumping," a voice said behind her. She spun to see Jaycen, his hair mussed by sleep, wearing a rumpled t-shirt and basketball shorts.

"What are you doing out here?" she hissed accusingly.

He rubbed his hair and yawned. "You know, I could ask you the same thing, but I think I know the answer."

"Oh, what? Now you're a mind reader?" she retorted.

"Nope. It's just that the only reason someone would be staring out at the ocean in the middle of the night is because they have something on their mind."

Marin frowned, angry at being so stereotypical.

"*And*, I know what's on *your* mind."

Duh. He was there, he saw her fail her dive test. Again. Of course he could guess. But not why. Never why.

Jaycen looked at her, a smile pulling up half his face. He sighed. "Not taking the bait? Well, I'll just tell you then."

She folded her arms and turned back to the sea.

"You're thinking about ... LOVE!"

She spun back toward him, spluttering and speechless.

"No use denying it. You're wondering how you can get Tui to notice you. Well, it's no use. He's only got eyes for Natalee. I wouldn't be your friend if I didn't tell you first. I'd hate for you to go pining away for him when there are so many other eligible bachelors for you to torment. But if you insist on throwing yourself at him, at least come armed with peach cobbler. It's your only hope." Jaycen stared down at her with such sincerity, that she stopped spluttering and laughed in amazement. She shook her head uncertainly. Jaycen continued, "We've all noticed. You might as well come clean."

Marin relaxed her shoulders and shrugged. "You are so lame."

"Guilty, as charged. So the next order of business is; what are you going to do about it?"

"Do about what? Your lameness? Forget it. It's incurable."

"No, about what's *really* on your mind."

Marin chuckled. "You mean my one-way romance with Tui?"

"No, about DeepWater."

The cold air raced down her lungs in one surprised breath, startling her inside and out. "Why do you have to do that?" she demanded.

"Do what? Read your mind? Oh, you are *so* mysterious, I could *never* guess what goes on inside your head!" He waved his fingers in the air above her like a sideshow magician.

"You know, we really shouldn't be out here." Marin moved toward the patio doors, but Jaycen blocked her pathway.

"Ok, tell me one reason why you are so worried about DeepWater? You seem to be great at everything. Any one of us would die to be on DeepWater. It's a guaranteed career in doing what we all love. It's why we're here! And you act like Gilbert gave you the death sentence." He stood with his arms out, determinedly standing as an obstacle to the doorway. She could get past him, but that would just give him an excuse to grab her and tickle her or some other random, stupid thing. Besides, if he'd noticed, others probably did as well. She flopped down on a vinyl chair facing him. He slowly sank into the other one.

"Look, I've been afraid of the water my whole life." She paused, waiting for him to crack a joke or start laughing. Instead, he just looked at her in surprise, so she continued.

"Ever since I was really little, I've had these awful nightmares over and over." She took a shaky breath, steadying herself. Other than Paul and her psychiatrists, she hadn't talked about this to anyone. She picked up a stray toothpick off the table and absently started jabbing it into the vinyl straps of her chair. "I'm lying in a bunk inside a houseboat, and a boat crashes into it and it catches fire." Jaycen furrowed his eyebrows, listening intently as she continued.

"Suddenly there's this huge explosion and the boat shoots forward and smashes into the dock and I fall onto my hands and knees. Water is coming in and there's smoke everywhere. The boat starts to roll and I'm trapped with the boat burning to pieces above me and sinking below me." She gave an involuntary shudder, cold, though the night was warm. "Then a hand reaches out of the water below me and pulls me under." She looked at him apprehensively, waiting for him to mock her.

"Wow! Did that really happen? Is that where you got those scars on the back of your neck?"

Marin reached up and pulled her golden brown hair around her shoulders, mortified that her scars were so obvious even in the darkness. "No! I …I don't know where I got them. Besides, it's just a dream. Uncle Paul says it's probably something I saw on TV or something when I was a kid." She played with her hair, making sure the back of her neck was covered.

Jaycen gestured to her scars. "Don't stress, they're not bad. I noticed them in the diving pool the first day. I thought they were some fishy tattoo or something. Like shark gills. Very intimidating. So who's this Uncle Paul guy?"

She felt her face get hot, hating how he always kept her off balance. That was more than she wanted *anyone* here to know, since Paul was the dive instructor at COAST. "I live with my Uncle Paul. He's my foster dad. I've just always called him Uncle Paul." She tried to steer the subject away from her unusual family situation. "So anyways, I've always had this thing with being underwater. It's just really, really hard for me." How did he get her talking about this, anyway?

Jaycen leaned his head back and looked at the crystal stars sparkling overhead. "Then why are you here?"

Marin flicked the bent toothpick into the air and watched it float on the wind to disappear into the darkness below. "Good question. Abusing my psyche, I guess."

Jaycen yawned and closed his eyes. "Not good enough. Pain is not a good re-enforcer. You must have some other motivation."

"You are impossible! Who are you, my therapist?"

He cracked open his eyes and smiled mischievously. "Sure. Do you need one?"

Marin's face flushed with anger and embarrassment. Did he know? She jumped up and started for the door without a word. Jaycen beat her to it, catching her arm.

"Ah, not so fast. I haven't spilled my guts to you yet."

She jerked her arm out of his grip. "Don't bother. I'm not interested in your guts."

Jaycen stood in her path indecisively.

"You know, if anyone catches us here after curfew, it would end your career here pretty quickly," she said. Jaycen's mouth opened and closed soundlessly, but he moved out of her way. She shoved past him and picked up her blanket and pillow, already heading toward the door. He followed her into the moonlit room.

"Mares, please, wait."

Something in his tone sounded so sad that she paused.

"Look, I don't know why everything I say makes you mad at me. I'm not trying to hurt your feelings or make you angry, or whatever I do. Just ... everything just comes out wrong around you."

Marin turned around to see if he was kidding or not, humiliation still pounding in her ears. He stood in the doorway looking at her with such open feeling that she simply stared back at him in surprise. He took advantage of that moment to walk quickly toward her. He put his hand on her arm imploringly.

"I know you probably think I'm a big jerk. You act like you hate me. But please ... don't." He brushed his fingers lightly across her forehead and stared into her eyes tenderly. She just stared back, confused.

Of course she hated him. He was obnoxious, immature, nosy, and right about his stupid hunches *way* too often. All he had going for him was his looks.

But, what if there was something more to him? She looked thoughtfully into his eyes, not daring to trust him, but wondering. He smiled back, moving closer. She could smell the clean fabric of his shirt.

"Marin, I ..."

Lights clicked on and blinded them completely. Suddenly Marin realized how uncomfortably close she and Jaycen were and stepped quickly away.

Dr. Sperry, the girls' dorm head, stood in the kitchen in a blue bathrobe with her red hair in a knot on top of her head. Her arms were crossed and she looked ready to slaughter someone.

Marin glanced at Jaycen and the pillow and blanket in her arms and back at Dr. Sperry in panic. "Dr. Sperry! This is not what it looks like at all. I swear. I was just really hot and I came in here to sleep on one of the couches. We were just talking, I swear!"

Jaycen shrugged and said, "I was just coming in to get a drink and saw Mares here feeling sorry for herself, so I thought I'd keep her company." Marin shot him an evil look.

"Well, both of you are breaking curfew. The rec room closes at 11:30 p.m.! I suggest you get to bed before I inform Dr. Gilbert of your activities!" She turned on her bare heel and started stalking toward the girls' dorm, angry that her midnight raid of the refrigerator was thwarted by teenage hormones.

Marin glared at Jaycen and started to follow Dr. Sperry down the hall, but paused and turned around when she realized Jaycen hadn't come with them.

She watched him turn out the light and drift back to the moonlight-drenched balcony. He stood silently, his gaze following the sparkle of a distant ship floating over the horizon until it tipped around the curve of the earth, disappearing with a small wink. He picked out a rock from a nearby planter and threw it as far as he could, where it landed in the white tipped waves below. She cast one last hesitant glance over her shoulder at his solitary figure, and wondered what thoughts had *him* staring out at the ocean in the middle of the night.

Blue sparkles moved across the ceiling in the warehouse pool, giving the room a zen-like feel, like an underwater grotto. The water was deep, sloping down to the rocky, natural floor leading out through the closed bay doors to the open ocean.

Marin sat on the edge with her feet gently splashing back and forth, trying to keep her heart from pounding every time she thought about submerging. Instead, she ran through some relaxation techniques and concentrated on breathing slowly. Suddenly, a hand touched her shoulder and someone shouted "Boo!" in her ear.

She jerked away out of reflex and found herself slipping off the edge, falling face first into the water. Fighting back a wave of panic, she broke the surface, gasping and coughing, gripping the edge with one white-knuckled hand. Jaycen was crouched by the pool, trying not to laugh, but his smile died when he saw the terror in her eyes.

"Oh no! Are you okay? I'm so sorry! I forgot ... you and water ..." he spluttered, trying to help her get out, but in the process he splashed more water into her mouth. She shoved him away angrily, still choking and glad that her face was already wet so her furious tears wouldn't show.

Paul Donnegan walked over and smacked the back of Jaycen's head. "What was that about, wise guy? Wanna drown her?"

Jaycen looked mortified. "I didn't mean to. I mean, I didn't think she'd fall in! I was just, you know, messing around, Mr. Donnegan," he stammered uncomfortably.

Paul's cheek twitched with anger. For a moment, Marin was afraid he was going to punch Jaycen.

"I'm okay, um, Mr. Donnegan," she choked out, finally getting the last stinging bits of water out of her lungs. Paul raised his eyebrows in surprise at her title for him, but then he relaxed and shrugged.

Marin looked up at him with pleading eyes. She wished she'd

thought to explain beforehand to him that it was bad enough feeling like she didn't belong here; if anyone knew she was related to one of the instructors, it would only make things worse. His expression hardened when he looked back at Jaycen.

"Careful who you're 'messing around' with, buddy," he growled. Putting one hand on Jaycen's forehead, he shoved him backwards into the water.

Marin pulled herself onto the cement and started putting on her tank, trying hard not to make eye contact with Jaycen as he climbed out of the pool and put on his fins. After a few moments, he slapped over to help adjust her equipment.

"Just because I'm slower than you does *not* mean I can't put a stupid hood on," she snapped, pulling away from him. He held up his hands.

"Sorry. I know. I just … I'm sorry. I completely forgot. That was so stupid of me." Marin glanced at him, surprised to see genuine concern reflected in his eyes. "I'm really sorry. I was only playing with you." He absently tucked a stray lock of hair gently into her hood. "Forgive me?" he asked, smiling hopefully down at her.

For a moment, her breath caught in her throat seeing him look at her so tenderly. For a moment she wondered if this overconfident jerk really did have feelings. Taking a step back, she let out her air and rolled her eyes. "Whatever, goofy," she said, heading back to the pool.

"What, was that almost a smile?" He followed, putting on his O2 tank and BC as he went.

"Don't push it," she said,

"Ah, but you did almost smile. That's progress. I'm totally satisfied." He grinned as he popped his regulator into his mouth and jumped back into the pool.

"*Mr. Donnegan?*" Paul asked once Jaycen was underwater.

Marin turned. "I'm sorry, Uncle Paul. I just really …"

"Want to be here on your own two feet?" he finished for her.

She felt relieved. "Yeah. Is that ok? I don't want to hurt your feelings or anything. I just, you know …"

He gave her a quick squeeze. "No worries, baby. Let's get you certified, and I'll be out of your hair. Well, mostly."

"Why is he here?" she asked nodding at Jaycen's form in the water.

"He's a second-year intern, and he's interested in search and rescue. Besides," he said, with a smile, "I thought maybe a cute guy along with us would be a distraction for you." He shrugged.

Marin scowled at him and slid into the water, still feeling angry and confused about Jaycen. She hardly noticed herself sinking into the depths until Jaycen swam into her view giving her the okay sign. She gave a reluctant okay back to him then did her best to ignore him, concentrating instead on remembering her signals. Glancing up, she thought for a moment about all that water between her and the surface. Her heart rate increased and her breathing became shallow and swift. Pain started building in her ears, along with a growing panic that she wasn't going to make it. She fought herself to slow her breathing. Holding her nose, she tried to depressurize her ears. Jaycen hovered in front of her looking worried. Paul sank to her side and waited. She ground her teeth down on her regulator in frustration as the pressure unbearably built in her ears.

Jaycen reached out to touch her and she jerked her hand out of his reach. There was no way she was going to mess this up and give Jaycen any ammunition to tease her with. He swam in front of her again, this time doing the okay signal. She glared and turned away from him. Why on earth did Paul want Jaycen along? The last thing she needed was to make a fool of herself in front of the cutest guy here.

Finally, with a pop of sharp pain, one ear cleared and then the other. The pressure was gone. She felt giddy with relief.

I'm fine, she signaled. Her fins touched ground and she looked down in surprise. She was already at the bottom of the pool! She didn't look up and see the water above her. Just knowing it was there made her hands shake. Jaycen swam in front of her again and she scowled. He was making it hard for her to pay attention to what she was doing. Paul was right, he was a distraction. She concentrated on how irritating he was and looked at Paul to begin testing hand signs. Whenever she started to feel shaky, she'd look at Jaycen, hovering near like an annoying puppy, and it gave her determination to keep going. He got close and touched her shoulder reassuringly. Maybe he was actually trying to be a distraction and Paul had put him up to it. She glared at Paul and he winked at her. Ugh! He had!

Paul pointed at the bay doors. It took her a moment to realize he was asking her if she felt up to going out into the bay so she could count it as an open water dive. She took a few uneven breaths, surprised that she was still holding it together. He watched her anxiously, but after a moment, she nodded.

They ducked under the bay door and swam out into the sunlit ocean. Shafts of sunlight pierced the water and the whole bay was lit in an iridescent blue, striped with lavender shadows cast by the boats parked above her. A tiny school of silvery fish, each no more than an inch long, darted past them. She stopped, looking in wonder at the beauty around her, finally understanding what had always made Paul so passionate about diving. She caught his attention as he drifted in front of her and nodded at him. The look of joy beaming in his eyes made her heart swell with love for this kind, patient man who had raised her. Her pulse still raced in her ears, and beneath her gloves her hands were still sweating and shaking, but right now she was doing it!

THREE

arin put on her dive equipment in two minutes, beating her previous time by .4 seconds. She smiled to herself as she glanced at the thick yellow dive watch on her wrist. After tomorrow, she would begin her mornings with a dive drill, because a basic knowledge of rescue training was required for everyone who worked on DeepWater. In a way, it reminded her of Uncle Paul, and she wondered for the first time if part of his training had been done here in this very room. She made a mental note to ask him the next time she saw him. It always amazed her how quickly he used to get in his gear when it seemed to take her forever. Until now. She smiled. Now if only going under the water would get easier.

She took off her mask and hood, shaking her hair loose down the back of her skin suit and smiling with satisfaction.

She had passed the first part of her dive test! *Barely,* the cynical part of her answered, tempering her triumph. And it wouldn't be long before she'd have to do a real dive. Just thinking about it made her mouth go dry. She scowled, angry at herself that she couldn't make this persistent fear leave her alone. It still made her heart jump to get into the water, but if she didn't put her head under at first, she could make herself do it.

What was surprising was she was now assigned to do a large part of her work with the subs, while most regular employees worked in the lab, analyzing chemical balances and mercury levels in the water and fish brought back from expeditions. She tried to tell herself she was imagining it, but she couldn't help feeling like the other members of DeepWater resented her on the team, especially the hands-on work she was asked to do, instead of "doing time" in the labs first. Even so, her coworkers and trainers were kind and brilliant, and she soaked up every bit of information that was given to her.

Dave, the lead engineer and Uncle Paul's best friend, walked in from the office carrying a bag of tools. "Hey, Mares! How do you like it here, huh?"

She smiled and shrugged. "The water hasn't killed me yet."

"Well, you know your uncle has me on the payroll to keep an eye on you, don't you?" he teased.

"I'm sure he does. What does he pay you in? Pizza?"

"No, free labor at my dive shop on weekends through the summer!" he boasted.

"Wow, you are one expensive spy! Well, I'll try to do something terrible and reckless sometime so you have something interesting to report."

Dave shook his head. "Nah, don't do anything stupid on my account. I'd better get back and see what your buddy there is doing to my sub," he said pointing to Jaycen.

She waved goodbye then tried to relax, soaking in the warm humidity, trying to talk herself into jumping into the water. Swinging her legs back and forth, feeling the drag of her fins in the water, she watched Dave clamp tight an assortment of air hoses on top of a bright yellow mini-sub in preparation for its next voyage.

The sub was tethered by two huge cranes, keeping it out of the water so work could be done to the mass of equipment all around the sub's body. In black, the name DELPHINIUS was painted across the nose of the small craft. Another crane held aloft the moveable workstation, which was a thick slab of steel that could let workers move heavy equipment and tools to different parts of the outer sub without getting wet. At the moment it was empty and parked in front of Delphinius, hovering over the water just below and under the nose of the dry submarine. Jaycen sat on the edge of it, attaching a reinforced cage containing twin cameras to the bottom cone of the submersible. The larger sub, Aquanis, slept in the next bay over.

She had work she needed to start on, but she loved watching the preparations for the deep dive, and for the first time she could remember, she felt really, really good. She allowed her mind to wander, marveling at how everything appeared black or yellow underwater. As terrifying as the whole idea was to her, it was also fascinating to think of how much engineering had gone into taking dry-land humans and giving them a portable habitat in a completely different realm. She smiled, and then Jaycen caught her eye and gave her a surprised smile back as he leapt to the top of the sub to help Dave attach hoses. She couldn't help but notice how nice he looked when he was just being himself.

"Agh! Mares! Grab that, will you?" Jaycen shouted as his tool clanged out of his hand and splashed into the water below his platform. The hose he was working on started hissing out oxygen. Marin looked down in concern as the tool started to sink. Jaycen noticed her hesitation and smiled encouragingly. "You can do it," he said with a quick thumbs up, before hopping off the platform and onto the flat top of the sub to help Dave try to wrestle the hose back into place.

"Shut off the O2!" Dave yelled. Jaycen grabbed the nozzle and turned it, but the oxygen pressure went higher, flipping the hose like a wild snake.

For a moment Marin considered picking up her hood and mask, but seeing the chaos on top of the sub and the tool sinking fast changed her mind. She didn't even take the time to unlatch her tank but slipped with it into the water, counting on its weight to take her down quickly beneath the platform near the belly of Delphinius.

She kept her eyes on the tool, trying not to think of anything else. The water pressed against her eardrums, but she cleared them and continued down, her hands trembling. Doubt creeped in, slowing her descent, but thinking of telling Jaycen she chickened out made her start swimming again. She forced herself to concentrate on the tool. *I just have to grab it and this will be over,* she chanted to herself.

Underwater, the thing looked like an oversized wrench with alligator teeth. It reminded Marin of an extinct dinosaur. She kicked harder, hoping to reach it before it hit the sloped cement floor. She didn't want it to start sliding farther down to where the cement ended and the rocky ocean floor began. She seriously doubted her resolve would let her go that far. Voices echoed above her; muffled background noise. She stretched out as the tool bumped the sloped side of the wall and began sliding downwards.

* * *

The oxygen hose kicked free and smacked Dave in the forehead, cutting a gash across his face and knocking him backwards. He fell on his back halfway hanging off the sub, feet tangled in the maze of hoses, wires and tethers at the top of the sub. Shouts were echoing off the warehouse walls as people came to help, alerted by the hissing and clanging of the loose hose.

Jaycen jumped to the solid ground of the cement deck trying to heave Dave to safety, but Dave's foot was tangled in the mess of hoses. He felt Dave's limp body weight sliding them both toward the water, the hose pinging spastically off the sub and beating Dave's legs mercilessly. With a groan, Jaycen braced his foot against the hull of the Delphinius and yanked Dave as hard as he could toward safety. Dave's boot was caught on a lever near the heavy tethers that held Delphinius out of the water. Jaycen gave a mighty heave before he realized what he had done.

With a sickening click, the emergency tether release that had been caught on Dave's boot flipped, releasing the front end of the sub with a tremendous splash that ripped Dave's boot completely off and sent Dave and Jaycen crashing to the dock floor on a wave of saltwater. The sub swung forward into the water, ripping the steel platform in front of it completely off its chains. It fell into the pool, sinking instantly. The sub shrieked, sliding against the cement until its tail caught, held partially aloft by the one remaining crane.

"No!" Jaycen screamed, scrambling to the edge of the pool on his hands and knees as a thousand pounds of metal plunged toward Marin like a Titan's fist.

* * *

Jaycen's wrench hit the cement wall with a bounce and slid a few feet before coming to a stop at the bottom of the cloudy water. Marin gave one last kick and closed her fist around the metal triumphantly, planted her feet on the floor and pushed off, headed for the surface with her trophy in hand.

Instantly a concussive wave of displaced water shook her, making her drop the wrench in surprise. Rotating upwards, she barely had time to register the huge shape falling toward her and attempt to spin away before the weight of the platform caught her, pushing her mercilessly back to the bottom of the pool.

Instinctively, she curled into a ball covering her head with her arm as the platform hit her with determined force, squeezing her down between the crushing mass of steel, the wall of the pool and the rocks below. The platform pressed down on her ruthlessly, forcing air out of her lungs and compressing her ribs. Her head connected with the metal and its thick bulk pushed against her, down, down, and further down, making her ears pop and her vision burst into stars.

It hit the wall of the pool with an unearthly screech and tipped at a slight angle, making a prison that trapped her as it settled. The pain in her body was so intense; it felt like every cell was exploding from the pressure. She squirmed and pushed, trying to find release from the pain, and for a brief moment, she felt something give and she moved backward, her oxygen tank scraping both cement and the steel.

Her hair was caught between the platform and the tank; a chunk tore loose and floated in front of her, pink blood dispersing before her eyes. She didn't register the pain, but kept pushing backward, away from crushing agony until her tank hit the wall of the pool, stopping her abruptly. The metal slab slipped farther, pushing, grinding against the wall and her tank, dislocating her right arm still trapped in the tank harness, until it caught the tank tightly. The tank buckled slightly under the weight, and she braced herself for the final pain of death when the movement stopped.

She shivered in shock, listening to the grinding, settling, waiting for the final crushing movement to finish her off, but it didn't come. The tank kept the metal leaning slightly against the wall, creating a tiny triangle of space for her. Her legs were splayed out under the end of the metal slab with her head and torso preserved and imprisoned between the platform and the unyielding wall of the pool.

Marin's head was spinning with pain and lack of oxygen. With her dislocated arm, she could feel the hose of her tank floating free beyond her fingertips, but there was no way to get it to her mouth. Still she fumbled with it, desperate to get air into her burning lungs, only to have it slip out of her hand, hitting the metal wall with a dull clang over and over again, the life-sustaining oxygen bleeding out in silver bubbles.

* * *

Jaycen kicked off his rubber work boots and dove into the water right next to the hanging Delphinius. Its nose was pointing down toward the metal sheet, a thick trail of oxygen bubbles streaming out of the still dis-connected hose. Marin was nowhere to be seen. His heart was screaming into his brain, panic ripping at his mind. *No, No, No, No, No,* he yelled to himself, scanning the water for any movement. He fought the need to breathe and dove to the bottom, clutching the sides of Delphinius for stability. When he saw a black flipper sticking out from the bottom of the thick metal, his scream came out in a broken stream of bubbles, "NOOOOOOO!"

A hand groped for him from above and pulled him to the surface, even as he fought to get to the bottom. A high-pitched emergency klaxon was sounding overhead somewhere and he prayed it meant there was help on its way. It wasn't until several black suited bodies dropped into the water around him that he allowed himself to be dragged to the top. Dave hauled him onto the deck then sat down dizzily to nurse his wet and bleeding face. Jaycen coughed and gagged, vomiting onto the deck, unable to take his eyes from the dark shapes of the divers below him. A black suit with a red stripe passed him on deck and jumped in with both feet. Gilbert. Jaycen fell back on his heels and shot a glance at Dave, holding a sopping wet rag over his forehead and dripping red droplets down his once white t-shirt. Dave looked grim.

"D-do you need anything?" Jaycen asked him, shaking with shock.

"I'll live. Don't even think about suiting up. You're a mess. You'll just get in the way."

Jaycen nodded mutely. "I'll get a clean towel for you," he said, getting unsteadily to his feet.

"You just sit yourself down and catch your breath. I'll be fine," Dave growled, eyeing him distrustfully.

Jaycen shook his head absently.

Dr. Gilbert broke the water's surface, yelling at everyone who was near. "Get the crane attached up here! We need something to pry against! Throw that transfer unit in here, quickly!" He pulled himself onto the deck. Dave was still holding the blood soaked towel against his head, yelling at people and trying to get the tethers cranked down from the crane into the water. Gilbert caught Dave's eye and shook his head severely.

"The platform is against the wall. If we attach it to the crane, it's going to right itself before coming up. She'll be ground to a pulp." Gilbert's face was white.

Dave stared straight through him, eyebrows furrowed in thought. His lips pressed together into a straight line and shouted to the closest man to him, "Go out to my truck and get my hydraulic jack!" he said, tossing the man his keys. Gilbert's eyes opened in understanding. He put his mask back on, waiting for the jack to appear.

Jaycen wandered away from the bay as tears started falling unheeded down his cheeks. The klaxon was making his head hurt. How long had it been? Two minutes? Five minutes? Ten? He didn't even think about it as he wandered into the locker room. He pulled his dive gear on and threw his mask over his face. He couldn't leave her down there when she was so afraid to begin with. The realization of her situation hit him so hard he fell to his knees, hanging on to a shiny wooden bench for strength. This was his fault. He did this to her. This crushing realization snapped him into action.

He forced himself to his feet and snatched up his tank, strapping it on as he went. By the time he reached the dock again, his mask was on and he was ready to go. He tossed a clean white towel to Dave, who yelled something angrily, and then he jumped feet first into the water. The crane from the dock had been lowered into the water, and several black forms were busily trying to re-attach it, while others were working with levers, trying to stabilize the sub. More were hovering around the slab, unable to make it budge. Jaycen swam lower, his hands and feet going numb as he saw Marin's still form trapped sideways under the massive slab. Nobody could survive that. In his heart he knew it was too late.

Jaycen reached the end of the slab, his irregular breathing filling his ears with noise. Everyone seemed to be working in slow motion. Hot tears kept squeezing out Jaycen's eyes, steaming his mask, but he kept moving downward. He had to at least touch her to see if she still lived. She had to know he was sorry. He never even had a chance to tell her how much he was starting to care about her.

He choked back a sob. She just couldn't be alone down here, with everyone crawling about like ants trying to move a mountain of granite. He swam next to the wall to reach her leg. He took off her fin, ripped his glove off his hand and held her foot tightly, feeling a slight pulse in her ankle. His heart leapt, remembering she'd had her tank. Bubbles squeezed through the gap in a steady stream, not a good sign. He tried to reach behind the metal to find the rest of her, but there was no room. He desperately tried to tap into some latent super human strength, willing himself to move it and reach her, but it was like the platform was welded to the bottom of the bay.

His ear was smashed against the wall, reaching for Marin when he heard tapping. Ignoring the voice of reason, he continued to force himself next to her legs to lift the enormous weight upwards.

* * *

Bright lights were exploding in Marin's vision. She fought the urge to exhale what little breath she had left, knowing there was no air to replace it, but her traitorous lungs insisted. Why did she ever come here? Her fear lashed out angrily toward her own stupidity. She had known something like this would happen! Her gaze fell on the heartless black slab poised to crush her to death and realized it didn't matter anymore. It was too late.

Time seemed to stop as bubble by bubble her last gasp escaped her mouth and floated upward, rolling gently over the metal hull and disappearing through a slim crack drifting up toward everything she knew and loved. *I was so close*, she thought sadly. Eyes wide open, she stared up at the tiny line of blue above her and thought of Jaycen. *Poor Jaycen. He'll think this was his fault.*

She vaguely felt her fin come off and a warm hand touch her foot. Pain made her body tremble as she tried to keep from inhaling. Her empty lungs screamed for relief, fighting with her mind that ordered her to keep holding on to that last empty breath.

Why do they keep looking so hard for life down here when all they need is up there? What could the ocean give them but a cold, lonely death?

With a shudder her body suddenly gave in to instinct; she opened her lips and sucked in the cold salt water, filling her lungs with stinging fluid. Her body jerked and shuddered, convulsing against the foreign element flooding her body. Pain shot from her arm, head, and burning lungs leaving her flailing and kicking uncontrollably.

* * *

Jaycen felt Marin's leg stiffen and her left foot swung wildly and kicked him. He screamed in helplessness, shoving against the unyielding platform, not allowing himself to imagine these were her death throes. Her kicks became violent, and then slowed. He beat the metal desperately with all of his strength, willing it to move. With a last stuttering twitch, her legs stopped moving completely and her body relaxed. Jaycen held her foot, weeping in the dark tomb.

* * *

Marin waited for the end, pushing the thick liquid in and out of her lungs, her body still hoping for air, her broken ribs crying with pain at every new breath. Strangely though, the panic she had felt was melting into peaceful acceptance. *So this is death,* she mused. It wasn't so bad once you got through the fear. The stars in her vision were disappearing one by one, like the end of a meteor shower at dawn. Still she waited, expecting blackness to come, or light, or nothingness. But nothing changed. She took in a lungful of water and exhaled, feeling strangely refreshed. Even the pain was going away! Amazed, she continued to wait for the end to come, but it refused. Again and again she took in water, and she felt her mind growing clearer and her body stronger.

* * *

Hands appeared around Jaycen and a short metal jack was shoved between himself and Marin's still legs. Chains were hooked together and slung around the crane hook. Gilbert began pumping the jack. When it made contact with the underside of the slab, it started moving upward. More hands groped under the metal, reaching for Marin's body. Jaycen pushed with all his might against the slab as the ceiling above her raised slowly, inch by agonizing inch.

* * *

Marin felt the world around her shift and she shuddered, bracing herself for the final pain, but it did not come. The slab let out a terrific groan, scraping against the side of the pool. She held in her breath, but the movement stopped. Then more scraping and banging and the movement began again. The iron cold pressure on her head released and water swirled between her forehead and the cold steel. She moved her neck slightly and found she could now move her left arm. The gap above her closed, but there was definitely more room below. She felt hands grasp her legs as she was dragged sideways under the flat face of the platform. Her tank caught and she panicked, but the hands kept pulling and the roof still rose until her tank broke free with a shriek. Suddenly she was free, floating face up under the water, dozens of black dive masks moving around her, pulling her to the surface. They pushed her out of the water and onto her face on the pebbled diving deck. Then more hands pushed on her lungs, unaware of the internal screaming of her ribs, pushing until the water rushed forward and she threw it up across the wet deck, sucking in a dry and painful gulp of air, rolling onto her back before pain finally filled her mind with blackness.

* * *

Jaycen raced to Marin and knelt in wonder near her head, dizzy with the hope that she was alive. He cradled her limp head on his lap, while silent tears of relief and joy rolled down his face. He didn't notice water slowly dripping out of six raw red lines on the back of her neck.

FOUR

The boat rocked peacefully, attached securely to its dock. It was hot outside, but the inside of the boat was cool and quiet. Marin's hammock rocked gently with the sway of the boat. She was home.

Not wanting to open her eyes and break the spell, she listened to the sounds of her life long lost; the murmur of voices coming and going on the dock, the hum of a motor coming to life. She heard water lapping at the back of the boat, and tapping coming from underneath it as her dad fixed the motor. In her mind she hopped down from the hammock and walked to the back of the boat, where a fiberglass circle came up out of the bottom of the boat topped with a solid metal door which could be closed when the boat was moving. The port was wide enough for a full grown man to fit through. Marin looked down into the open hole and saw her dad flash past, then he turned and swam back. His wet head popped up through the port hole.

"Hi, sweetheart! Have a good nap?"

Marin nodded, savoring the foggy memory of her father.

"Wanna go get your swim things on and come down with me? I'll be on the port side." He smiled a familiar smile and went back under.

Tears of joy prickled behind her unconscious eyes as she touched this long buried memory. *Faster, faster,* she urged herself. *Just jump in. Swim away! Hurry!*

Shouting outside brought the dream back into focus. It was too late.

She heard her mother screaming from the top of the boat and saw her go flying when the impact came. The boat rolled to its side, water pouring through the porthole in a crushing wave that knocked her from her feet and sent her swirling in debris. Smoke was filling the air. Instinctively, she ducked down into the water and clawed her way to the porthole, only to find the heavy door had fallen shut. Flames and heat were everywhere as she tried to find an escape. She went underwater searching for anything to help. Suddenly she saw a hand reach in through a crack in the hull. She grabbed it and held it tight, her clothes floating around her; panic and fear drowning her as her face sunk below the surface.

An alarm went off; an irritating, repetitive beeping coupled with echoing voices that dragged Marin out of the depths of unconsciousness. She felt claustrophobic and uncomfortable. What was going on? Opening her eyes to a bright light shining into her pupils, she pushed it away and sat up. Dave rocked back on his heels in surprise and a startled murmur moved through the crowd surrounding her.

She shook her head, confused. Remembering was like grasping spider threads that broke as soon as caught. She remembered diving for the tool and looking up as something huge fell on her, her mother thrown off the boat, drowning and breathing in the water, and breathing, and breathing. She remembered her father reaching through the hole to catch her hand. Then suddenly she was in the docking bay surrounded by staring people.

"What are you doing?" she demanded, glancing at Jaycen, Dr. Gilbert, and the ring of people on their knees or on their feet surrounding her on the wet cement. A red back injury brace was lying next to her and it looked like they were in the process of moving her onto it when she had awoken.

She noticed the congealed blood of a nasty cut across Dave's forehead and frowned, and then it all came back to her in a rush. Dave shook off his surprise and cleared his throat.

"Marin just lay back down. We need to get you to the hospital."

She got to her knees instead, ripping off the beeping O2 monitor clipped to her finger, making the intermittent sound change to one long flat line alarm. She reached over and clicked the machine off.

Dave stared at her in disbelief. "Marin, you're delirious. You probably have a neck or back injury. We need to get you to a hospital and have you checked out." He put his hands on her shoulders to gently push her back down, but she stood up instead, turning her head and twisting her back experimentally, to the collective cringing gasps of everyone in the room.

"I feel fine. I don't want to go to a hospital," she said simply. She walked over to a wooden bench against the wall and sat down, taking off the remains of her buoyancy belt and her remaining swim fin.

Nobody knew what to say. Dr. Gilbert shot Dave a look as he and Jaycen followed her to the bench.

Dave raised his voice.

"People, I know you want to help, but the best thing you can do right now is get working on cleaning up this disaster," he said, gesturing at the sub hanging drunkenly from one end.

Jaycen and Gilbert sat down on either side of her.

"Marin, I'm so sorry," Jaycen said, his voice cracking with emotion. "When you went into the water, the oxygen hose came loose and hit Dave hard. When I pulled him off the sub, his boot caught the emergency release and the sub slipped. It tore the platform loose and it fell ..." his voice broke and he couldn't finish the sentence.

"Do you remember anything?" Gilbert asked.

"Yes," she replied emphatically. "I could feel something hit the water, but it came down too fast. It pinned me. And ... I drowned," Jaycen's brows knit together in guilt, but she grasped his hand and stared into his eyes, lowering her voice. "It was okay! I could breathe. I could *really* breathe! Underwater!" Jaycen stared at her in astonishment. She continued, almost madly, "I know. It sounds crazy. But something else happened, too. I remembered a part of my life I've always thought was just a nightmare. It isn't. It was real. I *remember* the accident."

Dr. Gilbert's expression was unreadable. Jaycen looked down at his hands, still shaking with adrenaline. Marin was in awe. What just happened seemed so unreal that she felt she was losing her mind, living out what she wanted to believe rather than face reality. There was no way she wasn't hurt. She had been under without oxygen for over fifteen minutes, not to mention any trauma from the impact. It was beyond unbelievable. It was a miracle.

Dr. Gilbert put a gentle hand on her shoulder and looked into her eyes. "Marin. I know what you *think* happened, but I have an explanation. That space you were trapped in is the key. When the slab sealed you in, it crushed your tank. The oxygen was released, creating an air pocket for you that couldn't escape. It's a miracle, but a logical one."

Marin looked at him dubiously. He squeezed her shoulder and said, "Why don't you take a few days off and get some rest?"

She nodded and gave a quick, reassuring smile to Jaycen before leaving the scene of chaos and confusion behind her.

Marin closed the door to her room and lay down on the bed. She picked up her cell phone to call Paul, but her battery was dead, so she plugged it in, making a mental note to call him when it finished charging.

A stiff wind knocked branches against her window, and the light came in grey and somber. A storm was coming. She listened to the sound of the waves hissing against sand outside her window, glad to be alone to try to assimilate what had just happened.

Someone had mumbled something about needing therapy for post-traumatic stress as she had left the bay, and she wasn't sure if he'd meant for her or for the witnesses of the accident. She laughed at the thought. As far as she was concerned she was suffering post traumatic *relief.* For the first time that she could remember, she wasn't afraid anymore. She felt free, powerful, almost super-human. She had drowned. She knew it. And she had survived. There was something different about her, and whatever else it might mean she knew that the monster fear that had kept her prisoner all her life was gone.

Walking to the bathroom she filled the tub. Still in her wet swimsuit she let herself sink to the bottom of the tub, let out all her air and waited. She tried to force herself to breathe in the water but her body refused and pushed her to the surface with a gasp. She slammed her hand down in frustration and tried again. And again. Each time she kept herself down longer, but the air just above her was too much to resist and she couldn't make it happen. She sank down one more time, determined to drown.

A moment later, the bathroom door slammed open. Paul stood at the door, red faced with worry.

She came to the surface in a panic. "Uncle Paul? What's wrong?"

"What are you doing?" he shouted hysterically.

"I'm in the bathtub! Geez, why don't you knock!" she shouted back defensively. She snatched a towel and stood, kicking the drain plug out with her toe.

"Were you trying to KILL yourself? Marin, what were you just doing?" he insisted.

Her cheeks burned with embarrassment. "I was just, you know … relaxing."

"Underwater?"

She pushed him out of the bathroom. "What's the big idea, Uncle Paul?" she demanded.

"You tell me! I get a call that there's been an accident and they thought you'd drowned. I race over here and they say you're fine and when I come up to find you, there you are, six inches underwater." He pointed an accusing finger at the bathtub.

Marin leaned against the wall and took a slow, deep breath. "I'm sorry. I didn't know they had called you. I felt fine so I didn't think it was a big deal." She had never seen him look so upset. "I'm sorry, Uncle Paul, I thought about calling, but my phone was dead."

"Imagine my state of mind when I got a call like that. It's every parent's worst fear." His voice shook with emotion. "And you didn't think to borrow someone else's phone? Honestly, Marin!" He reached over to her and grabbed her into a fierce hug. She could feel his breathing coming in choking sobs.

"I'm so sorry, Uncle Paul," she whispered into his shoulder. "I'm okay. I'm really fine."

Paul huffed for a few more moments, then slowly deflated and sat down on her bed. "I'm sorry, I didn't mean to get upset at you," he said, hanging gingerly on to her hand. "It just scared me to death!"

She nodded and grabbed the quilt from the foot of her bed to wrap up in, then sat down next to him.

"You need to come home and get some rest."

Marin pulled back and shook her head. "It makes more sense for me to be here. You're going to be on call all the time anyway. Besides, all my stuff is here. And Dr. Gilbert said – "

"I don't care *what* Dr. Gilbert says, you need rest!"

Marin shook her head. "Uncle Paul, I *want* to be here. Dr. Gilbert said I don't have to do anything until I feel up to it, but I don't want to sit home and watch TV while this summer is evaporating around me." She raised her hands helplessly, trying to make him understand. "There's just over a month left until it's over, and I want to get every moment out of this experience that I can."

Paul shook his head stubbornly, opening his mouth to object, but she went on; desperately searching for logic he would listen to. "Just trust me to take care of myself. I really am okay. Besides, there are more people here if I need help, anyway." He grudgingly had to admit she had a point. "This feels like my own bed, I have everything I need, and I'm feeling fine." She surprised herself with how badly she really wanted to stay.

Paul took her hand again but didn't say anything.

Marin watched Paul's emotions playing across his face. She knew he was hurt and didn't understand, but she wasn't sure she did, either, and she needed answers. She decided to push him.

"Uncle Paul, where did I come from?"

His eyes darted sharply to hers and she knew he could tell what she was asking, but for a moment he didn't say anything. Then he cleared his throat.

"You know, Jessie and I tried to have kids for a long time, but it just never worked." He sighed heavily, the bittersweet pain of his earlier life playing across his face. "Finally we gave up and started looking at adoption. At first, we were looking for a newborn, so we could at least feel like we had raised this child from the start. But a friend told me about you in foster care, bounced around with no place to call home, and when we met you, I just felt like we were meant to have you in our lives. You were just three years old, and already smart as could be. And the cutest little girl I've ever seen." He smiled and traced a heart on the back of Marin's hand with his finger.

She didn't speak, silently urging him to go on.

"They couldn't find any records of your parents and it made things ... complicated. And Jessie was having struggles of her own that made things more complicated."

"Was it me?" she asked quietly.

"You? Of course not!" Paul retorted.

"I thought she left because she couldn't handle my breakdowns. She always seemed mad at me."

"She couldn't handle a lot of things, Marin. I didn't realize how big her problem was until it was too late. She was an alcoholic, Marin. And if the state had known how bad it was, we would never have been granted custody of you. Somehow, I thought if she finally got a child of her own to love, maybe she'd have the strength to stop." His voice grew husky with emotion. "She didn't. It only made it worse. And then she left us."

Marin steered the subject away from Jessie and the pain she left behind. "Uncle Paul, do you know anything about my life *before* you found me?"

He glanced up at her, obviously dreading where this was going, but she continued.

"Those dreams ... they're real. I know it. I *remember* it. I have to find out where I came from."

He looked sadly at her hand in his. Like any adopted father, she knew he wanted his child to have enough, to *be* enough without having to revisit the past. Still, somewhere inside he must have known this day would come.

"Uncle Paul, what happened today … it changed everything. I remember things that couldn't have come from a dream. I lived on a houseboat. There was an accident. My real …" she glanced up, "I mean, my biological parents were there, too. The boat sank and I was in it. And I couldn't drown then, either. Just like today." She stared at him intently, willing him to believe her.

He frowned, shaking his head.

Marin saw his hesitation. "Look, Uncle Paul. I know what you are thinking. But look at me! I'm not afraid anymore. I will never need to be afraid of the water again!" She continued in a rush before he could express his doubts about her sanity. "I just have to find out where I came from and I need your help to do it. You work for Search and Rescue; I want you to look up a boating accident that happened around fourteen or fifteen years ago. It was in a bay because the boat was docked." She bit her lip in concentration. "It was hot, so probably around June or July."

Paul glanced at her uncertainly, but she continued in a rush. "I swear I'm not crazy, I'm not delirious, and I'm not afraid of the water anymore! I'll prove it to you any time you want. Want to go diving? I'm there. Please, please promise me you'll take this seriously and look it up?"

Paul stood up and agreed with a sigh.

FIVE

After spending much of the next day resting and basically bored, Marin went back to work, though it was getting late in the day. No one who had seen her pulled from the water could believe she was alive, let alone working the day after being crushed and drowned. People shook their heads in disbelief.

It was strange being back in the docking bay again. Delphinius, the submersible that had almost killed her, sat innocently tethered across the pool undergoing a major overhaul, its wiring fried from its dunk in the water. She sat near the back tanks doing some of the paperwork that everyone hated to do. After the craziness of the past few days, the monotony of filing was strangely comforting and gave her time to reconsider the crazy plan she'd been going over in her head.

As the usual bustle of activity was winding down for the afternoon, Marin finished the last stack of papers. Friday night called most of the staff away for the weekend, so the timing was perfect for her experiment, with no prying eyes to question her. She made up her mind.

As the last people left the warehouse she melted into the pool and swam down, quickly moving past the man-made cement to the rock and sandy bottom near the opening of the bay doors, surprised and delighted with how fast and effortlessly she could move through the water. The huge metal garage doors were closed for the night, but they didn't touch the floor, and it was an easy fit to slip beneath them to the open water of the protected cove outside the door. Earlier she had left an underwater scooter tethered to the leg of the outer dock. She hoped some well-meaning employee hadn't found it and checked it back in, or there would be issues. She was relieved when she found it and had it untied in moments. The scooter was basically a motor with an enclosed propeller with handles, designed to tow divers underwater. She held its handles and started it up, the motor barely a vibration in her hands. It pulled her forward, providing what she lacked—high speed. She darted straight out the mouth of the bay, heading to the one spot she hoped no one would find her. Davey's Cave.

It had been over fifteen years since Paul and Dave had discovered Davey's Cave while hiking after work one weekend. The cave was tucked inside an inlet that was barely big enough for a boat to enter, could only be accessed by a 20 minute walk, and the entrance was pretty much buried in a landslide of scrub oak and sagebrush. But inside—oh, inside!

When she was about five, Paul took her to the ocean to show her his favorite diving spot, close to his job as a dive instructor at COAST. He was so happy to be able to teach her about his love of the ocean, and had grand visions of watching her grow by his side. When she was old enough, he pictured them diving together, exploring the ocean floor and discovering the underwater world side by side. Five-year-old Marin had followed him, whimpering whenever they got too close to the ocean. Paul thought maybe her feet were tired and carried her until they reached the scrabbly beach next to the overgrown hill.

She cried when the waves came close and Paul put her on his back to finish the hike down the hill. Carrying her inside the cave, he set her down on the shallow beach circling the water and clicked on his flashlight, expecting her to be dazzled by the deep blue water, as calm and beautiful as a private swimming pool, and the crystallized rock formations overhead that cast light around like tiny rainbows.

Instead, she screamed in terror, clawing on the slippery rock wall to find the way out and slipping into the cold water. Paul dropped his flashlight into the pool trying to catch her and it sank, throwing weird lights around them, swirling into the depths before shorting out and leaving them alone in pitch darkness with nothing but her echoing screams rebounding on all sides.

He had swooped her up and carried her home, cursing himself for his stupidity. She'd had nightmares about the place for months afterwards, as if all of her fears had found a face in that dark hole.

Now, however, she could think of no place better to disappear without anyone's notice. Buzzing through the cold Pacific, hugging the coast just enough to keep her bearings straight without getting tossed by the upper current, she slid at just over 20 knots to the rocky shoals that marked the submerged ocean outlet at the base of the cave. Paul had often told her how Davey's Cave was shaped like an elbow, with a short tunnel opening underwater, and a long upright part that could be accessed at low tide from the beach. Timing was critical in Davey's Cave, with its tube-like opening to the ocean; it filled completely when the tide came in. She glanced at her scuba watch and realized she had about 15 minutes.

Carefully maneuvering herself deep underwater to the rocky ocean floor, she aimed the scooter's powerful light into the black hole in the stony cliff and followed it into the cave. As much as she had learned since getting her diving certificate, this was the first time she had ever entered the subterranean cave, or ever gone alone into the open ocean for that matter. Her heart beat in her temples as she maneuvered the scooter through a narrow pass, praying she was in the right place and that nothing was lurking inside the dark depths.

Although she was relatively close to the top, only seventeen feet or so below the surface, she knew as well as anyone the dangers of being trapped in a dead end against the oncoming tide, and who knew what predatory animals might have chosen to take up residence inside the protection of the natural rock formation. Gritting her teeth, she pulled free of the tunnel and found herself in the calm but rising water of the glittering cave. A soft, sandy bottom covered the floor in rising drifts, responding to the pull of the water.

Half of her screamed that what she was trying was insane. She listened to the voice of Dr. Gilbert in her mind explaining how she had miraculously survived by the air trapped as the platform had fallen. It wasn't what she remembered, but the rational side of her demanded that she forget her memory; she had been in shock, her mind could have imagined everything and she was about to bet her life on a delusion. She bit her cheeks, rising to the top of the water. Numbly, she took off her diving mask and regulator, turning the knobs to the hoses off. The opening to the shore was already submerged, and the sandy beach she had stood on as a child was melting beneath the hiss of oncoming waves, yet there was still an opening large enough to let in the filtered evening sun which sent bright sparkles dancing across the surface of the surging water. Looking up, she watched the sparkling lights play across the salt stained crystals of the cave's roof. It was truly beautiful. She felt a twinge of regret for never letting Uncle Paul bring her back here.

Below her the tide was pushing through the sea tunnel and closing the gap between the exit and the water. She knew she had only moments to make up her mind. She shakily pushed the doubting thoughts away until only a firm resolve stood in its place.

Taking a calm breath, she released the straps attaching her tank to her back and let them drift swiftly past her grasp, hoses snaking out behind them onto the dark sand. She left the scooter's headlight on and let the vehicle fall, spinning its light in slow, dizzy circles as it came to rest near her oxygen tank, filling the cave with an eerie diffused glow. Holding onto the rocks, she kicked her fins gently, willing herself to stay calm. A new pulse of water pushed from below and the opening to the bay was buried in a foaming surge of water, pushing her against the cave wall. The light outside dimmed to a golden green as the pathway to the beach was flooded. She was trapped.

Glancing up at the ceiling, she knew it was only moments until she was out of air. In that second, her willpower broke. Terror ripped through her defenses, breaking through her mind with the force of the rising water, flooding her mind with the immense power of a lifetime of fear. This was insane! The sheer stupidity of what she was doing shut out all reason. All that was left was animal instinct. She had to get out!

Over twenty feet of surging seawater now separated her from her life-saving gear, and the force of it shoving through the submerged beach exit dragged her, spinning her around the rocky cave. Three feet of air was all that was between her and the dripping roof. Her fingers scrabbled to gain a handhold in the slippery walls, her legs fighting the current to gain access to the beach opening, ducking her head underwater, straining with all her might toward it, but the water pouring in beat her back.

Her mind spun frantically, jumping through stages in her life; despair at what Paul would think; angry at her stupid fantasy of living without the fear of the deadly water swirling around her. There was nothing but terror to believe in now. Who would be foolish enough not to be afraid of this living, breathing monster sucking the air from her lungs?

She thought of Jaycen, so unlucky to like someone so broken. The top of her head brushed the rocky roof and she pressed her face to the broken surface, screaming and crying and pleading for help. This was it; this was the end of everything. She clawed desperately at the rocks, crushing her face to the melting air, pushed by the hand of the merciless sea. The last pockets sifted noisily up through the rocky ceiling, through small cracks and fissures that led to the surface many yards above, merging her dying screams with the thin whistling pressure of the triumphant ocean, disappearing into the darkening sky.

SIX

Water forced its way into Marin's mouth and lungs, choking off her cry. Her body stiffened as the foreign substance forced its way into her and she thrashed uncontrollably. She fought the heaviness in her lungs, choking and kicking and spinning in protest, but habit forced her to breathe it in and breathe it out. Salt stung in her nose and throat, and she sunk, no longer held afloat by the buoyancy of air. Tears melted with the ocean as she said a hazy goodbye to life and let herself fall, no longer fighting death. She drifted like a piece of sand caught in the current down to the bottom of the cave.

The tide, now well above both openings to the cave, had ceased its tyrannical influx and had become a gentle swell and drop, pushing, pulling, and rocking her in its embrace. The light of her scooter shone in her eyes and she numbly wondered exactly how long it took to drown. Surely she should be dead by now. She took another breath of cold water, shakily forcing it in and out like the breathing tide. She looked around, feeling her mind slowly coming back to her.

The pressure of the water inside and out made breathing more laborious and she had to concentrate on making her body accept the work as natural. Her hands shook, not believing this was real. Was she really breathing water? Her throat and the back of her neck stung from the salt but other than that, she felt better by the minute.

She touched the top of her head where she had hit herself during her moments of panic and felt a small bump that was shrinking quickly.

Running her hand down the back of her neck she jerked in shock as she felt her old scars. Where there used to be smooth silver-pink skin covering the scars on both sides of her neck, there were now fleshy ripples protruding slightly. As she exhaled she felt water flowing out of them. She retracted her hands in shock.

What am I? She asked herself, recoiling from the touch. She looked around at the watery cave surrounding her and felt a blast of claustrophobia. She had to fight down an instinctive wave of primal panic at being under so much water with no way to breathe. Falling back on the relaxation techniques that Dr. Barton had made her use for years to coax down her fears of drowning, she forced herself to breathe deeply and calm down, focusing on the cavern floor. The irony that she was using Dr. Barton's tips to help keep her calm *after* drowning shook her from her panic and she suddenly burst out in laughter.

The water around her was growing dim, yet she could see surprisingly well. She swam down, flicked off the scooter's light, and looked out the tunnel. Even though the sun was setting, she could see a good distance into the water, a vibrant blue, and she tried to remember if she had always been able to see this well underwater. She laughed at herself, realizing that she had never before *been* like this underwater.

Full of wonder, she swam out of the tunnel and into the open, feeling freer than she had ever imagined possible. Turquoise water spread out before her in all directions, and the sea floor lay sloping downward. A small school of silvery sardines swung past her and paused, glittering like coins. She stared at them, open mouthed, wondering if they thought she was one of them. She reached out a hesitant hand to touch them and they skittered away into the darkness. She saw larger shapes in the distance swimming gracefully and she could feel the vibrations in the water as fishing boats trundled past on their way back to port. With her lungs filled with water, she had little buoyancy. She sank to the sand, touching the bottom.

Despite her amazing depth of sight, the light was getting seriously dim. Glancing at her dive watch, she realized how late it was, so she retrieved her things, slinging her tank over her back and letting her scooter speed her home.

The trip back went much faster, with Marin sliding through the water like a fish. She noticed different tastes to the water as she went, with patches that felt green with growth and spots that tasted like engine oil. Crabs and fish darted from her noisy vehicle. She vowed to come back again without it.

She raced to the warehouse and tethered her scooter to the pier. Only then did she come to the surface. Holding onto the dock for stability, she pushed her head out of the water. On impulse, she plugged her nose and blew water out the back of her neck, emptying the water from her lungs, and taking in a cold and almost unsatisfying breath of thin air. The movement seemed so instinctive that she paused, suddenly thrust back into a memory. She was holding onto the side of the port hole in the middle of their houseboat, she and her father both blowing water out of their lungs before pulling themselves inside to dry off and eat dinner. Her mother was at a small camp stove cooking soup.

The memory was so vivid it shocked her. She froze, captured by that happy moment, not wanting to move beyond it in fear of breaking it forever. Eventually, her dive watch beeped and shattered the mood, uncaringly warning of the late hour. Tucking her new memory into the shattered collection in her heart, she swam under the warehouse door.

Back in her room and after a hot shower, her wet hair wrapped tightly in a towel, she thought back to her attempts to breathe water in the confines of the bathtub with a laugh. Lying underwater in the tub with only centimeters between her nose and the easy temptation of air was too much of a task against the ingrained instinct to breathe. As terrifying as it was, she had known the only way to overcome it was to deny escape. And it worked! Strange elation flowed through her with a euphoria she had never before known.

She could never drown! The irony that her greatest fear was the one thing she need *never* have feared made her laugh out loud. She felt like a superhero, snatched from a lifetime of inadequacy and thrust into a future of complete proficiency. It was unfathomable. With these feelings rose a torrent of questions. What was she? Where did she come from? Who were her parents? Was there anyone else like her?

Suddenly all her thoughts about her previous and future life seemed disconnected. Her lost family, her fear of water, Paul, Jaycen—nothing seemed to fit right anymore. Was she even the same *species*? Could she ever have a relationship, get married, have children? Was she some kind of alien?

She ran her fingers along the back of her neck where her skin was smooth once again. Shaking her head in frustration, she stood up and flicked on her computer to start searching information about amphibians, reptiles, and deep water breathing. Nothing came up to give her answers, but she did find some accounts of Navy personnel learning how to adjust to breathing a highly oxygenated liquid called perfluorocarbon, which was extremely enlightening. She wondered why she hadn't looked this stuff up before she went to the cave.

The more she researched, the stranger she felt. Nothing out there came close to what she was experiencing. She didn't know what she was hoping for—some website for water breathers anonymous? Still, her earlier euphoria started seeping away as she realized just how different she was. It was frightening.

She cracked open a water bottle and took a sip. A knock at the door made her jump, spilling water down the front of her robe. The door opened before she could even stand up to answer it, and Jaycen poked his head in around the door.

"Hey, can I come in?" he asked, walking in anyway and sitting on her bed. The door swung shut behind him.

"Um, I'm not really … dressed," she said gesturing at her robe. Despite that, she was surprised at how glad she was to see him.

"Oh, I'm sorry. I didn't even notice. I just needed to talk to you for a second. I have to meet with Tui in a minute or I'd just come back when you've changed. Got a sec?"

She pulled her robe tighter around her frame and nodded. Everything in her reality shifted in light of her discovery when she saw Jaycen. The joy she'd felt earlier faded instantly. It was like looking at the world through unbreakable glass. Where Jaycen had seemed so attainable he bordered on annoying, now he felt off limits somehow. *What am I?* She started to feel ill. Tears simmered behind her eyes as she watched him run his hand nervously through freshly cut hair.

"I just thought you should know … I left my phone on the outboard after we came in this afternoon, so while I was on deck looking for it, I saw you swimming out from below the dock and under the warehouse door."

Marin felt ice run through her veins. "I … you did?" she stammered, but he continued.

"So I noticed you had a scooter tied up under there and that you forgot to check it in. I know *you* know what happens if you forget to bring in the expensive stuff, so I pulled it into the bay and locked it up for you."

Marin winced as she thought of the noise the huge bay doors made when they opened, which was why she had risked leaving the scooter out in the first place. She had planned on getting up at five when the first boats were scheduled to go out and bring it into the bay then, when the flurry of activity would cover for her. She couldn't speak.

Jaycen looked at her, an unreadable expression in his eyes. He watched her reaction curiously. "Why would you be taking equipment out, unauthorized, after hours *and alone?* I never pegged you as the rule breaker type, not to mention you are the least excited out of anyone here to go off exploring underwater in your free time." He got off the bed and squatted down next to her chair so they were eye to eye.

"Are you ok?" he asked quietly.

His tender concern stabbed her, breaking through to the complications her new reality presented. Tears behind her eyes rushed forward and she dropped her face into her hands to cover them, sobbing. Jaycen rocked back on his heels in surprise. She felt him awkwardly put his arms around her and let her cry into his shoulder. Tui was waiting for him, but that was going to have to wait.

Marin let all the stress and terror and amazement of the past twelve hours flow out of her, grateful for the warm, kind shoulder offered to her. She couldn't help noticing that he smelled like warm sand. It was several minutes before she felt in control enough to pull away, hastily snatching a tissue off her desk as she did. Jaycen knelt in front of her, looking completely baffled. He gingerly took her hand.

"What is it?" he asked.

Marin thought of all the ways she could tell him what was happening, but if she couldn't wrap her own head around it, how could she put it into words? And even if she did, how would he react? Wasn't she now the very definition of a freak? There were just too many unanswered questions and nowhere to begin. Again she felt a wall fall down around her, isolating her from everything familiar. All she could do to answer him was shake her head, slow tears still rolling down her cheeks.

"Are you in trouble or something? Is someone putting you up to this? Please, tell me Marin. I just want to help."

"I don't even know what to say, Jaycen. I just … I don't know. Yes, something is wrong, or right, or … I don't know. I'm not in trouble. I'm just …"

What could she say? She was a fish? An alien? A freak? All of the above? Then she remembered something Paul used to talk about and a different label came to mind. *A mermaid?* She let that thought hang in her mind as Jaycen waited for her reply, eyes wide.

Tui pounded on the door and they both jumped. He stuck his head in and said "Oi, Jaycen! We goin' or what?"

Jaycen jumped to his feet guiltily, glancing down at Marin's tear-stained eyes.

Tui followed his gaze and started to back out of the room. "Oh, sorry, Mares. Didn't know what was holding up Romeo here. Meet you in the car, Jaycen." The door clicked shut.

Marin stood up and wiped her eyes. "Guess you'd better go. He's waiting."

"He can wait. What were you going to tell me?"

She shrugged, her mind swimming. "I'll be ok, Jaycen. Something happened today that kind of shook me up is all. Don't worry, I'll be fine."

Jaycen didn't look anywhere near convinced. His phone started vibrating and he quickly silenced it, cursing Tui under his breath. "Look, whatever it is, I want to help." Marin let herself hope for a minute, believing in the daydream of someone to talk to, to help her find the answers. Someone to tell her she wasn't different or if she was, it didn't matter. Jaycen took both her hands in his. "Just tell me what I can do." His telephone buzzed again.

What could be done? The walls slammed hard around her and she whispered the cold realization aloud, "Jaycen, there's nothing anyone can do."

SEVEN

Paul sat at his desk flipping through his wallet until he found Dr. Barton's phone number, worried about Marin's obsession with the accident and a little hurt at her need to "replace him" as a parent figure in her life with this mystery family she could never have. He gave her a call.

"All adopted or foster children have a need to connect to their roots," she said. "It's part of developing their sense of self. In her case, it could provide a sense of closure that could be very beneficial to her. And don't worry, it doesn't reflect on your parenting negatively at all. On the contrary, it shows how safe she feels with you to reach out like this. Go along with it and be as supportive as you can," she suggested. Reluctantly, Paul agreed.

He didn't really think searching for boating accidents was going to turn anything up, but he'd promised, so he trolled the endless computer records half-heartedly until it was time to go home and sleep after finishing a long graveyard shift. He almost missed it as he started to close the files to shut down his computer, but a picture caught his eye.

A photo of a marina with several boats in flaming ruin, black smoke smeared across the sky; people on shore were staring, wide-eyed with shock. His hands began to shake as he read the report about a little houseboat neighborhood in a bay not fifteen miles from where he and Marin lived. A speedboat had raced into the marina and rammed into the back of one houseboat, causing an explosion as it hit the gas tank. The boats on either side had caught fire quickly.

Witnesses stated there were several people on board the boat on the left, only two of which survived initially, but died of severe burns within days. He felt eerie goose bumps rising on his arms as he read the true account of Marin's nightmares. The houseboat that had suffered the direct hit had a man and a woman on board. The woman's body was thrown into the water when it was hit. It was thought the man had been behind the boat working on the propeller and it was assumed that he and the driver of the speedboat had been incinerated.

He read on, heart pounding, disbelieving. In addition to the two doomed survivors, a small girl had been rescued from the wreckage. A black and white picture showed her, maybe two years old, lying on the sand in the arms of a black suited rescue diver. The article stated that she had been found in an air pocket in one of the sinking boats. There was no way to confirm her identity and nobody had come forward with information regarding her.

He stared at the article, shaking his head, feeling his world turned upside down. That couldn't be his little girl, could it?

He sent the email immediately to Marin and called her to listen to her reaction as she read it. He wished he'd just brought it to her in person. She was too silent on the phone.

"Marin? You okay?"

"That's it! That's me," she said triumphantly. "After years of being told I was crazy and imagining things, well, here's the proof I'm not, right in front of me."

"Are you sure?"

"Yes. That's me. What happened to the boats?"

"The boats?"

"Yes. The wreck. Of my boat. You know the one I came from? Where is it? Did they take it away or something?" Marin asked impatiently.

"The boat?" Paul asked, puzzled. "From the accident? I suppose it could still be there if it sank far enough. I'm guessing the fuel and oil all burned off, so there wouldn't have been much of a reason to pull any of them up."

She squealed in his ear in excitement. He pulled the phone away with a grimace.

"Uncle Paul, can you take me there? Can we go diving and look at it? Please?" He imagined her hands folded together, begging like she did when she really wanted something.

Paul leaned back on his chair wishing he'd had more than three hours sleep the night before.

Marin tried harder. "I don't have work today, you're not on call—I'll bring the sandwiches. Please?"

A grin spread across Paul's face. He'd waited a long time to have his little girl beg him to take her diving. How could he refuse?

"Ok. Let's go. I'll pick you up in an hour. Have you got access to tanks, or do you need me to pick some up at the dive shop?"

"I'm all set."

"Good. Don't forget—plenty of jalapeños on those sandwiches, ok?" he laughed.

"Gotcha. Thanks, Uncle Paul. It will be great! See you soon!"

An hour and a half later they were standing on the shore of a round cove filled with fancy houseboats, sailboats, and a marina already getting crowded with pre-weekend boaters. It was barely 8:00 a.m., but boaters got up with the sun. Paul got the chills as he pulled into the parking lot, passed a row of sun-bleached mailboxes and came to a stop. A chain link fence blocked off the entrance to the houseboats, but the gate was open and people were coming and going about their business.

Marin was enthralled. "It's like a little floating neighborhood!" she exclaimed, noticing the rows of geraniums planted on both sides of the fence, with the pier running down the middle of the boats like a sidewalk.

Paul watched her with a curious sadness. This could have been *her* home, *her* life, if not for a random stab from fate. He felt guilty for being grateful for the tragedy that lost her a family, yet gained him his. She stooped beneath the mailboxes and ran her fingers through piles of rounded stones surrounding the posts. They were beach rocks, beaten by water and rolled smooth by waves, their colors almost translucent. Paul strolled over and stood above her, silently stifling a yawn.

"These ... I remember them, I think," she said in a faraway tone. "I played here. I mean, it seems familiar; me sitting here and touching these stones. My jewels."

Paul held his breath so as not to break the spell. Marin ran her fingers through the rocks absently, her mind years away. She picked up a bluish one, considered it thoughtfully for a moment then stood, tucking it in her pocket. She dusted off her hands and studied the harbor.

"Well, let's go, okay?"

Paul followed her to the truck to get his gear on. He felt weird, like he was walking among ghosts and about to rob a tomb. He'd been around plenty of wrecks before, but none that had directly impacted his life like this one. He thought about the people that died that day. These ghosts were hers.

The water was fairly clear, and although boat traffic on a Thursday should be minimal, Paul set up a net of safety buoys around their dive site to ensure they could dive without fear of a speedboat coming by and running them down. The July water was still shockingly cool even with their wetsuits on. Splashing into the water, Paul watched as Marin adjusted her mask but paused before she put in her regulator. He saw her glance at him, and bite her lip uncertainly. He wondered if she was battling her old demons as, with a sigh, she turned on her hose and popped in the mouthpiece.

As they slowly sank down, the sparkling surface of the water darkened. They both switched on their lights and angled downward. It was only about a 60 foot dive before they hit bottom. The hulls of the houseboats hung over them like whales, their shadows adding darkness in patches along the bottom of the bay. Marin swam close to the bottom, inspecting every pop bottle, old shoe and piece of garbage that she came across. He assumed she was hoping for a flash of memory like she'd had by the rock garden.

Paul swam ahead, flashlight searching for the remains of the boats. He felt the pull of the tide and tried to calculate the amount of drift that might have affected the lay of the wreckage. The bay floor had a steep slope and about another 15 foot drop-off toward the middle of the bay where Paul bet the wreck would be. Positioning himself parallel to the pier he worked his way down the slope, his flashlight making broad sweeps in the murky water.

Paul kept an eye on Marin as she trailed behind, searching for pieces of the life she had lost in the rocky depths. She found another bluish stone buried in the silt and picked it up, sliding it into the pouch at her waist. Suddenly something caught his attention out of the corner of his eye.

Like the corpse of a monster, his flashlight shone on a mossy grey green hull, lying on its side.

* * *

Marin stared at the boat. It was bigger than she had imagined, and some-how looking at it made everything she had ever feared about the water come back in a rush. It was so … real. It was like digging up the remains of a dead relative. Tears burned in her eyes and brimmed over into her mask, clouding her vision, her breathing coming in sporadic gasps. Paul swam over to her and put his hands on her shoulders, trying to see into her eyes. She knew he would be freaking out, but was too overwhelmed to do much to stop it. He put his arms around her and towed her as fast as he safely could up to the surface. Emerging away from the buoys, he kept a lookout while she took off her mask and tried to slow down her breathing.

"You ok, Sweetheart?" he asked anxiously. Marin gulped a few breaths and tried to gain control of herself. "Let's head back to the shore, Marin, and grab our lunch. We can take it easy for a few."

Marin shook her head. "I don't want to get out yet. I just need a sec … just let me breathe." She shook off the urge to rip off her hood and breathe the cool water surrounding her. But this ability she had, what-ever it meant, seemed like part of something bigger, even dangerous, and she felt that the less people knew about it, perhaps even the less *she* knew about it, the better.

Taking a few calming breaths, she watched Paul, keeping an ever-moving eye across the water to keep her safe. Rescuer and protector. She felt a wave of affection for Paul, always standing in the shadows and pushing her onto her own feet to shine. Always willing to take calls when someone was in trouble, working two jobs, not for the money, but because he was good at what he did and wanted to make a difference.

As much as she loved Paul as a father, she couldn't walk away from this now. She had to follow this through and at least to try to find answers about where she came from. She concentrated on breathing until she felt in control again and Paul's expression relaxed. She put her regulator back in her mouth and gave Paul the okay sign. He nodded as she went back under. She kicked directly to the wreck, focusing on keeping her pulse even, her breathing regulated.

Layers of greenish brown moss covered much of the wreck. This close to the surface, sun filtered down and gave the moss an environment to thrive in; life springing from death. The broken stern of a speedboat lay nearby, its red fiberglass hull still glittering in the dim light; smooth, as if it was too foreign of a substance for moss to cling to. She swam over to the red boat, like a victim in court curious to see the murderer.

Most of the boat's back was gone. What was left was a twisted, melted mess, an open cave filled with settled rocks and tiny, darting fish. Paul had assured her before that any human remains found had been removed by police divers at the time of the accident. She kicked over to the speedboat's helm, running a gloved hand over the perfect steering wheel. The driver's seat was still intact, as well as one passenger seat, though it was buried under piles of sediment. The engine compartment in back was melted as well. She assumed the heat of the fire must have ignited the gasoline in the engine. It made her shiver to think of the driver of this boat, crashing and then caught between two huge fires with no way to escape.

She was surprised to see the useless key was still in the ignition, switched to on, its keychain coated in grime and swaying in the current. It somehow made her want to laugh. She pointed to it and looked at Paul. He shrugged indifferently, so she turned the key with effort and pulled it out, tucking it into her pouch. She looked carefully around the boat, but found nothing more than some corroded fishhooks and the remains of several beer cans that may have been debris from years of boats passing overhead.

Swimming over the mangled stern, she looked for any identifying features, especially where most boats put logos, names or silly marine phrases. She swept silt off ragged edges, looking closely with her high beam flashlight. She found some sort of mark curled under a piece of the upper stern. She looked closely, shining her light at all angles around the destroyed piece of plastic. Paul had read her the accident report the police submitted, claiming the event was a random tragedy, but Marin's attention to this small detail pushed him forward curiously.

She backed away so he could see what looked like a discolored black squiggle, a distorted wavy line. He backed up and shrugged, shaking his head. She fumbled into her pouch and pulled out the keychain, shining her light onto it, and onto the partial symbol on the boat. He took it into his hands, wiping some of the years of grime off and peered closely at it as she hovered over his shoulder. He traced the simple silver shape, not much wider than the chain itself, with his gloved finger. The shape in his hand matched the shape on the boat. A thin silver animal with two glinting blue eyes. She pointed at the warped line on the boat. There was definitely a blue eye on the design on the boat. It was a sea serpent.

Marin drifted off to the houseboat, leaving the keychain for Paul. Fueled by her discovery, she played her flashlight over the hull of her broken home with determination, looking for anything she might remember, some clue to help her find out who she was.

Like the red motor boat, the houseboat was listing to its side, its top leaning toward the deeper center of the bay. It was a two-story house-boat, but an older, boxy design. She could easily see where the motor-boat struck it, since that part was torn completely away, leaving a gaping entrance to the inside. She flipped up her headlamp and swam over the decomposing hull, searching for any identifying features, running her gloved hand over the rotting wood and fiberglass. It was hard to imagine this boat fitting inside the boat of her memories, lying skewed and decrepit in this twilight world.

Like an oyster, the sea claimed this object as its own, wrapping it in sediment and moss, tarnishing its brightness with saltwater, filling it with its own life forms. She felt an irrational anger that the sea had forever claimed all that was rightfully hers. Slick brownish moss clung to the surface, but wiped easily away when she brushed it with her hand. For a moment she thought that if she could just wipe it all clean, tip it back on its keel and bring it up to the land of the living, that she could somehow save it, this thing that represented all she had lost. Several small, silver fish darted out of the open back, startling her. She shook her head and moved into the cave-like hull.

She had a fun-house moment of vertigo as she floated into the tipped room. Warped wooden cupboards lay open, displaying thick plastic plates and cups sitting completely stacked, although leaning, waiting to be set on a table that was a crumble of rot and Formica. Marin reached in and picked up a sippy cup with rough teeth marks around the spout. She held it gently, realizing with surprise that those were probably *her* teeth marks. She had used this cup. This had been hers. With profound reverence, she held it carefully and moved on. The stainless steel sink was untouched except for a crab that scuttled into the drain, angry at being disturbed. Hardy marine carpet still clung stubbornly to the tilting floor, laced with sand. Paul drifted in, floating gently behind her, still clutching the serpent symbol in his hand.

Marin closed her eyes, touching the counter gently and willing those submerged memories to come to the surface. She was in a hammock, her favorite blanket tucked up around her chin. She opened her eyes and looked at a shelf above the table. Aluminum loops were embedded into the wall where a child-sized hammock once hung. She closed her eyes again, feeling the sway of the water and imagining it as the feel of

AQUA

the boat under her feet. Letting her mind roam free, she made herself
dream what it could have been like living here, even if it wasn't real. She
thought of the feel of the carpet on her bare feet. She thought of bacon
cooking on the small stove. She thought of a half gallon of milk always
kept on the lowest shelf of the door in the tiny green refrigerator so she
could reach it.

Opening her eyes again, she was surprised to notice that under
the grime, it really *was* green. She tried to pull it open. Paul came in
behind her and reached out to help. There was so much suction that she
wondered if it was still sealed shut after all this time. It was. The door
popped open and water rushed in, spilling its contents around her feet.
She looked at each item from the refrigerator, marveling that the last
time they had been touched her mother and father were alive.

Most things dissolved at the touch of the water, but several survived:
a container of cottage cheese, blackened pears in a Tupperware container,
a small jar of homemade jam, tiny sweet pickles. Marin put the pickles
in her pouch and Paul chuckled to himself. She repacked the refrigerator and closed the door, but it refused to close and hung loosely on its
hinges. In the door's lowest shelf was a browned plastic carton of milk.

She moved toward the back of the boat, her memories taking her to the
portal from her dreams. It was hard to find in the sediment and debris, but
there it was, hidden under the table. Only a large hole remained, ragged
and melted. She swam past Paul and through the bottom of the boat.

On the bay floor, she found what she was looking for. The heavy
circular door that belonged to the portal, buried in silt and debris. It
was still too heavy for her to move since it was half pinned under the
wreck, but she swept the grime off anyway. Paul came down beside her
and looked at the portal she was cleaning. It had a wheel on the top of
it, like the doors used in the Navy that are used to seal off an area from
water. Marin pointed to the hole in the boat above her and to the door,
as if they belonged together. Marin could see Paul looked thoughtful.
She knew what he was thinking, why would anyone want a portal *inside*
a houseboat?

Marin looked for symbols on the back of the houseboat as she had with the speedboat. The impact of the accident had ripped part of the back of the boat away, and it hung face down in the sand. She wished she could communicate with Paul down here. It was one of the frustrations about diving; everything was hand signals and gestures.

Her breath stopped as something caught her eye. "Marin" was printed in blue cursive that melted into twisted plastic on the back of the boat. It looked like the word had more letters, but they were indiscernible. She ran her fingers over the sparkly blue letters. Seeing her name on the bottom of the ocean like this made it feel foreign to her. *Marin ... Marin,* she said the name over and over in her mind until it didn't seem like a name anymore, just a strange train of sounds. So was the boat named after her, or did someone name her after the boat?

She turned to point out her discovery to Paul, but he was still under the boat poking around the portal. She waved to get his attention, but he wasn't looking her way.

Look over here! she thought forcefully, willing him to glance up. She sighed and started to swim over to him when suddenly a faint disembodied voice cut into her mind, sending chills down her back.

"Who is this?" it said. Images of the people who had died here raced into her imagination; voices of the dead calling to her.

She stopped, turning to look all around her, her heart pounding.

It came again, louder. *"Who are you? Amanda?"* Chills ran up her spine when she heard that name. She kicked her feet, racing to the safety and sanity of Paul.

"Where are you? Stay there and I'll come find you!"

"No! Stop it!" she thought desperately, trying to get away from the ghostly voice.

"Stay there! Please!" the voice demanded. *"I'm coming!"*

Marin crashed into Paul, breathing heavily. He caught her by the shoulders, looking into her wide, panicked eyes. He gave the signal to do an emergency ascent and she nodded frantically, kicking up and away from whatever was coming. Paul caught her arm to slow her down, reminding her they couldn't ascend more than 30 feet per minute. She glanced at the distance between them and the surface, feeling her old panic creeping in. Paul took her hand in his and she tried to stay at a steady pace next to him, despite the prickles down her spine that told her they were being watched. When they were almost to the top, she thought she saw something coming toward them from the shadows and she kicked harder. Once their faces broke the surface, Paul ripped off his mask.

"Are you ok?"

Marin looked around in the water below her, half expecting to feel something grab her legs and pull her down. Was she going crazy?

Paul caught her chin in one hand and said sternly, "Marin, what's going on?"

"I ... thought I heard something down there. A voice." She realized how crazy she sounded. "Did you hear anything?"

He creased his brows, frowning, but then relaxed visibly. "It must've been a radio playing. There are tons of boats out here. Water has strange acoustic effects. Sound can seem like it's all around you." He took a deep breath. "So you weren't having more ... you know ... trouble?"

She couldn't hear the voice any more. She shook her head in confusion as they swam to shore. Paul was right. It had to have been a passing boat playing a news station or something too loud. As they got their towels, she still couldn't shake the feeling that they were being watched, but the only people around seemed busy tacking up sails or laughing with friends.

Then, out of the corner of her eye, she saw what looked like a young man staring intently at her from the end of a pier, dripping wet, but in the instant it took to turn her head, he disappeared.

EIGHT

Finishing her sandwich, Marin watched a clipper gliding out of the bay and tried to sort out her thoughts. The sun was hot on her legs, so she pulled off the rest of her wet suit and let the sun soak into her skin instead. Paul downed the tail end of a can of root beer and wiped his mouth with the back of his hand.

"Uncle Paul, do you know my real name?"

Paul crushed the can between his two strong hands and placed it in the bag next to him before he answered. He sighed and looked at her sideways. "What's in a name? A rose by any other name would still smell as sweet, you know. At least that's what Shakespeare had to say about it."

"So, does that mean you don't? Or does that mean my name is Rose?"

"No, Mares. I don't know your real name. I'm betting they named you after the only clue they had to who you were; that name on the back of the boat. I know people tried to find out about you. Child Protective Services, the police, Search and Rescue, but there really wasn't much to go on. You could have been born at home, on your boat, or in some small hospital in Wisconsin. Here's something to blow your mind—you could have been born in another country." He let that sit on her mind for a moment, watching her try on the possibility. "Your name may be Helga or Dominica Maria Suave for all we know."

Marin paused hesitantly. "Could it be Amanda?"

Paul smiled and shrugged. Marin sat silently watching a boat leave the safety of the harbor, its huge sails unfurled like wings against a breeze she couldn't feel.

"Aren't boats supposed to be registered or licensed or something? How could they live here without having something saying it was ok?"

"Sure, there's all sorts of things like that. And rent, too, to live on a pier like this. But there were no records of them at all. According to the lease agent's report, they had just arrived and hadn't filled out papers, although there was testimony of two people saying they'd lived there for at least two months, maybe longer. It seems rather fishy, pardon the pun, but I read the report. The police seized all the lease agreements and nothing was there. The neighbors said they kept to themselves. That's all I could dig up."

"Well, what about the boat that hit us? Wasn't there anything about him? Or his boat?" she persisted.

Paul sighed in frustration. "No, sweetheart. The body was completely burned. The speed boat was just like a million others that come in here all the time for gas from anywhere up the coast. The best you could hope for was that someone had filed a missing persons report and they could link the two, but whoever it was either had no family to miss him or her, or the people that *did* miss him weren't going to say anything to the police about it."

Marin looked at him in shock. "You think he could have been a criminal?"

Paul said, "I don't mean there was anything criminal about any of this. I just think maybe he was a drug addict, or someone without a family. There are plenty of people in L.A. that fit that description."

Marin scowled. "Do you think *my* parents were criminals?"

She could see in his face that the thought had occurred to him. After all, how many people would live a life with no paper trail to identify them? Looking at her concerned expression, he shook his head.

"No, Mares. I think they just kept to themselves and hadn't filled out paperwork. There are lots of people that live on the water full time and move around when they want to. They don't like being tied down to one spot, and they don't like having 'big brother' looking over their shoulder. It's not so crazy to think they just didn't get around to filling out a rental agreement. It's a peaceful and adventurous life. The kind of life I wouldn't mind living, if you want to know the truth. Who doesn't dream of taking off in a boat and just disconnecting from the world to live life on your own terms?"

She nodded thoughtfully, accepting his answer and her thoughts drifted to the voice she thought she heard. It was just too weird.

"So, what was it you found down there?" Paul asked, changing the subject.

She reached over to her equipment where she had sat her things. "Just the pickles. Don't worry, I won't eat them. And this." She looked down at the sippy cup in her hand and passed it to Paul. He took it carefully, but water poured out of the ragged spout all over his lap.

"Hey! It's still full!" he laughed, wiping the water off his lap.

"I thought you might be thirsty," she joked. "What did you bring up?"

Digging in his pouch, Paul produced the key and chain. Marin scooted closer in and watched him shine the metal with a napkin.

"Hey, I think this may be real silver!" he exclaimed. "Look how tarnished it is." He opened up the crumpled paper his sandwich had been in and plucked out a stray pickle he'd left behind.

"Still hungry?" Marin asked.

"No, it's a science experiment." He took the pickle and squeezed it until a couple drops of juice dripped down onto the tarnished keychain in his palm. With one finger he gently rubbed the juice all over it, then wiped it off with his napkin some more. The keychain was still dark, but it had lightened enough to see the detail on it.

"Cool! Where did you learn how to do that?"

Paul smiled smugly. "The amazing properties of vinegar … third grade science."

Marin rolled her eyes. "Look how the end is all rounded, like a teardrop. I think this was bigger and it melted and this is just what was left."

Paul nodded thoughtfully, rubbing more pickle juice onto it and revealing more of its rich, silver shine. "The design looks warped, too. See where the scales are going different directions? Maybe this was a different shape originally."

Marin nodded. "Yeah. The shape on the back of the boat. A sea serpent or snake or something." Paul rubbed carefully around the eyes. Blue facets sparkled in the sun. "Do you think that stone is real, too?"

Paul turned it gently back and forth, making the eye glitter. He seemed lost in thought. "I don't know. Sure is pretty, though."

"It's a sapphire," she whispered. Something tickled at the back of her mind. She loved sapphires, but they always made her feel nervous some-how. She pulled the rocks out of her pouch. They were heavy, round, and about the size of an egg. She rubbed one with her napkin. "Look."

The rock was a translucent pale blue. "Wow. That's a keeper," he said, holding it up to the light. "Did you find this down there?"

"No. It's the one I found by the mailboxes. Here's what I found in the water." She shifted the other one around in her hand. It was a deeper blue, but had chunks of other rock clinging to it. "They're so pretty. Do you think they're real?"

"What, real sapphires?" he asked in surprise. "I doubt it. But I don't know anything about rocks." She tucked them back into her pouch.

Paul fingered the little silver keychain. "I want to spend some time with this and see if I can figure anything out about it, okay?" Paul asked.

Marin shrugged away her thoughts. "Fine with me. You can keep it." She threw the rest of her lunch into the basket and picked up her sippy cup. "Thanks for coming with me, Uncle Paul. You're the best." She gave him a one armed hug.

Paul turned his gaze back to the little object he held in his hand, with its blue eyes staring up at him, mouth open, poised to strike . "You know, this kind of reminds me of an old logo for a big time shipping company way up the coast near San Francisco or Oregon."

"Really? What was it called?" she asked absently.

"Leviathan."

* * *

Frank Gilbert was used to luxury. His leather chair was automatically warmed when its internal temperature became too cool, as it was now, with the heavy curtains drawn across the overlarge windows. A storm was stirring on the western horizon. He clicked his computer over to his 24-hour weather site and saw the forecast: rain was predicted for the next two days. He sighed in frustration. That would postpone his diving expedition. The door to his office opened and a small man with straight black hair and olive skin walked smoothly in, wearing a grey suit and white gloves. Gilbert stood.

"Mr. Hahn. How nice of you to drop by. Please, have a seat." The man sat down lightly on the edge of one of the chairs in front of Gilbert's desk, but didn't speak.

"Can I get you anything? Ice water? Maybe some herbal tea?"

In answer, Mr. Hahn clicked open his briefcase, producing several photographs which he picked up in white gloved hands and slid across the polished mahogany desk. Gilbert leaned forward to look and had to concentrate hard to hide his revulsion and keep his face neutral.

"How many test subjects did you use?" he asked, his voice barely more than a whisper.

"Two." The man spoke in a clipped European accent. "The photographs capture them in different stages. As you can see, only one survived, and he will have substantial modifications to his lifestyle. Nevertheless, we are counting this experiment to be a success. We will continue testing along these lines and soon we will accomplish our aims. We may no longer need what you have to offer."

The photographs flashed through Gilbert's mind and he shivered almost imperceptibly, but Hahn noticed and twitched a smile of satisfaction. Gilbert regained his composure and opened his desk, pulling out a handful of stones which he spilled gently on the desk. Hahn's eyes widened.

"You have them?" Hahn asked, astonished. He picked up the rough sapphires encased in Basalt, but glowing with inner beauty. Greed flickered in Hahn's eyes and it was Gilbert's turn to smirk. He enjoyed the look for a moment then continued.

"We have found a small amount several hundred feet down. It could merely be a random vein, but we are following the leads regardless. There is evidence of subterranean volcanic activity in the areas we've discovered."

"Why would you tell me this?" Hahn asked suspiciously.

"Because it means nothing. You won't ever find what you are looking for. It doesn't exist," he replied flatly.

The man replaced the photos and closed his case with an overloud click. He rested his gloved hands on the top of the case and stared at Gilbert with hard, obsidian eyes. "We shall see. When is the launch?"

"The loss of Delphinius pushed us back. We are prepping Aquanis, but it will take several weeks."

"Time is something you are quickly running out of," Hahn hissed. "I must remind you of the role you play in this, Dr. Gilbert. We will get our people in position one way or another. I am confident we are close to finding it, despite your pessimism. You know us well enough to know we will do what it takes to succeed. Need I remind you what happens to those who are responsible when we fail?"

Gilbert dropped his eyes to the pictures on his desk. "I'm well aware of your methods. I have no reason to fail."

"Good. And how many personnel will the sub require?" Hahn asked with a smug smile.

"Aquanis will carry two." Gilbert said. "We will bring the J.O.S.H.I.E. unit for remote exploration as well. It's a sophisticated motorized camera that can be controlled from Aquanis."

Hahn cleared his throat. "Aquanis is fitted for three, is she not?"

"Two are sufficient."

Hahn's eyes glittered. "Yes. Well. You must maintain the highest level of security. We will be very unhappy if our operations are disrupted by the untimely revelations of our program."

Gilbert frowned defiantly. "I am aware of the security protocol."

"Good. Then our business is concluded. Good day, Dr. Gilbert." Hahn rose and disappeared through the door. Gilbert stood at the window, watching through a gap in the curtains until he saw a black Mercedes Benz pull into the staff parking lot, collect Mr. Hahn, and drive away. Time was indeed running out. Back at his desk he opened a secure file on his personal computer marked "Hyper metamorphosis" and began reading feverishly.

* * *

Marin walked into the rec room to see Natalee sitting between Tui and Jaycen watching soccer. It was painfully obvious that Natalee didn't know or care about the game in the least as she cheered randomly for whoever touched the ball. Marin walked in just as a goal was scored for the other team and everybody groaned in unison, Natalee joining belatedly. Marin stopped in the doorway until she realized the groans had nothing to do with her, stabbed with a sudden blade of jealousy when she saw Natalee sitting so close to Jaycen. She sulkily continued inside to make herself a sandwich.

As she waited for the microwave to heat up her lunchmeat that had somehow been tucked in the freezer, she watched Jaycen's back. Natalee glanced her way but didn't say anything, which made Marin perversely happy. Natalee obviously wasn't so secure with Jaycen after all. The game moved to instant replay just as the microwave started to beep. Jaycen glanced over then turned back to the television. Marin felt her stomach constrict and suddenly she didn't feel very hungry anymore. She got a glass of water and gathered her sandwich up in a napkin. Suddenly Jaycen appeared at her side. Natalee sat on the couch staring daggers at her.

"Hey! Where have you been lately?"

Marin felt her face turn red as Natalee stood up as if to join them, but instead turned and walked silently out the door.

"I ... I didn't mean to interrupt your date."

Jaycen shrugged. "I hadn't asked her on one, so you didn't."

"I just came in for something to eat. I'll let you get back to your game."

"Yah, Jaycen! Get back to your game!" Tui yelled from the couch. Jaycen ignored him.

He wrinkled his nose at her soggy lunchmeat. "You call that food? Let me see that."

Marin hesitantly handed him her napkin-wrapped sandwich. He looked under the top piece of bread, made a face, and then dropped the entire thing in the garbage can.

"What! Why did you do that?" Marin cried out.

"I'm sorry, I just know that warm lunchmeat doesn't make a nutritious dinner. But to make it up to you, I'll buy you something else, ok?"

Marin stared at him openmouthed. Was he asking her out? Or just being really weird? She was speechless. He smiled and took her hand, dragging her through the main doors and out to his car.

"Do you like seafood?" he asked, helping her into his beat-up yellow Corolla. She nodded, still unsure if she had actually just been hijacked onto a date. "Great!" He pulled out his cell phone and made a call as he backed out the car.

"I'd like to make a take-out order. Yes. Hang on a sec, ok?" he leaned over to Marin, buckling her seatbelt and whispered, "Do you like shrimp?" She nodded. "OK, I'll have the Ultimate Feast and can you throw in some extra garlic biscuits? Yeah, I know! Those things are totally addicting." He threw his car into gear and headed toward the highway, still talking to the restaurant. "Um, yes." He pulled the phone away from his mouth whispered to Marin, "What do you want to drink?"

"Water?" she threw out tentatively. Jaycen scowled at her and shook his head.

"We'll take two strawberry lemonades, please. Yes, that's all. We'll be there in about ten minutes. Thanks." He hung up the phone and stuffed it in his pocket.

"Strawberry lemonade?" she said.

"Nothing but the best for my girl!" he smirked and laughed as she sputtered a protest.

"I happen to be allergic to strawberries!" she finally managed to say, enjoying the look on his face as the smirk disappeared.

"Oh, no! Are you really?"

"No. But it would serve you right if I were. Do you usually kidnap people, or is this a new hobby?"

"Only stubborn people who are impossible to talk to otherwise. So just you. But it is kind of fun. I may take it up as a sport."

"Do you at least plan on telling me where you're taking me?" she asked, trying to relax. His car smelled like Tommy Bahama cologne. It was slightly intoxicating.

"Sure. To my favorite place," he said cryptically. "But first, we'll stop at Red Lobster for a second to get your strawberry lemonade." He turned on the radio and they listened without talking until they got to the restaurant. Trying not to stare, she watched him out of the corner of her eye, his cheeks tanned and pink from the sun, his hair wild and unruly. He was extremely cute. His hands were calloused from working hard and he smelled slightly fishy, but in a good way.

She had to remind herself that there couldn't be anything between them, that there was no way a guy like Jaycen would really care about her. It had to be some joke.

But what if it wasn't?

Jaycen left the car running and trotted in to get their food. He came back with a huge grin on his face, handing her their drinks. "I had them switch it to raspberry lemonade just to be sure. I can never tell with you."

She faked a horrified look. "Oh, no! I really *am* allergic to raspberries!" She watched, stone-faced, while Jaycen tried to decide if she was kidding or not until Marin laughed and took the food and drinks onto her lap so he could drive. Jaycen shook his head in defeat. She punched in a straw and took a sip.

Jaycen drove back the way they had come then turned off onto a dirt road that led out along the edge of the hills overlooking the ocean. When he stopped the car and got out, he pulled out an old beach blanket, setting it down near the edge of the bluff overlooking the sea. She brought out dinner and sat down, admiring the setting sun.

"This is your secret spot?" She laughed at the irony. They were sitting on the bluff directly over Davey's Cave.

Jaycen nodded shyly. "I like to drive out here when I need time alone. Away from Tui, Danny and Natalee." He glanced up at her after he said Natalee, but her expression hadn't changed. "Don't get me wrong, I really like everyone in the group. But sometimes I just can't stand being around people. Anyone. I just want to think by myself."

He sighed and leaned back on his arms. "My mom used to bring me out here to watch the ships go by." Something in the way he said it concerned her.

"Is your mom, you know, still around?"

He laughed. "Yeah, I didn't mean to make it sound so final. She has multiple sclerosis so she has a hard time getting around. I try to help her out whenever I can. But a few months ago she started dating this military guy pretty seriously and it's been kind of weird."

Marin nodded sympathetically and helped herself to a biscuit. "So do you think she'll marry him?"

"I don't know. I'm not sure I like him all that much." He swallowed and looked out over the water. "She's worked her whole life to make sure we had a place to live, that I had opportunities for a better life. We even bought a little house a few years ago. I just don't want some guy to come in and take advantage of her and destroy all she's worked for, you know?"

She watched him with growing respect, touched by this moment of sincerity.

"It's always just been the two of us, I've always been the man of the house, and we've always taken care of each other. It would feel weird not to have that anymore." He leaned back on his elbows and sighed. "Still, in a way it would be nice to have someone there who she can depend on besides me. It would make it easier for me to go ahead with my own life, even though I feel like a jerk for even thinking that way."

They ate in silence for a few minutes, enjoying the peaceful scene below them of sailboats drifting in to harbor.

"So, what else do you think about when you're by yourself?" she finally asked, watching the sun reflecting in the ocean blue of his eyes. He seemed so real and wonderful out here away from everything. But how would it change things if he had any idea how different she was?

Jaycen shrugged. "Everything. Nothing." His face colored. "You."

Marin stopped chewing and swallowed hard, dropping her eyes. Jaycen reached over and took her hand, looking at her until she returned his gaze. He took a deep breath and plunged ahead.

"Marin. I want you to know how much I care about you." He searched her face for some reflection of his feelings, seeing none, but he stumbled on anyway. "I know you don't know me very well, and I really didn't plan on this myself, but when I saw you down under that platform and I thought ..." he paused as if forcing back the memory of that awful moment, "I thought I'd lost you. And I realized how much I've fallen for you. I just want to know if you would be willing to give me a chance." He glanced up hopefully.

She looked for some sign of the joke, but he was serious. For a moment, her heart leaped inside her, thinking how easy it would be to fall for him. But ...

She scowled in frustration. There was so much that was between them, no way to make him understand what was going on when she didn't even know what was going on herself. If none of this had happened, maybe. But now?

Jaycen caught her look and shook his head helplessly. "What's the problem, Marin? Obviously you don't care about me like I care about you. But I think I see glimpses in your eyes every once in a while, like just now. It's like you won't *let* yourself care. Why? I work next to you every day, and I can't stand it, feeling the way I do and not understanding why you won't even try." His face flushed with his confession, but he held her gaze.

For a moment, she wanted to believe she could let herself fall in love with him. Part of her already did care about him and now she knew he could see it. If only she could let herself be carried away with her feelings and turn her back on all the confusion. Maybe he would love her no matter what she was. Did it really matter all that much anyway?

Jaycen rose to his knees next to her and placed his hands on both sides of her face, caressing her cheeks gently with his thumbs. His hands trembled. "I care for you so much, Marin," he whispered. "Do you even want to try?"

The words formed themselves and slipped from her lips before she could stop them. "I do." He leaned forward, pulling her into a warm kiss. His arms circled around her, drawing her to him. Her heart tried to melt into his kiss, but there was so much blocking the way. The sun set behind him, bringing a cold wind up from the sea. He sat back and looked at her questioningly.

"What?"

She shivered and smiled sadly. "There are … things … happening right now that I have to figure out. I'm just not sure of anything, even who I am right now." She looked up at him, pleading for him to understand, but knew he didn't. How could he? She couldn't stand looking into his eyes, so full of hurt and confusion, so she pulled him close to her. He was warm and solid and he wrapped his arms around her lovingly, not understanding anything.

"Jaycen, I don't even know if I'm human," she whispered into his shoulder, not knowing if he could even hear her but terrified if he did. He didn't respond, but continued to hold her, stroking her hair until the sky went dark.

NINE

Marin spent a restless night, tossing and turning until she fell into a fitful slumber. At 5:00 a.m. she awoke with a decision. She wanted to see the wreck again. Alone.

It was her day off and still barely dawn. Perfect. She put on a wetsuit and disappeared into the ocean. The air in her lungs tried to pull her to the surface with its buoyancy, so, coughing slightly, she forced herself to breathe in the salty water. As the air left her lungs, she felt the weight of the water balance her body, letting her swim at any level easily, as if the sea itself was accepting her as one of its own. She ran a hand over the scars on the back of her neck in wonder, feeling water flowing out of them as she exhaled, amazed at how easy it was to transition to the water.

The ocean opened up for her as she exited the bay. She darted quickly along the coast, relishing the freedom of weightlessness and speed. Countless beams of sunlight cut through the water, precise as a razor's edge, painting the bottom of the ocean with stripes. Rolling onto her back, she could see the hulls of dozens of sailboats moving above her, casting shadows that passed softly overhead like clouds, with fish darting past like flocks of birds.

When she reached the wreck she tingled with anxiety. Somehow, this held the secret to who she was, what her parents were. The port in the hull proved that her parents had been like her, of both land and sea. Now she needed to find out exactly what that meant.

She sent a tentative *"Hello?"* into the water but heard nothing in reply, which relieved her almost as much as it disappointed her. She moved into the wreck. This time, she went slowly. There were no regulators to dictate how long she could stay under. She breathed in the heavy, salty water, tasting the mineral tang plus the bitter aftertaste of marine fuel. Something in the way the silt had been stirred up made her shiver. As soon as she drifted into the tilted boat, she knew something was different. Who else could have come down here? Paul? She doubted it. She hoped it wasn't whatever had belonged to that disembodied voice.

She drifted through flotsam of her life, plastic forks, a rusty bilge pump, shreds of mostly dissolved paper. She moved into the deep interior of the boat where it looked like the master bedroom had been. The mattress was covered with brown fuzz and tufts of orange sponge-like material stuck out in large holes along its surface. The water had a chemically stale taste that was harder for her to breathe. The cupboards in this room were undisturbed and she carefully opened them one after another. They were all completely empty.

Swimming back to the main room, a white square caught her eye on the warped countertop. Enclosed in a plastic laminate and stuck to the metal trim with a strip of magnetic tape was a well-preserved photograph. It was a tiny girl sitting next to a row of mailboxes, holding a rock and smiling into the sun.

It was her. The sight jolted her with memories of playing in the rocks under the shade of the mailboxes. Flipping the picture over were two words.

Find me!

Her skin began to prickle. Someone had deliberately placed that message here since yesterday. Someone who knew who she was, what she was. Her mind drifted back to the guy she'd seen on the dock. Could it be him? She searched the rest of the boat frantically but found nothing more, so she took her precious package and raced back to COAST.

She returned close to 8:00 a.m., breathless as she climbed out of the water and ran toward the dormitory. Jaycen was coming down the pier at the same time and she almost knocked him into the water in her haste to get to her room.

"Woah!" he shouted, catching her arm to keep from tipping in.

"Oh, I'm sorry, Jaycen! I gotta run."

She moved to pass him but he held onto her arms. "Marin, aren't you going out on the dive? You signed up last week, remember?"

She paused distractedly. "No, sorry, Jaycen. I've already been. But thanks." She hurried past him, leaving him staring at her retreating form.

"Where are your tanks?" she heard him call as the door closed behind her. She ignored everyone she passed, racing till she got to the privacy of her room. Grabbing a robe and shedding her wetsuit as quickly as possible, she took the picture to her desk, turning it over and over in her hands. The picture was sealed in what looked like a heavy pocket lamination, like on a driver's license, but she noticed it was thicker than a photo should be. Excitedly she snatched up her scissors and carefully cut the edge off the clear container. Carefully opening the package, two pieces of paper fell onto the desk. One was the photo, the other one was the folded page with the words "*Find me!*" scrawled in pen on the back. Unfolding the page she noticed a series of numbers scribbled on the back.

34.082237, -119.094887.

She held the paper up to the light, but all that was visible were the numbers. She shook her head in frustration.

Then she gingerly picked up the photo, soaking in every detail of the only picture she had ever seen of herself so young. On the back she read in faded pencil "Amanda's 2nd birthday. January 30."

Amanda? That was what the voice in the water said. She dropped the picture on her desk with shaking hands. *Amanda?* Her birthday was in April. She tried to do the math on paper because her brain had suddenly turned to ice.

Three months and seven days. She was three months and seven days older than she thought she was. She'd just lost a chunk of her life! She looked in the mirror. Everything she'd ever known or thought about herself, her life, Paul, *everything* suddenly felt fake, like it didn't belong to her anymore, as if she'd been erased and sketched back somewhere else by an untrained hand. Her whole world tilted sideways, shattered into shards never to be repaired. She slid to the bathroom, quaking, and threw up. Sinking down to lay on her back, she concentrated on the feel of the tile, letting the cold seep into her bones, connecting her to the earth.

She couldn't stop saying the name *Amanda*, feeling like a piece of driftwood in a hurricane, tossed and beaten until not even her own identity existed. She held one shaky hand in front of her eyes to check if she still had fingerprints. Her hands were still slightly shriveled from the water, but the whorls and swirls were visible. She traced them with her other hand, trying to connect herself together again. She lost track of time, laying her aching head on the tiles until she closed her eyes, finally drifting into a troubled sleep.

* * *

It had been a long day. Dr. Gilbert put everyone on alert, moving up the launch date for the Aquanis submersible by three weeks. It was unheard of. Several times launches had to be moved back to accommodate for weather or mechanical issues, but never had it been moved forward. No one understood why it would be changed, but nobody questioned Frank.

There was so much preparation to be done in such a short a time that everyone was assigned a piece of a new 24-hour schedule working exhausting hours. Dr. Gilbert was suddenly spending much of his time in the lab, working on a personal project that was supposed to go out with Aquanis, some time-sensitive test no one was allowed to see. He got so tired of incessant interruptions that he put Dave's team in total control of the expedition and its preparations so he wouldn't be disturbed. He could rely on Dave and his assistant, Ann. Jaycen had become Dave's right-hand man, so Gilbert reluctantly entrusted Dave to supervise him on the condition that Jaycen would not be included on the actual dive.

Gilbert was so close. He glanced at the data Hahn had left and stared into the microscope, willing the cells on his slide to look the way he wanted them to. He knew Hahn's line of research was off base, but perhaps there were other ways to get there? However, he certainly hadn't been able to change anything through his experiments. He re-checked to make sure his computer was completely offline before he entered more data on his private file. He knew how thorough Leviathan was. He compared his blood sample as a control with the other sample on his slide. The difference was disturbing. What might an organism with this altered blood look like? He shuddered to think about it. He sat back and rubbed his bloodshot eyes. He had one last avenue to explore, though he hesitated using it. Perhaps now was the time.

Certainly he didn't have much more to lose.

He ran his hands across his stubbly chin and closed his eyes, remembering the water weeping from those scars on the back of Marin's neck. Anyone who watched her would notice something was definitely different about her. He just prayed he was the only one watching. He pulled out his cell phone and had the office summon her.

* * *

Marin sat on the edge of her bed in her room, rubbing the crook of her arm where Dr. Gilbert had just drawn blood from her. She was happy to help with his experiment, but the way he looked when she was called into the lab almost scared her. He seemed overly tired and almost obsessed. When he had asked for her blood, she'd been worried. For a frozen moment, looking in his eyes, she was sure he knew about her. But he quickly explained that he was hoping she would be interested in going down in Aquanis, and that he just needed to test her oxygen levels so they would have a baseline to compare with when she returned to make sure she didn't have too much nitrogen in her blood.

It sort of made sense, so she let him do the blood draw, though he had taken several vials of blood from her arm, which seemed excessive. She felt slightly dizzy, so he had given her the rest of the day off to recuperate, even though she was feeling much better when she left.

Turning on her iPod, she sat down on her bed wondering what to do with her unexpected free time. The paper and photograph sat on her nightstand, and she scooped them up, leaning against the headboard with her feet tucked up in front of her. She had studied the photograph so often that she had every detail memorized—the three trees in the background, the blue Chevy truck parked behind her, a woman's shoe and part of her leg in the corner with the hem of a blue checkered dress. She wondered if maybe that was her mother walking behind as this picture was taken, and that would mean it was taken by her father. In some strange way, thinking about it like that made it feel like a family photograph.

She set it back down and stared at the numbers again with a sigh. She had tried assigning letters to the numbers, looking up cryptic codes on the internet and even tried calling variations of the numbers on her cell phone, but she still had no idea what they meant. She couldn't get them out of her mind. She knew she had seen something like them before, but it was driving her nuts trying to figure out where. She huffed in frustration. If they want to be found so badly, why wouldn't they have left a map?

She gasped as the realization hit her. Snatching up the paper, she ran down to the cartography room where boats plotted and registered their courses. The room was filled with filing cabinets, chairs, and desks overflowing with charts. The walls were covered with framed antique maps of the world. A draft board with an overhead lamp sat unused by the window, several maps lying on it, with scrolls scattered on top of everything. She searched through the layers until she found a close-up of the California coast. She felt a chill go down her spine as she looked at the numbers in her hand and realized where she had seen those numbers before.

They *had* left her a map. They were coordinates! She felt her vision swim in front of her as the revelation sunk in. Flicking on the lamp, she searched. Tiny numbers crisscrossed the map. Her hands shook as she ran her fingers down the paper until she found a number that matched one of the ones on the paper. She followed the line straight down the coast until it left the land and met with the other number. One mile off the coast of California. In the ocean. The paper fell silently to the floor. It was twelve miles up the coast and two miles out to sea. Her heart was pounding in her ears. She could be up the coast in fifteen minutes. She could be at the coordinates in forty-five minutes. She instantly made her decision.

Racing back to her room to change, she pulled out her cell phone.

"Jaycen? This is Marin. I know you're working, I'm sorry, but I'm off today and I need to ask you a really, really big favor. Can I borrow your car?"

Ten minutes later she was driving north up the coast. The sun made the car feel like an oven, even with the a/c blasting, but Marin couldn't help shivering. She couldn't even imagine what she would find. Were there others like her? If so, would they look like her? Could it be her parents? Maybe they were alive, just hiding.

She had grabbed her wetsuit, fins, diving compass, a heavy duty flashlight and a tool belt with a long diving knife attached, just in case. The road followed the water and several sandy roads branched off, giving surfers and partiers quick access to the beach. She glanced at her GPS and pulled off the road when she got close to her coordinate. The highway led to a naval base that was closed to the public, so she got as close as she could without being in sight of the base. Then she pulled the car off the road as far as she could and locked it.

It was noon on a hot California summer day and though the water was choppy with the brisk wind, there were several sailboats and surfers in the distance, as well as two Naval ships close to the base just north of her. She pulled on her wetsuit and strapped on the tool belt and knife. Nobody was close enough to notice her as she walked into the pounding waves and disappeared into the foam.

The noise and warmth from above vanished. She held her breath as she swam away from the shore, holding onto the buoyancy of air for a while and enjoying the light feel of it in her lungs. Besides, she disliked the feel of breathing in sand, and the rough surf was stirring up a lot of it near the shore. As her air soured, she slowly let it out and welcomed in the water, noticing the now familiar prickling feeling as her body adjusted. Filled with water, the pressure of the sea no longer affected her; she sank into the darker water below the surf. Undercurrents pulled at her body, dragging her back toward shore, but she fought it and finally broke free, following the dropping bottom of the ocean shelf.

Her ears depressurized and the canals filled with water as the ground dropped sharply away below her. She sank off the cliff until she found the sea floor again and flipped on her light to consult her diving compass. The numbers had burned themselves into her brain, so she aligned herself in the right direction and began to swim with powerful strokes, her fins pushing the seawater behind her.

The light was getting dimmer but the world still looked clear and greenish to her. Schools of fish darted away as she approached. She paused and circled occasionally to be sure there were no predators near. It amazed her how well she could hear, see, and feel underwater, and she wondered if that was part of her unusual heritage as well. Vibrations in the water came to her like sound – so tangible that she could tell when something was coming without even looking. It was like her whole body was an extension of her eyes and ears.

She felt the water displaced above her.

"Hello?" she called out experimentally in her mind. She waited, a feeling of instinctive fear creeping over her. Her hand went to her belt, withdrawing her knife. She held her breath, feeling something moving toward her quickly. She caught the shape of a Pacific Sleeper Shark passing a few meters overhead and her heart stopped in her throat. She waited, not moving a muscle and the shark continued to move away from her. It unnerved her how close it had been. She kept her knife out as she swam on, thinking about how stupid it is to dive alone and of all the ways you could die if something went wrong. She really should have left a note to Paul, but how could she put this into words?

The dark thoughts followed her, but still she swam on. She consulted her navigator again and realized she was nearly there. She reached the ocean floor and began to search. Rocks were strewn around, but nothing stood out to her as she descended. She adjusted her position, touching the sand with her flippers then saw something.

A three foot high rectangle of iron sat at the exact center of the coordinates. It was rusty and pitted and had a thick iron ring standing vertically on the top of it. It reminded her of some old fashioned weight, maybe from a shipyard. She ran her hands all over and around it, looking for anything that might make this object something important and not a wild goose chase ending with a piece of junk. She dug around the base with her fingers, but it seemed to go down for quite a ways. She took hold of the iron ring and pulled with all her might, but it didn't budge. She tried to kick it in frustration, but the water slowed her momentum and took out the satisfaction.

Why on earth would anybody want to send her to this thing? The excitement she had been running on melted away into worry. She checked her navigator one more time and made one last circuit of the area around the weight, then returned to it for one last inspection. She held onto the ring and looked closely at every side of the object, willing something to be there, any clue to who and what she was.

She felt a slight displacement in the water and grabbed her knife, shooting her beam of light around her in all directions, holding fast to the iron ring to give her more control, but she didn't see anything. She could still feel it, though. A humming sound—no, a vibration that seemed to be growing.

Her mind raced, trying to place the sound. A ship overhead, maybe? The sound grew closer and her pulse quickened. She shot her beam everywhere as she realized the sound was definitely coming from below the surface. Suddenly it stopped and she felt the hairs on her scalp prickle. She was no longer alone.

TEN

She held still, fighting the impulse to escape when she felt movement behind her. Her mind flashed back to her close call with the shark and she panicked, swimming blindly, straight up toward the safety of the surface. She could hear her pulse pounding in her ears as she shot upward, racing to the air. She knew she was being followed; it pushed her panic into overdrive. She felt her energy lagging and she fought against her fatigue, trying to reach the top before whatever it was got her. The light from the surface was getting brighter as she got closer to it, expecting at any moment to feel teeth slashing into her. She turned her beam of light below her without seeing anything, but when she swept it back in front of her she dropped it in fright. In the glimpse of light a meter or two away from her, easily keeping up with her was a man. She screamed, her voice nothing but a garble of vibrations and kicked harder against her burning muscles to keep going. Her flashlight stopped falling and started moving upward quickly, keeping her in a halo of light. When it came level with her, she felt the handle pressed into her hand.

Her legs refused to kick any longer and she slowed, pulling in deep breaths of water. Shaking, she shone the beam of light on her pursuer to see him better. It was a young man, bare from the waist up but with black dive pants on the bottom. He had long flippers attached to his feet which he kicked almost lazily as he swam parallel to her. She tried not to notice how muscular he was, from his thick thighs to his bulky chest. No wonder he had no trouble keeping up with her. He had dark hair that floated behind him. He held out his hand to her and she heard words form in her mind. It was the same voice she had heard at the shipwreck.

"Are you Amanda?" He looked at her expectantly, smiling.

She shook her head in disbelief, stopping her ascent completely. She had not seen his mouth move at all. Amanda?

"I'm Marin," she tried thinking to him.

He nodded, thinking for a moment. *"Marin."* Somehow she didn't feel like he believed her. He gazed at her for a long moment. *"Marin."* He nodded in understanding. *"That name is on the back of your boat. That's not your name."*

"You!" she said accusingly. *"You were on the dock when I went to see my houseboat!"*

He raised one shoulder in a half shrug. *"I was in the bay and heard you call out. I was hoping it was you."* She could feel the joy in his voice and for a moment was overcome with borrowed happiness.

"I am Marcos." He looked overhead. *"Did anyone see you come into the water?"* Marin shook her head and he continued. *"We should go; it's very dangerous this close to the surface. Will you come with me?"*

Her heart caught in her throat. If this was what she had been searching for, why was it so frightening? She could hear—no, *feel*—his voice speaking into her mind as clearly as her own thoughts. His words had a heavy Mediterranean accent.

"Where are we going?"

He smiled at her confusion. *"To Portus. You don't need to worry. We will be there soon."* He started swimming downward in powerful strokes and she kicked slowly beside him. He stopped for a moment, then took her flashlight and placed it back in her belt. Then he put both her hands on his shoulders. *"It will be faster this way. Do you mind?"* She shook her head and they started down again, this time holding onto his massive shoulders.

The moment she touched him, her vision changed. Suddenly she could see herself through his eyes, feel his heartbeat as if it were her own. She snatched her hands away in surprise and her vision returned to normal.

His brow furrowed. *"Did you feel that?"* he asked. She nodded. Hesitantly, he touched her again and she instantly felt the connection to him, pulling her into his mind. She could feel his feelings as if they were her own.

"Can you tell me what you feel?" he asked.

"I ... I can see everything you see. I can hear what you are thinking. It's like I'm inside of your head or something. How can you do that?" she asked, pulling away once again.

"I can't. You are doing it. I can feel your presence inside me but I don't seem to have access to your sight or thoughts like you can mine. Interesting."

They heard a sound and Marcos shook his head. *"Aaron is waiting for us. We should go."* He put her hands on his shoulders again and started swimming back down.

She tried to block her mind, amazed at how fast he could swim as he pulled through the water with powerful strokes, and hoped he really couldn't hear her thoughts as easily as she could hear his.

They swam diagonally to the sea floor. Floating near a rocky shelf was an open vehicle shaped like an M with a point connecting the two sides. Inside one of the halves was another person, also naked to his waist, watching them expectantly. He looked younger than Marcos by three or four years, making him around fourteen or fifteen. His hair was short and curly. The boy smiled shyly at her. Marcos swam to the other half of the craft and took her hands, guiding them to the center portion, where there were controls and a handhold. She noticed there were handholds and controls at the top of each arch in front of the men as well. The vehicle looked like it was designed for one, two, or three people to use.

"Hold on," Marcos thought to her. She felt his amusement and anxiety as he thought the words to her, then the emotions cut off as he placed his hand on what looked like a power switch. The humming began again as she realized what she had been hearing earlier was the sound of this vehicle. The engine was in the center, below her. It seemed

like an advanced version of her underwater scooter, pulling in water and shooting it out forcefully behind. They rose from the sand and they spun around to face the dim twilight of the open sea.

The younger boy looked at Marcos mischievously and pulled back on the controls. The vehicle shot away, pulling hard at Marin's arms so quickly that she almost lost her grip. Marcos moved something and the ship slowed. He reached over and lightly punched the kid in the shoulder.

"*Are you ok?*" Marcos asked her. She nodded. "*Good. Aaron is young. Please forgive his prank.*" Aaron ignored her. The machine still moved so quickly that she had to strain to keep her hold. Marcos adjusted something on the handles and a small shield slid out of the front of the machine like a windshield, giving them all more protection. Aaron glared but didn't say anything.

"*This will be easier for you. I forget that you may not be used to traveling this fast yet.*" Marin just held on. She felt Marcos and Aaron exchange thoughts, but couldn't make out what was being said. She opened her mouth and tried to speak out of frustration, but it just was incoherent vibrations. Marcos turned back to look at her, laughing in his mind. "*Be patient. We are almost there.*"

The machine started to descend into the deeper ocean. She felt numb with cold and anxiety. Who were these people? Could they read minds? Was this her family? The water was darker and she began to feel the flow differently, as if the water was moving up around an obstacle. They began to turn parallel to the shore as they dropped.

They were entering a canyon that had formed into the continental shelf. The shelf itself stretched out like a cliff on both sides of them as far as she could see, but the place they were descending into looked like a massive spoon-shaped opening, protected on all sides. They dropped halfway down the left side of the rocky face heading straight into the cliff. Her muscles braced against the inevitable impact, but the skimmer ran into a gap and kept going, moving upward into a tunnel. She felt the water getting warmer and saw a glow up ahead.

Before long they broke the surface in a submerged cavern lit with clear, blue light. A natural shelf jutted into the water making it look like a large room surrounding a luxurious natural swimming pool. Marin watched the young men plug their noses and push water out of their lungs, but she couldn't see any lines on the back of their necks. She was filled with conflicting feelings and wonder. Every question tumbled into more questions. Who was she? What is this place? Who are they?

She surfaced, their dripping echoes sounding extra loud after the muted water. The cavern looked natural, with long stalagmites hanging down, but there were fluorescent lights hung in the ceiling.

Marcos pulled his machine into a small cubicle carved into the rock below the ledge. She noticed several of these storage caves all along the rim of the bay, each occupied by a vehicle. Did this mean there was an entire community?

Aaron pulled himself up on the rim and stared down at her curiously. Marcos pushed himself up and reached out to help her up onto the ledge. On the rocky shelf, she sat with her legs hanging into the water, shivering until Aaron ran over to a counter, brought back a fluffy towel, and wrapped it around her, sitting back on his heels to watch her reaction.

She absorbed the warmth of the towel before she realized how unusual it was to have something dry hundreds of feet below water. Marcos and Aaron shook their hair and Aaron trotted off down a hallway. Marcos knelt down beside her, studying her, smiling. She tensed that he was so close to her, strength radiating from him. He had a cleft in his chin, making him look like some kind of movie star.

He touched his lips with one finger, then leaned toward her and whispered, "Amanda, please wait here quietly. I will return shortly." His voice was warm and deep, and like his thoughts, his accent more pronounced. He looked younger than she had first thought. He turned quickly and walked down the hall after Aaron.

She sat on the edge of the pool, absorbing her surroundings. The air was heavy and humid and had a hint of a sulfurous smell. She felt a wave of dizziness sweep over her unexpectedly and she put her face into her hands, hoping she wouldn't throw up. Slowly the feeling passed, leaving her a little shaky. She couldn't imagine where she was or how deep. There were metal cabinets and a drafting board not unlike the one in the cartography room back at COAST, as well as five or six computers. She shook her head in disbelief. Some kind of underwater research facility? She stood up and wandered over to the computer desk, wondering what was taking her host so long to return. It wasn't long before she heard a shriek.

"NO! You didn't!"

Her stomach turned to ice. She strained to hear Marcos's reply, but his voice was low and she couldn't make out his words. Feet slapping against the stone brought her attention back to the hallway. An older woman emerged with crazy grey hair and a bathrobe around her and they stared at each other in shock. She brought her hands together to her mouth, and then swooped her into an enormous embrace.

"Oh, Amanda!"

Marcos watched, smiling. The woman stepped back and looked Marin over, tears welling in her eyes. She sniffed, pulling a Kleenex out of her robe pocket.

"It's like you've returned from the dead."

She had an accent that Marin couldn't quite place. Maybe English or Australian. The woman considered for a moment and extended her hand to Marin, laughing.

"I've forgotten my manners, Amanda. I hope you'll forgive me. I'm Aggie, short for Agatha. Me mum was a fan of Agatha Christie and cursed me with her name. So it's Aggie for short." She cleared her throat emotionally. "I never dreamed I'd ever see you again."

Marin frowned. "I'm not Amanda. My name is Marin."

Aggie smiled sadly. "No, my dear. You are Amanda. I was there when your mother named ye."

The color drained from Marin's face. "My mother? Do you know my mother?" Her voice caught as she said the words, her heart aching.

Aggie sighed, recognizing the longing in her voice. "Yes, of course.

Very well. Ye look just like her." Aggie paused, considering, then she continued. "She was my sister." She watched, wanting Marin to figure it out for herself.

Realization flared in Marin's eyes. "You're my aunt?"

Aggie beamed. "I am!" She embraced Marin again, gruffly. "I am your aunt, fluffy robe and all."

Marin patted the back of her aunt's robe awkwardly, feeling overwhelmed. This woman under the world, smelling of sulfur and bacon and sounding like she came from England was her *family*? So, what were they? Mermaids; mermen? She glanced at the muscular man who had brought her down here. What was he, then—her brother? She really hoped not.

"Well, now you're here, we'd better figure out what to do next." She turned toward the tunnel entrance, pulling out a tissue and blowing her nose noisily. "Come along, dear. You'll catch your death of cold in here. And you look like you just might have a wee bit of pressure sickness."

Marin tried to process everything, but exhaustion and emotional shock was beginning to take its toll. She felt shaky and dizzy again, her vision slightly blurred. She didn't move to follow the woman. After a few steps Aggie turned and looked at her expectantly. "Come along, Amanda. You look just about beat, and you can't sleep in the bay."

"Sleep!" she blurted, her panicked voice echoing, making the others wince. "I can't *sleep* here! I have to go back!"

The woman looked at her in surprise, taking a few steps forward. She wrung her hands uncomfortably. "Oh, but me dearie, I'm truly sorry, I am. You *can't go back.*"

Marin began to panic, her mind grasping at all the reasons she couldn't stay. "I borrowed someone's car to get here. It's just sitting on the dunes. I have to give it back to him. And what about my Uncle Paul? He'll think something awful has happened to me and he'll just … die!" She felt herself starting to lose control, old feelings of being trapped underwater melting together with a new fear of leaving her life without even a chance to say goodbye.

"There are things you don't understand. You know too much now that we can't let ye leave," she said apologetically.

Marin felt her reality sliding out of focus. She noticed the roof tilting above as her eyes rolled back into her head and she tipped, unconscious, onto the cold stone floor.

* * *

A short time later, in the deepening twilight above Marin, someone walked out of the ocean with borrowed keys and got into a yellow Toyota. He drove it back down the highway, parked it at COAST and hid the keys behind a tire before melting back into the waves.

ELEVEN

As the sun went down, darkness drifted in on the lab, entombing Gilbert with blackness. He didn't care. The computer gave him light enough, and a small table lamp shone on his microscope. The day staff had long ago called it a day and the night shift was busy out on the rig. He relished the quiet, but since it had been two days since he had slept, it was difficult to keep his eyes open without the constant clamoring around him. He rubbed his tired eyes and squinted into the scopes again.

He took a deep breath. Finally he was seeing the change he was looking for! Marin's cells were unmistakably different from his own, but changing those cells to match his was difficult. Everything he had done so far had killed the cells. But this time, they were still alive, though not metabolizing like they should. Still, he knew he was finally onto something. He kept the mangled but living cells in a dish carefully placed on a shelf above the computer.

A new slide of Marin's blood was placed under the scanner. Another test. He had lost track of how many he had run today. He had to find the back door. If the change could be undone, he would know the recipe and the key would be his. The back of his hands itched and he absently rubbed lotion into the leathery skin while his mind fought against fatigue. So many questions. How much does she know? What is she capable of? He forced his mind to bend to the task at hand, ignoring all else.

* * *

Jaycen held a bunch of daisies he'd picked from the front of the dorm wing. He knocked on Marin's door, hoping the flowers didn't make him look too corny, then waited and knocked again. Puzzled, he walked out to the back windows of the hallway that overlooked the parking lot. He could just make out his car in the darkness, parked under a burned out streetlamp, so she had to be back. He returned to her door and tried the knob. It was unlocked, so he let himself in. Her bed was rumpled and unmade, the bathroom light was on, and her iPod was quietly playing.

"Marin?" He stepped into the bathroom, but there was no sign of her. He frowned. He found a cup in her bathroom, filled it with water, put the stolen daisies in it, and then arranged them on her nightstand. A photograph leaning on the lamp caught his eye; a small girl near a mail-box. He picked it up and studied it, wondering if it might be a photo of Marin as a child. He read the back and noticed the wrong name and birthday. He assumed it was a cousin or a friend and set it back down. Concerned, he left to search the campus more thoroughly.

* * *

Marin opened her eyes slowly, feeling disoriented and sore. A faint sulfurous smell irritated her nose. Her legs ached and felt rubbery but she couldn't remember where she was or why she felt so tired. It was absolutely dark. Not the darkness of a bedroom; the darkness of a tomb.

She reached out to turn on her bedside lamp and couldn't even find the table. Her clothes felt rough and unfamiliar, and her bed was hard. She stood up blindly, feeling around for the walls but instead of the cool, smooth walls of her dorm, there was rough, uneven stone.

With a horrible jolt, she remembered where she was. And what was she? A prisoner underneath tons of water? Why couldn't she go back? Nobody would ever find her here. It would be like the earth had swallowed her whole.

She tried to calm down and look for a way out. The room felt circular and irregular. It wasn't made by humans, but carved by nature herself. There had to be a way out, or how did they get her inside? She felt a crack in the wall and a stretch of smooth metal. Then a doorknob. Expecting it to be locked, she was shocked when she turned it and blue-white light poured in.

Squinting against the light, she stepped out of her room into what looked almost like a modern home. Rugs covered the floor; small lamps were lit and rested on bookcases. Several stuffed leather chairs, a small couch and even a big screen TV sat in the middle of the spacious area. One corner of the large room was a kitchen, complete with a refrigerator and a microwave and stove. A delicious smell made her stomach growl before she even had a chance to realize she was hungry.

"Oh! Amanda! You're up. I'm so glad. I was about to bring you a spot of breakfast." Marin jumped at the voice. Aggie came into view from behind the door of the stainless steel refrigerator. She barely came up to the top of the door, and her silver grey hair matched the appliance almost perfectly. Marin stared at her. She was dressed in jeans, but had the same fluffy pink bathrobe on with the addition of thick sheepskin boots. It was hard to decide how old she was, because she moved quickly and with a surety that made her seem younger than her grey hair implied.

"Come on over to the table and have a bite, will ye?" She carried a plate of bacon and eggs and a cup of orange juice to the table and sat down expectantly. "I bet you're starved! Tuck in!" Marin moved over hesitantly, her traitorous stomach growling loudly, and sat down across from her aunt, the stranger. "I do hope you are feeling better. Just a touch of pressure sickness, I'm sure. It's to be expected."

Marin stared at the food, trying to figure out if it would look different if it was poisoned, but realized she was being ridiculous and started to eat. The bacon was good, but had a strange texture, chewier somehow. The eggs were tasty and seasoned with basil and garlic. She realized as she was chewing how hungry she was. The woman sat back in satisfaction.

"That's more like it," she laughed cheerily. "Hope you don't mind the robe. It gets so dreadfully damp sometimes that I can't stand the chill. It's just the two of us this morning. The rest have all gone off to work, and I get to stay in and get you acclimated."

Marin dropped her fork. "Morning?" She thought of Jaycen's car, parked next to the dunes being towed off to the impound yard and police investigating her disappearance.

"Oh, yes dear. It's about eight a.m. There's an atomic clock over the stove there. You had a good long sleep. Hope you feel better."

"What day is it?" she asked.

The woman laughed. "It's Saturday. You haven't been here more that fifteen hours." She watched Marin's reaction.

Fifteen hours! How could she have been here that long? People might be looking for her! She was supposed to go out on a dive this morning with Jaycen, Tui and Natalee. "Where am I?" Marin whispered.

Aggie grabbed a damp cloth and started washing crumbs off the table. It seemed she couldn't sit still for long without doing something. "You've met your cousin already. He was in on the plan to find you, the rascal! Remember, yesterday? He was in the skiff that brought you here."

Her heart sank. So the handsome merman guy *was* related to her. Figures. She swallowed a mouthful of eggs, suddenly not very hungry. "Yes, I remember. Marcos."

Aggie laughed. "Oh, no. He's not one of mine. He's Malcolm's son. You'll meet Malcolm later. I meant *Aaron*. That's my little ragamuffin. He's fourteen. Well, technically, he's not truly your cousin, not by blood, anyway. But I've raised him and he's the only child I've ever had. And I'm the only mother he can remember, so it all comes down to the same thing." She shook the cloth off into a trash can.

"I can see how you could confuse those two boys, though. Aaron is practically Marcos's shadow. A bit of hero worship. Personally, I think it's also a bit of topside envy. Marcos's been raised up top, and Aaron has been raised below, and of course the kelp is always greener across the bay, eh?"

Marin wasn't sure she followed her, but she smiled uncertainly. Her smile dropped quickly, though. "Listen, Aggie. I don't understand. What is this place? Who are you all really? *What* are you?"

Aggie sat back down and placed a hand over Marin's. A frown creased her face. "I know, love. You have a million questions. And you will learn the answers soon enough. Any answer I give you will just generate more questions at this point." Aggie sighed. "I fear Marcos was so anxious when he found you that he took matters into his own hands." She turned around abruptly. "He's the only one his age, you know. So you can't blame him for wanting to believe you were still alive." She smiled. "And here you are, alive and well and we get to adjust things a little." Marin opened her mouth, but Aggie put up her hands to stop her. "I know you have a lot of questions, but for now, until we know what to do with you, I'm afraid you'll have to learn to live with them. It's safer that way. For you and for us."

"Can't you tell me anything? What are we? Human? Mermaids?" she exclaimed, frustrated. "And I can't just stay here. I have to go back. Soon. They'll be looking for me." She dropped her fork to her plate. "I didn't plan on staying here forever! I have a family, work, a life up there." She pictured Uncle Paul and her stomach twisted just thinking about what her disappearance would do to him. It would utterly destroy him, and she knew it. She swallowed hard, determined not to let that happen. "I can't just vanish. There are people that care about me, and I care about them."

"Amanda, although you don't know us yet, you have people down *here* that know and love you, too. There hasn't been a day gone by that I don't think about your mother and father and what happened to you." She wiped her eyes uncomfortably with the back of her hand and stood up, bringing her dish over to the sink and washing it with her back to Marin.

Marin shook her head. "I *have* to know what we are, Aggie. Who we are. Are you aliens or something?"

Aggie turned and looked at her with raised eyebrows. "No, of course not, dearie. Well, actually, perhaps some of us are, but that's because we never bothered to get American Visas." She laughed at her joke, but Marin just creased her eyebrows.

"Sorry, dear." She said, more seriously this time. "No. We are not aliens; you are not from outer space. You, and all of us down here, are Arydians." She said spreading her hands out in front of her.

"Aggie, what …"

"I told you, it's just going to make a lot more questions, and I don't want to address them until we can meet with the Council," she said, drying off her hands. "Trust me dear, you'll be better off if we tell you all at once." Marin stared down at her plate of unfinished eggs, unsure of how to proceed. After a lifetime of searching, she was here, among family in a place that held the answers. But was she any closer to those answers? And what was the cost?

"Hmm. Don't like my eggs? Never mind. I'm sure you'd rather take a look around now wouldn't you, dear?" Aggie took her plate to the counter. "Would you like to go for a swim so I can show you your new home?"

Marin shrugged, still troubled. Aggie continued, "Well, then. I've got a skin for you to wear. It may be a little big, but it'll have to do. Come along into the bay."

Marin followed her and wondered for the second time about the clothes she was wearing. Someone had taken her out of her wetsuit and put her in some cotton drawstring pants and a brown shapeless overshirt. She scowled uncomfortably at the thought of strangers undressing her. "Where did my wetsuit go?" she asked, padding into the cavern behind Aggie.

Aggie smiled knowingly. "Don't worry, I took care of you. No, the boys were not present, and yes, we still have your wetsuit. It's right here." She went to a series of sturdy plastic closets and opened one. Marin reached out for it, but Aggie stopped her. "Oh, no, dearie. That won't do. Trust me, you'd much rather swim in a *skin* down here."

She pulled out a heavy, grey, body-shaped suit and handed it to Marin. "Go on over there behind the changing screen and put this on. I'll nip over and put mine on as well."

Marin took the burdensome load and with an effort carried it over to the screen where she changed. The inside was thick and gelatinous and stuck to her body. When she put it on, she felt like she had gained fifty pounds of flab.

As she emerged from the screen, Aggie was just pulling her own suit up over her shoulders. She patted her skin and asked, "What do you think of your new suit?"

Marin wrinkled her nose.

"Ay, it does take some getting used to. But you'll be glad for the warmth it offers. It's my own design, so be careful what insults you sling at it," she laughed jovially. "It's a special silicone gel that replicates whale blubber and acts as an insulator without adding buoyancy. It's all the rage down under!" she said, nodding to the water. "Shall we?" She finished zipping her suit and put a swim cap over her shortish hair.

"Listen, Aggie. I have to go back. Just for a little while. I can come back; I just need to take care of a few things."

Aggie shook her head, but Marin kept talking.

"I know where you are now. I can come back anytime to visit. It's not far at all."

Aggie's face grew stern. "Amanda, you don't understand. You can't just leave and come back anytime. There are things going on beyond your understanding, and people who wouldn't hesitate to kill you for the little bit you know of us. You absolutely can't leave."

"Aggie, I'm not going to stay down here forever. I have to go back."

Aggie's mouth set in a firm line. "Amanda, there is more at stake than you realize. I'm sorry, I truly am, but we can't let you go back." Aggie's eyes softened and she put her arms around her. "Don't fret, Amanda. We've taken care of everything. The boys took the car back. Nobody saw them. They will never know."

Marin stared at her, battling her emotions, overcome with the thought of being trapped down here forever. Never having a chance to explain, to even say goodbye. They will never know, she realized in alarm. She couldn't leave Paul wondering forever what had happened to her. She was all he had!

She leapt into the water before Aggie could say anything else and started swimming frantically for the tunnel entrance. Despite her desire to understand, her mind rejected everything she had seen and heard. All she wanted was to retrace her steps and go back to normal. She didn't want this other world with its other people. She just wanted air, sun, home, Uncle Paul, Jaycen and reality.

She felt water displaced behind her and realized Aggie had jumped in after her. She pushed herself with a burst of speed and broke out of the tunnel and into the open sea. She headed straight up, kicking toward the light of day with all her strength. She felt Aggie's voice calling out to others, but couldn't understand what she was saying, even though she felt the urgency in her voice.

She redoubled her efforts to reach the surface. She felt vibrations swimming toward her, coming from other tunnels in the cliff face. She kicked out, her foot impacting against something warm. Strong arms wrapped around her waist from behind, stopping her. Hands reached out to pull her down. She screamed, her voice nothing but shapeless warbles. She saw the sparkling sun above her getting farther and farther away as the weight of bodies holding her brought her down. She kicked and thrashed violently at the people surrounding her. A woman's face pressed close to hers and thought into her mind, *"Please be calm. We will not harm you, Amanda."*

"Let me go! I'm not Amanda!" she screamed in her thoughts, startling the woman. She kicked the woman in the stomach and twisted to get free, spinning in her captor's arms so she was face to face with the man holding her. It was Marcos. She didn't know if she could talk to only him, but she tried. *"Let me go!"* she pleaded looking into his eyes. *"If you can hear me, please let me go!"* She placed her hand on the bare skin of his chest, pushing thoughts toward him, demanding he let her go.

Marcos stared at her compassionately, but shook his head. *"You do not know the danger you are in, the danger you are putting us all in. We must go down now, right now. Please, come with me and all will be explained. I promise we will not harm you. Please trust me."* She didn't answer, but stopped struggling. It was pointless anyway. He held her so tightly it was all she could do to breathe. He continued to hold her close as they descended. She could feel his concern for his people; his guilt that he had made the wrong choice in bringing her down to them. She removed her hand to break contact with him.

Marcos called out a series of sounds, different than anything she had heard before. She felt his tension as he waited for a reply, still moving them both downward rapidly.

A new sound began; a rumbling tremor that filled and shook the water. Everyone instantly stopped moving, waiting. It was coming closer. She tried to imagine what could be making such a violent noise, and then remembered the Naval Base so close above them. She wasn't sure, but she thought they must be close to it, if not directly below it. Certainly *they* had any number of ships that could shake the water like that. Whatever it was seemed to be moving closer overhead.

The emotions of the people around her made her tremble. It was terrifying to them all. Still, they continued to sink with barely a movement. *"Do not move, just drift down!"* Marcos thought to her. Time seemed to freeze as a monster ship came close overhead, dread and terror sitting loudly in the hearts of the people around her.

Suddenly, a sharp keening sound filled the water and Marcos relaxed noticeably. She could see shapes moving quickly toward them through the water from the open sea. Marcos sent out a piercing chirp that was met in kind with other chirps and squeaks. Marin stared until the shapes came into sight.

Dolphins. Dozens of bottlenose dolphins shot out around them, swirling and dancing, bumping them with their smiling snouts. Marcos reached out and stroked one as it went by, loosening his grip on her slightly. She was too entranced to notice. The sea was filled with squeaks and groans and chattering, the water stirred up by turbulence. Marcos pointed to the surface and many of the dolphins broke off and raced to the surface to jump into the air, disappearing from sight and then crashing back down again in a graceful curve. The rest continued to swim around the people, herding them in a roundabout way back to the cavern opening. One by one the people disappeared and the dolphins would wander off to join the throng at the surface. At last Marcos and Marin entered the tunnel mouth. He released her, but held her hand tightly as they moved back into the tunnel leading into the underwater cavern.

TWELVE

Jaycen got up at 6:00 a.m. and did a few reps of push-ups and curls to start his day, still wondering where Marin had taken his car yesterday. Surely she was back by now. He resolved to ask her when they went diving this morning with Tui and Natalee. He knew Natalee wasn't thrilled to be paired with Tui, but it wasn't really like a double date even though Tui thought it was. Truthfully, Jaycen was hoping it would turn out to be one as well.

With everyone scuttling to get the launch of Aquanis underway, all recreational activities were suspended. However, the summer tides were changing, as were the migratory routes of the many species that COAST was responsible for tracking, so an obligatory group was sent out to gather samples. Jaycen had volunteered himself, Tui, Natalee, and Marin as soon as the post came open. No other members of the permanent staff had volunteered, already feeling stretched from the extra hours and overtime they had been expected to serve.

Dave signed up to captain the boat, anxious to get out of the way of Frank, who had become increasingly short tempered. No doubt he was relishing the idea of some fresh air after spending a week cramped in the hold of Aquanis making sure she was wired correctly and her mechanics functioned fluidly.

Jaycen cheerfully helped Dave load the boat, keeping an eye out for Marin, surprised that she wasn't there to help. She hadn't answered his texts or phone calls, and she still hadn't shown up. As it got closer to departure time and Natalee and Tui found their places in the stern of the cabin cruiser, Jaycen ran up to Marin's room looking for her. After knocking, he walked in to find the room exactly as he'd left it the day before. The bathroom light was still on, her iPod still playing in its dock, and his stolen daisies drooping in the cup on her bedside table. He frowned. He picked up his cell and called her, but realized as it began to ring that her phone was on the desk across the room, vibrating noisily.

He picked up her cell and hung up, his concern deepening. Where could she be that she wouldn't have taken her phone?

He scrolled through her phone and saw she had a bunch of missed phone calls, most of them from him, and one from someone named Paul. He was startled when his own phone started vibrating.

It was Tui texting him, *Oi! Get a move on!*

He wrote back. *Hold your trunks on, man!*

He picked up the picture next to Marin's bed and gazed at it without seeing it. Suddenly he realized he didn't know anything about the girl he had thrown his heart at so recklessly. She had certainly tried to keep her life a secret. Somehow he felt that there was more to her puzzle than he'd ever imagined.

Move it or lose it! Tui texted. *We are going to leave without you, bonehead.*

Go on without me. I can't find Marin. Cover for us, will you? I don't want Dave thinking I'm a flake.

Why not? Because you are one?

Yeah. Go jump in a lake.

Plannin' on it. Have fun, buddy.

Yeah. You too.

Jaycen leaned back on her pillow. The soft scent of Marin's peppermint shampoo surrounded him and he breathed it in deeply. Marin's phone started ringing. For a moment he was tempted to answer it and ask whoever it was if they knew where Marin was, but he quickly realized how crazy it would sound to be on Marin's phone, asking about her. Shortly after, it vibrated with a voice message. A moment later came a text, which he opened.

Hey, Mares. Give me a call when you get a minute, ok? Love you.

He fought down a flare of jealousy and hoped the text was from her uncle Paul, not another guy.

* * *

There were over forty people crowded in the underwater cavern. Nobody seemed to be moving anywhere in particular, and Marin wondered what they were all waiting for. Many had satchels hung around their shoulders and long tools of some sort. Some had strange eyewear on their faces. She could feel their thoughts humming around her, but though none were directed at her, she felt by their glances that they were definitely talking *about* her. She realized Marcos was still holding her arm. Apparently the ability to see through his eyes only applied to skin to skin contact, because she felt nothing but the pressure of his fingers closed around her flubbery dive suit. She shrugged her arm and he released her, but stayed close to her side.

"*Can you hear me?*" she thought to him. He nodded distractedly. Everyone seemed to be holding their breath, often looking up toward the rock ceiling. Waiting.

"*Can everyone hear me, or just you?*"

He glanced at her, and then returned his eyes to the ceiling. "*Just me if you're speaking just to me.*"

"*Can you hear everything I think?*"

He shook his head. "*Only what you tell me. Or what you say out loud to everyone. You can speak to anyone like this underwater.*"

"*How is that possible?*" she asked, amazed.

He shrugged. "*It's just how we are. My father believes all animals have the ability to communicate this way to some degree. Think about a school of fish—thousands of bodies swimming together, yet with only millimeters between them, they never collide. It is much the same with us. We are, in essence, a school of fish. Thus we can communicate. Try this.*" He took her hand. "*Concentrate.*" This time, his thoughts came with pictures. She could see millions of tiny silver fish swarming in a shining tornado, sunlight flicking off their iridescent scales. It took her breath away.

"How did you do that?" she asked in wonder. *"I can see that like it was right in front of me."*

"Really?" He seemed amazed. *"You're not supposed to see anything. Just impressions and thoughts. It's faster through contact, though."*

Marin shook her head. She didn't know if it was a good thing or a bad thing.

He shrugged, letting go of her hand.

The people around her jostled and someone moved toward them.

"What's happening? Why is everyone waiting?" she asked him.

Before he could answer, Aggie appeared, pushing through the crowd and looking angry.

"Oh, Amanda. Why? A whole day wasted before it was even begun. As if we don't have enough trouble looking for us! All I asked for was some patience. Why would you throw us to the wolves before you even know anything about us?"

Marin just stared at her, not knowing what to say while feeling trapped, angry, and attacked. She decided that aunt or no, she was not particularly fond of Aggie. She glared back and said, *"My name is Marin!"*

Aggie put her hands up in frustration. *"Marcos, you'd better show her around down here. I'm likely to toss her in the vent. I'll talk to you both when things calm down."* She addressed her thoughts to the crowd. *"Best go to the lower banks today, everyone, until the coast is clear."*

"So, what was all that about?" Marin repeated. Instead of answering, Marcos turned and led her down through a narrow tunnel. Several other people followed, but they dispersed along the way into small caves leading off the main path.

"Don't judge Aggie so harshly," he said. *"She is truly very kind at heart. It's fear and responsibility that makes her sound so tough. She cares for us all very much, and is a good mother to Aaron. A good mother to all of us, really. It's a hard life down here, and as the leader, Aggie must be hard as well. I know she would die to protect any one of us."* They turned yet another

corner and dropped straight down several feet. *"I've heard her speak of you fondly many times over the years, and I know she loves you very much."* He shook his head. *"She never told anyone where you were. I know she was trying to protect you, but it just made me more curious, so I was always looking. I should have talked to her about it when I first saw you. And I shouldn't have brought you down here without telling her. I'm sure she is very worried about the shock waves it may produce."*

"I'm sorry. I don't mean to be a problem," Marin said. Marcos stopped swimming.

"Are you? Sorry you're here?" he asked.

She shrugged, feeling awkward. She hadn't *asked* to come here. She'd been invited. By him!

He took her hand. *"Because I am not sorry at all."* She blushed, feeling his warm feelings flowing through her, washing away all her doubts.

"This is where many of us live," he said, pointing to the many twisted paths that led off their main tunnel. *"They are above our thermal vents and warmer than most of the other caverns."* He led her through the labyrinthine passageway, his powerful legs making it hard for her to keep up.

The farther they got from the surface, the darker it became. As they descended, however, a yellowish glow began, strengthening as they went. Finally, it opened into an enormous submerged cave. It was larger than a football stadium, bleachers and all. The light was brighter here, emanating from glowing pipes spidering over the walls.

"This is the upper banks," he said with a tinge of pride. *"I work here often, as do we all, but today it's not safe."*

"Not safe because of me?" she asked a little sheepishly.

Marcos nodded. *"Perhaps you know our neighbors upstairs? The naval base is very close to us, only a mile or so above. Their radars and sonars have become very sensitive. Sometimes we can't even watch futbol."* He laughed and touched her hand, his touch showing her several people huddled around the television watching a soccer game on the big screen TV.

"As long as we stay close to the ocean floor as we travel around the base, we are safe, but when someone is screaming and kicking and thrashing the

way you did, right under their noses … well, they get nervous and want to find out what it is."

He paused so she could catch up to him. *"The caves protect us, but we can't be sure of them picking up vibrations if they are looking closely, so it's best we stay deeper in the caverns. Do you mind if we go faster?"*

He took her hands and placed them on his bare shoulders, towing her with more power than she could have ever managed. She couldn't help but be mesmerized by his accent that slipped out occasionally. She found herself waiting for his next words to see if they would betray where he was from.

"What was with the dolphins?" she asked, wanting to keep him talking.

"Sometimes when the military is looking too close in our area, we call our friends to cover for us. On radar and on the surface, they see dolphins playing and they stop worrying."

"You call dolphins?" she asked dubiously.

"Yes," he said simply. *"They help us when we need it in return for our discarded food. But it all depends on how close they are. Today we were lucky, they were close."* He floated off the ledge and paused. *"It almost makes me sad to think of the help they give us when we repay them with garbage, but they seem to think it's a fair trade."*

"You're saying that you can really talk to animals?" she repeated in disbelief.

"No. Not all animals. Just intelligent ones. And only underwater. I could never get my horse to listen to me back home. Maybe if I'd thrown him in the water it would have been different," he laughed.

"What happens if they find you?"

"I would guess they would drop something dangerous on us and destroy everything then figure out who we are later. That would be the safest for them. Or maybe they catch us and try to find out why we live underwater, run tests on us, torture us. That seems like the worst to me."

Marin shuddered at the thought as he continued. *"Can you imagine what the world would do to us if we were found out? How many people would fight to know what we know? It doesn't take a genius to realize that he who controls the sea controls the world."*

As horrible as it was, she had to agree. *"If it's so dangerous, why do you live under a naval base?"*

"Because it's perfect for us. Let me show you. Do you want to see my farm?" He pointed to the bottom of the cavern far below them.

She shook her head in awe. He put her hands back on his shoulders and they plunged to the cavern bottom. The cave was broken up into patches that resembled a quilt. Dozens of different kinds of plants covered the entire floor, but it didn't end there; patchwork gardens crept up the walls and covered the ceiling as well. Every inch of space was put to use. There were mossy lichen patches, long swaying grassy pastures, even strange fruitlike orbs growing on what looked like a shaggy tomato plant.

"What's that over there?" she asked, pointing to a huge silver machine with tubes jutting out like a monstrous inverted octopus. The glowing tubes branched off into the caverns, emanating both heat and light.

"We call it Mother, because it makes all this possible. See, we are next to a cleft in the earth's crust." They swam closer to the machine.

"You've harnessed a geothermic vent! Brilliant!" she said in amazement. Marcos beamed at her, pleased at her reaction.

"We are close to a seismic rift, but not too close. Mother has a great arm that has been sent into the vent, to collect the heat and gasses that rise from the vent. We use the heat to make the Upper and Lower banks grow, as well as to heat everything."

He gestured to a huge opening at the bottom of the cavern with yellow light streaming from it. *"Down in the lower bank, she has a turbine that is turned by the gasses rising which gives us power and runs our water purifier and the television and so on."*

He took her hand again and started toward the wall. *"Come see my farm."* They swam to a patch on the floor that had a variety of bluish bulbs growing with leathery leaves. He picked a piece of one of the leaves and offered it to her.

"Taste?"

She looked at it uncertainly. He took a small nibble to encourage her.

She popped the piece in her mouth and chewed. It tasted weird because her mouth was already full of salt water, but as she chewed it, it changed to a heavy flavor that reminded her of beef.

"Do you like it?"

She couldn't find an honest way to answer, so she just shrugged. *"It's different. What is it?"*

"It's a species of beet. It has a lot of iron. The leaves taste very good to me. It reminds me of spinach, but has a taste of meat. It is very good for you. Also, the bulb of the plant can be shredded and taste like eggs, and they have no cholesterol!"

She wrinkled her nose, wondering if that was what she had eaten for breakfast with Aggie earlier.

"I created this plant," he continued. *"All of these plants were developed by us, under the guidance of the Council. All of the Council leaders are scientists. We could not survive without their knowledge."*

"Who are the Council?" she asked, trying to suck the taste of salty, raw hamburger out of her teeth.

"You will meet them, later. Aggie is one of them." He glanced at an intricate dive watch on his arm and said, *"We should go down to the lower banks until we know we are safe."*

They started toward the brightly lit passageway below them. Her curiosity finally got the best of her and she asked, *"Marcos, where are you from?"*

"Originally?" he asked, swimming easily on his back as they entered the large tunnel. She nodded, matching his speed, but with much greater effort.

"I was born in San Francisco. Just up the coast." He smiled. *"I am an Amer-ikan,"* he said playfully, over-emphasizing his accent.

"Oh."

"But I was raised in Agios Nikolaos, on a small island just west of Greece. I went to an English school, so my English is very good, no?"

Marin smiled, glad they were not touching in case he could hear how insanely gorgeous she found him.

This tunnel was much larger. She estimated she could drive a semi-truck through the opening with plenty of room on either side. She reached out and touched the walls, snagging her finger painfully. The walls were prickly, made from cooled lava.

She had a sudden sense of vertigo as the passage opened up and a massive valley floor dropped away below her. The cavern was enormous!

Dozens of men, women, and even children seemed to be picking rocks off the eastern wall, dropping some, and putting others in the long bags slung across their backs. She noticed that only a few people were wearing Aggie's wonder suits and she wondered if the reason was that they were too rare, or too weird.

Marcos stopped in the tunnel mouth, his legs churning the water almost lazily as he drifted a hundred feet above the ocean floor. It seemed like he was superhuman; floating on air, his dark hair flowing behind him, a halo of light highlighting his every feature. He took her breath away.

"Aggie said maybe I shouldn't show you this. It would be too dangerous for you and for us, but she had to agree that everything you have seen is dangerous." He took her hands in his, hovering on the edge of the abyss.

"Why can I feel what you are thinking when I touch you?" she asked, sending her thoughts. He let go of her hand. The connection dimmed, but she could still sense him if she concentrated. Marcos looked thoughtful.

"What about now?" he asked.

"Yes, but not as much."

"This is important. We should tell the Council when you see them. Can you sense the thoughts of anyone else down here?"

She tried to concentrate on Aggie, and felt a wave of anger and frustration directed at her. *"Yep. I can feel Aggie. She's still mad at me."*

"How about anybody on land. Can you feel them?"

She thought of Paul, then guiltily of Jaycen, but couldn't make contact, although she suddenly remembered again that she was missing the dive Jaycen had signed them both up for. She hoped he wasn't freaking out. *"Nope. I can't feel anyone."* She felt Marcos relax and she wondered just how much he knew about Jaycen, if anything.

He took her hand and pulled her slowly into a close embrace, surprising her and taking her breath away. *"Does the amount of contact change what you can feel?"* he asked casually.

With a rush of sensation, she could feel his arms around her from his perspective as well as hers, like she was both of them at once. Her face flushed as she could feel his attraction to her and knew he could sense how she felt about him, too. The feeling was intoxicating; intimate and frightening. He pulled her closer until it was almost impossible to think objectively. She tried to separate their thoughts and mentally step back. Suddenly she didn't know what to do with her arms. Hug him back? Just let them flop to her side where they were? She could feel his heart beating faster in his bare chest and tried to keep her mind in line. Finally she managed a coherent reply.

"It's a little ... different when I'm holding your hand than when you hug me. What does that mean?"

He released her to arm's length. *"I don't know. We should talk to the Council about ... most of it."* They stared at each other uncomfortably.

Marcos shook his head and cleared his throat, turning toward the bottom of the cavern.

They sank halfway down the wall when Marin's eyes focused on a woman filling a bag over her shoulder. She gasped in surprise. *"Those rocks they are putting in the sacks—they're sapphires!"*

"Yes."

"That whole wall is made up of sapphires?" she asked incredulously.

Marcos nodded again. *"Most of this cavern has sapphire within its walls. They are often found around geothermic activity,"* he said.

Suddenly she realized how significant the Arydian's civilization was. It wasn't just about living and breathing underwater. The ability to tap into the resources found at the bottom of the sea, from natural gas to veins of gold, could make someone rich a million times over! People would look at the ocean like Spain had once looked to the Americas; a land overflowing with natural resources that would fill the pockets of anyone brave enough to look. No wonder Aggie was nervous about her leaving. *"You're right. Those who rule the sea could easily rule the world."*

Marcos watched the understanding grow in her eyes. *"You see why this is such a dangerous secret, now. Not only do we have the biggest source of gems known to mankind, but we have the ability to get it easily. Think what that would do to the greedy ones of the world."* They descended to the bottom and he picked out a rock the size of a grapefruit, twinkling like fire in the orange light.

"This is unbelievable!" she exclaimed. The floor was covered with enormous gems; more beautiful than any she had ever seen. *"Why would they drop these?"*

He shrugged. *"We can only use the smaller, less refined gems. The better ones would raise too many alarms. The world has nothing up there to compare with the quality of these. People would demand to know where they came from and Leviathan would have our distributors before they had time to think. As it is, they risk their lives to help us."*

"So you throw them away because they are too perfect?" she asked, astounded. Marin took the gem in her hand and was hit with a flood of forgotten memories. She remembered bags of uncut gems sitting in the back of her houseboat. Her father would let her pile them up and make little houses with them. She had been playing with priceless gems as a toddler!

She dropped the huge stone and let it fall to the ground. *"What is Leviathan?"*

Marcos gave her a dark look. *"The Council will explain. But they are the reason we live here, and I would give my life to destroy them."* He cocked his head to the side as if listening to something. *"The ships have left. We can return,"* he said, taking her hand. Without a word, he led her back into the darkening tunnel. Marcos took Marin into the main cavern by the bay while he went to change, giving her time to do the same. She went behind the screen and stripped off Aggie's wondersuit and put on the heavy woven garments she had worn earlier. She felt chilly and reluctantly had to admit that the suit had kept out the cold better than any wetsuit she had ever worn.

There were people working at the long tables surrounding the bay, and in the living area a couple of men were cooking something prickly that smelled a lot like cabbage. Everyone was talking in hushed tones and she wondered if it they were still under some kind of alert.

She wandered to the room she had spent the night in and dried her hair with a towel she found lying at the foot of the bed. She closed the door and crawled under the rough covers and closed her eyes.

It was probably about 7:00 p.m. The staff would be just finishing dinner and Jaycen and the rest of the interns would be tying up the boats for the night. She had been missing for more than 31 hours now. Had they called the police? Did Paul know? She was tempted to go to sleep and forget about life for a few hours, but the smell of food finally coaxed her out into the main cavern again.

She found Marcos in the living area, wearing a white t-shirt and a pair of the same kind of rough knit pants she was wearing. He was talking softly to a young girl with long yellow hair and for a moment she felt a rush of jealousy at this strange girl until she chastised herself for laying claim to a guy she'd known for only a day. Besides, as she got closer, she realized the girl couldn't be more than twelve.

She couldn't help but notice how extremely handsome Marcos was. It was the first time she had actually seen him dry. His hair looked black underwater, but it was actually dark brown, with golden highlights around his face. It hung long and wavy almost to his shoulders and his skin was a deep bronze. When he saw her come in, he stood, and she noted he was at least a full head taller than she was. She suddenly felt shy, like the person standing in front of her was a complete stranger, not someone she'd spent the day with, holding his hand for most of it. This guy looked like some Greek god, and he took her breath away.

He smiled, further dazzling her senses as she walked toward him. "You look lovely," he said, his voice deep and rich like honey. He met her halfway, kissing her softly on both cheeks. She stopped breathing for a moment. The girl on the couch looked up and smiled, making Marin feel bad for the mean things she had been thinking about her.

She stood quickly and spoke in a soft voice to Marin. "I'm Tania. I am so happy to meet you, Amanda. Are you hungry?"

Marin nodded gratefully at her and all three of them walked to the kitchen area. Marcos busied himself scooping food onto plates at the counter near the table.

"I'm surprised there are children here," Marin commented. "Were they born here?"

Tania laughed lightly. "No, other than Marcos, we were brought down later and changed when Portus was almost finished. Only family of the Council and those who may have had any knowledge of the project were brought down, one by one and in small groups, so Leviathan could not find us." A frown creased her brow, "Although we have stopped changing people since …"

"Have some dinner?" Marcos cut across their conversation, placing an unappetizing looking plate of food in front of both girls. Marin started to ask Tania more when Aaron walked out of the hallway, eating a plate of slippery looking food.

"Hey. My mom is in a meeting with the Council. She said Amanda is going to have to meet with them tomorrow."

"Tomorrow?" Marin looked shocked. "Why can't I talk to them now? She knows I can't stay here! I have a job. I can't never go home again!" she spluttered, missing the pained look Marcos shot her. "I … I don't even have clothes or … or a toothbrush!"

Marcos smiled. "You can stay in the room you slept in last night. We have all the clothes you need. And I can get you a toothbrush from the supply room. Tania, will you get her a change of clothes?" He turned to her. "We'll be right back." They left before she could protest.

Aaron grinned mischievously at her. "So. Do you like Marcos?"

Marin rolled her eyes at him.

"No, seriously! Do you like him?" he persisted, undeterred. He swallowed a mouthful of food.

"Like I'd tell you if I did! You're his best bud."

Aaron brightened up. "Really? Did Marcos say that?"

THIRTEEN

Marin woke in the same dark room and stretched. Even though the bed she slept on was hard, she'd slept surprisingly well. The room was so dark and quiet; she had no idea if it was noon or the middle of the night. Opening the door a crack, she looked in a mirror hung on the wall, wishing for a brush. She scrambled her long hair into a twisted knot at the back of her neck, realizing for the first time that she didn't really have to worry about anyone saying anything about her scars. It was refreshing to wear her hair up. She walked out of the room and right into Marcos.

"I'm sorry!" she said.

"Don't be. I was just coming to get you for breakfast!" he said with a warm hug. She soaked in his embrace, loving the strength of his arms around her.

They ate a spongy material for breakfast that was chewy and slightly sweet. Marcos finished quickly and sat back watching Marin.

"Can I ask you a question?" he asked. Marin nodded and he continued, "I don't mean to make you feel uncomfortable, but I noticed the lines along the back of your neck."

His comment shocked her. "I … they're … well, how I breathe the water. Don't you have them?"

Marcos pulled his hair away from the nape of his neck, showing his flawless skin. "So you are different from the rest of us. Interesting."

Great. So even among the freaks, she was freakier. "How would I be any different from you?" she asked, feeling defensive.

Marcos leaned close to her and touched the lines along the back of her neck. "Well, you have these. And we have these." He leaned his head to one side and showed her lines similar to hers, only his ran just behind his ear. He noticed the concern on her face and hurriedly added, "They are not big differences."

"Yeah, well, the difference between an elephant and a chicken is a tiny strand of DNA."

"Don't worry. Different is not bad. You perhaps have more talents than the rest of us because you were born to it. We were all given Arydia by injection and then we changed. You inherited it from both your parents. So of course you would have differences."

"Differences? You mean there's more?"

"Well, yes. I mean you are basically the first generation of a new species, are you not?" He looked at her half-eaten spongy food. "Do you not like your food?"

She swallowed and shrugged, suddenly not hungry. She didn't know what to think. A new species? She frowned at the thought of it, and then realized he was still waiting for her response. "It's just … different."

Marcos laughed. "Let me guess. In this case, different means really bad?"

She smiled and set down her fork.

"I need to get down to the garden and pick some Althos Beta." She shot him a puzzled look and he smiled. "It's the egg substitute you had yesterday. We use it in many of our dishes." He rose and rinsed his plate off and set it in a tray to dry. "I've neglected my duties during your stay," he said sheepishly. "I would take you with me, but Aggie and the Council want to meet with you as soon as they come back from the lower banks. It shouldn't be long." He said over his shoulder.

"You're leaving me here alone?" she asked, surprised.

His mouth hardened into a line and she realized he was giving her a chance to earn Aggie's trust now that she knew the risk of starting another crisis like she had the day before. "Will you be ok?" He asked pointedly.

"I promise I won't try to run away," she met his gaze steadily. "I promise, Marcos." His eyes met hers for a moment and then he nodded, walking toward the bay.

Alone in the cavern, Marin wandered down hallways that seemed half man made and half volcanic exhaust tube. The floor was smooth, but the walls were littered with holes and rough basalt. She opened a door to a round room with a steel table filling it. There were maps and charts covering all the walls and a couple of shelves along them. She looked at the ones on top, careful not to disturb their order, wondering if perhaps this was where the Council met. Blueprints were laid over the table and she recognized the bay and the canyon wall where she was now. It said "Portus" at the top. So this place is Portus. She wanted to move it and look at the other drawings, but didn't want to disturb the pile and alert anyone that she had been snooping around.

On the nearest table, a file folder caught her eye and suddenly she didn't care what papers she was upsetting. She snatched it up. On the outside was the word A.M.A.N.D.A. Several pictures of her as a small child fell onto the desk. She picked them up and studied them carefully, touching the faint memories that they produced. One picture showed her as a newborn, being held by a woman with long dark hair. With a catch in her throat she realized she was looking at her mother for the first time.

Aggie cleared her throat, making Marin jump, dropping the folder in the process. "I see you found the Council room well enough," Aggie said flatly. It was obvious that she was still feeling flustered and angry about Marin's attempt to leave. Several men walked in behind Aggie and sat down around the table, nodding to her.

One of the men leaned forward in his chair and said, "It is good to see you again, Ama …Marin." he corrected hastily. "We will address your questions now and decide what is to be done."

She took the pictures and slid them into her pocket, throwing a defiant look at Aggie. She sat down in one of the chairs at the table. "Great. I have a lot of questions. First off, who are you guys? And what is Arydia? What—"

"Let us start at the beginning, shall we?" Aggie interrupted. "These are the original members of AQUA, or as we are now called, the Council. I will write down their names as they introduce themselves to you so you will remember. Of course, you know me already. I'm Agatha." Marin watched as she produced a dry erase marker and wrote Agatha across the top of a white board standing beside her, feeling like she had been dropped into some kind of bizarre kindergarten class. She glanced at the other members, looking for some hint of emotion, but they all seemed engrossed in her reaction.

"Uh, okaaay," she said.

The man nearest to Aggie spoke next. He had a thick, musical accent, heavy eyebrows and a shaggy mane of graying hair. "I am Malcolm Stefanos. I am from Greece, and Marcos, your friend," he said, waving his hand toward the door, "is my only son." Aggie wrote Malcolm underneath Agatha on the white board.

"The next member of our original group was Ahsan Ahmed." She wrote his name on the board underneath Malcolm's. "Ahsan was from Bangkok, but unfortunately he was killed before the exodus. His family, however, resides with us, and you may have seen some of his dear children."

"What's the exodus?" Marin asked. Malcolm held up his hand to stop her.

"Please, allow us to finish. You may see only one drop of paint, but many together make a picture. Watch."

A lithe Japanese man spoke next. He smiled hugely at her and bobbed his head in welcome. "I am Noburu Sasaki. It has been long since I have seen you. I am happy you have returned to your family."

Marin smiled weakly in return. Aggie wrote the word Noburu on her list. Marin was beginning to wonder if Aggie was slightly insane, but the others didn't seem to see anything amiss.

Aggie spoke again, writing a name on the board as she did so. "Douglas was next, but he was met with an accident as well. We all miss him dearly. He was your father, my brother in-law, and Emily's husband."

Marin's breath caught. Emily? Her father was one of these council people? Questions boiled through her brain, but her voice refused to cooperate and all that came out was a pathetic squeak. Aggie turned back around, and Marin was surprised to see that she looked upset.

"I am Alexei Kordovic," the remaining man stated in a deep baritone. He was large and his thinning hair looked like it had been blonde at one time, though it was now laced with grey. His voice sounded as if he might have been from Russia, Bulgaria or somewhere else in Eastern Europe. Marin felt like she was sitting in on a mini version of the United Nations, and couldn't help but wonder what brought all these people together.

Aggie stood next to the board and looked at her expectantly. The others stared at her as well, waiting.

Marin shifted uncomfortably, wondering what they wanted, feeling confused and very awkward.

"Don't you see, Amanda?" Noboru asked.

"See what?" she asked, completely dumbfounded.

Aggie rolled her eyes in exasperation and took her marker to the board. She underlined the first letter of every name and then sat back down with her arms folded.

Suddenly it struck Marin like a tidal wave. A.M.A.N.D.A. The first initials of these people she had never seen before spelled her real name.

* * *

Dr. Gilbert treated himself to a short walk out onto the deserted pier. Early morning was his favorite time of day, with the fishermen taking their boats quietly out of harbor, no speedboats or tourists or students clogging the beach and water and, best of all, nobody needing him for anything. He squinted in the sunlight as he stretched his back. The sun had just appeared in the periwinkle sky, shooting barbs of light to reflect off every wave in the ocean below him.

He spared a moment to savor the warm salty air and remember a time when he was a boy, looking out at the ocean by his father's beach house and imagining himself sailing the open sea or diving to the depths to discover new worlds just like Jacques Cousteau. He lingered on the memory for a moment before he shut it down. The contrast between then and now was so stark it was painful. As if on cue, his phone started to vibrate but he waited, knowing that whoever was calling needed something: a signature, permission, information. It was always something.

Reluctantly he pulled it from his pocket, accidentally pushing the button to answer the call. The phone stopped ringing and the face of Mr. Hahn filled the screen. Cursing to himself, he brought the phone to his ear.

"Mr. Hahn. How are you?"

The clipped voice on the end sounded tinny and far away, yet severe. "The operation must be moved ahead immediately. My sources tell me that our target is extremely viable. There was another anomaly yesterday. This is most certainly the correct site and I am certain we will find them there."

Gilbert panicked, knowing time was vanishing too quickly for him to react. He remained silent for a moment, steadying his voice. "I understand. When?"

Hahn's voice rose in pitch. "Immediately!"

Gilbert forced his dry mouth to work and his voice not to betray his anxiety. "We're not ready. The sub is still at least three weeks away from launch. There's no way we can have everything in place before then."

"You seem hesitant, Gilbert. Perhaps your heart is not completely committed to our endeavor," Hahn said silkily.

"No. But I am concerned about the safety of my crew."

"Perhaps if you spent less time on your 'project' and instead worked on our mission you would find success."

Gilbert's heart stopped.

Hahn waited, knowing his words hit their mark. "Do not think, Dr. Gilbert, that we do not protect our interests. We watch them very carefully. You have one week to complete your preparation to launch. If you are not ready, consider our agreement at an end." The phone went dead.

Frank woodenly put his phone back in his pocket, fighting the urge to be sick over the side of the dock. All the beauty of the morning had turned dark and cold. He bit his cheek and turned back to the lab.

* * *

Seaman John Mcneil the Third enjoyed writing reports. His grandfather and his father had both served in the Navy and had seen action in their respective conflicts, so it was expected that he, too, would join when he came of age. For John, the glorious stories of battle and camaraderie held no appeal in real life and were much more enjoyable between the pages of a book. Still, the family expectation had to be upheld, thus, after the pain and discouragement of his basic training were over, he was delighted to find himself assigned to a coastal cruiser, patrolling the calm waters of the Southern California coast. He had two days off out of every ten to enjoy the laid back California lifestyle and when he was assigned to port, he worked in the office, filing mountains of minor incident reports and translating them into concise records added to the military's massive database.

He paused at his next report, perusing the details of a strange incident. Sonar had detected a disturbance just a mile off the coast inside the Naval Base's sea boundary. Seismic activity was usually to blame, but the report had claimed the sounds were "suspicious," whatever that was supposed to mean. Whatever it was, it caused enough concern that the base was notified.

By chance, a cutter had been nearby with personnel suited up for a training dive, so they were diverted to investigate. The cutter had sent divers in, but all they found at the coordinates was a large and restless pod of dolphins. According to the incident report, the dolphins became aggressive, severely injuring one man and the mock rescue had become a real one.

Mcneil took off his hat, wiping the sweat off his forehead with the back of his hand and wishing for the millionth time that his office had better air conditioning. He dumped the remains of a cup of melting ice into his mouth, relishing the coolness of it. A notification came through on his phone. *Dentist appointment,* he read to himself. Dang! He'd forgotten.

He sighed and turned back to the page in front of him. As he typed the report, he frowned to himself, thinking of two things about this report that bothered him. First and foremost was that dolphins are rarely aggressive unless they feel threatened, and it seemed strange that six divers would constitute a threat.

The second thing that disturbed him was the fact that this was not the first time a report like this had come across his desk recently.

He finished typing, then logged into the record archives. Maybe he could see something in comparing the two incidents that would shed light on the mystery. Maybe the Coast Guard was experimenting with training dolphins to carry sonars, or feeding them strange chemicals to increase their intelligence—he'd seen a movie about that once.

Scrolling down the dates, he struggled to remember when he'd filed it. It had been several months ago, he remembered, and then it hit him. The day before his mother's birthday. It caught his attention because his mother was a nut for dolphins, and he'd mentioned it to her in his phone call to her the next day.

Ah, yes, here was the date. He scrolled through the information, but couldn't find the incident report. He opened up the files for the previous day, then the following day. He searched thoroughly, but the file was gone. He couldn't figure how the file could've vanished. He was sure he remembered typing it up. Could he have accidentally deleted it? He certainly hoped not. There were severe punishments for messing up military records. Could somebody else have deleted it? He laughed at the absurdity for a moment, wondering who would care enough about a stupid dolphin sighting to tamper with the records.

He sat back in his squeaky chair, perplexed. "Ah, I must be going nuts!" he muttered to himself and went back to the next paper on his pile.

FOURTEEN

"This cavern and all you see in it are all that remain of an idea that was meant to change the world. And you are the first and only child to be born into it. Your mother named you after each of us," Aggie stated simply, as if that would explain everything.

Marin waited, not sure which of her pile of questions to offer next.

Malcolm spoke. "Twenty-six years ago, we were chosen from our respective countries because we are the best minds from the around the world, at least that is what we were told when we were approached by Leviathan." He tilted his head to one side and shrugged. "They offered unlimited resources to solve an impossible problem, and this is the result." Malcolm gestured to everyone in the room.

Noburu put a hand on Malcolm's shoulder and stepped in. "An international company, Leviathan, recruited us all to work together to find a way for humans to live in the last frontier; the depths of the sea."

He waited until she nodded her understanding. "Your father and mother were among us, though they hadn't met at the time we began." He smiled at her again. "She and her sister, Aggie, worked at a university in England. Your mother was a biologist, Aggie was a chemist."

Aggie lifted her eyebrows in challenge. "Was? I still am!"

Noburu nodded. "Forgive me."

Aggie nodded and went back to studying the desk. "Each of us had received a related degree in more than one field, which we believe set us apart to be approached. The project was called, simply enough, AQUA."

The Council members nodded their heads and Noburu continued. "Our main objective was to create a way for humans to live underwater for extended periods of time, similar to the many mammals that inhabit the ocean, our cousins the dolphins, for instance." He waved a hand towards Aggie. "Aggie developed a suit to accomplish that end, but that was not enough in itself to assure life underwater. The body must resist the physical trauma of extended submersion, the intense pressure of water had to be overcome, and obtaining oxygen had to be addressed as well. The mechanics of creating a habitat for humans that could withstand the tempests of the changing currents was critical, as well as finding out the psychological impact of changing your entire environment." He sat forward in his chair, eyes intense. "Learning what to grow, how to eat, how to get the vitamins the body requires, what the impact on bone structure would be, how to find fresh water. It was a project to rival setting up civilization on the moon."

"Yes, but harder because the moon doesn't have as unpredictable a climate," Alexei grunted, and the others chuckled mirthlessly.

Noburu nodded. "Precisely. But at least the ocean is local for most. Regardless, this was the task we set out to do, and we were thrilled and challenged to our utmost abilities for the next seven years with no thought given to cost or equipment. We learned and worked without limits. It was every scientist's dream." The small room fell silent and Noburu looked at Aggie.

She nodded and picked up the story. "It was during this time that your father and my sister fell in love and were married. They had so much in common—they were both brilliant biologists and AQUA had them working on some of the same aspects of the project for so long," she sighed. "I suppose it was inevitable. We had all become close while working together. We were more like family than co-workers. Though, of course, we had others that worked with us, we, as department heads, met together frequently and made the decisions and discoveries that shaped AQUA. And it was your mother who discovered the secret."

Noburu began again. "Emily isolated a hormone that is produced by a special genus of frog during its last stages of metamorphosis from its life as a tadpole. By isolating this gene and pairing it with certain species of fish, this hormone became the key to all you see here. The drug was named Arydia."

"Fortunately, Ahsan began asking questions," Alexei interjected. "He was wise enough to ponder not only the questions of how it can be done, but also *why* it should be done, and *if*. He was a quiet, thoughtful man. A good man." He looked down and said quietly, "A friend." He cleared his throat and continued. "He knew that what we found would be a powerful tool, changing the world in fantastic ways. But, perhaps because of the war-torn world he grew up in, he realized it could also be a formidable weapon that could destroy everything as we know it. He knew that controlling the sea is critical in controlling the world." Marin nodded in understanding.

"So, he started watching. He cautioned us to guard our knowledge until we knew more about our benefactors. While we spent our time perfecting the gene and planning the ideal place to stage our great experiment, he spent part of his time digging and learning everything he could about our parent company, Leviathan. He became our spokesperson with Leviathan. They trusted his reports and included him in some of their plans. Thus, he knew before any of us what we had done."

"In a way, Leviathan was an amazing accomplishment. People from all over the world, businessmen and women, had come together for one purpose. If only our governments worked that closely," he said wistfully. "Ahsan learned that Leviathan's objective was to create a new government. A new *continent*, underwater. Imagine that! Imagine, Amanda, what would happen if a huge parcel of land appeared with its own weapons, its own army and its own belief in what the world should be. Imagine the chaos and wars that would ensue. And imagine if this country bordered every continent. Their armies could plant weapons right on top of your borders and nobody would be able to do anything about it. These people we worked for, who had seemed to be visionaries and explorers like Christopher Columbus and Neil Armstrong, now looked more like Attila the Hun or Hitler, do you see?"

Marin nodded.

"The information we had was too dangerous and we made plans to destroy it all. It was heartbreaking, but we knew it must be done. Ahsan was brilliantly deceptive. He had led Leviathan to believe we were further behind than we were, putting our early attempts up as most recent, and encouraged us to move ahead with our plans for destruction quickly before we were found out. However, Leviathan grew impatient and had their own plan to entice us to further our work. They had been doing their own research, you see." Alexei paused then continued in a cracked voice, "They took those we loved ..." his voice cracked completely and he was unable to continue.

Aggie stepped in. "They looked for our weaknesses and exploited them. Children, wives, husbands, parents. They were taken to an island off the coast of Canada and held there as ransom until we finished the job we were expected to do."

"Didn't anybody call the police?" Marin interrupted, unbelieving.

Aggie rolled her eyes. "People go missing all the time, Marin. And a handful of people scattered across the globe—who is going to put that all together? Besides, they left us no doubt as to what they would do if we went to the authorities. As a token of their commitment, they sent us the left small finger of each of their hostages, as well as a photo of each of them with their mutilated left hand to leave no doubt about what they had done."

"We wondered, but now we knew; we were not dealing with scientists as we believed, but terrorists." She paused, letting this information sink in.

Marin recoiled in horror. Everyone in the room looked haunted by the memory. She couldn't imagine how horrible it must've been for each of them. Part of her mind didn't want to accept that it could be true. She didn't want to believe people like that existed on her planet.

"At that point we realized that the only way out of this was through it. Ahsan was our expert in Archaeology and Engineering, Alexei is our geophysicist and they had been working together to create an underwater habitat off the coast of Tortugas, Mexico. It was a bio dome with dry land as well as access to water, sparsely furnished and Spartan in every way. However, Alexei had discovered a better place, off the coast of California, near an uncharted geothermic vent. It was also extremely close to a naval base, which had made it ill-suited in Leviathan's eyes for the AQUA program and also difficult for us, but it had the benefit of protection from the worst of our enemies if we were found. We were, in essence, hiding behind our mother's skirts."

Alexei blew into his moustache, ruffled at the comment. "Yes, a mother who is constantly patrolling these waters and listening with bionic ears. It was extremely difficult to bring our equipment out here without arousing suspicion."

"How did you do it, then?" Marin asked, completely enthralled.

Alexei shrugged and said, "We are not without connections. Malcolm's family owns a shipping company in Crete. Ahsan's cousin owned a building supply company. My brother in-law was a jeweler in Seattle. There were ways to get help. We would buy the supplies we needed, seal them in waterproof containers and adhere them with magnets to the bottom of ships. Then, when we got near to our destination, we could release the magnets and let the containers drift to the ocean floor, where we would bring them in with our skiffs. It was difficult, but Ahsan quickly devised a way to deflect sonar and radar on our crafts, using technology your military has used for years."

Marin was confused. "Wait, why did you make another hideout? I thought you were going to destroy all your work and leave?"

Noburu smiled at her. "Ah, you are good at puzzles, just like your mother. Yes, we were going to destroy all our work, but the knowledge we had," he tapped his index finger against his temple, "was alive as long as we were. It became apparent that we would never be allowed to walk away from this project. Terrorists do not reward those they use except with death: those we love first, and eventually our deaths as well. So, we made a monumental decision. We all had to die."

FIFTEEN

Seaman Mcneil had taken a long lunch to have a tooth looked at on base. His left front molar had been giving him trouble every time he chewed something sweet. The Navy dental office was small and businesslike. There were no fancy chairs, no relaxing music. The overworked dentist had taken a few x-rays and told him he needed a root canal, which they promptly started and filled with a temporary filling while his crown was sent away to be made.

Seaman Mcneil rubbed his jaw, muttering about his bad luck as he walked back to work. He popped some ice in his mouth from a drink he'd bought at the cafeteria on the way back, wondering how a guy who brushed so religiously would need a root canal. Perhaps he drank too much soda. He shrugged off the thought and set his drink down next to his computer terminal.

Pulling out a chewed pencil he used as a place marker from his pile of papers, he started where he had left off. He was halfway through writing about a missing clearance card before he noticed he had already filed that report before he went to lunch. He flipped through the papers and realized he was several incidents ahead of where his pencil was. His pencil had been moved! Unnerved, he looked over his shoulder at the rest of the office to see if anything else was out of order or missing. Finding nothing unusual in the small room, he went through his papers, comparing them to the data he had put on the computer. Everything seemed normal. He was about to chalk up the experience as a result of Novocain-induced amnesia when it hit him. The report about the dolphins was missing.

He started for the door and pushed the intercom button. "Captain?"

* * *

It was a cool evening for summer. Jaycen waited on the pier for Tui and Natalee's boat to return. He sat on the edge, dangling his shoes into the lapping waves. He had spent the better part of the day searching COAST from top to bottom, and then he had taken his car driving along the coast. He told himself he was probably just being obsessive, but something nagged at the back of his mind that something was wrong with Marin's disappearance. And something about his car had made him nervous, too. When he'd gotten in, he had to pull his seat forward to reach the pedals comfortably. He was fairly certain that Marin's legs were shorter than his. So why, if she was the last one to drive it, would it have been pushed back so far?

Frustrated and angry about fretting over Marin, he had driven into town for a couple of hours to visit his mom and have dinner with her and her fancy pants military commander boyfriend, who spent the evening telling war stories, trying to become Jaycen's buddy, and dropping not-so-subtle hints that he was thinking about becoming his new stepdad. He'd driven back to resume his vigil in an even worse mood.

It was like Marin had vanished off the earth. He'd even slipped into her room and checked her cell phone a couple more times, but the only one to call had been that same number. Now he sat waiting for Tui, who texted him almost a half hour ago, asking him to "quit being a flake and help unload."

Silent sailboats skimmed across the horizon, their silhouettes dark against the rust sunset. A liner's bright lights twinkled far out to sea. He wondered what it would be like on a cruise ship, sailing off the end of the continent until there was nothing but ocean. He pictured himself standing on the deck of some fancy ship, drinking some fruity drink in the warm sunset, holding hands with the one he loved. Which brought his thoughts back to Marin. Frustrated, he slapped his hand onto the deck and renewed his worn out vow to quit thinking about her.

Finally, he heard the hum of a motor coming closer as the cutter entered bay. As they pulled up, Jaycen was shocked to see a couple in the bow of the boat. Tui had his arm around Natalee, a triumphant grin on his face. Somehow it made Jaycen mad, as if Tui and Natalee had stolen his daydream. Natalee looked up at Jaycen with a strange look of surprise but didn't move out of Tui's circle of arms. Maybe if he and Marin had gone on this trip, it would be them smiling and looking … together.

"Hey, loser! 'Bout time you showed up!" Tui joked, leaving Natalee and hurling a coil of rope onto the dock.

"How was the dive?" Jaycen asked, dropping a bumper down to protect the side of the boat.

Tui's face split into a huge grin. "It was fabuuuulous!" he said, jumping onto the dock. "The weather was perfect, the nets were almost empty, and my girl here found a spiny dogfish." Jaycen raised his eyes when Tui called Natalee his girl, and Natalee blushed and looked away, as if she wasn't quite used to the idea. "So, since you spent your Saturday off the clock, it's only fitting that you bring in the equipment and specimens while we go grab some dinner." He took Natalee's hand and helped her off the boat and put his arm around her as they walked away down the pier.

Jaycen grumbled, jumping on deck. Dave was already stowing the nets and life preservers. The sun dipped behind the horizon and turned the world an inky blue. Jaycen flipped on the deck lights by the stern.

"Hey, I'll help you, Dave." He strode over to the tank that Dave was struggling to lift on his own. Dave nodded. He looked tired.

"Thanks. I'm sorry you weren't feeling well. We missed you on the dive." For a moment Jaycen had forgotten that he had told Tui to cover for him. He supposed in hindsight he should have texted Tui and asked him what story he had told Dave.

Jaycen nodded. "Thanks. I'm feeling a lot better. It must've been something I ate."

"Yeah, Tui told me you couldn't leave the john." Jaycen scowled and vowed to punch Tui the next time he saw him. They picked up the heavy tank and Dave continued, "Speaking of the devil, where did lover boy run off to? And did Marin ever turn up? It's not like her to ditch something. Hey, hold on a second." Dave undid a valve at the bottom of the tank and let a steady stream of water pour onto the dock, then tightened it back up. "We've only caught a couple dozen today. No need to carry all that water." They heaved it up over the side of the boat and together they brought it into the warehouse lab before going back to the boat to finish putting it right.

"No, I didn't see her today. But I was the one to sign her up, so maybe she just didn't know. Looks like it was a great day for a dive. Where did you go?" Jaycen said, hoping to change the subject. As concerned as he was for Marin, he didn't want to cause problems for her.

Dave straightened up and rubbed his sunburned neck. "We went up the coast a couple of miles toward the naval base, but there were a ton of ships in the area. It looked like they were preparing for some heavy exercises. We didn't even have time to put out the buoys before they called out their dogs and told us to go somewhere else. So, we just turned around and went straight out from Neptune Net. Don't know what they're doing up by Point Mugu, but they look like they mean business."

Jaycen frowned uneasily.

* * *

Gilbert stopped by Marin's room on the way back to his office and tapped on the door. He heard music inside, but there was no answer. He was tempted to open the door, but realized how inappropriate that would look. He waited for a moment longer before walking to the elevators for a silent ride up to his office. When he sat down he sent a quick email to Marin asking her to call and meet him as soon as possible in the bay lab. Then, hesitantly, he checked his own email. He winced as he saw that Mr. Hahn's secretary had sent three emails in the last four hours.

He wondered why Mr. Hahn hadn't contacted him directly. He pulled out his phone and realized it had gone dead, probably hours ago. He muttered under his breath and opened his email.

"We must move the schedule up. We have only two or three days at most. Contact me immediately to verify you've received this!"

Two or three days! It was impossible! All this work for nothing. There was no way to move forward. Exhaustion and fatigue took over. He let his head fall onto his arms folded on his desk and wept.

* * *

Marin sat back in her chair, stunned. "Die?"

Malcolm looked at her, his eyes dark under thick brows. Aggie cleared her throat and explained. "The hormone had been tested on certain mammals to see if it would work, however it had not been used in humans yet. Ahsan learned it was never the intention of Leviathan to keep us after the human testing stage had begun. They had recruits that were enlisted to be test subjects and *we* were to be held at arm's length until the testing had proved successful, and then disposed of. None of us by this time had any hope that our loved ones would be released, or that we would be allowed to live while we held knowledge of Leviathan's great secret." Aggie's eyes clouded over at the memory.

Noburu smiled at her sadly and took over the narrative. "Your mother knew time was running out for us. She administered the hormone to herself when she was alone, but she couldn't test it without, in essence, drowning. The physical demand for oxygen was too great, and she found she would always panic and come up for air. In order to assure it would work, she took a boat out and went to a dive site she'd seen and used handcuffs to lock herself to a weight dumped by the navy years ago. She took her scuba gear off, locked herself up and let herself drown." Noburu leaned back in his chair, watching her reaction.

Marin was quiet, remembering her similar experience in Davey's Cave. The terror of those final moments still shook her.

Malcolm sighed. "Your mother was very brave to do what she did."

The others nodded thoughtfully, and Noburu continued with a laugh, "Your mother was very proud of herself! She was delighted that it worked, and showed us immediately."

Aggie jumped in at this point. "Leviathan was getting suspicious. We knew then that it was time to put our plan into action. She administered the drug to each of us, and we each took our turn locked to that terrible weight and drowning, only to come alive again. We became, in essence, a new species and called ourselves Arydians, after the compound that changed us. We stole every scrap of our research from Leviathan, hid it in their own submersible, and transported it down here. Then we burned Leviathan to the ground."

Marin was shocked. "Burned it?" She was accosted with thoughts of mad scientists running through a watery warehouse with gallons of gasoline and flamethrowers. Who *were* these people, anyway?

Aggie read her expression and pursed her lips. "Leviathan isn't full of people out to discover the last frontier and make their own civilization. Their sole purpose is to use the ocean to control the world, no matter the cost. This is a war, Marin. With more at stake than you realize."

"It became extremely dangerous for anyone left behind as well. After a few years, Leviathan started to suspect we were not all dead. They discovered a few of our people, and when they would not talk, they were tortured and killed. Aaron's parents for instance. Aaron was just a little thing, barely able to walk, but he was left for dead in the wreckage of their home; discarded like a piece of trash," Aggie spat out bitterly. "We found him, brought him under, and I raised him."

Aggie shifted in her seat. "He was the youngest child at the time to be given Arydia. He had some reactions to the drug, but in the end, he was changed and has lived with us ever since. We then started to bring down as many of our contacts as we could, and eventually their families. It became too dangerous to leave anyone who knew of us behind."

The door swung open and a woman of about forty walked in, breathless, eyes wide with panic. "Divers!" she exclaimed.

Marin felt a surge of adrenaline change the temperature of the room. Everyone but Marin stood and rushed toward the door. As Malcolm walked by her, she reached out her hand to stop him.

"What happened to the hostages? The ones they had taken from you?"

He stopped and looked at her hand on his arm, not meeting her gaze.

"They killed them. They killed them all," he said gruffly. She released his arm and he shuffled past her and out the door.

* * *

Captain Drake Savage stood aboard a steel grey cutter in the fading light. The boat was larger than most cutters, and fully armed for combat. By the dim light he could still make out his diving buoys bobbing around behind the boat. He didn't hold out much hope that his men could find anything so late in the day, but he wanted them to look anyway. Besides, it was good training for them in night maneuvers. He could see their headlamps like tiny stars in the water below him. He allowed himself a moment to enjoy looking up at the stars which were beginning to gleam in the clear night above him and the star-like lights below him, surrounding him like he was standing in space. He exhaled noisily, and then clicked the intercom.

"Kill the lights. Go to infrared."

"Affirmative, Skipper," the voice crackled back to him.

A moment later the glittering lamps were extinguished below him, leaving him staring at the black water. Twenty-two men and three women were in the water below him, searching for who knows what. Unusual dolphins? He'd read the report twice and talked to the nervous rookie clerk who had the crazy idea that someone was tampering with Naval documents to cover up unusual activity in the area, but he couldn't help but believe that it was some glitch or error the kid was making into a big deal. Still, Savage's commanding officer had given the order for an investigation, so here they were. He'd give them another forty minutes and then he'd call the whole operation a wash. He pulled up a metal deck chair and sat down to watch the stars.

* * *

Marin had never seen so many people moving so soundlessly in her life. It was eerie. She looked for Marcos in the main room, but people were rushing everywhere, shutting down computer banks, unplugging appliances, and switching off everything.

Noburu grabbed her wrist and silently switched on a small, dim, flashlight. He led her to the bay, where everyone was gathering. Every desk and shelf around the walls was being emptied into large metal containers with locks. She felt all the Arydians, even the children, moving with a sense of urgency but with a precision that told her they had done this before. Noburu led her to the wall, handed her one of Aggie's dive suits and indicated that she should put it on.

She started to ask him what was going on, but he waved her silent with a look of panic. He put his index finger to his lips, and then pointed to the roof. She nodded, though she didn't understand and slipped behind the screen to pull on the heavy wetsuit. When she emerged, people were sliding the containers into the water. They moved themselves into the dark water like eels, with no noise whatsoever. Noburu returned just as they flicked off the rest of the light, leaving her in blackness so absolute it took her breath away. He took her hand and led her to the edge of the floor, sliding down into the water and pulled her toward it as well.

She sat down on the edge and dropped quietly into the cold. She brought water into her lungs slowly and let it out again. Under the water her vision improved greatly. People were everywhere, around and below her. She watched in amazement at this three dimensional world where people could be above, behind, and around you without care of gravity.

"Can you hear me, Marin?" Noburu thought to her.

"Yes," she responded.

"*Good. There are divers in the area from the Naval Base. We must hide. They are using sensitive sonar equipment, so we must not make a sound. Despite the shelter of the cave, sound can travel through the water to the opening. The lives of every one of us depend on your silence. Do you understand? Not a sound.*" She felt the anxiety in his voice, and she knew he didn't trust her not to freak out and try to break away as she had earlier.

"*I'll be good, don't worry,*" she assured him.

Noburu nodded and took her hand. She felt weird holding onto this strange older guy she barely knew and wished Marcos was there instead. He led her off the main tunnel into a small alcove and let go of her hand.

"*Can you be trusted to stay here? We have much to do.*"

"*Alone?*" she asked anxiously. "*For how long?*"

Noburu faced her and looked into her eyes. "*For as long as the situation requires. We are trying our best to protect you as well as ourselves. Please trust us. You are brave. If something happens, I swear someone will contact you. You will need to get out as fast as possible and get as far from here as you can as quickly as you can. Follow the tunnels back through the upper bay and you will emerge on the far side of Portus. Otherwise, please stay here and don't make a sound.*"

Marin nodded and Noburu swam away down the tunnel, leaving her alone in the darkness of the room.

"*Marcos?*" she whispered in her mind, hoping only he would hear her.

"*Yes?*" he answered back.

She jumped at his mental contact, both relieved and alarmed at the clarity of it.

"*Where are you?*" she asked hopefully.

"*I am busy right now. Where are you?*" She was surprised at the brusqueness of his response.

"*I'm ... just alone,*" she stammered, embarrassed that he could feel her fear, and suddenly feeling like she was three years old and scared of the dark.

"*Look, I've got a lot to do right now.*"

"I'm sorry. I didn't mean to bother you," she said, trying to hide her hurt and confusion.

After a while she felt him contact her again. *"I didn't mean to be short with you. Things are difficult right now. I need to concentrate."*

"What's going on?" she asked tentatively.

"It's kind of hard to describe. I'm just trying to call some help to cover for us."

She closed her eyes, hating the feeling of being trapped inside the cocoon of rock she was in. She held onto her connection with Marcos like a lifeline, trying to imagine where he was and what he was doing when suddenly she felt the world shift. Opening her eyes, she was in the open water at the base of the cave.

Looking down she saw her hands were no longer her own, but Marcos's. It was more than seeing what he was seeing. She felt like she was really there. She could see the shapes of others waiting at the mouth of the cavern, trying not to make a sound as they watched several divers slowly moving through the water far above them. The Arydians had meter-long spears attached to packs on their backs and were clearly ready to use them. Through Marcos's eyes she could see the metal hull of a ship showing up as a black shadow floating almost a half mile up directly above them. She reached her arm out and felt it collide with the rough wall of Marcos's room. Her eyes didn't register that her arm had moved at all, however.

"What are you doing?" Marcos shouted into her mind in alarm. She flinched at his shout and cut off her connection with him in reflex. The moment she did, she found herself back in the room, staring at the uneven floor.

"Marcos?" she sent out tentatively, bracing herself for the world to shift again, but nothing happened.

"What did you just do?" Marcos demanded.

"I don't know! I was just thinking about you and suddenly I was there! Is that normal?"

"No, definitely not."

"Oh." She stared at the walls for a few minutes in silence not knowing what to say, thinking about the shapes moving around and above them. Who were they? She tried to curl herself into a ball and think of other things, but she wanted answers. Finally she asked, *"Can I try it again?"*

Marcos didn't answer for a minute, and then he said quietly, *"Okay."* She put her hand out to steady herself on the rock bottom of the cave and closed her eyes to follow his link with her until she felt like her eyes were opening and she could see what he was seeing. It was like watching a movie, but she was totally connected to every sense. She could hear the sounds; feel the vibrations as Marcos called to the dolphins as if she was making the sounds herself. She touched her throat to make sure it wasn't really her. She could feel his heart beating as if it were her own. He felt her surprise as she thought, *"Wow! It worked!"*

"Yes, hello." He seemed disturbed and a little annoyed with her. She couldn't help but feel amazed at the sensations she was having. It was like she was a ghost possessing his body. She tried to rub her nose with his hand.

"Stop that!" he demanded.

"Can you tell what I'm doing?" she asked in awe.

"Yes, you are messing with my head. This is a crisis and I can't afford to make a mistake."

She could feel his feelings without him even telling her; his concern for the safety of his friends and family and his unwillingness to put them in jeopardy, but she could also feel his burning curiosity about why she could enter his mind at will. She could also tell that he at some level liked the closeness of the contact. The thought made her face warm.

"I'm glad you like me, too, Marin."

She was shocked, dismayed that the contact went both ways. What had he discovered while she had been probing into his emotions?

She pulled away a little bit, until she was just observing the surroundings.

"I'm sorry."

"This may not be the best time to experiment with this," Marcos commented dryly.

Marin hated to leave the action to go back to waiting in her forgotten corner. "*Can I just watch? I won't do anything but watch.*"

Marcos could feel the fear woven into her words, and despite his better judgment, he agreed. He opened his mouth and made the sound again, crying mournfully into the water. This time it was answered. They both felt movement in the water as animals came gliding along the ocean floor. The water started to come alive with dozens of fins and flippers, rising from the sand like spirits from the grave.

SIXTEEN

Frank awoke at his desk with his arms numb and a crick in his neck. He glanced at the darkened window and realized with a start that he'd been asleep. Cursing himself, he refreshed his email and saw another three messages from Hahn. He steeled himself and clicked open the most recent.

Sending support team for upcoming launch.

He slammed down the cover of his laptop. Locking his office door, he stalked back to the lab and began another test.

* * *

Captain Savage checked his watch. It had luminescent hands that glowed softly in the starlight, and was a gift from his mother over thirty years ago when he'd graduated from the Naval Academy. The watch was one of his most treasured possessions for both its sentimental value and for the fact that it was always reliable, despite the many punishments he'd inflicted upon it over the course of its life. He thought wryly how he wished people could be so forgiving and dependable.

The team had another seven minutes until the exercise was over. He was just moving to signal his people when the water came alive with dorsal fins. Dolphins! Delighted, he leaned out to get a closer look.

"Captain?" His speaker crackled from the dive team.

"Yes, I see them. Careful on your ascent. You may want to come up on the port side."

"Captain? Do you see them?" the lieutenant squeaked into his mic. "Captain, the sharks, they're everywhere! Request assistance."

Sharks! He flipped on the overhead lights and shone a beam into the water. His blood chilled at the sight surrounding his boat. They were everywhere, writhing across the surface, churning up the water like a boiling cauldron. He caught a close glimpse of one as it thrust out of the water, sliding over the back of one of its comrades. Mako Sharks. Fierce, quick and deadly. They acted like they were in a feeding frenzy, a phenomenon where sharks go mad at the smell of blood and devour anything in sight, including each other. He quailed to think what his team was feeling right now. He had to get them out of there fast.

"Lieutenant Davidson, talk to me. What's everybody's position?" He paused, listening. "Davidson! Talk to me!" Radio static crackled into his ears. Savage beat his hand in frustration on the railing, willing someone to answer him.

"Sir, this is Ensign Larson. Lieutenant Davidson is unable to respond."

Unable to respond! Dead? The feeding frenzy ... Captain Savage swallowed and moved on to the living. "Status, Larson!"

"All accounted for, sir. Holding at thirty-five feet. Davidson is having trouble with his hose. Trying to help. Please advise."

Good. Davidson wasn't dead, yet. That was a small relief. "Visual?"

"Yes sir. They are swarming all around us. We are holding. Please advise!" He could hear the veiled panic in Larson's voice. He reminded himself to give Larson a commendation if he made it back alive.

"Can you move to the port side without attracting attention?"

"Sir, we already have their attention. I fear any move we make will provoke them. Davidson is convulsing."

"I have 15 minutes left on the tank ... verify."

"Yes, sir. Fifteen. But he is sucking O2 fast. Please advise."

Advise? Larson's repeated plea was shaking him. What advice could he give? He steeled himself and opened the cabin of the boat. Two helmsmen stood at their posts, ready to move at the first sign.

"Gentlemen, we have a problem." He explained to his two officers the situation, and while one radioed base, the other came out on deck. "I need ideas, and I need them now," he said with forced calm.

"Could we scare them away with our air horn?" the helmsman suggested.

Savage shrugged hopelessly. "I don't know that it wouldn't enrage them more."

"Maybe we could draw them away with the light."

"They weren't drawn to the light to begin with."

"Do we have anything on board we could feed them with?"

Savage looked thoughtful. They did have a pound of bait in the freezer. "But wouldn't that make them more inclined to stay here? We've got to get them out of there! Davidson is failing. The situation is critical."

* * *

Marin recoiled in horror as she saw sharks rising past Marcos toward the surface. Everyone else withdrew to the safety of the cave. Only Marcos stayed out, barely hidden by the overhang, sending the animals shooting by like deadly torpedoes.

"Why?" Marin asked. She couldn't wrap her head around these people. She could maybe see why they would want to kill Leviathan, but these divers were just ordinary men and women doing what their superiors told them, trying their best to serve their country. These were people like Paul! Paul had been in the Navy for twenty years!

Marcos seemed distracted. "Why, what?"

"Why would you want to kill these sailors? They're innocent!"

Marcos seemed confused. "I'm not killing anybody. Let me concentrate! These guys are hard to handle!"

Marin watched for a moment, unsure what to believe, then tapped deeper into his mind, hoping he wouldn't be able to tell.

She felt thoughts and words flowing to the animals, riling them up, making them angry, yet still controlling them. She could see flashes of sight from the sharks—open mouths, frothing water, tails lashing, black dive suits sitting still like strange trees floating in the darkness. She could feel their anger and scorn at the weak humans, but also the primal fear of them and memories of their sharp weapons. Through their eyes, she saw one man thrashing around, clawing at his mask. *"Weak one! Kill it, kill it!"* She felt their intense desire to bite the one that stood out from the rest. She pushed Marcos's mind to see it as well.

"Help him!" she screamed at him.

"I can't! We can't let them see us!" She could tell he felt torn, but his loyalties were stronger with his people. She knew he wouldn't move.

"Something's wrong! He's dying! You won't be able to hold them back much longer!"

"I'm sending them away." The outlying sharks started drifting, but those in the heart of the frenzy were falling beyond reach. She felt his mind pushing the sharks, trying to calm them down, but all of their eyes were on the one who was struggling, blood lust on their tongues. Marcos didn't have the strength to quell their primal instincts.

She pulled away from her connection with him and found herself back in the cave, gasping water in huge, panicked gulps. She couldn't shake the image of that man in the mask, his panicked eyes opened wide, mouth gasping for air. She knew that feeling, and she knew she had to get out of there and help him. She left the cave, following her connection to Marcos. She could feel every bit of his concentration trying to manipulate the creatures and calm them down. His mental strength was failing. Within moments she was shooting past the opening and into the open water, surging toward the enemy and a mass of deadly sharks.

She rose to the center of the maelstrom. She felt him crying out to her to stop, but she couldn't make herself turn back. Instead, she reached through his thoughts to touch the animals again. She could see them circling around the dying man, forced to resist the impulse to tear him apart. The battle was making them anxious, and they fought to break free of the mental contact. She joined her mental energy with Marcos's, trying to push the sharks away from the man while racing to reach him in time.

* * *

"Ok, launch!" Captain Savage yelled. The bait flew off the starboard side of the boat, scattering bits of squid and mackerel across the surface of the water thirty feet away from the vessel.

"They are circling Davidson. We can't get to him!" the ensign shouted into his microphone.

Savage pressed the knot that his stomach had become with his crossed arms. This could easily become a blood bath. These were the times when he hated command. Who was he to make the call to leave a man behind to his death? He paused and then uttered the hated words.

"Move out."

"They are looking at the bait." Larson reported. "I am waiting for a clear shot of Davidson."

"Get out of there. Port side! Now!" barked Savage fiercely.

"What about Davidson?" Larson asked.

"What's his status?"

"Still surrounded, but Captain I can't just ..."

"That's an order, Larson. Move out!" he barked back, his heart breaking.

"Yes, sir."

"God help him." Savage whispered.

* * *

Marin pushed through the throng of teeth and fins to the man. He was convulsing, and his pupils were like tiny dots. She knew he had mere moments before he would be beyond help. Looking at his tank, she decreased the oxygen. She was relieved to smell the bait in the water that the ship had thrown overboard. Instead of repressing the instincts of the sharks, she and Marcos could divert it. The swarm of animals decreased, but three or four still circled angrily around the dying man and his rescuer. She pushed her thoughts into the minds of the remaining sharks, *"Follow the others, food is close."* One by one they caught the scent and slipped away.

Carefully, moving slowly, she looped her arm through the back of his buoyancy vest and towed him to the surface. Soon she was next to the well-lit ship along with the few remaining members of the dive team. The last sharks surfaced, causing the divers a wave of panic as they scrambled onto the back of the boat. She pushed the unconscious man close to the dive platform, staying underwater and out of sight, hidden partially by the curve of the hull. A hand reached out and took the burden of the man out of her arms, and voices drifted down around her, shouting. She turned to flee below the ship, but as she kicked downward, she felt a hand close tightly around her wrist. Her arm was pulled hard toward the boat.

"Marcos!" She cried in panic, yanking her arm as hard as she could. She kicked off the boat, trying to break the grasp, but someone jumped in the water and hands closed around her chest, pinning her arms behind her back and she was helpless. She squirmed and fought fruitlessly against her captors and caught sight of Marcos reaching out to her as she was dragged out of the water and onto the dive platform of the ship.

Bright lights flicked on with an electric hum like a bug zapper, forcing Marin to awaken, squinting. The rough mattress she was on, even though fastidiously clean, smelled strongly of booze and vomit, and the woolen blanket scratched her arms. It took a moment for her eyes to adjust to the bright light shining down from the ceiling and she wondered what time it was, as there were no windows.

She sat up, nursing a painful headache behind her eyes. She felt nauseous and wondered if it had anything to do with coming to the surface too fast last night. Had she tried that with air in her lungs, she'd probably be in the intensive care unit. A moment later, the door opened and a middle aged woman with a clipboard came in, carrying a folding chair which she unfolded next to Marin's bed.

She smiled as she sat down.

"Good morning, Marin," she said, glancing down at her clipboard. She said her name as if they were playing some sort of game and Marin was a pretend name they had both agreed upon.

"Yeah. What time is it?" she said, rubbing her eyes.

"It's about oh nine hundred."

"Can you say that in English?" Marin asked testily.

The woman pursed her lips and replied, "Seven minutes after nine."

Marin sighed. "Is that a.m. or p.m.?"

"A.m. You've slept in."

"Yeah, well you guys kept me up pretty late last night."

"For obvious reasons."

"Not to me! All I did was try to help someone."

"We just want some logical answers," the woman said in exasperation. "What were you doing in restricted waters, at night, alone?"

Marin sighed, tired of every word she said being questioned. "I went over this last night. I was surfing, I got a little too far out in the water and couldn't get back in. I saw your boat and tried to make a swim for it. I thought you would *help* me," she said, adding the emphasis for guilt. It didn't work.

The woman wrote something down on her clipboard, and then put her pen down. "Where is your surfboard?"

"I don't know."

"Where did you park?"

"I was dropped off at the dunes by Mugu State Park."

"What about your wetsuit? A little hi-tech for surfing, don't you think?"

Marin bristled, hoping her defiance would mask her pounding heart. "It's European. Very expensive. I got it on eBay. P.S. I want it back."

There was a swift knock at the door and an elderly man in a white lab coat came in. Marin judged he was a doctor by the stethoscope around his neck and the confident aura he exuded.

"Ah, you're awake. How nice." He turned to the woman in the chair. "That will be all, Lieutenant Ruiz." She looked up at him in surprise.

"I'm sorry, but I'm not finished here, Doctor," she replied coldly.

"Yes, you are," he said in a calm voice.

She glared at him, but his gaze never wavered and she backed down. "Fine, Sir. I will return later."

"Don't bother. I can take it from here. Dismissed."

She got up and moved to gather her chair, but the doctor sat down in it first. She stood, flustered for a moment before turning briskly and walking out the door.

"Now then," he said, getting comfortable. "Let's see how our little hero is doing today, shall we?" He pulled out his stethoscope and listened to her lungs and heartbeat. He took a light out of one of his deep pockets and looked in her ears and nose. "How do you feel this morning?" he asked in a friendly tone.

"I have a killer headache and want to barf. Can I go home now?"

The man smiled indulgently and patted her knee. "Don't worry, my dear. I have arranged transportation to take you back where you belong." He went to a cupboard and pulled out a plastic pink bowl shaped like a kidney. "Here, just in case."

Marin sat up but was hit with a wave of queasiness and instead leaned back against the wall. After a few shallow breaths, she felt okay to try talking again.

"So I'm not under arrest?"

The man laughed. "Goodness no! You're in the hospital ward. Did you think you were in a jail?" He chuckled, looking at the bare walls. "I can see where you'd get that idea. Unfortunately, the military doesn't care too much for aesthetics. No, you were just in the wrong place at the wrong time. Or perhaps in the right place at the right time. I think if you hadn't come along when you did, we would have lost a good officer, and you may not have fared so well, either." He shifted in the uncomfortable chair.

"I'm sure drifting alone for so long you must be fairly dehydrated. You may not have lasted much longer yourself. So, you see. You helped us, we helped you. It worked out very nicely, don't you think?"

Marin nodded, not knowing what to think, but relieved that she would be allowed to leave.

The doctor produced a rubber band, three empty vials, and a syringe and placed them next to her on the bed.

"What's that for?" she asked.

"We need to check you are well enough to go home."

She shook her head. "You're not taking my blood."

The doctor frowned silently, and then shook his head. "Now, I'm not supposed to tell you this," he said, leaning toward her conspiratorially, "but the Navy has been doing some chemical testing in the water in this area. Something about lowering PH levels and retarding algae growth. But in large doses, it can be very harmful. So, I need to run some blood tests to make sure you haven't absorbed too much into your system." He held out a rubber band with a smile.

"No."

His smile faded. She stared at the needle, bile rising in her throat. "I don't like needles."

"I really must insist," he said, bringing the needle closer to her arm.

"No!" she said, jerking her arm away. The movement was too quick. Her vision swam; she leaned over the pink bowl and threw up everything she had eaten in the last twelve hours.

* * *

"We've got to get her back!" Marcos yelled, pacing in the main room of their underwater home. "Who knows what they'll do to her!"

Malcolm shouted at his son. "What they'll do to *her*? Your actions have caused a chain of events that could lead to the death of us all! How could you be so careless?"

"You are blaming this on me? Am I the one who called the divers? Am I the one who brought them down?" he yelled, outraged.

"Yes! You should never have made contact with her! There was a plan in place and you forced us to abandon it because of your silly *crush!*" Everyone who had been in the room had drifted away, except for Aggie who waited awkwardly by the kitchen.

"Think about others for once, Marcos!" He threw his arm out, pointing at Aggie. "Think about how hard it was for Amanda's own flesh and blood to see her raised on land with strangers, never being able to see her, to be part of her life?" Malcolm pulled at his hair in frustration. "And why make such sacrifices? To protect her! Leviathan knows who we are. They have never stopped looking and because of that, we've lived in danger of them every moment of our lives. However, they didn't know about her. She was safe, and those of us who truly care about her have worked hard to keep it that way," he said eyeing his son pointedly.

Marcos stared at his father, overcome with anger and despair. Words bubbled to his mind faster than he could sort them to speak, so he said nothing.

Marcos broke eye contact first and sank to the worn sofa. He let his head fall to his hands, his dark curls hiding his face. Malcolm lowered his hands with a tense sigh and sat beside his son. After a moment, Marcos lifted his angry eyes to his father.

* * *

"What can I do, Father? I think I love her!" The despair in his voice broke Malcolm's heart.

Malcolm put his large, rough hand on his son's shoulder. He took a deep breath. "My son, there is no guarantee she would return your love. She does not even know us. She has different dreams, a different life and people up there that care about her." Marcos shot him an angry glare, but Malcolm continued.

"And, unlike us, she may never *have* to leave the surface. You think she's one of us, but you know she is different. She didn't take Arydia like everyone else down here, she was born to it. On both sides. Who knows what that means for her future?"

"Father, in just this short time, I could feel it. She even found a way to see through my eyes! Like she was inside me, watching everything I was doing, and I could tell she was already starting to care. There is something there, I know it! We just need time!"

"What would you have us do, then? Storm into the Naval base and demand she be released?" Marcos looked up hopefully and Malcolm threw up his hands in exasperation. "Look, Marcos. There is a chance they will release her without much thought. There are a lot of swimmers, divers, and surfers all along this coast. It isn't too outrageous to think they might have come upon one at night who got in trouble. But we have to prepare for the possibility that she might tell them about us. We have to prepare to evacuate."

Marcos rose in protest. "She would never betray us!"

"Maybe not in her words, but she was wearing one of Aggie's suits, that could be enough to prove her story false. Regardless, we need to be prepared. There is just too much at stake. You must not do anything foolish."

"If we leave, she will never find us."

"I'm sorry, Marcos," he said softly.

Marcos sat, tense, his muscles aching for action, his heart battling his mind. Finally, he nodded.

SEVENTEEN

Two uniformed Naval officers drove Marin back to COAST. Jaycen was playing a game of football on the front lawn with Nick, Danny and Tui when the white Navy jeep pulled into the parking lot. Jaycen came running as they pulled Marin out of the back seat. She stood up unsteadily, letting the officers each take one of her arms. Jaycen ran to her side, dropping the ball and letting it wobble under a car.

"Marin! What happened? Where have you been?" he cried, edging the officer out of the way and taking her in his arms. She stepped back from his embrace unsteadily, feeling embarrassed and disoriented.

"Do you know this woman?" one of the officers asked him.

"Of course! She works here with us. She's been missing since Friday!" The taller officer nodded to the other officer who pulled a phone out of his pocket and started talking as he walked to the other side of the vehicle. Danny and the others gathered around Marin curiously.

"If two of you would be willing to sign this paper and note your phone numbers, we'll release her into your custody." The officer produced a sheet of paper and a pen. Jaycen nodded and signed his name without even glancing at the words. Nick shrugged and signed below Jaycen. The uniformed man got into the jeep and they drove away, leaving Marin surrounded by her co-workers.

"What happened? Who were those guys?" Jaycen demanded.

"Did you get arrested?" Tui asked in amazement.

Marin put up her hands. "Look! It's been a really weird weekend, and I feel like throwing up … again. Can I at least sit down?"

Jaycen put his arm around her waist and helped her into the building and up to her room. Nick, Danny and Tui followed, crowding into her small space. Jaycen sat her down on her bed and put a pillow behind her.

"We've been looking everywhere for you!" Jaycen exclaimed almost angrily.

"I'm sorry," she said, resorting to the lie that had worked for the Navy. "I just went out surfing and got pulled out too far and couldn't get back in. I drifted into the Navy base waters and they rescued me. It's not a big deal. It's just kind of embarrassing and I feel …" she searched for some reason to feel the way she was feeling and thought of the doctor. "I feel dehydrated. They had their doctor look me over."

She leaned back against the pillow, the straightened immediately. "Dang it!" she exclaimed. "They kept my wetsuit, the jerks." She slapped her mattress in frustration, worried about what it would mean for the military to have one of Aggie's wondersuits. Great, another way she'd endangered Marcos and the Arydians. She rubbed her face with her hands, worried about what Marcos would do, hoping he wasn't trying to get into the military facility to rescue her. Suddenly exhausted, she looked up at Jaycen. "So then they let me go. That's it."

"Did they take your blood?" a voice questioned from the door. Tui moved aside so Dr. Gilbert could walk in. "Excuse me," he said to Jaycen, who stood and let him take his place.

Marin glanced up curiously. He looked at her with a mixture of concern and something else—maybe despair?

"How much did they take?" he whispered.

"They wanted to do a blood test but I wouldn't let them. They said something about chemicals in the bay to stop algae growth. They wanted to see if I'd been exposed," she said, wondering why Dr. Gilbert would care about the tests they wanted to do.

He slipped the syringe he had been holding into the pocket of his jacket and folded his arms. "There may be some truth to that. Would you be willing to let me run one on you? If you have been exposed to something, it would be best to know what it was," he said.

She hesitated. "Yeah, okay," she replied. At least he was someone she knew.

"Good." He ran a hand across her forehead and let it pause there, checking for fever. He brushed the hair gently away from her eyes and sighed.

"You need to rest. And plenty of protein. I'll order up a steak and some orange juice immediately."

"Uh, I don't think I could keep anything down right now," she said, suddenly feeling very self-conscious with all these guys in her room looking down at her. Why couldn't they just leave her alone and let her sleep?

"Nonsense. Protein will help you feel better. Trust me. I *am* a doctor, you know." He smiled a genuine smile. Marin was surprised at how a real smile transformed him from the formal, single-minded boss she had always known into someone much more human. "I'll be back in a few minutes to get that sample. Don't worry, it'll be painless."

She nodded grimly and Dr. Gilbert rose. "Gentlemen, let's let our girl here get some rest while she waits for some nourishment. Out!" He indicated to the door and they all left, Jaycen glancing over his shoulder as he was escorted out the door. Gilbert closed it behind him and she relaxed into her bed, glad to be alone. She had barely closed her eyes when her door quietly opened again and Jaycen slipped back inside to kneel by her bed.

"Hi," he said, taking her hand. She felt a lump rise in her throat. How could she have forgotten how endearing he could be? It felt like she had been gone for months.

"Hi."

"What really happened?" he asked, squeezing her fingers. She sat up, unprepared for his direct question.

"What do you mean?"

"I mean that you don't surf. At least you've never talked about it before, and there have been plenty of opportunities to talk about it. You don't even *like* water, and you're telling me you suddenly know how to surf? And if you were lost at sea, how did my car drive itself back here? And with the seat so far back. It's almost like it wasn't you driving it. That's pretty much what I mean."

She stared at him for a few moments. What could she say? She was hanging out with her cool new fish people and causing them trouble with the military? She just shrugged and shook her head with a sigh.

"Look, people here were seriously worried about you. I've been going crazy looking for you, *and* trying to cover for you. All I'm asking is that you let me in. I'm sick of this, Marin. I know it's obvious, but I care about you so much I think I'm going crazy, and I need to know what's going on."

Jaycen squeezed her hand tightly. "If you don't feel the same about me, fine." He took an unsteady breath. "But for mercy's sake, please tell me what's going on with you. Is it some other guy? Are you dating someone from the base? Because that's the only thing I can come up with and it doesn't even come close to filling in all the gaps."

Marin's jaw dropped in astonishment. With all the crazy stuff going on, Jaycen's explanation seemed so simple and ludicrous that she started laughing hysterically, her stress turning it into tears, then strange, laughing sobs. Jaycen dropped her hand, looking baffled and hurt.

Finally, she was able to speak, but the thought still made her laugh, it was so far from the absurd truth. "No, I'm not dating anyone from the base. I'm not on drugs. I'm not a terrorist. I'm probably insane, but who wouldn't be?"

She stared at his confused look and leaned forward, feeling suddenly reckless and fed up. "Ok, you want the truth? Fine! I'm a mutant mermaid created by a bunch of crazy scientists who were trying to change the world for good, but instead were empowering a group of power hungry terrorists to take over the planet. I spent the weekend getting to know my fish family and learning how to read minds and control dolphins and sharks and getting the fish guys in trouble with the Navy who doesn't know they're hanging out inside their borders until I saved a guy who was drowning and got captured and probably blew their cover, so now they will be hunted down and destroyed or captured to be experimented on, changing the planet as we know it and maybe tipping the earth into world dominion by evil forces!" She leaned back against her pillows, shaking. "P. S., I have no idea how your car got back here or who drove it, but it was probably Marcos or Aaron or one of the other fishy guys."

Jaycen raised his eyebrows and blinked twice. "Wow. So … you *were* hanging out with guys on the base."

Marin growled in frustration and slammed her fists down on the bed. "Jaycen, you are the most obsessed, jealous nut job I have ever met!"

The door clicked open and Dr. Gilbert appeared with a Styrofoam container in one hand and a cup of orange juice in the other. He looked at Jaycen in surprise. "Am I interrupting something?" he asked innocently.

Jaycen's ears turned red and he stood up quickly. "No, Dr. Gilbert." He glanced down at Marin still scowling on her bed. "I'm just leaving." He pulled the door shut behind him.

Gilbert set the food on her bedside table and opened the container. "I had the kitchen whip up a steak for you, medium rare. It will do you good. Also, Lois in the med lab sent up a couple of iron supplements for you."

The smell from the steak actually made her mouth water, reminding her she hadn't had land food for days. Gilbert produced silverware wrapped in a real cloth napkin and popped a straw into the orange juice. Marin waited for him to leave, but he just stood watching her then he sat down on the edge of her bed. He set the container on her lap, so she opened it and started cutting into it. The steak was a little squishier than she liked, but it tasted delicious. She wondered why the staff never got steak when *they* ordered at the cafeteria. Ah, the privileges of being the boss.

She looked up and noticed Gilbert watching her with a strange look in his eyes that quickly disappeared when their eyes met. He seemed to want to talk about something but didn't know how to start. She ate her steak, too tired to care what he had to say, but knowing she was probably in trouble for something with the way this weekend had gone.

He produced a syringe and several empty vials. Taking her left arm in his, he tied a band around it and started drawing blood. Marin continued to eat with her right hand, trying to ignore everything Dr. Gilbert was doing.

"I hope you start feeling better soon," Gilbert said sincerely. She nodded, chewing. He pocketed the vials and put a bandage on her arm. "You should be back on your feet by this evening. I'm sure you've noticed that you heal astonishingly quickly."

Marin shrugged. Gilbert cleared his throat again. "We launch the Aquanis soon. Things are going to be very hectic around here. I think it would be wise for you to stay close until the launch."

She swallowed in surprise, waiting for him to explain. He furrowed his brows and then stood up. Pausing at the door, he said, "Marin, please, for you own good, keep your door locked. And don't go anywhere alone." Before she could open her mouth to ask him anything, he shut the door and walked away.

Marin awoke disoriented. Late morning light was streaming into her dormitory window. She lay on her back trying to figure out where she was. She had been dreaming she was in the dark, cave-like room she stayed in while she was underwater. Everything here seemed too light and frail and fast somehow. She realized as she got up and dressed that she'd slept in a different bed three nights in a row. It felt weird to be hopping into the shower and getting ready for the day like nothing ever happened, like she could just go back to her life and forget about it all. Already it seemed to be something out of a dream. She smiled wistfully, thinking of Marcos. She knew he would probably be frantic with worry and that she should try to let him know she was ok and that nothing bad happened, but later. For now, the hot water splashed her face, warming her from head to toe, and she let herself pretend she was just getting ready for another day at work.

She snapped open the shower curtain and glanced at her cell phone, still sitting near the sink where she had left it days ago. "Dang!" she muttered angrily, turning off the water and wrapping her robe around her as quickly as she could. It was almost nine o'clock on a Monday! She had a test she was supposed to be running with Steve on a tank of jacksmelt for the government report right now. She threw on her clothes and yanked her wet hair into a ponytail, cursing her phone's alarm for not going off. As she kicked on her shoes she checked her phone. The ringer had been turned completely off.

"Ugh!" she grumbled in frustration, looking at the fifteen messages, mostly by Paul and Jaycen. She sent off a quick text to Paul.

Sorry! It's been a really busy weekend, and forgot to check my phone. I'm ok, but late to work. Love you! Call you soon! She hoped that would be good enough and shoved her phone in her pocket before taking off to the holding tanks.

The day passed quickly, with everyone stressed and excited about the move-up date for Aquanis. Launching was so expensive and time-consuming, that even with luck and funding, COAST could only plan a launch *at most* every two and a half years. There was a frenetic energy that kept people moving quickly during the long hours but tempers often flared at the slightest provocation.

So much of the workforce was focused on the launch that the menial tasks of cataloging species, testing, and so forth often got delayed or pushed off onto the less critical employees.

Marin was grateful to be one of those less critical employees, content to fish Chinese Mitten Crabs out of a tank and attach tiny electronic tags to their shells to help the institute track their migration. It turned out that Steve had been pulled off the jacksmelt study, so nobody really noticed that she was late and she had been able to run the tests herself. At the end of the day, she planned to take a Jet Ski out and release the fish back outside the bay, and try to contact Marcos to let him know everything was ok. She hadn't had a chance to even dip her foot in the water so far.

In the meantime, she tried to relax and concentrate on not getting nipped by the crabs. She enjoyed working in the back of the huge open building, watching everyone bustle around with their self-important tasks. The three bay doors were up, letting the sunshine and the fresh salt breeze wash in, pushing out the humidity that tended to build up in the warehouse. It felt nice to just work and be alone to think. As the afternoon shadows lengthened, she thought about her future.

Everything about what she was doing felt good, warm, and familiar. After seeing life down below, she realized how hard it must be to live and thrive like they did. Even mundane things like grocery stores and dentists were luxuries they didn't have. It made her think of early pioneers taking their few belongings on their backs and traveling into the west, knowing they had to use the materials around them to eke out an existence or die. She didn't know if she could be that strong.

Marcos's life haunted her. Unlike the other children down below who were changed when they were too young to remember much, he had known life on solid ground. He'd even started taking pre-college classes up top. It made her ache to think of all he lost. Every time she thought about him, her heart started pounding.

She didn't know what to think about the strange connection she felt with him. Was it because of him? Or her? Or a combination of the two? The romantic part of her wanted to believe there was some mystical link between the two of them that made such profound contact possible. The scientist in her wanted to conduct experiments to see if it was an ability she alone possessed. There was one way to find out, but she felt guilty for even considering it.

As if on cue, Jaycen appeared at her side, rubbing his kinked neck. "Watch out," he said, pointing to the crab she was holding, "they bite." She glanced up at him, taking her eyes off the baseball sized crab she was tagging. It chose that exact moment to grab her finger and pinch it hard.

"Ow!" she shouted, jerking her finger away, scowling. She put the crab back in the tank and looked at the small cut on her finger. Jaycen took her injured hand and looked closely at it, laughing.

"I would say 'I'm sorry,' but I did warn you."

She tried to pull her hand away, but he kept it. "How come I can do this all afternoon and I don't get pinched until you come along? You distracted me!" she said accusingly. A drop of blood oozed from her finger.

"So I'm distracting? Nice," he said mischievously. "Looks like it broke skin. Wanna bandage?"

"I'm ok."

"In that case …" He kissed her wounded finger.

She jerked her hand back. "Ew. I'm not five, and now you have blood on your lips."

Reflexively, he drew his bottom lip into his mouth and it came out clean.

"Ok, now I'm seriously going to be sick," she said, looking disgusted. "Tell me you did not just lick my blood off your lip."

"Mmmmm. Tasty. Salty." He shrugged. "Why is it I can't have a normal conversation with you? It's like you are always ready to fight." He said it casually, as if noticing for the first time.

"Because the second you come near me things go weird. And you make me angry."

"Weird? I really thought you would say 'wrong.' Weird I can live with."

Marin rolled her eyes, but had to laugh grudgingly.

"Wanna go catch a movie?" he asked unexpectedly.

"You're asking me on a date? I thought you just kidnapped your girlfriends."

"See, you just said girlfriend! This is really getting somewhere."

"And see, I'm getting frustrated because things are getting weird!" she said.

Jaycen nodded. "And you're getting angry. I'm beginning to see a pattern. So what about the movie?"

Marin got up from her stool and stretched. Jaycen seemed so relaxed, not like the hopeful, desperate guy she sometimes thought he was. Maybe thinking she had a guy on the side was good for him. She startled herself by realizing guiltily that she sort of *did* have a guy on the side. She saw Jaycen was still waiting for an answer.

"Yeah, that would be great. But I have to release the crabs and the Jacks today. We've had them almost a week."

"Ok. Are you taking out a boat or a Jet Ski?" He reached up out of habit to rub his stiff neck.

"Probably a Jet Ski. Why?"

"I'll come help you."

She thought of Marcos for a moment but guiltily agreed.

EIGHTEEN

In the late afternoon, Jaycen and Marin started loading the fish and crabs into a portable holding tank. Between the two of them it didn't take long to strap it to one of the larger Jet Skis tied up to the pier.

"Are you sure Dave won't have a cow if you come with me?" she asked as she stepped into the driver's seat and tied her hair up in a messy bun.

Jaycen scowled. "I've put in eleven hours today. At the very least, I deserve a break by law. He can make me work all night long when I get back if he wants. But right now, I'm leaving." He got on behind her, slid his arms around her stomach and pulled her close as the engine roared to life. They moved slowly out of the marina and past the buoys at the bay's entrance.

"Let's get out of here," he whispered into her ear.

"You got it!" she yelled back to him, kicking the throttle into full gear, shooting them into the open rolling plains of the sea. Her hair worked loose of its elastic band, whipping around Jaycen as he buried his face in it, smelling the minty scent of her shampoo, soaking in the feel of her so close in his arms.

Strangely, she didn't seem to mind him holding her. She sank back into him and let him support her as she took them up the front of the heavy swells of the incoming tide, and down their smooth backs into the green valleys. She took some waves that made him nervous but she had a good feel for it and they always made it to the top.

He had to admit to himself that he was impressed. When he'd first met her, she'd seemed so afraid of everything. Now it felt like she was daring the sea to swallow her. She shouted out in triumph as they mounted a large roller and caught the crest as it pushed them back toward the shore. He could feel her joy and energy like electricity in the air. They raced down the coast, away from Point Mugu, keeping the shore in view on their left. Sailboats dotted the horizon, racing soundlessly, taking advantage of the last hot breezes before the sun went down and took the wind with it.

When she was about five miles from the shore, Marin slowed the motor down and killed it. The waves were softer, bobbing them up and down gently, and without the sound of the Jet Ski, the distant wash of the waves and the cries of the gulls reached out to them. Marin relaxed into Jaycen's arms and let her head fall onto his shoulder. He pulled her closer and rested his face next to hers, loving the quiet joy of this moment, willing the sun to slow its descent and let this warm, perfect day linger just a little longer. He wanted to engrave it into his heart, so no matter what happened between them he'd at least have this moment to relive forever.

* * *

The sun was getting close to the horizon and Marin knew they would need to turn back soon. She could feel his chest rising and falling behind her and tried to match her breathing to his, but his was so much deeper and slower she couldn't manage it. She fought with herself for being so cruel as to want to get him in the water and try to communicate with him, to hold him, just for the sake of her own curiosity. She decided that he would probably go along with it even if he knew it was just an experiment, but it didn't make her feel any better. She let him hold her, savoring the tenderness without guilt or obligation, knowing the moment was going to come for her to either give in to her curiosity, or give up and just release the fish and go home.

He made a stretching movement with his back and she sat up, realizing that he had been supporting both of them for a while with nothing to lean against himself.

"Don't leave!" he said quietly, pulling her back to him. She resisted, throwing her leg over the seat so she faced the side of the craft, still not sure what she was going to do, regretting the loss of that perfect moment.

"I'm hot," she said slipping off her sandals and pulling her t-shirt off her swimsuit and throwing them in the bulkhead cabinet.

"Yeah, you are," he said, smiling impishly.

She rolled her eyes but grinned. "I'm going to get in the water. Wanna come in?" She attached the tether to her arm then slid into the cold Pacific.

"Really?" He looked around to make sure no big boats were coming in their direction. Marin swam on her back looking up at him. He took off his shirt and set his cell phone in the bulkhead cabinet as well. "Okay, watch out!" Standing on the seat he jumped into the air, cannonballing into the water beside her with a splash. She laughed and sank under the water, tempted to breathe in a lungful and swim around below him like a shark. He sank beside her, holding out a hand to her.

She concentrated her thoughts to him and asked, *"Can you hear me?"*

He kicked his way up to the surface and she followed.

"Wow! You were way under there! I thought you were nervous about the water," he said, catching his breath.

"Jaycen, did you hear anything when you were underwater?"

He continued to wipe the saltwater off his face and shook his head. "No. Did you?"

She ignored his question and frowned. "Jaycen, can I try something?" she asked, holding her hand out to him.

"Sure," he said, taking her hand in his.

"Okay. Hold your breath. Think of me, okay?" They both submerged and she tried to connect to his thoughts. She didn't feel it working. He pulled her hand and she realized he needed to go up for air. She followed him up and joined him, wiping the water from her own face.

"Are you just showing off how much longer you can stay under water than me?" he laughed.

She smiled and shook her head, still puzzled as to why she couldn't reach him. There was only one test left and she really didn't know if she should do it.

"What are you trying to do?" he asked, steadying himself with one hand on the rim of the craft.

She seemed flustered. "I'm just wondering about something. I want to see if water helps people ... sense each other better. You know, like fish. And if maybe contact can be a conductor for that sense."

Jaycen stared at her, his wet hair dripping salt water down his cheeks. "Let me get this straight, professor. So, you want to conduct an experiment with me to see if we can sense each other better if we make contact underwater?"

Her face went red, but she nodded sheepishly.

He grinned slyly. "Ok. Let's see if you can sense this." He pulled her into an embrace, letting go of the Jet Ski and pressing his wet lips to hers as they sank into the water. He held her close, kissing her passionately in the emerald green water, then rising up for air long before she wanted to.

"So, did it work?" he asked, still holding her closely to him.

She didn't want to hurt him, but couldn't hide the disappointment she felt. She pushed gently away and pulled herself up onto the Jet Ski. He glanced up at her, confusion etched in his face, then silently climbed up behind her.

"I guess we'd better release the fish," she sighed. She opened the container the crabs were in and shook them into the water where they sank gratefully into the deep.

He nodded, turning around in his seat to undo the latch to the tank. He tipped the tank on its side and the fish came out in a silvery waterfall. Most of them swam away, but a few lay on the top of the water, dead from too long in captivity. Their bodies drifted silently away toward the shore.

"I always feel bad for the ones that just don't make it to see freedom again. If they had just known it would be temporary, would they have been able to hang on?" Marin asked pensively.

Jaycen draped an arm around her, not answering, watching the silver fish floating into the waves. "Maybe things are better for them wherever they are now. You know a great big ocean without predators or something like that."

Marin looked at him, surprised. "You mean fishy heaven?"

He shrugged, his face reddening. "Why not? All God's creatures and all that. I'd like to think heaven is a lot like this. Only better. And I can't imagine heaven without the sea." He looked out at the boats sailing past and fell quiet.

Marin watched his silhouette in the sunset, reminding her of a sailor longing for the sea, his heart full of love for the ocean. The sunlight streamed through his blonde hair making it look golden in the lowering sun. He really was almost beautiful in his handsomeness. No wonder the other girls thought she was crazy for not falling for him instantly.

She wondered what life would be like if she could let herself love him. Or if he could love her if he really knew what she was. It would probably be a lot like this, she realized. Living and working on the ocean, warm arms and tender moments. It would be a good life. If …

"Jaycen?" she asked impulsively, "Would you feel the same for me if there was something … wrong with me? Like some strange birth defect? Or if I was … say … an alien?"

Jaycen burst out in laughter until he caught the earnest look in her eyes. He cleared his throat. "Well. You mean … like would I still like you if you were a mutant mermaid like you said?"

Her eyes widened in shock. She'd forgotten she'd said that.

He smiled and pulled her close, whispering in her ear, "I'd consider myself the luckiest man on earth. What sailor doesn't dream about falling in love with a mermaid?"

* * *

Dr. Gilbert took another slide from his microscope and replaced it with a new one. He focused it and sent the image to the computer screen where he could see it in greater detail. Everything he added to her blood samples changed them just enough that the cells would no longer reproduce. He rubbed his eyes, willing them to keep looking. The answer had to be somewhere right in front of him, if only he could figure it out. The samples he had taken were slowly used up slide after slide as he searched for the key. The precious blood was almost gone.

He leaned back on his chair and let his eyes stare briefly at the dark ceiling of the warehouse lab far above him. A knot of worry sat in his stomach and wouldn't release him from its grip.

Now the Navy was involved in all this. He fought back the panic that threatened to black out all rational thought.

He stared into the darkness until his eyes started to close involuntarily, then shook himself awake, forcing his mind to focus on the slide in front of him. He prepared a slight variation to the hormone soup he was working with and was about to apply the new mixture to the cells on the slide when he noticed something that made his heart stop. The untampered cells had reproduced at an amazing rate. He watched them moving around frenetically, duplicating themselves over and over again. He couldn't believe what he was seeing and turned to the nearby sink to splash cold water on his face to wake up. Looking back at his computer screen, he saw it again. It wasn't a hallucination. Why hadn't he seen that before? He stared at the screen, heart pounding in his chest, head exploding with everything this could mean to him.

No wonder Marin got better so quickly after the Delphinius accident. It gave him chills to realize she really might have come out of the water with broken bones. They just didn't stay broken.

An idea suddenly hit him. He tore off his lab coat, searching for the cut he'd received on the way to the lab yesterday. It was fairly deep and still stung slightly.

Hands shaking, he let one drop of Marin's precious blood from the microscope slide fall onto his arm and seep into his wound, not daring to believe the crazy ideas blasting through his mind. Even if she had the power to heal herself, it wouldn't mean it could work on someone else's cells … would it? He stared at his arm, not trusting his brain when he could no longer feel the sting of the scrape. He waited, breathless, for a few more seconds before taking a piece of gauze and wiping the blood off his arm. The cut was almost completely gone.

* * *

The wind turned chilly as the sun dropped below the waves. Wearing their wet swimsuits made it seem even colder. Jaycen offered to drive on the way back and Marin was grateful for the protection his body gave her from the wind. She held him close with her face pressed against his bare back for warmth. They slowed down as they reached the buoys and she looked over his shoulder to see that the warehouse doors were shut and most of the employees had called it a day. There was no sign of Dave, to Jaycen's obvious relief.

As they pulled into the bay, the dying rays of the sun illuminated a lone figure sitting on the edge of the pier. Marin's heart fell into her stomach when she realized who it was. She released her hold on Jaycen, but not before she felt him tense up, wondering who the stranger was that seemed to be waiting for them. Waiting for her, she realized. They pulled up alongside the pier as Marcos stood and walked over to them, graceful as a cat. He threw them a line.

Marin didn't dare make eye contact with Marcos as he reached down to tie off the rope right next to her.

"Thanks," Jaycen said, taking the hand that Marcos offered to help him onto the dock. He turned and they both put their hands out to Marin. She looked up at them, side by side with their hands out to her and felt her mouth go dry.

"Come on up," Marcos said in his rich accent.

Hesitantly, she took both their hands and they pulled her onto the dock. On land, she noticed that Marcos was a couple of inches taller than Jaycen.

"So … are you new here?" Jaycen asked hesitantly. "I don't think we've met. I'm Jaycen." He held out his hand to Marcos, who took it and shook it heavily.

Marcos smiled, his white teeth gleaming in the twilight. "Marcos. Oh, you haven't met me. I do not work here. I've come for Marin." He turned his smile to her and she felt her knees wobble. She felt like she would rather melt into the boards than be here with these two like this. Was he there to take her back?

Jaycen was suddenly frosty. "Come for Marin?" he repeated suspiciously. He glanced at Marin for an explanation. Her face turned a burning red.

"What, have you two got a date or something?" The words came out bitterly and laced with bubbling jealousy.

Marin was surprised at his comment and she looked at Marcos, shaking her head. Jaycen smiled triumphantly and placed an arm around her protectively.

"Because if you *thought* you did, you were wrong. We've got a date tonight that we'll be late for if we don't get going soon." He started to walk, but when she didn't follow he stopped.

"I have no wish to intrude," Marcos said smoothly. "But I was under the impression that she was in distress the last time I saw her. I wanted to make sure of her safety." He bowed slightly to Marin and she nodded, but Marcos made no move to leave. The tension was getting unbearable. "I promised I would not take you anywhere against your will," he said to her in a low voice.

Marin put her hand on Jaycen's arm. "Jaycen, I need to talk to him for a few minutes. Can I catch up with you? I won't make us late."

Jaycen's mouth closed into a straight line as if jealousy was burning a hole through him. "Fine." He took the rope and pulled the Jet Ski into the warehouse.

"What are you doing here, Marcos?" she demanded when Jaycen was out of earshot.

Marcos looked down into her eyes, and reached out softly to touch her hair. "I had to know you were okay. The last thing I knew was you being taken away by the divers. Why didn't you try to contact us … contact me?" He said everything evenly, but his emotions were crackling with electricity.

Marin looked around her, feeling very conspicuous. She wished she could talk to him without the risk of anybody else hearing or seeing. For a moment she thought about jumping into the water where they could talk without fear of Jaycen overhearing, but realized that would only raise more questions.

"Come on. Let's walk down the beach a little ways, okay?" He smiled and made to take her hand, but she refused. Jaycen would most certainly be watching them out of the common room the second he could get up there. She knew *she* would be, if the situation was reversed, but the bay curved out away from the windows and nobody could see them if they walked the north beach. When they were out on the sand she relaxed a little. They sat down by some pine trees near the water's edge.

"How did you know I was out on the water?" she asked.

"I saw you leave and followed you."

Marin's air froze in her chest. She held her breath, wondering miserably if Marcos had seen her out swimming with Jaycen.

"I couldn't keep up with you so I came here and waited until everyone else had left. I know it should have been enough to know you were safe, but I wanted to talk to you."

So he hadn't seen the kiss. She let her breath out slowly. "I'm sorry. Everything happened so fast, and I didn't know how to let you know I was okay."

Marcos looked at her sternly. "You couldn't have called me from the water? I would have heard you."

Marin looked down at her hands. "I didn't even think about it. I'm sorry. It's all so new to me." Her hand dropped to the sand between them. He covered it with his hand and she moved to pull it away, but he pressed down on it.

"I don't think he can see," he said nodding to their hands. She sighed and reluctantly agreed. "So. Is he the one that keeps you from me?" he asked bluntly.

Marin sighed. "Marcos, I barely know you. I don't know what to think. I don't want to feel like I have to choose my life right this second. I don't know if I *can* give up everything I know, like you and Aggie and everyone else did. It's not you; it's … everything."

Marcos looked hurt. "Don't say you don't know me, Marin. You have touched my thoughts and seen through my eyes. No one will *ever* understand me as you can," he said gravely.

She knew it was true and felt awful. But still … to give up life, earth, air? Now that she had it back, she wasn't ready to lose it again. Forever.

He leaned back and looked up at the stars gleaming over the pine trees. "I understand what it is like to give up everything you love. I miss the world." He spoke with such loneliness that it took Marin's breath away.

She turned her hand over so their palms were touching. His wavy hair hung below his bare shoulders as he stared up at the sky and breathed the air he had been exiled from. She couldn't be sure, but it looked like there were tears in the corner of his eyes, shining in the starlight. He was right; she did know him better than anyone. She tried to connect with him, to talk to him soul to soul through the contact of their hands, but it didn't work.

"Do you love him?" he asked suddenly. He turned his eyes to hers and asked forlornly. "Do you really love him?"

The question meant more than the words it contained. It was an accusation, misery, desperation and despair. Maybe someday Jaycen could find another. But Marcos …

Marin shook her head sadly. "Marcos, I've worked with him for weeks. I care about him, yes. But love is bigger than that. I care about you, too. I feel caught between air and water and I don't know which to choose. I'm sorry, I know you don't want to hear that, but I have to be honest with you. I just don't know if I can leave all this, even if it means we can be together."

"What if I was willing to give up *my* world to be with *you*? Would that make a difference?" he asked, lifting her hand and grasping it tightly.

"Could you even do that?" she asked, caught completely off balance by his offer. "Leave your father and Aaron and everyone?" She thought his answer would be no, but what if it was yes? Everything seemed to be moving so fast, decisions flying at her faster than she could cope. She wanted time to get to know him better, to learn if the feelings she had for him were real or just attraction. Somehow she doubted she'd ever get that time.

He laid back into the sand, looking straight up into the sky. "If I could, I would." He picked up a handful of sand and let it fall onto his bare chest. "I miss being dry." He chuckled bitterly.

"What did Aggie say about everything?" she asked, pulling her knees up and wrapping her chilly arms around them.

"They wouldn't let me come after you at first. They were very concerned."

She nodded guiltily, hoping the Navy hadn't come down looking for answers. Marcos seemed to read her mind. "They were not just concerned about our people. We were all very worried something bad would happen to you. But to draw more attention to ourselves could be fatal. I left to find out if you were okay …"

"And come get me?" Marin added. Marcos nodded. "You're supposed to take me with you?" she asked, her mouth dry.

Marcos looked offended. "I gave my word to you that I would not, and I told them I would not as well. I *refuse* to force you to leave the world, no matter how I feel about you, because of how I feel about you."

Marin didn't know what else to say. They both heard a noise on the dock and turned in the darkness to see what it was. Marin was fairly sure it had something to do with Jaycen wanting answers, tired of waiting.

Marcos sighed and stood up. "Your date is waiting." He held out a hand for her and helped her stand. They stood together awkwardly for a moment before Marcos folded his arms determinedly. "Look, you don't have to commit to anything yet. But I want a chance to be with you and

I don't want to lose it to some landy just because he happens to live in the same element as you. Will you go on a date with *me*? Tomorrow night?"

Marin nodded, feeling like a cad, and he pulled her into a quick embrace and kissed her cheek gently.

Marcos whispered in her ear, "Meet me under the dock at dusk."

She heard the water lap around his ankles as he disappeared into the waves.

NINETEEN

Jaycen sat on the dock throwing rocks out into the sea. Everything had seemed so perfect just an hour ago and now … Marin sighed as he tossed another rock.

"Hey." Marin sat down beside him. "Can I have a rock, too?" Jaycen didn't answer, so she took one and threw it with a satisfying plunk. They sat in silence for a while until finally Jaycen couldn't stand it anymore.

"So who was that?" he said, trying to sound causal. It came out strained and she wasn't fooled for a second.

"Well, he was one of the people I met over the weekend. He came here wanting to make sure I was okay." So far, so good. Not lying.

"He seemed pretty familiar to you for just having met him," he said, throwing a rock hard into the water. Marin flinched, hoping Marcos wasn't getting pelted. She stopped throwing them just in case.

"Yeah. It really does seem like I've known him a long time. Ever met people you felt like you already knew when you'd only just met them?" she wondered aloud.

"Yeah, I felt that way when I met *you*. But apparently it was only my delusion."

"Can we go? We're going to be late." She hoped Marcos wasn't hanging out under the pier listening. It was getting harder to stay neutral in this conversation.

"What's the point, Marin? You seriously feel like going to a movie after meeting up with your *other guy* right in front of me? Do you have any idea what I feel like right now?"

"Please, let's go. I know what this looks like, but it's not what you think."

"Oh, so you're saying you're not interested at all in Mystery Muscle guy?" he shot at her accusingly. Her pause told him everything. He shook his head in disgust and turned back to the water.

She slowly stood up and started walking down the pier toward the warehouse. Jaycen stayed where he was, heatedly throwing rocks into the bay. She opened the door and walked inside, feeling like she just destroyed whatever chance she had with anyone she ever cared about.

She leaned back against the inside of the door, shaking and feeling ill. After several minutes, she heard Jaycen's footsteps coming down the pier and the door was flung open, knocking her down against the corner of a metal footlocker.

Marin glared up at him from the floor. "You just plowed me over!" she yelled, all her anxiety and pain raging into fury.

Jaycen started to yell something back, but saw blood pooling around her elbow. Still hurt and angry, his expression softened anyway. "Are you okay? I didn't even know you were there. I was just trying to catch up to you." He knelt down next to her and tried to look at the cut on her arm.

She yanked it away from him, wincing. "I'm fine. Leave me alone."

Jaycen sat back on his heels, anger, concern, and offense playing out across his face. Then he broke into laughter.

Marin scowled at him. "What's so funny? Are you sadistic or something?"

He laughed even louder. "I really am starting to see a pattern here. Things get weird, you get frustrated and then you get angry." He stood up and offered his hand to her. "At least it was good for a little while longer before it got weird this time. Maybe the pattern is changing?"

She took his hand and stood up, offering him a watery smile. Walking to the sink, she washed the blood off her arm. A pink line was the only trace of her injury. Jaycen whistled in amazement.

"Lucky. It looked a lot worse than it was."

Marin shrugged. "How about a late movie?"

"You're on."

* * *

Across the world, several people met in a nondescript high-rise in Bangkok. Most had not seen each other in person in several years. Instead they spoke through secure channels and coded messages, and kept their own silent tabs on each other daily. One didn't become part of this organization without learning how to watch all aspects of a situation, especially one's back. The last time they met, the news was catastrophic. This time, however, redemption was being offered. Each person present was infamous, powerful and deadly—so, like a warped version of King Arthur's knights, they met at a round table with no hierarchical order.

Mr. Hahn sat at the round table, his face looking calmly at the men and women who spent their lives building invisible empires of tyranny on the backs of thieves, politicians, and princes in their various countries. For twenty-six years their organizations aligned toward a common goal: complete and total domination. They called the coalition Leviathan. The name was a trademark as familiar in the marine world as Nike is in shoes. Fishing industries, cruise lines, even an internet telecom were among the many offshoots from the parent company Leviathan. Headquartered on the Oregon coast in the Coastal Reef Center, Leviathan was making a strong comeback after a terrible fire that destroyed much of the center well over a decade ago. A catastrophe for which Mr. Hahn had been blamed.

Mr. Hahn was pleased to be the one holding the information on his lap. He cleared his voice and the room became quiet as a tomb, the hard eyes of each person centered on him.

"Our patience will soon be rewarded. As we long suspected, our project was not abandoned, but stolen. The thieves have been found." He paused, letting the murmur of astonishment drift around the room. "The thieves have been using our technology to create a working habitat off the coast of California, not far from our old friend, Dr. Gilbert. And it has proven to be completely viable." Hungry looks met him on all sides. He felt almost giddy with the satisfaction of being right. He sat quietly, savoring the way his colleagues were hanging on his every word. There was more, but he wanted them to ask for it. He didn't have to wait long.

"Prove it," Freidrich Dutrich demanded, leaning over the table, his thick arms resting on its glossy surface.

Hahn placed his briefcase on the table and clicked it open, producing photographs of a soupy substance that looked like swamp water and passed a copy around to everyone at the table, along with a data sheet.

"These are the contents from the stomach of a girl the Navy picked up in the area we have been monitoring." Several noses wrinkled in distaste. Hahn smirked internally, never letting the expression touch his face. "If you will turn your attention to the laboratory analysis you will find the data extremely interesting. Partially digested Benga Floradie, Althos Beta, Chindrae Colida, all of which were developed in the AQUA laboratory in Oregon. This should remove all doubt about it."

Glancing around the room, Hahn noted the grudging nods from each member of Leviathan, knowing none of them beside himself could really understand half of the information on the paper in front of them. But why should they? AQUA had been his idea; they were not scientists. They were businessmen and thugs and warlords.

"We must move quickly, then! Catch them and make them pay. And then we may begin," a man with dark skin and black eyes, known only as Zar, hissed, leaning forward eagerly. Others nodded their agreement. "Send down the sub!" he said, slapping his calloused hand on the table.

Hahn created a patient smile. "We will launch on Thursday. All is running according to schedule. And then you may begin your parts of the plan." He stood up, signaling the meeting was over.

Chita Vasquez sat back, watching carefully, calculating. She alone was looking through the data Hahn provided. She sat forward and motioned with her well-manicured hand. Hahn turned his attention to her. "This girl picked up by the Navy. Do you have her?"

He kept his smile in place through the lie. "Of course."

* * *

The next day Dr. Gilbert was in the warehouse supervising the preparations for the launch. With only two days to go the activity was intense. Marin kept well back from the action and stayed busy writing toxicity reports for the government surveys. She didn't see Jaycen at all, since Dave had him in the sub constantly to run tests on every wire and piece of machinery packed into the machine.

Dave's co-pilot, Ann, was annoying everyone by insisting that she practice with the grappling arms, even with so many people running around the outside of the sub. Ann spent her day in the cramped back seat of Aquanis moving the mechanical arms up and down, side to side and picking up random things from the dock and the floor of the ship. Occasionally she forced some unlucky employee to stand in front of the arms holding a piece of paper so she could try to grab it from different angles, scaring them half to death at each attempt. Dr. Gilbert put a stop to the live testing when he finally noticed what she was doing.

Jaycen came by around two and Marin offered him half of the sandwich she was eating for lunch. He gratefully accepted and wolfed it down in three bites. "Did you see the investor with Dr. Gilbert?" he asked her, stealing a drink from her cafeteria carton of milk.

Marin stood so she could see over the table to the pier. "The little guy?"

"Yeah. I guess he's some international big wig investor that owns a lot of stock in COAST."

"Hmm," she said, clearly not interested. She sat back down and looked at her screen, scrolling through files of water temperature and migratory changes.

"He's having an argument with Gilbert." She glanced at them again. They appeared to be having a quiet, yet intense conversation.

"What would he want to argue with Gilbert about?" she said, half-listening to him.

"Me."

She looked up questioningly. "Why you?"

"Dave picked me to go on the dive!"

"Wow, that's amazing! Congratulations!" she said in surprise.

Jaycen crossed his arms and scowled. "Yeah, but Gilbert doesn't want me to go. I overheard him before Dave told me to go take a lunch. The little guy is insisting it's too late to change plans. I think he's my new hero."

She put down the pen she was using to keep track of her place on her data sheet. "Why doesn't Gilbert want you on the dive?"

"I don't know. I couldn't hear much before I got sent off. It sounded like Gilbert just wants Dave and Ann on board. He must've had his head in a hole not to notice they were planning on taking me. I mean, I've been working on this for weeks now." He glanced over his shoulder at the men. Gilbert looked furious, but the smaller man seemed cool and nonchalant. "I thought it was too good to be true to get this opportunity. I've dreamt about this all my life, and when Dave said I was going down with him, I seriously didn't believe him." He took a deep breath. "I don't blame Gilbert for not wanting me on the sub. He probably thinks I'll sink it." He dusted the crumbs off his hands. "Even so, he should've said something before now. He can't jerk this away from me the day before launch."

Marin refrained from saying; *Of course he could jerk it away. He's the boss.* Dave crawled out of the sub and joined in the conversation. His voice boomed across the pier.

"You can't mess with this right now, Gilbert. We've been on this for weeks and I don't have time to work it with someone else! If he doesn't go, the sub doesn't go."

As if someone had pushed a pause button on a movie, people all around the warehouse stopped what they were doing, straining to hear the exchange. The workplace became unnaturally quiet.

Jaycen whispered, "You tell 'em, Dave!"

"So the sub doesn't go," Gilbert said evenly. With the lack of activity, their words could be easily heard. Everyone gasped in disbelief.

Mr. Hahn stared calmly into Gilbert's face. "That would be most unfortunate, Doctor. I know the amount of research you have put into *your* project. It would be a shame to have it all … disappear, just to keep the boy from going. I'm sure if he came along, neither one of us would have any cause to worry."

Dr. Gilbert stared defiantly in the man's face, but after several tense moments, he looked down, defeated. He turned to Dave. "Carry on," he said to him and walked back into the building. Slowly people started moving again, mumbling to each other in awe over how close they had come to their project being wiped.

Dave turned back to the sub, but not before making eye contact with the investor and giving him a slight, imperceptible nod.

"Sweet! I'm back in business!" Jaycen said, hopping off the desk. "Guess that means I'll be working late tonight. You doing anything special?" he asked, trying to sound as if he didn't care.

She sighed internally. "I don't really know what I'm doing tonight. I may be doing some swimming or something," she said as casually as she could. Was that lying? She really didn't know what they were doing. Just whom she was doing it with. Fortunately he hadn't asked that question.

"OK. I'll see you later maybe?" Jaycen smiled hopefully at her and headed back to the sub.

Marin left at five to get ready for her date. She couldn't believe how nervous she felt. She took a shower and started to do her hair, but realized she didn't know if they were going to be on land or in the water, so she put on boy shorts and a swim tank under her clothes just in case. The bay was still buzzing with activity when she came back, so she crept out the warehouse delivery door and went down the south beach before coming around below the pier. She slipped under, enjoying the cool, swampy shade and found a seat to wait on a large pile of rocks. Up above she could hear Dave barking out orders and Jaycen responding. As far as she could tell, Dr. Gilbert hadn't come back to the dock for the rest of the day, so Ann was working the arms again and stressing out subordinates with her experiments. Water splashed into her face. She spluttered and looked around, but couldn't see where it was coming from. Just before she got hit with another splash, she caught sight of a hand flipping up out of the water several feet out in the shade of the pier.

Marcos rose silently out of the water, grinning.

"Hey!" she whispered, wiping salt water off her face.

"Sorry. You just looked like you needed to get wet. Are you ready?"

"For what, exactly?"

His smile got even bigger. "To come with me." He held out his hand to her.

The words sent a thrill of excitement through her. It looked like they were going to be in the water. She slipped off her shoes and pulled off her t-shirt and shorts, putting them in a neat pile with her phone far enough up under the pier that they wouldn't get wet when the tide came in. Then she gingerly picked her way around the rocks to the cool water, taking his hand.

"Wait," she whispered. They stood, ankle high in the water, holding hands.

"Can you hear me?" she thought to him. He just smiled down at her. They sank lower and lower and she repeated the question until they were both completely underwater and he finally replied.

"Yes!"

"Why can't we communicate out of the water?" she asked.

"I have a theory," he said, leading her out into the sparkling green water of the bay.

"Really? What is it?" she asked, struggling to keep up with him. He placed her hands on his shoulders so they could swim together, his stronger body moving them both faster through the currents.

"It's like sound waves. Like echolocation. Something in the genes and hormones used to create us give us the ability to communicate with each

other under water as if we were our own species or pod. Something to do with electronic pulses of thought passing through the salt water, blah, blah, blah. I'm not a scientist."

"What are you, then?" she asked, surprised that among a new race of underwater physicists and biologists and engineers that he didn't consider himself a scientist.

He paused for a moment, thinking. *"I guess I'm a farmer,"* he said, shrugging at the sound of the title. *"I showed you my garden, remember?"*

She laughed and nodded. The current pushed harder against them as they made their way out of the protection of the bay and into the open sea. *"So according to your theory, how is it you can talk to dolphins or sharks if they are a different species?"*

"I can do it because I have taken the time to learn their dialect. Dolphins are intelligent beings. They can learn our words and phrases. Why could we not learn theirs? Dogs can understand a lot of words and commands, and Dolphins are much more intelligent. Besides, they can communicate with us on a basic 'frequency' already when we are underwater. Sharks also, but they are less ... civilized. Still, as you saw, you can appeal to their instincts and control them to a certain extent." They were headed up the coast and following the pacific shelf.

"Where are we going?" she asked, eyeing the abyss to her left.

"I forgot where I parked my car," he said chuckling into her mind. They came upon a line of mossy boulders which spilled off into the darkness. *"Ah, here it is."* He helped her hang onto the controls of the skiff he'd used the first day he met her, just last week. She could hardly believe it was only that long.

"Did you talk to the Council about why I can see what you see and feel your feelings?" She could feel him flush with embarrassment.

"They thought it might be an emotional connection. That's my belief too. Maybe it is because your parents both took Arydia and you were born with it in your blood. That would make you different from us. But Noburu thinks it may be more. He thinks maybe you have a deeper connection to everyone down here."

"Why?"

"Like lions on land, there is a natural leader. Nobody knows why, but there is always one that is designed differently than the rest. One who is born with extra skills that help him or her lead and keep everyone safe."

Marin was thunderstruck. *"Noburu thinks I'm born to lead you guys?"*

"Well, in the dolphin world, their leader is someone who can tune into everyone's frequency. Doesn't that sound like you?"

"Well, yes. And I guess that would explain why I couldn't hear ... anyone else underwater. Like other swimmers," she added, hoping he hadn't followed her train of thought to Jaycen. She felt like such a two-timing jerk. But at the same time, she hadn't committed to any relationship with either of them, so she didn't know why she should feel bad. Still, she did.

"I would assume anyone that's not of our species wouldn't be able to communicate like we can," he said pointedly, starting up the silent engine and making her feel even more self-conscious that he had at least touched on her thoughts of Jaycen. She turned her attention to their ride as she felt the skimmer begin to vibrate under her hands. She held onto one side of the powerful vehicle and he to the other as they dove off the edge of the cliff into the depths of the ocean.

TWENTY

The speed took her breath away. Marcos put up the shield and she hung on tightly to her half of the bowlike device. He reached over and put his hand over hers and instantly her experiences multiplied, living through both their eyes simultaneously. The machine reminded her a bit of a motorcycle; leaning would accentuate turns and dips. The connection between them allowed her to anticipate every move, making it possible to take spins, turns and jackknifes with surgical precision. It was unbelievable. Gravity was irrelevant. She felt like she was flying through the water, over canyons and cliffs with no fear of falling or drowning. He began a corkscrew descent, spinning them tighter and tighter, lower and lower, until their legs were tangled like twin tails on a kite. Finally they reached the bottom, laughing breathlessly. Marcos slowed the machine and they drifted through the darkness.

"That was incredible!" she said joyfully. She felt Marcos's emotions rush over her like a wave of delight. How could she have forgotten how intimate the connection between them was? It was like she could feel every emotion doubled and amplified, not just her happiness but his as well. *"This could be addicting! Can you feel what I'm feeling as well?"* she asked. He nodded, his eyes shining brightly.

"This is the happiest I have felt in my life, Marin. Thank you." His touch brought such a wave of love and longing that she drew back in confusion. It was baffling to actually feel how much someone cared about her. She felt her cheeks turning red and decided it was time to

change the subject. She pulled her hand away from his and the intense emotions subsided.

"So, do you ever get used to living in the twilight down here? I can see better than I think I should. Is that part of being Arydian as well?"

"You get used to it. Besides, you use your senses a lot more down here anyway. Can you feel it yet?"

Marin was confused. *"What am I supposed to be feeling?"*

He touched her hand and she understood. There was something huge ahead of them. The way the water moved in front of them had changed, like how a forest changes the eddies of a breeze.

A moment later she stopped and gasped in awe. They were at the foot of an enormous ship. The mast was broken and buried point-first into the ocean floor, like a huge finger pointing down from the center of the boat. Mounds of silt-like sand dunes were heaped around the ruined prow. Everything on it was furry with sea growth, blunting all the edges to rounds.

Marin stared up at the masthead above her and could barely make out the shape of a carved woman with a tail that wrapped around one side of the bow. A mermaid. She realized Marcos was watching her, waiting for her reaction.

"Do you like it?" he asked. They let the skimmer settle on the bottom of the sea, raising a puff of sand. The ship rose up before them like a ghost. It had settled onto the sea floor almost directly on its keel. It looked like someone parked it in the water.

"It's huge! What is it?"

He looked at her, completely dumbfounded. *"It's a ship!"*

She laughed. *"I can tell it's a ship. I mean what kind? It looks ancient!"*

"It is ancient. Between two and six hundred years old, I believe. Come." He took her hand and they swam onto the deck. The dark shadow of a large fish swam away from their approach and dozens of tiny white crabs dotted the deck, scurrying for safety. *"I think it's a carrack or a caravel. The bow is sunken in and it's pretty buried, but its railing looks rounded like a carrack."*

"A what?"

"Sorry." He shrugged. *"I'm a history nerd, not just a farmer. The carrack was used in Christopher Columbus's time. You identify that kind of bulging bow type with pirates or pilgrims. The caravel later replaced the carrack because it was a little more stable. But look at this."* They swam to the stern of the craft. The wood had collapsed slightly, sinking it to a crazy angle, but it was the original helm; the wheel almost perfectly preserved. Marcos drifted up to it and ran a finger across the filmy surface. *"You can just imagine the people working on this ship, running up the ropes."*

"It's kind of sad. And scary."

"Yes. I was nervous when I found it, too. But look around. It's quite amazing."

She laughed at him.

"What?" he asked.

"It's just your accent is interesting. Nobody says things like 'quite amazing'."

"Well, isn't it?"

"Yes. I suppose it is." She gazed at the tangle of wood around her. *"It's hard to believe this could be over two hundred years old. Maybe older than America itself."*

"Well, of course America is much older. But the organization of the country would be younger, yes."

"You're right. You are a history nerd," she laughed. *"Marcos, this is the most amazing thing I have ever seen! I bet nobody has touched this since the moment it sank."*

"Nobody has. Except for me." He smiled. *"Want to come inside?"*

She considered the crumbling deck apprehensively. *"Is it safe?"*

"I've been inside many times." He led her through the open mouth of the hold and down the stairs. It was darker inside but still they could see fairly well. He let her explore several rooms, scattering small schools of fish as they went, looking at tin lanterns, scattered table legs, sea chests open and full of silt.

"Are there ... you know?" She swallowed after stepping on a long piece of mossy wood in her bare feet.

"Bodies?"

"Yeah."

"I'm sure there were. But this is a recyclable world. Pretty much everything edible gets eaten at some point. One hundred years would give something a long time to dispose of bones, and this has been here longer than that. Don't worry."

"Okay," she said hesitantly.

He stopped and pushed on an ornamented door. It swung soundlessly open to reveal the largest room yet. They were at the stern of the boat in what could only be the captain's quarters. A heavy table sat in the middle of the room as if placed there, not dropped through fathoms of water in a sinking ship. Dim light filtered through surprisingly unbroken windows. An old candle chandelier hung heavily from the ceiling, laced with grey-green silt.

"Why didn't the table get tipped when it crashed?"

"It's nailed to the deck. Probably kept people from getting hurt in rough seas." He watched her move around the room, touching the glass of a decanter in a cupboard, with a golden emblem etched in the side, running a finger over the stained glass windows. *"Marin?"*

"Hmm?" she responded, running her hands along the ornately carved bed frame built into the wall.

She had been so engrossed in this new world that she stared at him for a minute, not understanding what he wanted. He moved close and touched her hair lovingly, pulling her closer, and then kissed her.

As their lips touched, she felt his memories, his loneliness, his hope and love come rushing toward her. Everything he felt about her flooded through her mind as real as her own thoughts. It shocked her, and she could tell it shocked him as well, but he didn't pull away, letting his soul stand bare before her without apology.

His memories shot through her mind like a movie on fast forward. She could see glimpses of his early memories, before he could even speak; almost feelings rather than thoughts, laced with pictures, hazy around the edges—his mother smiling, an apple tree heavy with sweet-smelling blossoms like snow, and the smell of sea grasses that grew almost to their doorstep on the beautiful island home he loved. She felt his terror as strangers stole away his baby sister, Katrina, in the middle of the night, tearing his world apart. She saw his mother and father screaming in hysterics, desperate to get her back.

She felt the childhood perfection of his early life shattered, his mother crying, always crying, wasting away in heartbreak until her heart stopped beating. She saw her buried, feeling the confusion and loneliness of a toddler who didn't understand why his mother was gone. She felt the emptiness of their home and his father's stern despair as they locked the door and left forever, moving far away because something bad had happened at Father's work. The images and feelings became sharper in more recent memories. She knew his friends, his school and lived with him as his father would travel all over the world, often leaving him alone as he grew into a young man. She felt his rage when his father told them they had to leave the land. Arguments and anger and fear and, finally, saying goodbye to the sunlight and sand and making the transformation that brought them to the world below.

She saw him alone again, below the sea in a ruined ship, lashing out in anger and despair, knowing he could never be allowed to return, that he would always be alone, with only the adults and young children to keep him company for the rest of his life. Then she felt his hope when Aggie mentioned there had been another like him. The possibility that Marin might have survived. Someone who might one day come to them and maybe end his loneliness.

She kissed him, watching, feeling his entire life wrapped up in this one moment, this one dream, knowing that all he wanted in this world was for her to stay with him and heal his battered heart. He could feel her hesitation, but he refused to let it kill his hope. Her tears mingled with the salt water around her as she pulled herself away, breaking the connection.

He looked at her tenderly, the green light from the window playing shadows on her face. *"Now you know me,"* he said simply. *"I don't know how you did that, but now you know."*

She shook her head, the memories of his lifetime still a storm in her heart. *"I'm so sorry!"* she said, overcome by the sadness in his life. She felt like she had trespassed through his soul.

He spoke softly. *"No. There is nothing to be sorry for. It is all who I am. And now you are a part of me."*

She didn't know what to say. She had never imagined it was possible that she could actually *feel* the life and memories of another, see how someone else saw her, feel the love someone had for her. The experience left her in awe. This sad, gorgeous, wonderful, person loved *her* that deeply. It was precious, terrifying, sacred and beautiful beyond description. And all he wanted was for her to love him back. They were the same, like they were made to be together.

He brought her close, resting his cheek on her head. *"Your touch is something special,"* he said. She smiled, comforted by his arms around her.

He released her with a look of sadness that confused her and gestured around the room. *"This place is mine. I have spent a lot of time here, especially when my father forced us to leave the land. I knew why we couldn't go back up, but I hated being sent into this exile."* He ran his hand across the table's edge, and then stared at her pointedly. *"I didn't choose this. I felt like every choice was stolen from me, my whole life ruined."* He paused for a moment before going on.

"I was a junior in high school when we left. I had a job after school training horses at a ranch near our home. I was getting good grades. I had friends. It was the longest we had stayed in one place and I wanted it to last." He laughed mirthlessly.

"Now, my dreams of college, going back to Greece to see my homeland, having a normal life and family—all gone. I didn't want any of this," he said, pointing at the submerged world around him.

"I decided I needed something that was away from my father and the Council and everyone else who expected me to be like them, to be okay with what we were doing; what we had given up." He leaned against the bed

frame, raising a puff of silt. *"I wanted a chance to choose my own destiny. So this is it. This is my sanctuary and my hope."* He moved to a corner and she followed.

He removed the wooden lid of a built-in window seat and stepped back. She looked inside and gasped. The entire space was filled with gems, gold coins, jewels, rings, cups. Her mouth dropped open. It was a real, honest-to-goodness treasure chest, probably worth millions.

"You found this here?" she asked incredulously.

"Some of it. Some I've picked out from other wrecks along the coast. Some are just pieces taken from the mine back at the base, you know, sapphires and such. Remember how the really good ones get tossed and we look for the grainy, second and third class gems, the kind people find up top? There is so much more on the ocean floor than any of the stuff upstairs," he said, pointing upwards. *"They just have no way to get it. So, I took some."*

She reached in and picked up a heavy stone the size of an ostrich egg. Part of it was encased in rock, but over half of it looked like a giant emerald.

"It's green," she said.

He laughed. She was surprised that she could still see so well in the dim interior, even colors. It just looked like a room on a very cloudy day. She knelt down beside Marcos's treasure. Dipping her hands in it, she picked up handfuls of thick gold disks with unfamiliar symbols and faces on them, letting them slide out between her fingers and fall heavily onto the piles below. *"This is amazing!"*

He sat down next to her, grinning hugely. *"It's my dragon's hoard."* She laughed. He reached into the pile and brought out a pearl the size of a dime attached to a ring of finely worked gold. Smaller twin sapphires glittered on either side of the pearl. It was breathtaking. She held it, loving the pearl's inner glow. Gently he took it from her and put it on her finger, his brief touch sending a jolt of hope and joy through her heart. *"This is for you."* He kissed her cheek, making her face warm.

She looked into his eyes, seriously considering for the first time the incredible life she had waiting for her in this vast new world.

He returned her gaze, but his smile slowly slipped away. *"There is something that nobody has told you yet, Marin. Right now, you think there is a choice, that we can choose between land and the sea. But things have been happening to everybody. It is why we no longer allow others to be changed."* He reached out an arm and pointed to a rough patch of skin on the back of his hand. *"Nobody knows why, but this is how it starts. For some it happened fast, others are just starting to show the signs. Their skin gets cracked, they can't see as well on land, and soon they can't breathe out of the water, at least for very long. And they cannot have children."* He paused and bit his lip. *"Some have already died. We have created a race that will soon be extinct."*

"But, then, how do you explain me?" she asked, not wanting to believe him.

Marcos shrugged. *"Aggie said your mother suspected there were problems with Arydia and was experimenting with something to counteract its effects. She thinks your mother chose to test her experiment on herself rather than put any of the others at risk. Something must have worked, because she had you. We don't know if this is why you have slight differences than the rest of us, or if it is just a gift of your birth. But whatever it may have been disappeared with your mother."*

"But, after all this time, can't you fix it? I thought you were all super geniuses or something!"

"Of course we are running experiments; keeping some out of the water as much as possible to see if it slows it down, eating different food, trying to take hormones to counterbalance the effects of the injection we all had. But we have had no success."

He caught up her hand in both of his. *"I gathered all this treasure so I could leave the water and build my own life, but now I don't believe that was meant to happen."*

Her blood ran cold at the thought of never being able to leave the water. Ever. Then the significance of it hit her. She felt like she was being told she had a terminal disease.

"Do you think there's a chance this might happen to me, too?"

He looked into her eyes sadly. *"You may be different. Some think that there is something about you that can be used to help us; something in the way you were made that might stop the change from happening to us, or reverse it."* He frowned, his eyes filled with sympathy. *"I am sorry I had to be the one to tell you about this. But I believe you have the right to know."*

She shook her head. Her thoughts were swimming in circles. Was he right? Was she destined to live the rest of her life in the shadowy world of the sea? Never to walk on land again? She remembered the night Marcos had told her how much he missed being dry and shivered. Then her breath caught in her throat as she thought about Paul and Jaycen. The tears that came to her eyes merely drifted into the sea unnoticed. She sank down near him in the silent tomb of the ship, shaken. Shock took over and she sat sobbing silently into the soundless water.

* * *

Marcos drifted from the room and let her have time to cry, to take in the truth of everything without disturbing her. Waiting. Remembering how he'd felt when they discovered what was happening to them.

He sighed. Aggie and the Council had sent him to bring her back to Portus, by force if necessary. He wasn't going to do that. It would do no good to keep her here; at this point, he knew she would just run again. And he didn't want this forced on her like it was on him. She could never learn to love this world, or love him, if she blamed him for keeping her here, just as he blamed his father. He held onto his one last hope that, like the rain, she would eventually return to the sea.

TWENTY-ONE

Marin was silent on the way back, though she did allow Marcos to keep his hand over hers as he drove the skimmer, showing her the beauty and mystery of the world around them. An enormous blue whale came up behind them so close that they could see its shiny black eye. They slowed the skimmer and stared at it, filling the ocean like a building tipped on its side.

"It's magnificent!"

Marcos seemed equally in awe. *"We are looking at the largest animal on the planet."* They felt insignificant in comparison to the hulking body before them.

"I can't believe something so enormous lives on the smallest food source in the ocean," Marin thought, shaking her head in disbelief. *"Do you see these a lot?"*

"I have only seen one other, and it was not this close. They are more common out here in the depths, and I am forbidden from coming this far from Portus alone."

"You're not supposed to be out here?" she asked as the behemoth turned and swam away from them. The engine began to hum and they started moving again through the water.

"No. But I come anyway. What can they take from me that I've not already lost?"

"Do you really hate being down here so much?" she asked.

"No. I don't hate it at all. I just hate the thought of never having a choice.

And I especially hate the thought of being here the rest of my life alone."

She swallowed hard at feeling the hope and longing directed at her, but it was tempered with his determination to let her choose. It made her respect him even more. They moved in silence for a while, each in their own thoughts. *"Marcos, how old are you?"* she asked, realizing she had no idea.

"Nineteen. I'll be twenty in August. I'm wondering, am I older than Jaycen?" She felt a wave of jealousy in his thoughts.

"No. I think he's older than you by a little bit."

"Older in years, maybe, but I am older than him in my heart."

"Yes, you seem like it," she had to agree. They reached the rocky outcropping and left the skimmer by it.

"I'm supposed to bring you back to our home tonight. They say it's not safe for you up top anymore. When the Navy examines Aggie's suit, they will come looking for you, as might others."

Marin froze, glancing at him uncertainly. *"You're not, though, are you?"*

Marcos shook his head. *"I want to."* He took her hand in his. *"I want you to be safe. And you know how much I want you with me. I won't force you, but I will ask you from the depths of my heart, please come back with me, Marin."*

"Marcos." Her feelings for him crowded through her heart, and part of her wanted to take his hand and let herself fall, to see where their life could lead. But all the things she could never have or do again raced through her mind. Things as random as potato chips, snow, trees, and dirt.

"I can't. Not yet. I need more time."

They swam on in silence, lost in thought. The water was warmer when they got into the bay. Lights from the warehouse shone down on the docks where people were working on the huge ship that Aquanis would soon be loaded onto. They swam to the far side of the bay, away from the activity humming around the docks and stood just under the surface of the water.

"I guess I'll say good night to you here, if you can get in all right."

"Yes, I'll be fine. They won't notice me." She prepared herself for the intense emotional experience of kissing him again, but he just wrapped his warm, strong arms around her and pulled her close, holding her tightly. *"When will I see you again?"* she whispered.

He rested his cheek on the top of her hair. *"I have to go for a few days. But I will find you when I get back. Be safe! You know that Leviathan was not destroyed by our people. Only crippled. They are still out there, looking for us. Trust no one,"* he said, releasing her. He gazed at her for a moment, barely able to make out her features in the darkness, and then he turned and with one powerful stroke disappeared into the black water.

She dressed silently in the dark under the pier, hoping she wouldn't step on a crab or anything sharp in her bare feet. Her eyesight had gotten much better in the last few weeks, even on land. She wondered if eventually her other skills might work up here as well, given time.

There was a lot of activity above her, but she decided to risk trying to melt in with the bustle and go through the warehouse rather than make her way around the entire complex to the main entrance. The main bay door was open so she made her way past the wooden walkways of piers to the largest and headed in. Spotlights were trained on the largest ship, Star Chaser, lighting up the deck. She didn't see Jaycen, but he was probably jammed inside Aquanis because Dave was outside it tapping on the port window and yelling. She turned the corner and slammed into Dr. Gilbert who had been standing just inside the bay doors.

"I'm sorry, Dr. Gilbert!" she said, backing up. He nodded, but didn't move aside to let her pass.

"Did you enjoy your swim, Marin?" he asked.

She glanced at the water, wondering how much he could see from the dock. "Swim?" she asked, trying to sound casual.

"Yes. The one you just returned from."

"How did you—"

He held out her cell phone. "Your phone was ringing under the dock. I found your shoes and clothes. Your hair is dripping wet, and your clothes are damp. So, did you enjoy your swim?" he asked conversationally.

"Ah, yeah," she stammered, taking her cell and putting it in her pocket, cursing herself for forgetting to turn off the ringer. "It was a hot day. It was a nice swim."

"Yes. Did you happen to see anything unusual on your outing?"

"Um ..." she thought of the sunken ship, the piles of scavenged gold and jewels, a huge whale, not to mention the gorgeous merman. She didn't know what to say so she just shrugged.

He glanced down at the ring on her finger, but she couldn't tell what he was thinking. He leaned in close, an intense look in his eyes. He reached out and held onto her arm.

"Marin. There are things you don't know about or understand." He glanced around, as if afraid of someone listening. "I thought I made it clear to you, do not go anywhere with anyone! Do not go into the water. Do you understand? It is extremely dangerous." He looked up quickly as someone walked by with a laptop in their arms and waited until they were out of earshot. "Do you understand?" he repeated.

Marin nodded, confused. Gilbert let go of her arm and gave her a quick, sad smile. "Good. Get some rest. And lock your door." He turned and strode out into the dock, leaving her confused and alarmed.

Instead of going to her room, Marin grabbed some leftovers from the cafeteria in a Styrofoam container and went out on the porch of the rec room to eat and think. Directly below her, the prep crew still scurried around trying to tie everything up for the dive in the morning. She felt sorry for anyone down there tonight, as tensions were running high.

Dave seemed to be in a fever of anxiety, making everyone double and triple check every system. It was good practice, but everyone who had been looking forward to the dive was now just looking forward to it being over. Who knows when any of them would sleep tonight. She finished her ham fried rice as she watched them, feeling like a spy. A hand reached out from behind her and clamped over her mouth. In shock, she tried to break away before a voice whispered in her ear.

"Shhhh! I don't want them to notice I'm missing." Jaycen released her with a grin.

"You scared me to death!" she accused, shaken.

He looked genuinely surprised. "I'm sorry. I really didn't mean to scare you. I just wanted to get away for a second and catch my breath, and when I saw you up here I snuck away to join you. I only have a few minutes before I head back down. It's going to be an early day tomorrow. I hope he lets us sleep for a few hours."

She took a deep breath and tried to calm herself. "Good luck tomorrow."

He sat down heavily on one of the wicker lounge chairs. "Yeah, thanks."

"You seem nervous. Are you ok?" she asked, sinking back into her own chair.

"Yeah. I am worried about tomorrow. There's so much that can go wrong, and Dave is acting so crazy it's making me feel like we're never coming back."

The thought had never occurred to her. "You could drown," she said in amazement.

"Well, yes. That is the worry. Or be crushed. That would be bad, too. But it's the drowning part that I don't like."

"I never knew *you* were afraid of drowning," she said, astonished.

"Now you do."

"So why go into this line of work?" she asked, burning with curiosity.

"Probably the same reason you did. I love the ocean. I'm great at biology. If I could get over my fear of drowning, it would be a perfect match. Sort of like us if we can get past the weird/angry cycle."

She rolled her eyes. "I don't know if weird will ever *not* be part of my life."

Jaycen gave her a sly smile. "So, I ran into your Uncle Paul earlier. You could have told me who he was, you know. I wouldn't care. We had a nice talk."

"What?" she asked, mortified.

Jaycen grinned mischievously. "He gave me 'the talk.'"

She slapped her face with her hand and groaned with embarrassment.

He stood and took her hand from her face, pulling her to stand with him. "Don't be sad. It actually made me feel really good. Like maybe I have a chance." He laughed. "Did you tell him I kissed you?" he asked, pulling her into his arms, smelling the warm scent of her hair.

She laid her face on his shoulder, glad he couldn't see her face burning crimson, and enjoyed being held without answering.

"You did?" he asked in amazement, pulling her away to verify it by the look on her face. "Ha!" he said triumphantly and brought her back into his arms, hugging her.

"I didn't tell him! He just sorta … guessed."

He beamed, his cheek against the top of her head. "That's even better!" he said happily.

"Why?" she demanded.

"Because he could tell!" he said, happiness etched into every line on his face.

"Jaycen," she said pulling away. "Stop making me get all comfortable with you!"

"What?" he asked confused.

"You think that you can just love me and I'll break down and love you back! But it doesn't count because you don't understand!"

Dave's voice yelled from down below. "*Jaycen*! Somebody find that kid, NOW!"

Jaycen just stared at her, but she didn't say anything more so he opened the door to go inside, shaking his head. Just as he crossed the threshold he turned back. "I don't *have* to understand. And love always counts, Marin. Always." He turned and walked away.

* * *

Jaycen lay in his bed with the lights off, staring at the ceiling. He threw a tennis ball up and caught it, even in the dark. Somehow, the rhythmic motion helped him think. He was careful not to let it go so high as to hit the ceiling, since there were offices above him and they had complained about strange bumps at night when working late. It had to be close to three in the morning, but he kept his throws low anyway, since he could never be too careful with the kooky workaholics around here.

There were only a couple of weeks left until the internship ended. Nobody had said whether he could continue working at DeepWater when it finished, or if he was expected to return home with the rest of the interns. He didn't want to ask and stir the pot, but living in uncertainty was wearing on him. He felt frazzled and edgy, like the sky before a big storm.

Earlier in the afternoon, he took a quick lunch break. He'd sat with Natalee and Tui while they smooched and tried to ignore them while eating his sandwich and watching the news. Gas prices jumped almost a dollar per gallon overnight and people were panicking. Normally something like that felt like it belonged to another world; the adult world of politics and stock markets and commodities that he didn't quite feel obligated to participate in, at least not yet.

But his car was a gas hog, and he emptied his tank on Saturday when he'd driven out to see his mom and he didn't get paid for another three days, so he was effectively without a car until the weekend. There was talk about government corruption and price fixing that weighed heavily on his mind, mixed with Marin and DeepWater, making him feel helpless and manipulated, like a piece of driftwood pushed by the pounding surf. He felt like everything was wrong somehow, and there was nothing he could do to make it right.

His ball flew too high and it bounced harshly off the ceiling and back into his hand. He didn't know what to think about Marin. She really did sound crazy, but if he thought about it just right, it was crazy enough to fit some of the circumstances. He shook his head and mentally kicked himself for wanting to believe she was a mutant mermaid. The truth was, he just wanted there to be some explanation other than she had borrowed his car to pick up that Marcos guy, who then drove back to COAST before they went off together for a couple of days and who she'd been seeing off and on all week.

He tossed the ball higher, knowing he should make himself sleep, but knowing it was pointless, especially when his alarm was going off in just over an hour. He sighed and threw the ball harder at the ceiling, making a loud bonk and smacking his hand hard when it returned. From somewhere upstairs, he heard a foot stamp hard on the floor in return. Sheepishly, he let the ball drop as he rolled over to try to force some sleep into his brain.

* * *

Marin woke to the sound of a knock at her door. She struggled to drag herself awake, as it seemed like only a couple of hours since she'd talked to Jaycen on the balcony. She had gone to bed torn up and miserable, but still locked her door before falling asleep.

She tried to rub the sleep out of her eyes. The darkness outside her window was complete and her digital clock read 4:00 a.m. She sat up and turned on the bedside light.

"Who is it?" she asked groggily, hoping whoever it was, probably Jaycen, would hear the fatigue in her voice and leave.

"It's Dave. Can I talk to you?" a gruff voice answered.

She blinked in surprise and stood up, pulling her wrinkled clothes into some semblance of daytime use and unlocked the door. Dave walked in, wiping his grease stained hands on a red rag. He seemed so out of place, and she realized she had never seen him alone. He was always with someone in the warehouse bay or working in his dive shop or going somewhere with Paul. He looked agitated, but he flashed a weary smile at her.

"I'm sorry to barge in on you so early, Mares, but we have an emergency. Ann was scheduled to go down in Aquanis with me in the morning, but she had an accident and won't be able to make it. I need a replacement, and you are the most likely candidate since we launch in an hour and you are already here."

"What?" Marin stared at him, stunned. Her mind still felt fuzzy from sleep, and she couldn't wrap her head around what he was telling her.

Dave pursed his lips causing his mustache to stand straight out. She had to refrain from laughing. He spoke in clipped words, accentuating every syllable. "I am offering you a once in a lifetime chance to go to the bottom of the sea in a manned submersible. Dr. Gilbert suggested you as a replacement because of your biology background. I need you to fill a slot so we can do the dive in the morning or it will be canceled." He looked flustered and upset, wringing the dirty rag in his hands as he spoke. "We've all been working too hard to let that happen. This is vitally important, Marin, as well as a good opportunity. I wouldn't suggest passing it up." He looked at her expectantly, and she could feel his frustration as she hesitated.

She blinked at him, confused. "Dave, there are people lined up out the door to go on Aquanis. Why would you be choosing me? I have no experience."

Dave's eye twitched slightly as he stared at her. "You're right. There are a lot of people who would like to go. But they're not here and we're prepping for launch right now. So you get the lucky number—right place, right time and all that. I'm offering this chance to you because I know how hard you've worked for this. Paul and I have been friends a long time, Marin. I've watched you grow up. And I can't think of anyone I would trust more than you to help on this mission."

He rubbed his face wearily. "So, are you good to go?"

She couldn't find words to answer him. Suddenly she felt like she was being offered a ride to the moon and truthfully she didn't know if she really wanted to take it. He read her thoughts and frowned, pulling out his trump card in desperation. He pulled the door shut behind him and lowered his voice. "Marin, you don't realize the importance of this mission, do you?"

She shook her head, not knowing where this discussion was going.

He lowered his voice further. "Marin, I know about Arydia." She caught her breath as he plowed on. "This entire mission has been funded by Leviathan. They are looking for the Arydians, and they think they know where to find them. The only chance we have to help them is to make Leviathan think they are looking in the wrong place. I can't trust anybody else to help me falsify the information we collect but you."

She stared at him in shock. "How …?" She couldn't understand it

He smiled knowingly as if reading her mind. "I worked on the AQUA project, Marin. I knew your mother and your father. I've been one of the Arydian's contacts for years."

"But, then we need to warn them!" she spluttered. Dave put a calming hand on her shoulder.

"They have been warned. They are preparing to leave as we speak. But we've got to find a way to stall Leviathan long enough to let them get away. Can I count on you?" He searched her eyes, watching her as she thought. As she nodded, she was surprised to hear Dave's sigh of relief, as if he didn't know she had no choice.

"Good. Get ready and meet me at the dock. And remember, don't tell anyone!" He turned, but paused at the door. "And stay away from Dr. Gilbert. He's one of them." He said over his shoulder as he walked out, clicking the door shut behind him.

As soon as Marin arrived in the warehouse Dave hurried her onto Star Chaser, the ship that would deliver Aquanis to its drop point. Aquanis was hanging securely by four sturdy cranes built into the ship on its port side with weathered metal steps leading up to its open door. He gave her waterproof pages and a wax pencil and told her to do a pre-dive check inside the sub. Other than Dave and her, the place was deserted, but after a few moments she heard talking on the dock and poked her head out briefly to see the weary, yet excited employees gearing up for the expedition. She crawled back into her cramped seat before anyone could see her.

She sent a quick text to Paul to tell him what was happening and not to worry, making a mental note to call him as soon as she got back since she was pretty sure he wouldn't check his messages until he woke up. By that time they would be submerged, but she wanted someone other than Dave to know where she was.

She heard people on deck and Dave appeared in the doorway looking grim.

"We are ahead of schedule, and I'm hoping we can get this thing moving before Dr. Gilbert gets here," he whispered, pausing as someone passed by outside the sub. Marin nodded and he went on. "I don't like the thought that he might tie you to the Arydians, so I want you to stay in here out of sight 'til we get out on the water, ok? Don't get out until I come get you." He closed the door and twisted the pressure lock, sealing her in.

A throaty rumble began below her as the Star Chaser's engines were started. Within moments, the boat started moving. The sub rocked heavily on its cranes as she struggled to get herself back into her seat and attach her harness.

* * *

Dr. Gilbert spent the night in his office, crammed in the army cot he kept in the corner. His phone had been ringing incessantly with calls from Dr. Hahn, but he refused to answer or to allow himself to think of the consequence of not answering. There were more important issues to solve now, and he couldn't allow anything to waylay him. His phone was set to go off at 4:30 a.m., an hour before the launch.

The sound of an engine tore him from his sleep at 4:20 a.m. The Star Chaser! He panicked, racing out the door in nothing but his boxers and a t-shirt, taking the stairs two at a time instead of waiting for the elevator. Even so, he was too late. He cried in anguish as he watched the Star Chaser growing smaller as it left the bay, taking his life with it. He stood with his bare feet on the cold deck, fighting the urge to jump in an outboard and chase them down.

Think! He cursed himself for his shortsightedness, tearing his hair in frustration. He raced to his lab, snatching several hypodermic needles, four vials of fluid, and a small wireless remote control, which he prayed would work, and stuffed them into a mesh bag. Growling with impatience, he waited for his personal computer to boot up and had to wait even longer for his virus to download and melt the memory. Grabbing a pair of discarded swim shorts, he threw them on, jumped into a cabin cruiser, and drove off knowing he was never coming back.

TWENTY-TWO

The Star Chaser didn't have long to drive before they arrived at the dive site. Marin had been watching the shoreline as the early rays of sun started lighting the sky, nervous and confused. Thinking of Dr. Gilbert as an enemy of the Arydians disturbed her, especially remembering the special interest and favoritism he had consistently shown her. She always thought it was because he knew Uncle Paul so well, but now? She realized with a shock that Dr. Gilbert *knew* about her. He had known she was different longer than *she* had. She wrapped her arms around herself to fight off the chill she was feeling inside and out. And what about Dave? If he was part of the Arydians, why didn't they tell her? As if summoned by her thoughts, Dave appeared next to her.

"Betcha have a few questions for me, don't you?" he asked genially. He acknowledged her nod. "Best not to talk up here. Come into the cabin," he said, holding her elbow. He could feel her hesitation and smiled. "Don't worry. Remember, I'm with the good guys."

Reluctantly, she followed him into the dim interior of the cabin. "I'll take over," he said to the driver, who vacated the captain's chair and left. Dave circled the ship once and let it idle, then turned to face her.

"There are people that are desperate for the secrets you know, and they will do *anything* to get them from you. Dr. Gilbert suspected you were one of them. I needed to get you away from him as soon as possible."

She shivered when she thought of Gilbert taking her blood and rubbed her arm, though the mark had long since vanished. And the Navy—had they learned anything about her while she was there?

Dave continued. "He found out something you may not be aware of. We saw him on our surveillance cameras do something very interesting. Do you know that your blood can heal others?"

She shook her head, shocked. "What? No. That's impossible."

"Have you ever been sick? Hurt? Betcha got better pretty fast if you did. Unnaturally fast. Like when you got crushed under that platform?" he asked knowingly.

Her brow furrowed as she thought back to every time she could remember falling down or getting bruised. It never lasted long. And she'd just walked away from the accident with the sub. When she thought about it, she realized she *had* no memory of ever being sick.

"Let's try something." He smiled knowingly and took her hand. "This might hurt a bit," he said, producing a safety pin that he deftly jabbed into her index finger. She winced as he squeezed a few drops of blood out of the wound and let them drip onto his thumb, cracked with years of working in salt water. A moment later he wiped his thumb clean. The wound was pink and healing, the divot already filling with new flesh.

"That has bothered me for years! I can't believe it actually worked!" he breathed in awe. "Do you know how valuable you are? Everyone on earth will come clamoring to bleed you dry," he said with a hungry look in his eyes. She backed up, bumping into the wall, and he relaxed and smiled.

"Now do you see why we need to get you safely underwater with your people?"

She nodded uncertainly, wondering if she would ever be allowed to see the sun again. "What are we going to do?" she whispered.

Dave glanced out the window and gave a signal to the workers below. "We're stopping just outside the protected waters of Point Mugu Naval base. Then you and I will take Aquanis right down to them. We have arranged for what will look like a little accident and Aquanis will be another tragic loss to the cruel sea. They'll guide us in, and return me to land when everything has settled. I'll start a new life under a new name. I've done this many times before. Don't worry."

"What about Jaycen?" she asked, puzzled.

Dave's head jerked up at the sound of a boat motor, his face hardening. "Dr. Gilbert is coming. We've gotta go!"

They raced to the deck as she searched through the faces for Jaycen, wanting to see him one last time if only for a moment. Dave swung open the hatch and boosted her inside. She turned to look over the heads of the crew, wondering if this was the last time she would see the light again. In the distance, she could see Dr. Gilbert's boat closing in on them. Dave put a hand on her head and pushed her inside. As he pulled his leg up to crawl inside himself, Jaycen appeared in the doorway.

"What's going on, Dave?" Jaycen demanded. Marin could hear the boat approaching fast and someone yelling. Suddenly, a faint pop was heard and Dave grunted in pain, his shoulder blooming red.

"Dave!" Jaycen cried, helping steady the older man as he dangled half in and half out of the submersible. Peeking out over Dave's shoulder, Marin saw the boat closing in on them.

"What's going on?" Jaycen repeated desperately.

Dave looked at his useless arm in agony and appeared to make a quick decision. Grabbing the front of Jaycen's shirt he pulled him close. "If you want Marin to live, get inside. I'll explain when we get launched. I need you to pilot." He crawled the rest of the way in and Jaycen didn't hesitate to follow, pulling the door shut behind him and twisting the lock.

"No! Jaycen!" she cried out in alarm. "You have to get out!" He had a life; he couldn't just disappear like Dave could!

He just shook his head and fastened his restraints. Dave crawled into the driver's seat and activated the crane arms. The sub started rocking as they moved out and away from the boat.

"Hang on!" Dave said as he manually released the safety arms and they fell seven feet, hitting the water with a tremendous, jarring splash.

Jaycen flipped on the oxygen tank and activated the motor. The sub came alive with yellow lights and a myriad of control panels.

"Take her down, Jaycen," Dave said through gritted teeth.

"What is going on up there?" Jaycen demanded. "Was someone *shooting* at you?" he said, looking at Dave. Blood pooled around Dave's fingers where he was holding onto his shoulder. He nodded grimly.

"Somebody *shot* you?" Jaycen repeated incredulously. "Why would someone be shooting at you?"

"They are after her," Dave said nodding his head toward Marin in the back of the sub.

"Who is after her?" he demanded.

Marin spoke, her voice shaky. "Leviathan." She whispered the name like it was poison.

"What's Leviathan?" he asked, turning the sub to a slight downward angle. The light from the water outside turned darker green.

"I told you already. Remember? Secret science experiment, mutant fish people?"

His eyes bugged out. "You are not serious. Things like that don't exist."

"Ask Dave," she said angrily.

Dave laughed faintly, and then winced. "So," he said through gritted teeth, "I seem to have misplaced the exact coordinates during the, ah, excitement up top." He looked at Marin. "It's going to have to be up to you if we're going to make it. Do you remember the numbers? You need to take us down to them."

She thought back to the package in her houseboat Marcos had hidden for her with the coordinates and tried to adjust it farther north and away from the coast. "I think I can get us pretty close." She wrote down her best estimate and he punched them into the computer.

He sat back, relieved. "Thank you. Whew! That was easy!" he said. He glanced at her and chuckled. "Don't suppose you'd want to bleed on my arm, would you?"

Marin laughed uneasily, feeling like he was only half-joking. Dave reached under his chair and picked up a small computer screen and re-entered the coordinates. The submarine began its descent to Portus and the Arydians.

The radio crackled to life. "Aquanis, this is Star Chaser. Abort mission. Repeat. Abort mission!" Marin was surprised to hear it was Dr. Gilbert's voice.

Dave smiled a wide, relaxed smile. "Looks like Dr. Gilbert finally made it on board." He laughed and leaned into the microphone, flipping the toggle to activate the radio. "Unable to abort, Star Chaser. Technical difficulties."

The sub creaked and groaned as the pressure increased. The radio screamed to life.

"Dave! Don't do this!" Gilbert pleaded. "You don't know what you're getting into! These people are not going to let you go! Whatever they've promised, it's not good enough! Dave, please respond!"

Dave chuckled, enjoying the panic in Gilbert's voice. Marin and Jaycen exchanged uneasy looks. The sub rocked as it hit the heavy current coming from Mugu lagoon. She knew they were getting close. What would Jaycen think when he found out she had been telling him the truth? His hands were white on the controls; she knew he was struggling to hold it together already.

"We are experiencing turbulence. Cannot comply," Dave said smugly.

"Dave!" Gilbert's voice warned. "Don't make me do this!"

Marin's eyes went wide at the threat. Do what?

"There's no turning back, Douglas. We are committed," Dave said into the microphone. "You need to think about the innocent lives you've involved in this before you do anything stupid. And guess what? I brought insurance."

Marin froze. Douglas? She thought his name was Frank. She turned to look at Dave, a sinking feeling growing in the pit of her stomach. "Who is Douglas?" she croaked.

Dave turned and looked at her, his eyes dark. "Dr. Douglas Franklin Gilbert, of course."

She looked down, stunned, feeling like she was seeing her life

KATHERINE ARMSTRONG WALTERS

through a tunnel, scenes flashing in front and fading away. Dr. Gilbert giving Paul a job, taking them out on the boats, referring her to her psychologist to help her overcome her fears, always there, always in the background, choosing her for COAST, making it so obvious she was his favorite, warning her of danger, locking her door, always touching her life. She saw his face with perfect clarity, his high forehead and brushed back hair, and a thin white scar running the length of his brow, never hidden, as if wishing to be recognized. A scar from a wound when his boat was destroyed on the day his family was taken from him?

Her father had been there all along! Her eyes met Dave's. He was watching her carefully connect the dots and arrive at the correct conclusion.

"They're nothing more than hostages, and you know it!" Dr. Gilbert shouted into the radio. "Please! Don't take her! For pity's sake, please! Don't make me do this!" he begged.

"I believe we are arriving at our destination, ladies and gentlemen," he said over his shoulder, breaking eye contact with Marin. They felt the craft slow.

The radio crackled to life one more time. "Marin! Jaycen! I don't know if you can hear me, but …" Dave clicked the radio off.

* * *

In the cabin of the Star Chaser, the radio fell silent. Dr. Gilbert dropped the receiver to the floor, grabbing the doorway for support. He took several deep breaths to calm himself, and turned to the captain. "Forty knots, starboard, quickly! Aquanis has been sabotaged!" The ship roared to life and entered military waters. Within minutes, there were boats racing toward them, their intercoms blazing out warnings.

"Send them a distress call. We are on a rescue mission," he commanded. The captain immediately picked up the radio and started explaining the situation. When they were as close as he dared get, he took the small remote out of his bag and pressed a button, praying that

God would forgive him. The two minute delay was set, there was no turning back. Then, while everyone was on the fore deck waving off the military, he skinned off his shirt, took one last glance at his ship, grabbed his bag and dove into the water.

* * *

The submersible settled on a rocky shelf, popping and creaking under the pressure of tons of water. "Now, my dear, we wait for your escort," Dave said nervously. "They will pick you up and we'll be on our way."

"What's going to happen to Jaycen?" she asked in little more than a whisper.

Within a moment, a tiny plink echoed inside the hull, followed by a hiss and the acrid smell of smoke. Dave blanched. He ripped off his restraints and dived toward the sound. A small medical kit was fastened to the side of the sub. He yanked it off its base and cursed. Underneath were the remains of a small glass jar containing a tiny electrode. Water was shooting out in a fine mist into the submarine.

"Liquid nitrogen. I would have never found that. Ingenious." He was alarmingly calm. "He's broken the gasket." He nodded at Marin in approval. "Your father is really quite brilliant."

Jaycen's eyes went wide. "He broke the oxygen coupling? We have to get topside, now!" He attacked the controls of the sub, trying to push energy into the motors, but nothing responded; just the dull hum of the generator and a continued hiss coming from the wall of the sub. He grabbed some long nosed pliers and tried to tighten the bolts around the oxygen coupling, but the rubber gasket had been frozen with the liquid nitrogen and the seal shattered. He put the pliers into his shirt pocket numbly, knowing there was no way to stop the leak.

"I'm sorry, Jaycen," Dave said evenly. "I've cut the power. There is no way to restart it. It really is a pity. You were my insurance policy, but apparently, Douglas has called my bluff." Dave was beginning to look slightly hysterical.

"Look at me, you idiot!" Jaycen said, grabbing Dave by his wounded shoulder. "We will die if we don't get the engines moving!"

Dave pulled his arm back hissing in pain. "No, Jaycen. *We* won't. *You* will."

Marin grabbed the heaviest thing she could find and hit Dave across the head with it. He crumpled into his seat, moaning. Jaycen flung him out of the way in a heap and tried to get the controls to work from the pilot's seat. Nothing happened. Outside the window, a dark shape moved past. Marin caught her breath, touching the small porthole with one hand. What was that?

TWENTY-THREE

J aycen tore the sub apart, looking for anything to help them start moving again, fighting his panic as he felt his sneakers getting wet. Already the temperature was dropping alarmingly low.

Marin just watched him, cursing herself for walking so blindly into this trap, leading Jaycen, Marcos, and all the Arydians to their deaths. She had given them the coordinates willingly, trustingly, just as Dr. Gilbert ... no, *her father* had warned her not to.

The dark shape moved past her porthole again and she caught a better look at it. It paused outside, its eye coming close, like *it* was looking *in*. She shrieked in terror when she saw it. The thing charged at the window, its misshapen head resembling a shark, but it's lateral and posterior fins had fingers protruding out of them. It hit the glass, rocking the sub and increasing the mist into a spray before rebounding into the darkness.

Jaycen was yanking the control panel apart trying to hot wire the engine. "Mares, help me!" he said, grasping her hand and shoving it into a tangle of wires. "Hold this one," he said, shoving a wire into her numb fingers. He struck it with another wire and the engines coughed and died. He tried it again and again, each time the light grew dimmer. Cold water was filling the bottom of the sub.

Jaycen sat back on his heels. "He's got some stupid override hard-wired into it, cutting the power every time it catches. It's like he *wants* to die!" Jaycen said, throwing his hands down in frustration.

Marin's eyes filled with tears. "I'm so sorry, Jaycen. I'm so sorry!"

Jaycen gave one last hopeless look at the controls and then turned, sloshing through the rising water to hold her.

"This is all my fault," she cried into his shoulder.

His hands shook as he held her close to him. "It's nothing to do with you. He went crazy. It's not your fault," he said hopelessly.

"I don't want to watch you die," she said, dissolving into sobs. "This is what they planned. They want me to watch you die!"

"We're not going to die! Someone will help us. The Navy is right above us. They've gotta have subs somewhere around here."

She didn't bother to point out the odds of that were low. They had maybe half an hour left, if that. They both knew they were empty words meant to fill in the hollow of hopelessness they were in. Even if the sub could move, at the rate they were taking on water, they would drown before they got anywhere near the surface. She felt anesthetized with shock.

Another large shape swam close by, rocking the sub and knocking them both into the water pooling on the bottom.

"What *is* that thing?" Jaycen said, spluttering to take a look out the window. Another monster streaked past, this one eel-like, with long, saber fangs. A human torso stood out in relief against its grayish body and hair streamed out behind its head.

So this is the face of Leviathan, she realized. Of course they would have tried to continue their experiments. These monstrosities must be the result. There would be no escape for either of them. Jaycen turned back to the wiring, praying for a miracle.

Marin wondered where the Arydians were. Did they have any idea she had led Leviathan straight to them? She had to find a way to warn them! She pressed her face to the window, straining to see anything, willing them to hear her.

"Aggie! Marcos! They know where you are! They've found you!" she screamed mentally, willing her thoughts to travel through the glass and to the people she had endangered.

Again the ship rocked, cutting the lights for a moment, leaving them in utter blackness before they spluttered back on. Shapes flew past both ports. Jaycen pounded on the control panel in frustration.

"The engine relay is gone. Someone must have a remote access to cut power to the engines." He sank back onto his heels and dropped his head into his arms. The sub had tilted enough that the spray coming in was now underwater, filling the sub in a gentle, bubbling fountain. Marin couldn't contain the hopelessness surrounding her. For a few moments, all was silent except for the tiny fountain ticking off the moments of Jaycen's life like a water clock. She reached over and touched his shoulder. He raised his red eyes, tears streaming down his face.

"I'm sorry. I just ... thought there was going to be more time." He laughed a strange sobbing laugh. "I was going to a basketball game with Tui tomorrow. And my mom was going to come out Saturday. She got off work because she wanted to meet you."

Marin didn't know what to do but wrap her arms around him and hold him close, feeling his warmth and beating heart, his breath on her neck for the last time. She could think of no way out of this for him. And when the air was gone, they would come for her.

Jaycen held her tightly, like he was clinging onto life and they both cried, feeling the water creep slowly up their thighs. Jaycen pulled back, his hands entwined in both sides of her hair and held her face in his palms. "I'm honored to share this last moment with you."

The water was rising past her waist. All the worry and wondering if he would love her and if she should love him back dissolved as she looked into his blue eyes and realized it didn't matter anymore. "Jaycen, I love you."

He smiled sadly, pulled her close and kissed her as the water climbed relentlessly up his chest.

* * *

Douglas Franklin Gilbert swam as if his heart would burst. He glanced at the remote he held in his hands, honing in on the location of the submarine. He caught a glimpse of it settled on the top of the rocky cliff and breathed a sigh of relief which turned quickly to panic as he saw a swarm of creatures circling the sub, waiting.

* * *

"We're under attack!" Noburu relayed from the submerged entrance to the cave. Minds echoed the warning and everyone came alive in a flurry of practiced movement.

"Mum! Leviathan found us!" Aaron cried, running though the empty kitchen to the council office, slamming the door open. Aggie and Alexei were stripping the files from shelves of the nearly empty room. Aggie straightened.

"So. They have come at last. Have Malcolm and Marcos returned?"

Aaron was out of breath, his eyes wide with panic. "No! They should have been back hours ago! What if they were taken?"

Aggie walked to her son and put her hand on his shoulder, looking straight into his eyes, knowing composure often meant the difference between life and death. "You are the oldest of the youth. You must take charge and get them into the back cavern. Wait for Malcolm and Marcos. If they don't come, we must still go ahead with the plan."

Aaron was shaking, but he met his mother's eyes and dipped his head. She pulled him into her arms and held him close. "Be strong, son."

"I love you, mum," he said, trying to steel himself. He turned and ran down the hallway to the submerged tunnels in the back.

Aggie turned back to Alexei. "It's time to go."

The large Russian pursed his lips grimly, following her to join the other adults in the water at the entrance.

* * *

Jaycen shook as the cold sank into his bones. "Do you think it hurts to drown?" he asked. A sound drew his attention toward the unconscious form of Dave. The sub had slowly been rolling until it tipped almost sideways and Dave hung over his seat, his face near the roof, still moaning.

Marin ignored Dave. As she answered Jaycen, her voice caught in her throat. "No. It feels weird, but once you get over the panic, it's almost like drifting off to sleep. Everything goes dim and you just fade away." She squeezed his hand, willing there to be some other way.

Jaycen chuckled. "You say that like you know." His body shuddered. "I guess you came pretty close under Delphinius. I'm still sorry about that," he said, running a finger down the side of her face. "I never meant to hurt you."

"You didn't. It was the best thing that ever happened to me," she said meaningfully.

"Right," he laughed bitterly. "Just promise me something, Marin. If there is a fishy heaven … will you find me when we get there?" There wasn't time for her to answer. The sub was hit again and they were sent rocking until it righted itself. The air was almost gone. They pressed their faces to the roof, willing there to be more time.

She couldn't watch him die. She sank below the water and threw her arms around his chest, sobbing. He wrapped his arms around her and sank as well, holding his breath.

Movement caught her eye and she saw Dave rolling off the seat, flailing in the water. His head broke the surface and she could hear him screaming in frustration. She knew Jaycen couldn't fight his instinct to breathe for long, and he pushed his way to the top, searching for air in the diminishing gap between the water and the ceiling. She watched from below, her heart tearing in half as she heard the echoes of his sobs, reliving the terror of Davey's Cave, but knowing no salvation awaited him.

Dave dove underwater, clawing under the bottom of his chair. He found a small packet and ripped it off, tearing it open with his teeth. A tiny green pill floated out which he popped greedily into his mouth, chewing desperately. Immediately, green foam formed around his lips and spilled out into the water. Marin recoiled, thinking of movies she'd seen where the traitor took a cyanide pill to kill himself when no hope remained. She couldn't understand why Dave would want to commit suicide when he was obviously going to die within moments anyway. She held her face against Jaycen's chest, not wanting to watch. Dave started thrashing, churning up the water. And then he started changing.

* * *

Gilbert could see creatures battering the sub, impatient for their prize. He couldn't understand what they were waiting for, but he knew time was running out for Jaycen, if it hadn't already. *"Aggie! Hurry!"* he screamed. As if in answer, all around him he could suddenly feel the jumbled and angry thoughts of the monstrous creatures focus on him.

As if drawn by his thoughts, one of the creatures streaked toward him, mad with rage. It seemed like an uneven blend of manta ray and human, with a strange, pale face and human eyes staring menacingly out of the white bottom of an enormous ray. Hands and a semblance of feet hung out of the edges of its body, making it look like an enormous human bat. As it swept by Frank, he caught a glance at the creature's left hand. He stared at it, not realizing the importance of what he was seeing until it spun around to come at him again. The thing was missing its left pinky finger. His stomach contracted when he realized in an instant who these monsters were.

"It's them!" he screamed to the Arydians, projecting the horror of his image into their minds. *"It's our families!"*

The group responded with a chorus of surprised and anguished voices. How could they fight them? Their wives, husbands, and children, turned into these monsters sent to destroy or capture them.

"No!" Aggie shouted, silencing everyone. Frank could see her take up her spear, fasten it to the battery pack on her back and shove herself to the front of the group. *"Thomas is dead. Those people we loved are lost. These are beasts now, nothing more. What was left is gone. This is about survival. We must move forward in order to live."*

The group moved out from the overhang and Aggie pointed an electric rod toward the creatures, signaling the attack. It drew the attention of the creatures and they charged toward the Arydians.

Frank used the distraction to streak down to the sub.

* * *

"Marin, can you hear me?"

She shook herself. Hope surged through her heart. *"Dr. Gilbert?"*

She felt the sob of relief and joy in his voice. *"Yes! Yes, it's me! Open the hatch! I'm here to help. Is Jaycen still alive?"*

"He's dying!" she cried. *"He's drowning!"* She fought her way past Jaycen's thrashing body and grabbed the wheel on the door above her head and turned it with all her might. The wheel moved slowly, and she cursed it, pushing against the wall of the sub to give her more strength. The wheel turned completely and stopped. *"Help me!"* she cried.

"I am. Push it out!" She strained against the door, feeling the water shooting around it and filling the rest of the cabin with icy sea water. Jaycen stopped thrashing.

"Jaycen!" she cried in despair. Dr. Gilbert reached his hands under the rim of the door and pulled, heaving it open and gliding inside. He pulled a syringe out of his bag and shoved the needle into Jaycen's arm.

Marin drifted close by, crying, and holding Jaycen's cold hand.

"Come on, kid! It's not too late. You can be ok. Just take it and wake up!"

Frank pulled a slender device out of the pack on his back. It had a short rod with a cord hanging from it. He touched a button on it and a humming sound began. He touched the end of it to Jaycen's chest. His body jerked spastically. Frank shocked him again and Jaycen's hand flew up, hitting Marin in the mouth, but she didn't even notice. Frank looked up, hopeless.

"I didn't want him down here!" he mourned. *"I tried to get him out of this!"*

Marin couldn't allow herself to give up yet. *"Would mouth to mouth work down here?"* she asked.

"I don't know. It's worth a try," he said flatly.

Marin placed her lips over Jaycen's open mouth and forced water in and out of his lungs. It took a huge amount of effort to push all that volume, but she managed to push several breaths through him before she felt a flutter under her hand.

"His heart!" she exclaimed. *"Feel it!"*

"Jaycen! Come on, kid!" Dr. Gilbert cried, hope igniting. Jaycen's body took a shallow breath of water and then another and another. Marin kept her hand over his heart, willing it to become stronger.

"Jaycen! Come on! Fight for me!"

His eyes fluttered and he took a huge lungful of water and expelled it, convulsing.

"What's happening!" she cried, looking at her father in alarm.

"I don't know."

Jaycen flailed in panic, his eyes open, breathing in shallow gasps. Marin took his face in her hands and mouthed the word "Jaycen." He stared at her, wanting her to come into focus, willing her to be real.

"He's coming around! I think he's still with us!" Dr. Gilbert crowed in delight, throwing his arm around his daughter.

"Jaycen?" Marin asked. *"Can you hear me? Are you okay?"*

He blinked slowly several times and shook his head as if to clear it.

"Is this fishy heaven?" he asked.

* * *

Aaron and twelve other children gathered in the warmth of the deepest part of the cavern where he paired the other children up, oldest to youngest, so there was an older child and a younger child together. He kept the youngest, Rene, who was only six, with him. Each of the children over the age of eight had been taught how to drive a skimmer and participated in numerous drills to prepare for the possibility of a quick escape, so this was nothing new to them. This time, however, something felt different.

They could hear the calls of their parents, uncles and aunts as they gathered for battle, and fear kept them silent and watchful, like springs about to be released. News of Marin's ability to see into the minds of the others spread and everyone had been trying to see if they all possessed the gift to do the same with limited success. Images and glimpses could be caught by most of them, but they didn't last long.

All the children heard as Aggie relayed the message that the monsters coming to destroy them were their own families. Most of the children were too young to remember the loved ones people had lost to Leviathan's cruelty, but they all knew of the effects of it, losing mothers, fathers, or siblings.

Aaron and another child exchanged pained looks. He caught the glimpses through the adult's eyes of a huge squid-like being, bearing down on his mother and the others. It took all of Aaron's restraint not to rush to her side and protect her. Instead, he concentrated on the task at hand.

He grimly pulled out four heavy satchels and threw two over each shoulder then carefully checked the equipment inside every one. Each had one detonator, double protected, to be used simultaneously when the signal was given. At the base of the cavern, a huge submarine arrived, filling up the lower bay with its huge bulk.

* * *

"They're coming!" Aggie said. *"Stay close and don't let them get behind us into the bay."* Suddenly she cried out and grabbed her head, doubling over as the creatures caught her thoughts and replied with waves of tortured screams. In a moment, all the Arydians were struggling in pain against the mental onslaught the monsters were sending out to weaken them before the attack.

Noburu moved to the front of the group, wincing. *"They can hear us as well,"* he shouted to everyone over the cacophony. .

Aggie almost collapsed with despair. *"Is this what they have suffered all this time?"* she lamented. *"How can we hope to fight this? To fight them? What if they are still inside there somewhere?"* Aggie screamed in pain and frustration.

Noburu shook his head, trying to shield himself from the chaos raging within, trying to dismiss the thought of his young son tortured and twisted into a creature from a nightmare. *"We must fight the dead to save the living."*

The monsters arrived and dove at the Arydians with sharp, precise movements, coming at them from every angle. Each Arydian held a short spear attached with a wire to a battery pack on their back that would send an arc of electricity jolting through the monsters' bodies, forcing a temporary retreat, but there was no defense against the waves of mental torture. The beasts backed off just out of reach of the spears and circled their prey hungrily.

TWENTY-FOUR

Paul brushed his teeth, getting a refreshingly late start on his day off. Today was a great day to take the boat out for a little fishing. He smiled to himself, feeling rested for the first time in days. Putting his toothbrush away, he checked his phone and noticed a text from Marin.

Dave needs me on Aquanis. We're going out at 4:30 a.m. Talk to you when I get back. Love, Marin.

He put the phone down. Why on earth would they change plans so late in the game? And why choose *her* to fill in that spot? Something felt wrong about this. He slapped on his shoes and grabbed his keys, jumped into his truck and screeched out of his driveway.

He threw on his sirens as he swerved the six miles from his home to the COAST building, jumping curbs and scaring commuters. Trying not to panic, he called Dr. Gilbert over and over, but his phone wouldn't pick up. When he pulled into the parking lot, the whole place looked deceptively quiet and deserted after the chaos that had been going on for weeks. He finally found Tui in the common room making a hot dog.

"Where is everybody?" Paul demanded.

Tui looked up at him in shock. "Uh … gone? Aquanis launched today. Dr. Gilbert gave everybody the day off. I'm just here to grab some lunch. We don't have to be back until seven tonight when they get back. Did you need something?"

Paul, an average-sized man, reached out to the hulking Tui and grabbed him by the shoulders. "Why did they take Marin?" he asked, his voice icy.

Tui looked alarmed. "I'm sorry, Mr. Donnegan. I didn't know they took her. I don't know anything about it, except that they'll be back tonight."

Paul ran down to the warehouse and pulled the launch coordinates off the computer. He snatched the keys and took out a Jet Ski, gunning it toward the launch point.

* * *

Giddy with relief, Aaron saw the nose of the Arydian craft move into the water of the back cavern. Marcos and his father maneuvered the massive sub to its dock and opened the pressurized port. Aaron and the children crowded into the safe belly of the machine, all rushing forward to speak at once.

"What is happening?" demanded Marcos, looking at Aaron.

"There's a land sub, and Leviathan sent creatures to attack! They found us!" Aaron said breathlessly. "They say the creatures were made from our captured families!"

"What?" Malcom roared in disbelief from the cockpit. "How is that possible?"

"That's all I know," Aaron said helplessly.

With a look from his father, Marcos sealed the door behind them. The submarine was the only one of its kind to have ever been created, designed with the ability to fill with water and defy the pressure of the deepest sea trenches on the planet, as well as operating light when filled with oxygen. Right now it was operating light and capable of transporting the entire remaining colony of Arydians, though it would be an extremely tight fit. As soon as the airlock was secured and the water expelled, Malcolm lowered the lights and carefully backed the machine out of the rocky cliffs into the open water. Settling behind a range of volcanic stone, he turned off the engine.

"What should we do?" Marcos asked in a whisper.

Malcolm closed his eyes, trying to smash down hope that his daughter might still be alive and could somehow be saved. There was no way to save themselves from the changes occurring, let alone reverse what had happened to the poor souls warped into these hideous beasts. But he could not force his heart to obey. If his daughter lived, he had to at least try. "I must help them," he said.

"But what about the children? Are you saying we leave them?" Marcos asked anxiously. Aaron strained to hear, wanting to be asked to come along and fight.

"No. You must stay. You and Aaron can pilot. If the battle goes badly, you know what to do. For now, step outside the airlock and stay in contact, and call your friends to help us if they will. If it looks like we won't succeed, we will retreat through the back and meet you here."

Marcos nodded, signaling Aaron to move to the cockpit and take his place. Both Marcos and his father moved through the airlock, closing it securely behind them.

A wave of thoughts assailed them as they stepped outside. Tortured wails rang like sirens through the water, making them dizzy with the noise. Marcos grabbed his father's hand, amplifying his thoughts to be heard. *"Be safe, father."*

Malcolm gathered his son in a massive hug and held him for a moment. *"I will. You as well."* He released him and swam toward the fight.

Marcos summoned all his mental energy and called to dolphins and sharks alike, praying they were close enough to be heard.

* * *

Movement in the back of the sub drew Dr. Gilbert's attention. Dave began thrashing again. Chills ran up Marin's spine. Dave should be dead.

"Let's go!" Dr. Gilbert said, pushing Jaycen through the open port-hole. Waves of sound blasted them from the creatures below. Jaycen

was still disoriented and weak, and Dr. Gilbert had to work to get him through. As Dr. Gilbert reached back for Marin, the lights failed completely and she was left in utter darkness, save a dim blueness filtering in through the four windows and the open door. Something moved in the darkness, blocking the doorway. It raced toward her and she screamed.

"It's time for us to go, Marin. Our escort is waiting." Marin heard Dave's voice in her head and shuddered, unable to contain her thoughts.

"Why aren't you dead?"

He laughed, moving closer, but still blocking her way out. *"I can't drown. I'm just like you now."* He reached out and grasped her arm with claw like fingers. Something was wrong with the way they felt. They were leathery and smooth, like the skin of a shark. In one quick movement, he enveloped her in his thick deformed arms. He held her so tightly she could barely move as he wrapped something around her. She fought frantically, terror taking away all reason.

"Marin!" Frank shouted from outside the submarine. Jaycen spun back toward the sub and grabbed hold of the edge of the door as Frank tried to force his way back into the cramped vehicle. The door was blocked by a leathery back. *"No!"* Frank screamed. *"You can't have her!"* He kicked the shape, trying to break Dave's back.

"Stop!" Dave rasped, moving deeper into the sub. *"She's coming through. If you make one move, I will crack her spine."* Marin was pushed roughly through the opening, a wire taut around her waist held by a muscular webbed hand. She could barely breathe because the wire was so tight. It felt as if it had already cut through the skin around her waistline. Jaycen grasped her hand, stunned with shock and fear.

Dave pushed himself through the opening, struggling through the narrow door. Frank recoiled. Dave's face was wide and elongated with rows of sharp, pointed teeth. His nose had completely disappeared and his ears had melted into his mutated skull. His neck was gone, making his head and torso one long, muscled unit. Arms of a sort came out from his side with fins connecting his elbows to his body. Tatters of his shirt and pants still clung to him in useless rags. His back was humped and misshapen and Marin realized that beneath the remnants of his shirt was probably some form of a dorsal fin trying to emerge. All of his skin was mottled brown and grey. The first cohesive thought that came to Marin's mind was Tiger Shark.

* * *

Marcos heard her cry and his mouth went dry. "*Marin!*" he yelled, eyes scanning the water until they found the submarine perched on top of the cliff. He hesitated for only a moment, praying Aaron wouldn't need him and lunged toward the sunken craft.

He called to the dolphins again and to the sharks, but the only response he heard was the discordant shrieking of the beasts.

"*Marin?*" he asked, slowing as he neared the sub.

"*Marcos! Stay away!*" she cried. Pain and fear laced her thoughts. Behind her a creature emerged. His stomach twisted as he realized she was bound to the creature somehow. He waited, listening, looking for an opportunity, moving forward slowly. Carefully, he slid a blade out from a sheath at his waist.

* * *

Noburu commanded everyone to pull together in a tight, circular formation, poles sticking out like a puffer fish.

The creatures circled. Noburu's calculating mind observed in a detached way how difficult it was to defend oneself when the enemy can strike from any point on the plane, rather than just from your front, rear or flanks. Very much like how fighting in space would be, with a 360-degree axis. The creatures wove in and out around the ball, sometimes coming closer, testing the power of the Arydian's spears over and over again. They seemed to be waiting for something.

With a sinking feeling he realized what they were waiting for.

The power on their battery packs wouldn't last thirty minutes against use such as this. Time was not on their side.

* * *

Aaron waited silently in the dim interior of the ship. The side windows were so small they were almost useless. He felt cut off from everything and everyone except all the stupid kids on the ship. He knew protecting them was important, but why did *he* have to do the job? He was old enough to be out fighting, protecting their home and his mother instead of babysitting. At least Marcos was stuck here with him.

After several agonizing arguments with himself, he decided to open the door and at least *see* what was going on outside. He picked up the detonator bags, telling the kids to be quiet until he got back. He went through the airlock and was assaulted with screams of the ocean gone mad. He threw his hands up over his ears, but it was no use. The sounds were inside his head.

He shouted Marcos's name but Marcos was shooting away from him; away from their people, battling for their lives against a horde of living monsters, and speeding towards a small sub perched on the cliff. Aaron paused for a moment of indecision before darting towards the melee.

* * *

Jaycen looked like he was in a living nightmare. Through her haze and pain, Marin could see him struggling to understand the situation he had awoken from the dead to find himself in; deep in the middle of some other world war with unimaginable creatures evolving around them.

He shook his head as if to wake himself, but then looked into Marin's eyes. She squeezed his hand, wincing as she did. His eyes hardened and he gave her hand a small squeeze back

Dave's thoughts grated on their brains. *"Don't try anything, any of you. I am more powerful than you could ever dream. I'm not going to kill her, but she will be coming with me. You can either live with that or die with that, but it won't change anything. Move away."*

Marin released the pressure on Jaycen's hand but he wouldn't let go. Instead, he took the long-nosed pliers out of his pocket in one smooth movement and stabbed them into the hand Dave was using to hold the wire. Dave roared in pain, jerking his arm, pliers embedded in the back of his webbed hand and slamming Jaycen into the side of Aquanis. Frank snatched Marin and started swimming toward Marcos as fast as he could. Marcos shot toward them, knife ready to defend her.

Dave ripped the pliers from his hand and kicked his powerful fins, covering the distance to Marin in seconds, before they even reached Marcos. Dave growled savagely and snatched her up in his jaws, biting into her abdomen. She shrieked in agony as his jagged teeth sank into her skin, not enough to puncture her organs, but enough to lock her in place. In shock and anguish she struggled to maintain consciousness against the pain. Frank stopped short as Marin was ripped from his grasp, crying out in despair. Marcos breached the distance, slashing his knife in Dave's face.

"Stay away. Her life is mine, now," Dave snarled.

"You will not leave here with her," Frank hissed at him. *"We would rather see her dead than with you. I will not give her to you to be tortured like her mother. You will never get the secret to Arydia."*

"Fool! We knew you were a traitor, pretending to us all this time to search for the secret to trade for her life back. We have been watching everything. You can be assured you will never get her back now. We have no further need of her or of you. We have your daughter. The secret lies in her blood."

TWENTY-FIVE

"*Conserve your batteries,*" Noburu said calmly. Aggie nodded, trying hard to think of a way out of this. She felt her heart begin to pound, feeling unspoken energy moving through the water. Soon they were going to make their move.

A huge squid-like creature swam slowly in front of Aggie, its human eyes meeting hers, mangled arms mingled with tentacles reaching for her. The pain in his face was unbearable.

"*Thomas?*" she cried in disbelief, letting the tip of her pole drop.

The creature jerked in mental pain, his face changing to a mask of tortured rage and lunged for her before she could raise her spear, snatching her out of the group. Her agonizing scream was cut off as it broke her in two.

* * *

Aaron cried out in anguish as he watched his mother's body drift to the bottom of the sea, her dying cry echoing in his mind.

The creatures raced in for the kill.

* * *

Jaycen shook his head, feeling nauseous. He was lying across the back of Aquanis. Twenty feet away, Marin was dangling from the mouth of the beast he had once known as Dave. He reached into the hull of Aquanis and pulled out a pry bar and swam behind him, murder in his heart. Marin twitched in the monster's mouth, blood pooling around his teeth. Marcos reached out a hand to touch her.

"Don't!" Dave snapped into their minds, jerking her away. He sucked in a mouthful of water around her bleeding body. *"My friends here will take care of you. Goodbye, Douglas."* He turned to the waiting beasts. *"Kill them."*

And then he began to shudder. His head started shaking, his body convulsing. He spat out Marin and grabbed his face in pain. Marcos and Frank caught Marin's hand as she fell. Jaycen swam to her and helped them support her. Suddenly Dave's eyes opened wide when he realized what he'd done.

"Her blood!" He shrieked, spitting out what was left in his mouth. It was too late. It was starting to heal him, changing his cells to what they once were. His fingers emerged from the rubbery flesh surrounding them and his face became smaller. He screamed, but the words drifted into nothingness as he lost the ability to communicate. The leathery covering of his body became soft and unprotected. He writhed in panic as his lungs no longer accepted the oxygen from the water. His body convulsed, shutting down under the pressure of the water as he was quickly healed to death. The two creatures circled his body uncertainly, their twisted minds trying to process what they were seeing.

Frank, Marcos and Jaycen watched, holding Marin as Dave sank into the depths below the cliff. Shocked, it took them all a minute to realize the significance of Dave's death. Frank shouted to the others.

"Lure them into the cavern and trap them! They'll need air soon! I think they can be healed!"

Marcos, the strongest swimmer of the group took Marin's hands over his shoulders. *"Can you hang on to me?"*

Marin's breath was coming in ragged gasps but she opened her eyes slightly and nodded. Her wounds were still bleeding profusely.

"Don't touch her blood!" Frank cautioned. *"Don't breathe in any water*

that's been tainted. I'm not sure if it affects us yet. Marcos, try to make contact with them. Give them hope!"

Jaycen followed, staying out of the wake of pink water trailing behind them and tried to make sense of it all. Marin really was, for all intents and purposes, a mermaid. And here he was, living and breathing underwater as well. Suddenly everything she said to him and the strange way she always acted made sense. Was it only this that had kept them apart? It broke his heart to think how things could've been different if he had only known. Watching her fading in and out of consciousness, he wondered if he would ever get the chance to tell her that none of this would have changed how he felt.

* * *

Marcos pushed his thoughts out to the chaos in the water around him. The creature that killed Aggie was reaching in past their defenses and pulled two more people out, breaking them like discarded toys. Noburu was shooting bursts of electricity into the water behind them, covering the Arydians as they backed into the cavern and scrambled out of the water.

"Seal the bay once they are in!" he cried. Soon the water in the bay was full and the surface boiled with the thrashing monsters, clambering to reach them. Alexi turned a wheel on the wall and a grinding door of stainless steel slid shut, trapping everything inside.

Frank, Jaycen and Marcos had to drag Marin the long way around Portus since the main cavern was sealed, maneuvering as quickly as possible to the hidden entrance in the back, close to where the Arydian submarine was concealed. Once inside, they swam the labyrinth of convoluted passages through the back side of Portus. Finally they hit a dead end in a large, partially submerged cavern, and pulled Marin's limp body up steel rungs that were pitted and dripping with moisture. Once out of the water, Frank raced through the corridors, through the living area to the bay, where the surviving Arydians were crowded around a pool of ghastly creatures.

"Make room! Get a medic kit now!" he yelled, forcing his way to the edge of the bay. A moment later, Jaycen and Marcos pushed their way through, amid gasps of alarm. Marin's unconscious body was drenched in blood.

"Bring her over here where the floor tilts downward," Frank commanded. They carried her gently and laid her down on the rocky floor, her blood pooling around her and merging into a rivulet that poured into the waters of the sealed bay.

"You're not going to let her bleed to death, are you?" demanded Jaycen.

Noburu appeared with a medic kit and Frank snatched it from his hands. "Of course not." He elbowed Jaycen aside and pulled Marin's shirt up over her waist. Her stomach was a bloody mess. "But if her blood can change these creatures back into the people we love, I'm going to use it. Get me fresh water!" He winced as he tried to assess the damage. Someone brought a pitcher of clean water, which he poured over her wounds, increasing the flow of red fluid pouring into the bay. The razor teeth marks were spaced evenly around her middle, like a gory belt. He touched one wound, watching the blood puddle around his finger. "She should be starting to heal already!" he said, his voice laced with concern. He started patching up the wounds with gauze and tape, folding whatever skin he could find back over the wounds.

Noburu moved over to him and leaned down to say in a quiet voice, "I'm sorry. You may not know, but we lost Aggie."

Frank glanced up at his longtime friend, and let out a heavy sigh at the loss of his sister-in-law. He shook his head, biting the inside of his cheek. Noburu put his arm around him.

"We will all miss her. She was a good leader and friend." Frank wiped his eyes with the back of his hand, nodded, and went back to work on his mutilated daughter.

"Look!" Alexei cried, pointing at the water. The surface was foaming with movement. A human head rose up out of the water's edge and uttered a garbled moan. Tania and several others reached into the water and pulled out a man with black hair, plastered to his wet head.

"Kazu?" Noburu raced to his side, staring at the man in disbelief, trying to find the child he lost in the face of this man older than twenty. The young man shook his head in confusion, heaving salt water out of his lungs. He fell to his knees, retching.

The Arydians pressed forward as another head appeared, and another. Four, then seven more humans were pulled from the pool and given towels to cover themselves. They expelled water from their lungs, their loved ones gathering and trying to identify them. The remaining creatures swarmed like sharks around the blood in the water, clawing each other to swallow a dose of the healing elixir. One by one, transformed to one degree or another, they were pulled onto the shore.

Frank wrapped Marin's abdomen to stem the bleeding, while Marcos and Jaycen knelt around her still body, willing her to live. Malcolm made his way to the circle and found Marcos.

"Why are you here?" he hissed in anger. Marcos looked up at him in surprise. "You left the children alone?" he continued in disbelief, his voice rising, drawing the attention of those around him. Marcos's face blanched. "Go to them! Now! Bring the sub!"

Marcos looked down at Marin's pale form sadly and let her hand fall to her side. Then he stood and ran back down the corridor. Jaycen took up her hand and held it close. "What can we do?" he asked Frank.

Gilbert laid his head against her chest, listening for a heartbeat. For a moment his breath caught, not hearing anything, but then a faint whisper of a flutter let him breathe again. "She's lost a lot of blood. She needs to get some or her heart will fail." He glanced up at Jaycen. "You've had the hormone I derived from her blood. Nobody else has the same genetic makeup. What's your blood type?"

"O positive."

Gilbert set his mouth in a straight line. "You'll do. Lay down."

* * *

The Jet Ski flew through restricted waters and into the middle of a maelstrom of activity. Three U.S. Navy cruisers surrounded the Star Chaser and smaller boats were moving between the vessels. Paul pulled his Jet Ski next to the Star Chaser and climbed aboard. A Navy captain was in hot discussions with the captain of the Star Chaser, Captain Jack Cunningham. Paul pushed his way into the discussion.

"What happened?" he demanded of Cunningham.

"We've lost contact with Aquanis," he stated flatly. Paul's heart caught in his throat. Cunningham introduced Paul to the Naval Officer. "This is Paul Donnegan, an employee of COAST," he said briskly.

The Naval officer sniffed. "This isn't something we need to involve extra civilians in." He turned to Paul. "I hope you understand. This situation could quickly get out of hand."

Paul straightened and glared into the man's eyes. "I'm also Retired Commander Paul Donnegan, Navy SEAL, and a member of the California Department of Search and Rescue. And my daughter is on that sub!"

The officer took a physical step back and all authority drained from his face. "I'm so sorry, sir! I-I had no idea."

Paul held his glare for a moment longer then turned to Cunningham. "Let me hear their last transmission." They turned and moved into the cabin to replay the last communication between Star Chaser and Aquanis.

* * *

When Marcos reached the sub, Aaron was nowhere to be seen. He went inside to find the children in hysterics. "Where's Aaron?" he demanded. Nobody knew anything except he'd gone outside and hadn't come back.

Marcos went back out through the airlock, calling for Aaron, but he didn't respond. He didn't want to think about what might have happened to his young friend. After a few minutes spent looking for him, Marcos returned, took the helm of the ship and guided it into the belly of Lower Bay and turned off the engine. He reassured the children that the fighting was over.

"You must stay here. The others will be coming to the sub soon. If you see Aaron, send him to the work room." He left the ship and raced back, praying Marin was still alive.

* * *

The water became still as the majority of the creatures were pulled out of it. Malcolm cried out as he saw a young woman lying face down in the water, her long black hair spread out around her, her body partly changed. He dove in, despite the shouts of disapproval and grasped her, swimming back to the shore with one arm. Other bodies bobbed to the surface in varying degrees of change, and others dove in to rescue them.

Some of the survivors were strangers, unfortunate people who crossed Leviathan in one form or another and were absorbed for experimentation.

The creature—now a man—that had killed Aggie sat sobbing, his feet hanging off the ledge. Alexei squatted down and put a hand on his shoulder. "Thomas?" The man nodded, covering his face with his hands, shoulders shaking. Alexei sighed, not knowing how to comfort him. "It wasn't your fault-what happened to Aggie."

The man looked back with hollow eyes. "Not my fault? I killed her!"

Alexei sat down beside him, not knowing what to say.

"You don't know what it is like, hearing them inside your head every moment of every day! They can make you do things so the pain will stop, but the pain never stops. Not completely. They made me *kill* her." He looked at his hands in disgust.

"Don't hate yourself. Hate Leviathan. You were not in control. You must let it go and think ahead. Aggie was raising a young boy, now he's alone. You can help him!"

Thomas glared up at Alexei, his voice rough from years of unuse. "I can never be free of what I've done. Do you know what it feels like to hold your wife in your hands and destroy her? I will *never* be free from this." He looked at Alexei, haunted. "What kind of father could I be to the boy? I killed her. In front of him! I know he saw her die! I heard his cries!" Thomas stood, an insane look in his eyes.

"No, Thomas. There is more to life than this tragedy," Alexei said fearfully.

"There is only one chance I have to escape this." He choked in sobs and nodded to himself. He looked at Alexei for a long moment. "Tell the boy I never made it back." He raced to the wall, grunting as he hefted a double load of dive weights and dove into the water before Alexei could react.

"Stop him!" Alexei cried, diving into the water after him, but it was too late. Thomas sank like a stone out of Alexei's reach. The cave bay was deep and the pressure crushed the air out of Thomas before he ever reached the bottom. A funnel of bubbles, the last of his breath, broke the surface.

* * *

Outside the sealed doors of the bay, one solitary monster felt his mental control slipping. The creatures were no longer listening to his commands—they were changing! He cursed as his army was reduced one after another to nothing, falling into the welcoming arms of his enemies. It was impossible! His features were partially hidden within a fishlike face, but there was rage flaming in his eyes as he resolved to use his final weapon. Mr. Hahn raced back to his waiting submarine.

TWENTY-SIX

Marin sat up, feeling queasy. She was wet and her body ached all over, particularly her stomach and back. It was dark, but the open door was letting in some light. Her muscles and the skin around her waist felt raw. She lifted her head and saw her shirt was torn and bloody around the hem. An IV was attached to her arm, and she followed it to Jaycen, who was lying on his back asleep on the cool floor in a puddle of pink tinged water. Jaycen, resurrected like herself, and now unable to drown ever again. She felt so grateful to her father she thought she could cry.

She wondered what Jaycen would think of all this. Watching his face, relaxed in sleep, his blonde hair still damp from sea water, she let herself wonder what it would be like, now that he knew. Better than just knowing, he was part of her world now.

She didn't have long to ponder; somebody shouted out in the bay and Jaycen startled awake.

"Marin!" he said, sitting up. "Are you ok?"

She nodded, slightly lifting her shirt to show him a zigzag of pink but healing wounds around her waist. "Are you?"

"Yeah." He seemed to be bubbling over with things to say, but instead exhaled and just scooted closer to put his arms around her. "Why didn't you just tell me?" he said softly into her hair.

"Because it's crazy. You wouldn't have believed me," she replied.

He backed up and leaned against the wall. "Yeah. Crazy." He rubbed his face with both his hands and winced as he kinked the arm with the IV in it. He smiled mischievously. "Does this make us blood brothers or something?"

Marin glanced down at the tube. "Thanks. For saving me." She looked up and smiled at him.

"Hey, anytime. I was just returning the favor."

"Technically, that was my ... um ... Dr. Gilbert. But I helped."

"So, he's your dad?" he asked.

Marin nodded thoughtfully. "It's weird, but now that I know, it just makes so much sense. I'm really surprised I never wondered about it before. I mean, he's been around me pretty much all my life. But I never thought of him as anything but Paul's boss."

"So, what will Paul think of all this?" he asked. "You don't have to answer if I'm being too nosy."

Marin shrugged. "I don't know. He'll probably be sad. But he likes Gilbert. Maybe he'll be ok with it." She furrowed her brow. "I wonder if they'll change him, too. I bet he'd like that."

"Yeah, you're probably right," Jaycen agreed. "I guess that means your real name was supposed to be Marin Gilbert. Weird."

"Well, actually, it was supposed to be Amanda Gilbert. But that's a long story." She stretched, wondering if she could take the IV out of her arm by herself, but she decided it would be better to let someone with experience do it. "So, what do you think your mom will say when she finds out her son has joined the fishy club?"

Jaycen leaned his head back and sighed. "I don't know. I really don't even know how to tell her." He turned and laughed at Marin. "She'll probably think I'm crazy and won't believe me."

"Yeah, I know the feeling," she chuckled back, and then grew serious. "Jaycen. People know you and I came down in Aquanis. I don't know how we can go back. Leviathan won't give up. They'll be looking."

"What's Leviathan, anyway? Is that what Dave was?"

Marcos appeared in the doorway, blocking out the light. "Leviathan is a faction of revolutionaries. Terrorists. They are the reason Arydia was created." Marcos knelt down next to Marin and peeled the tape off the inside of her elbow, pulling the tubing out and placing a cotton ball over it. He bent her arm for her, holding it. His hands felt hot.

Marin tried not to notice how beautiful he was as he crouched down so close to her, speaking to her with his eyes. Marin flushed awkwardly. "Keep it like this for a few minutes to stop the bleeding." He kept hold of her arm. Jaycen cleared his throat and Marin looked away, suddenly interested in the pattern of the floor.

"So, can I just yank this out? Or were you planning on doing that?" Jaycen asked shortly. Marcos moved toward him and peeled off the tape, jerking the tubing out. He handed him the cotton ball. Jaycen scowled and covered up the spot of blood welling out of his forearm. "Thanks," he said dryly.

"She's right. Leviathan will find you if you go back up top. Maybe they will kill you, maybe not. They will certainly kill anyone else that matters to you."

"So, what are you then? *Not* Leviathan?" Jaycen asked him.

Malcom walked by the door and Marcos sighed. "I must go back to the sub." He brushed past Frank on the way out.

Frank smiled at Marin and sat down on the floor next to her. "We are Arydians. Leviathan paid for the development of the chemical, Arydia, which they wanted to use to give them power to inhabit the water and control it, and through it, the world. We created Arydia, and then tried to destroy Leviathan and all their research to stop them."

"So, how do you explain those creatures?" Jaycen asked accusingly.

"Leviathan had the beginnings of the research. And they had Marin's mother, who is the only one who knew the entire formulation."

Marin gasped and covered her mouth. Frank put his hand on her arm. "The day our houseboat was destroyed was the day she was taken. We were one of two families that hadn't gone under when Leviathan was destroyed. The other was Marcos's family. His father, Malcolm, and his cousin sold the sapphires we mined to help finance Portus and pay for the materials we needed to stay alive. The money from the sale of sapphires was kept in small accounts up and down the North American coast. Your mother and I lived on a boat, making deposits and withdrawals, buying supplies, and delivering them to Portus. It was a good system."

"How did they find us?" Marin asked slowly.

Frank shifted. "Leviathan found out about the sapphires from Malcolm's cousin who couldn't keep his mouth shut." He scowled bitterly. "By this time Marcos had already lost his little sister and mother. They were travelling all over the world to spread out the distribution of the gems, only selling the irregular and unimpressive ones. Still, Leviathan noticed the deposits and formulated a plan to capture us.

"It was our fault, too. Your mom and I stayed too long in one place. It had been a while since we had seen any sign of Leviathan and we let our guard down. Plus, we'd had a baby."

Marin realized he was talking about her. She pictured her parents living a life where they were always moving, always hiding. It made her sad. She could vaguely remember being on the boat. She had a fuzzy memory of wishing she could have a swing set like she'd seen on their little television.

Frank continued. "As soon as Leviathan found us, they acted immediately before we could move again. They had divers stationed at the mouth of the bay with nets. They had tied a man to the helm of a boat, controlled it remotely, and crashed it into the back of our boat, killing the man, who was Malcolm's cousin. They knew we'd swim to safety and Leviathan was ready for us. The primary target was your mother, Emily." His voice caught and he paused, spinning the ring on his left hand absently.

"When the explosion hit, your mom was thrown overboard. She was hurt, but not badly, so I told her to run and I went back for you. They caught her almost immediately. I heard her screaming while I tried to get to you through the bottom of the boat." His voice shook. Marin leaned her head against his shoulder, waiting until he could continue.

"I could barely touch you. I didn't know if you were alive or dead. A rescue diver appeared next to me and I pushed his hand in through the broken hull to touch you. I had to make a choice."

He looked into her eyes through the tears. "I'm sorry, Marin." He whispered. "I left you. I went to find your mother and left you to the rescuers. And when I got to your mother, they captured me as well. The only thing I could pray for was that you were alive and that they would never figure out who you were." He sighed heavily. "It worked. They were so focused on us that they never gave you a second thought. Neither of us breathed a word to them about your existence and you were free of this awful legacy. I stayed away from you, stayed away from the Arydians. But I couldn't make myself stay completely out of your life. It was selfish of me, I know." He cleared his throat, and brushed his eyes with the back of his hand.

"Your mother would never tell them the compound and I didn't know it. No matter what they did to her, she would not betray you, the secret of Arydia, or the location of Portus. Eventually I was sent back to COAST, charged with devising a new variation of the Arydia. Instead, I spent my time working on bogus compounds of Arydia, while secretly trying to find a cure for it. Your mother was kept hostage, underwater at Leviathan headquarters, to give me incentive to keep moving forward. They had a new team they were using to replicate the compound at Leviathan, and they had your mother's DNA. But, though they tried, they never could find the secret. The creatures we witnessed were the results of the experiments of their version of the serum. We had thought they had been killed, but Leviathan used the people we loved, even the children, as guinea pigs for their vile experiments." He shook his head sadly. "Your mother was the bravest woman I have ever known."

Marin sat silent for a long moment, digesting the horror of her family's history. She wanted to know what happened to her mother, but couldn't bring herself to ask.

He turned and tentatively reached out to brush the hair back from her cheek. "Amanda," he said, his voice choking with emotion. "My little Manders."

Marin's eyes filled with tears. Something in that nickname brought her back to sitting on the shore as a tiny girl, holding a fishing rod in her hands, her father sitting beside her, his dark hair wild with the breeze.

"Daddy?" she said, trying it out for size. Frank's tears broke free and ran down his face. He put his arms around her and pulled her close, sobbing into her hair. She cried, too, for all the lost years and sadness.

"I'm sorry I ever left you," he said, holding her tightly. "Can you forgive me?"

She nodded, pulling back and wiping the tears with the back of her hand. "If you hadn't, they would have gotten me, too," she said, smiling sadly. He nodded.

"I know. But not a day goes by that I don't think of some way I could have made it turn out differently."

"It's okay," she said, thinking how she would have never known Paul, never even lived on land or gone to high school. Perhaps she would have spent her life as a prisoner like her mother, tortured, or changed. She shuddered at the thought. "It's okay," she whispered again.

Someone walked in and flicked on the light, making them all wince. Frank looked up in surprise.

"Ahsan!" he crowed, standing up and embracing his long lost friend. The man looked shaky, ill, and thin, his shoulders wrapped in a woolen blanket. He smiled vaguely. "Amanda, this is Ahsan. He is one of the founding scientists from AQUA. He and Malcolm designed and built this place. We thought he had been killed when we burned Leviathan."

The man nodded weakly. He cleared his throat several times before he could make sound come out of it. When he did speak, it was gravelly and rough and no more than a whisper.

"They are coming."

Frank's face went white. "When? How?" he said. He stepped outside and yelled without waiting for an answer. "Get everyone to the sub. Now!" he said.

"They are close," Ahsan wheezed.

* * *

Paul stood on the deck of the Star Chaser, watching people moving around him like busy ants. He knew there was nothing anyone could do but wait. He also knew, deep in his heart, that Aquanis would never rise again. He listened with mild curiosity as people passed him, deep in the drama and anxiety of not knowing. A louder buzz started to fill in the conversations around him and he heard the words "Dr. Gilbert missing" and turned to hear more. Could Gilbert be one of the people Marin had said was responsible for this whole mess? In the recording, it definitely sounded like he had been threatening Dave. Paul had worked with both Dave and Dr. Gilbert for years. He couldn't imagine either one of them wanting to hurt his daughter or sabotage a mission.

* * *

The Arydians pushed into the sub, moving in through its stainless steel hull and trying to find a place in the severely overcrowded craft. Marcos caught sight of Frank and wove his way through to touch his shoulder.

"I can't find Aaron," Marcos said. Frank frowned and Marcos continued grimly, "He has the detonators."

Frank let out a frustrated breath. "We don't have time for this," he said, stress making the veins in his neck stand out. He pointed to Malcolm and Noburu. "We need help. Aaron is missing and he has the detonators." Both men moved out of the sub and dropped into the water. Frank turned to Marcos. "You have maybe five minutes. Do you think you can find him?" Marcos nodded and slipped through the throng of people. He walked over to jump into the water to call to him but stopped and rushed back inside the sub and found Marin standing in the back near Jaycen, talking.

He fought down the rage of jealousy that possessed him. He wanted to hate Jaycen; part of him truly did, for being there, for loving the girl he loved, for moving in, even to this world that had been his own. He had killed any hope Marcos had of happiness. But he couldn't give in to that hate now. He walked up to her and touched her hand.

"I need your help. I have to find Aaron. Can you come with me to help see through his eyes where he is?"

Marin nodded, following him before Jaycen had a chance to object. They moved quickly through the crowd and into the bay, jumping into the water hand in hand. Marcos tried to shield his feelings from her; he couldn't afford to distract her from their task, but he could tell she could still feel the waves of anger and hurt buried deep below the worry and immediate responsibility weighing on his shoulders. When they were deep inside the tunnels, he stopped and turned to her.

"Can you hear him?" he asked desperately. He knew she didn't know Aaron very well, and wasn't sure how to contact him, but he closed his eyes and tried to project images of Aaron clearly into her mind.

"I can't sense him anywhere," she cried in despair. *"No, wait!"* He could see she had caught his trail. She kept hold of Marco's thoughts as if she were holding his hand, following the connection and bringing him along with her until they were touching Aaron. They looked down through his eyes and saw blood on his hands from a cut on his palm. They could even feel the pain, but it was nothing compared to the agony within. Marin must have felt it more intensely. She doubled over with reflected anguish, holding her stomach to keep from throwing up as they felt him reliving the horror of his mother's death replayed over and over in his mind. Gasping, she pulled them both away and slammed down mental walls to stop the torture, bringing them back to the darkened tunnel.

"Could you tell where he is?"

He shook his head, shaky with the intensity of Aaron's emotions still pounding in his veins.

"Aggie's been killed! Does anybody know?" she asked weakly.

Marcos nodded gravely, and then pushed the tragedy to the back of his mind, refocusing on the present. *"I couldn't see as clearly as you. Do you have any idea where he is?"*

She shrugged helplessly. *"I can see it, but I don't know where it is. Couldn't you see it by touching me?"*

"Not clearly enough." Marcos frowned. He took her face in his hands and kissed her, pushing into her mind, searching for Aaron in her thoughts. When he found what he was looking for, he pulled away, leaving her breathless. He touched her face sadly.

"I'm sorry," he said softly, and turned to race down the corridors to a secluded cave at the dead end of a narrow tunnel. She followed silently behind him.

Aaron was drifting in the darkness when Marcos and Marin arrived, the four detonator bags hung over his shoulder.

"Aaron," Marcos said calmly. Aaron didn't respond. *"Aaron, I'm sorry. We all loved your mother. Nobody wanted this to happen."* Aaron didn't move.

Slowly, Aaron's eyes focused on Marcos. *"You!"* he hissed. *"It's your fault! You could have saved her!"*

Marcos inched closer. *"I'm so sorry, Aaron. I don't blame you for hating me. But, we have to leave. Now. Leviathan is coming!"*

"I watched you. You went right by her and chased after your stupid girlfriend instead." He turned his eyes to Marin, boiling with hate. *"None of this would have happened if you hadn't come here!"*

Marin backed away from his gaze. The water around him seemed to radiate his pain and rage. He rose from the back of the cave and shot toward her like a coiled snake. Marcos saw the glint of a blade in his hand, and knew she wouldn't react in time. Marcos dove between them, pushing her against the wall. Aaron plunged the knife deep into Marcos's belly. Marin screamed, catching Marcos as he curled in pain, the water turning red with blood.

Aaron fell back, horrified at what he'd done. *"I didn't mean to!"* he stammered. *"I didn't mean it, Marcos!"*

"Get the bags Marin!" Marcos gasped. He held the knife tightly, folded over it in agony. She moved to take the knife out, but he stopped her. *"No! It will bleed more. Just get the bags! Now!"*

She reached over to Aaron. He flinched like he expected to be hit, but she only yanked the bags off from around his neck and threw them over her shoulder.

"Help me get him to the sub!" she barked, her voice full of panic and anger.

Aaron hesitated, gulping down sobs, and moved to take Marcos's legs. Marin put one arm around Marcos's chest and began swimming back toward the sub. He fought to keep conscious as he heard her scream out in her mind for help, her voice scared and full of despair. Noburu found them and took over for Aaron, who followed, crying silently.

* * *

By the time they reached the sub, Marcos was breathing in ragged gasps. Marin willed his heart to keep pumping; fearing each gap between heartbeats would be the pause that never ended. Malcolm appeared at the edge of the bay and cried out when he saw his son, pale and bleeding to death. Aaron shrank back, but Noburu pushed him forward and onto the shore. They pushed the water out of their lungs and struggled to carry Marcos inside the sub. Aaron disappeared into the back of the sub, hiding from the accusing gazes.

"Make room!" Malcolm's booming voice pushed people back. They laid Marcos down between dozens of pairs of feet.

"Leave him to us." Noburu said to Malcolm calmly. "There is nothing you can do for him. But you must get the rest out of here. Now."

Malcolm caressed his son's damp forehead and nodded, moving toward the front of the huge craft. The engines started with a heavy thrum and people swayed as the sub turned to the open mouth of the cavern.

Marin knelt by Marcos's side. She had only seen wounds like his in movies. She was terrified for him.

"Marcos?" she whispered. He didn't respond. The knife still plugged the wound, but blood ran down his bare stomach covering the floor around him. "Please don't die. Please hang on to me," she cried, holding tight to his hand, pushing his cold fingers onto hers with her other hand. He started shaking.

Frank Gilbert pushed his way to them and dropped to the floor, bustling feet around him. Marin looked at her father's face and was filled with despair when she saw him assess the wound. He shook his head.

"He can't die. He can't. He was trying to save me," her voice cracked with despair.

Marcos was breathing heavily, his dark curls hung damp against his forehead. He didn't respond to the touch of Dr. Gilbert's probing fingers. Frank frowned grimly.

"We have to get the knife out. He's ripped up inside. He needs surgery to stop the bleeding." He shrugged helplessly. "Hold him," he directed. Marin positioned herself over Marcos's shoulders and held him down while her father dug out several wads of gauze from his bag, and holding his breath, withdrew the knife. Marcos shuddered in pain, but didn't make a sound. Blood gushed from the wound and pooled around him. Frank pressed the gauze against the wound, slowing the flow. The knife fell, clattering, to the floor.

Jaycen appeared through the throng of people and knelt hesitantly by Marcos's side. Marin glanced at him briefly and turned her attention back to Marcos's pale face. Even in the dim light and in all his pain, his beautiful Greek features were breathless. She held his bare shoulders, feeling the strong muscles and not believing that they could ever stop moving. She closed her eyes against the memory of holding him deep in his hidden ship, wanting her to understand him. Marcos's whole life felt like a succession of tragedies, and now to die like this, for no reason but the irrational anger of a heartbroken teenager, seemed absurd. Tears raced down her cheeks and dropped to his face. Frank held the gauze tight against the wound and looked at Marin helplessly.

Suddenly Marin opened her eyes in determination. Before she could think or change her mind, she snatched the bloody knife off the deck and sliced it along her forearm. Frank recoiled with a gasp and she pushed her father aside letting the blood run onto his stomach, mingling with the blood still coming from his wound.

"It won't work. The damage is on the inside," Frank said quietly.

"Then put my blood on the *inside* of him, like you did with me and him!" she demanded, pointing accusingly at Jaycen.

Frank shook his head. "You're not even his same blood type. It will just make you sick and won't help him at all."

"You don't know that! Look at him! He will die if we don't try. Just do it! Quickly!" she cried.

Frank looked at his daughter and shook his head, but took out the IV kit from his bag. Jaycen took a pad of gauze and pressed it against the gash in her arm, wrapping it with tape. Within moments Frank had the tube and the pump hooked up to his daughter and Marcos. People tried to move out of the way the best they could while watching everything in shock. He took out a needle and silk and tried to stitch up the wound to stop the bleeding.

"I just pray that by some miracle you have enough left of whatever magic you hold inside you to heal this boy." Frank said, his grim look silently reminding her that a portion of her blood had recently come from Jaycen. It would probably diminish whatever effect she hoped to have on Marcos. She closed her eyes and added her prayer to his.

TWENTY-SEVEN

In the pilot seat, Malcolm drove steadily, trying not to think about his son bleeding to death a few feet away. Instead, he concentrated on moving them quickly away from Portus, keeping his eye trained on the water for the sub that Ahsan claimed was bearing down on them. He heard movement and saw Ahsan easing himself into the co-pilot's seat. Ahsan looked at him questioningly and Malcolm nodded, so he relaxed as he sat down. Malcolm couldn't help but notice how pale his friend looked, his dark Arabian skin still leathery and somewhat shark-like.

"How are you feeling?" he asked, still watching the sea carefully.

Ahsan swallowed, easing his voice back into use. "It is good to breathe." He smiled weakly. "It has been a long time."

"You've been underwater this entire time?" Malcolm asked in disbelief, morbidly curious.

Ahsan nodded. "They needed to test out each variation of their method. We were logical choices. I was among the last, though it didn't do what they planned since I had already been changed with Arydia." He shuddered. "I was kept in a cage no larger than a closet for eleven years, fed on scraps from the world above. Me and all the others. They are not content to simply make an army; they want to control it, body and mind." He pulled the blanket tighter around his shoulders. "They tried everything they could think of to bring our minds under control." His face hardened as he spoke. "They found the means when they realized we could speak to one another. They used ultrasonic frequencies to force

261

thoughts into our minds. Then something changed. Hahn found something that could mimic the effects of Arydia. It is different from Arydia, but has some similar properties. I worry they must've broken through on some level." Ahsan shuddered again, his voice raspy and tired.

Malcolm frowned dismally.

"Where do you think their sub will be about now?" Malcolm asked.

"It will be close enough. I hope it hurts," he said bitterly.

Malcolm reached under his seat and took out the brown bags he had taken from Marin. His son's blood was splattered on the brown canvas. "Will you do the honors?"

Ahsan looked at the detonators inside and sighed. "All that work," he said regretfully.

Malcolm nodded. "It was always part of the plan. You know that more than anyone."

Ahsan tilted his head in agreement and pushed four buttons at once.

* * *

Paul stood at the bow of Star Chaser, watching the waves below him. The Navy had nothing to offer to help rescue the Aquanis. They re-routed a sub on patrol, but it was still miles away. It was two hours since they lost contact and the sun was getting high in the summer sky. The crew was silent and in shock. All their work and planning and three crew members just sank into the sea like a rock, never to see the sun again. And Dr. Gilbert vanishing into who knows where—it was too hard to believe.

They clung to hope that their rational minds knew was ill-founded. Oxygen would have run out over an hour ago. Nobody could have risen through the pressure. There was no scenario anyone could provide that ended with survival for the explorers below, or explained how Dr. Gilbert vanished. So they kept a silent vigil in a huddle with two Navy ships, waiting for the Navy sub to show up, or something to float to the surface to signal the end.

Suddenly, Paul felt a concussion deep in his chest. A sound? A feeling? He gripped the railing and stared at the water below. The sea fell still as glass and then started trembling. He could vaguely hear the scream of sea birds along the coast, taking off in unison and streaking away in panic. Something was coming. The vibration was getting stronger. Waves jumped in choppy peaks, irregular, ignoring the pull of the tide. The air was filled with a growling that sounded like thunder, deep and massive and coming from everywhere, though the sky was clear and calm.

His hands turned white as he heard the ships start blaring alarms and with a detached part of his brain he wondered what good it could do. It didn't appear there was anywhere to run.

The engine of the Star Chaser roared to life under his feet and backed away from the cluster of ships. The two Naval cruisers started to move away as well. Shaking like a lid on a boiling pot, the boat deck rattled beneath him. He held tightly to keep his footing, watching the unnatural movement of the ocean below. He saw bubbles rising to the surface off the port bow several meters away, followed by a mass of swirling pale blue, like an enormous balloon in the greenish water.

"Here it comes," he said aloud to no one in particular. He held his breath as it broke the surface as a massive geyser, shooting water one hundred feet into the air and knocking everyone to the deck with its concussive blast. The closest ship rocked hard to starboard and threatened to roll, its motors screaming, trying to back away from the massive eruption.

The water reached a peak in the sky and turned, hammering down on the boats like a waterfall. Paul clung to the railing, feeling the water pounding the air out of him, trying to drag him into the ocean with raking hands. He held his head tucked under his straining arms to shield it from the blow, praying the beating would end. Water filled his ears and nose, deafening and smothering. He felt the boat shuddering with the punishment. His grip started to slip as water forced itself between his fingers, prying them from the railing. He realized the water was going to win, and then suddenly it was gone.

He struggled to his knees, gasping for air, shaking. Waves buffeted the boat from every direction. Crew members threw ropes to help anyone that was cast overboard. One Naval ship was listing to its side and another ship rushed in to help keep it afloat, fighting the treacherous sea.

* * *

Far beneath the surface, Mr. Hahn watched from a thick glass window as Portus collapsed within itself. A trail of bubbles marked the path his warhead forged to the cliff. Not a soul came out of the cave. They must be inside.

He smiled in grim satisfaction as he pictured the traitorous group being ground to death in the collapsing rocks. Perhaps he didn't capture the girl, but they were close enough without the Arydians. Killing them all was the next best option.

As his sub backed out of the rocks, his eyes widened in panic. He saw orange clouds boiling out around the disintegrating cliff. Frantically, he ordered the sub to drop as the blast field expanded, hitting the top of his sub and throwing it spinning into the deep.

The walls of Portus folded in on itself, erasing its existence away. The explosives were set in strategic places to simply collapse the caverns, but the missile Hahn had sent penetrated deeper into the earth. The volcanic vent that sustained life for the Arydians complained and reached out to touch its sister, the San Andreas Fault for justice. Together they united to punish the earth for daring to disturb them.

* * *

The trembling below the Star Chaser slowed for a moment and the water seemed to be recovering when the growling started again, deeper. Something shifted deep in the earth. Paul felt the water drop below him several feet at once and the ship dipped as if falling in an elevator.

Paul blanched and grasped the railing, praying another explosion was not coming. Instead, he felt the water dragging the boat away from the shore, piling up into a huge mass. Whatever happened below had triggered something huge. He fought his way to the cabin. Throwing the door open, he locked eyes with the captain, and realized with a chill that they both knew what was coming. The captain turned the boat out to sea and pushed the engines, screaming with speed, to race the tide, praying to get past it before the giant wave formed a crest. They sent a warning out by radio to every channel they could think of.

Paul felt another concussion shake the boat and they slid down the back side of a surge of water that swelled up between the Star Chaser and land, racing toward the shore like a train. The swell continued to grow until it blocked his view of the coast. He watched it break against the shore where the sand picked up the wave, land moving like water in a hump that travelled inland in a long, ropy line. He realized in awe that he was witnessing the sine wave of an earthquake. Dust and debris filled the air of the coast in seconds. He closed his eyes and offered a prayer for anyone in its way as they sailed west as fast as they could to escape the inevitable tsunami that would soon follow. All hope died in his heart of ever seeing Marin again. Nobody could survive whatever happened down there.

* * *

Forty miles away, Malcolm and Ahsan felt the shock wave arrive several minutes after the explosion. The impact pushed them west with much more force than they anticipated. Lights dimmed and flickered inside the cabin and they could hear the alarmed voices of their passengers trying to keep their footing as the sub rocked unsteadily.

Noburu left his son and made his way to the front and entered the cabin. "Did we do that?" he asked in disbelief.

Malcolm scowled, concerned. "We didn't have that much firepower in there. It was just rigged to collapse the tunnels and bays."

Noburu blanched. "We must have triggered something in the thermal vents," he whispered, horrified.

* * *

Marin was feeling dizzy and nauseous, but she didn't want to tell anyone, knowing they would stop what she was doing. An annoying buzzing was filling her ears, and her lips and hands felt numb but she didn't care.

It should have been her. The pain of this thought made her breath came out in a sobbing gasp. She couldn't bear the thought of Marcos, kind, innocent Marcos, dying for her. Surely there couldn't be that much injustice in the world. She'd already watched Jaycen die in front of her and come back—she had to believe Marcos could do the same. She willed whatever was in her blood to knit him together and bring him back to her.

The sub rocked, rolling her closer to him, and the lights flickered. She could hear gasps of alarm and children calling out, crying for their parents. She reached out to hold Marcos's hand. It was cold. The sub shook again, tossing people to their knees. She felt her stomach constrict, and she realized she was going to be sick, but the buzzing grew deafening and her world went black.

* * *

Paul's phone rang constantly with calls of help for Search and Rescue but with no way to help, he had turned it off until he returned to shore on board the Star Chaser. As it pulled up to the remains of the dock at COAST, everyone was stunned at the devastation caused by the earthquake and subsequent tidal surge. Half of the building had fallen to the sand. He could see inside like it was a doll house with the back taken off. Furniture, computers, life vests, and papers lay strewn like flotsam across the debris-filled bay. The warehouse doors were still intact, but the company yacht had rammed the large main door, buckling it inward.

The boat was on its side, taking on water and leaning against the door sideways.

He looked around at fallen trees and sunken boats numbly. Somehow, the sight of the destruction didn't shock him. In that single instant when Marin was torn from him, his whole world was demolished, outside as well as in. The city looked like he felt; crushed, mangled, wholly and completely destroyed. While the crew tried to tie up the ship, he numbly turned on his phone, doubtful if he could answer the calls even if he wanted to. It buzzed with a text.

This is your only chance: 33.682068,-118.597412, 1900

He frowned, staring at the numbers. He thought maybe it was some spam that had gotten through his firewalls and was trying to give him his lucky numbers for the day. He was just about to push the delete button when the clock on his cell caught his eye. It had just switched to 1800, military time. 1900, seven o'clock? He looked carefully at the other number, his heart throbbing. Instantly it came into focus. The other numbers were coordinates. He jumped up the steps, squeezing in past the captain and raced to the navigation charts. Quickly chasing the numbers down, he found himself looking at a point in the open sea directly between Santa Monica and Santa Catalina Island. If he left immediately, he could be at that point by 1900 hours. But why?

Who sent that text? Dr. Gilbert? Or Marin? For a moment he felt a spark of irrational hope. Shaking his head, he was needed here, in the city. It was his responsibility. The coast was hammered. Every able body in Search and Rescue and any other branch of public safety would be on call. He walked out to the leaning pier, hopping over the several missing boards until he could see the parking lot of COAST. The space he parked in was now covered with part of the northern wall of the main building. His truck was demolished, crushed like a tin can. It made his decision that much easier.

The lights were out when he went inside the warehouse, water sloshed against his feet, but he made it to the smaller bay door and strained against its bent frame to open it just enough to pull out an open bow boat. He entered the coordinates and set off through the clogged bay and into the open sea.

A little more than an hour later, he pulled the boat into a holding position, circling the coordinates, feeling like a fool. There was nothing in sight for miles around and his boat was extremely low on gas. He didn't have enough to make it back to COAST, and it was doubtful whether he'd make it back to dry land at this point. He was hungry, exhausted and emotionally spent, plus he was feeling the beginnings of heat stroke from lack of water and too much sun. Behind him, fires burned in the hills around Los Angeles, filling the sky with columns of smoke that turned the air an eerie amber in the twilight sky. It reminded him of the look in the air the morning he first saw Marin. Wiping his eyes with the back of his hand, he turned off his motor, determined to wait another five minutes before trying to get back to shore. He crossed his arms over the steering wheel and closed his eyes.

A sound startled him awake. Darkness had fallen around him. A chilly wind blew against his sunburned face. His watch read 2100 hours. He'd been asleep a long time. He scanned the horizon, seeing nothing to account for the humming he was feeling in his feet. He began to panic that it was the beginning of another earthquake. Behind his boat, the water began to rise, pushed up by something unseen. His blood was pounding in his ears as he prayed, *please, not again.* He didn't think he could survive another explosion and hammering like he received earlier. The water continued to bow upward until the black hull of a strangely rounded sub breached, rising above the surface of the ocean. Paul blinked in surprise. A hatch opened above the choppy waves and a man got out and moved toward him.

"Gilbert?" Paul said, not believing his eyes.

Frank nodded, smiling. "Need a lift?"

TWENTY-EIGHT

Night had fallen, and the sub was quiet. The lap of waves could be heard through the open door, and warm night air spilled in. Most of the people on board had chosen to sleep outside after the two harrowing days they had spent crammed together in the sub. Jaycen sat near Marin as she slept deeply, still oblivious to the changes to her world. He hoped when she woke he wouldn't have to be the one to tell her about *him*, because he knew it would be one of the first things she would ask about. He pushed the dark thoughts away, looking at her and loving her, yet feeling so far apart. Her hair had grown over the past few weeks and fell in a wavy golden brown tumble around her face. He wanted to reach out and touch it, and hold her like he had before, but so much had happened that he doubted they could ever find their way back to where they once were.

He swallowed hard, knowing someone would have to tell her about Marcos. It was obvious she cared about him, but impossible to tell how much. But there was nothing he could do. His path was set before him, and it led away from her. He sat and watched her sleep, wishing he could find a way for things to be different.

* * *

Marin could hear seagulls crying. She opened her eyes and looked around her. Late afternoon sun slanted through the open door. Jaycen was near her on a chair with his head back, sleeping. Nobody else was around. She could hear the hiss of water on the sand, and the air was hot and humid. She was definitely still on the sub, but why was sunlight spilling in the doorway? And where was Marcos? Marin closed her eyes and shook her head numbly. She didn't want to think about warm and beautiful Marcos, cold and dead. She thought of his strong hands, his dark eyes, and his charming accent. She couldn't open her eyes and face the truth, wanting to ask Jaycen, but fearing the answer. She tried to swallow and realized her throat felt like glue. She tried to make a sound but it died as a pathetic croak.

Jaycen snapped awake. "Marin?" he asked hopefully. "Are you awake?" He moved to her side, bringing her a glass. "Come on, try to drink something," he said gently.

Reluctantly, she swallowed, easing the discomfort in her throat. Her head felt heavy and slightly ached, but the drink felt good. Jaycen sighed with relief.

"What is this?" she questioned, looking at the murky grey drink.

"It's water mixed with coconut milk. It's really good for you, has a lot of electrolytes. Really, Gatorade should market this stuff," he laughed softly. He watched her for a moment, his face turning solemn, and she wondered where the careless prankster was that she had first seen in him. His eyes looked stormy. Something bad happened; she could see it all over his face. With a cold dread she thought again of Marcos.

She sat up, leaning against the curved wall for support. "What happened?" she asked, staring into her glass, bracing herself for the news.

He shifted uncomfortably. "There was an accident. An explosion and an earthquake," he said quietly. "We are on an island off the coast of Mexico. We had to come up for repairs. It hit us pretty hard."

"What? How?"

"It's bad. The Arydians blew up Portus to destroy the evidence. But it got way worse than they ever imagined. It triggered something and it looks like the San Andreas Fault slipped. The whole coast is a mess.

A tsunami wiped out everything for miles all along the coast. A lot of people got hurt. A lot of people died." His frown deepened.

Her breath caught as she thought about Paul. Was he okay? Was he alive? She couldn't even imagine what he would be thinking or where he would be right now. Jaycen seemed preoccupied and rubbed his face tiredly. She remembered belatedly that his mother lived in Los Angeles too. "Do you think your mom is okay?" she asked gently.

He shook his head. "There's no way to get in contact. Not without leaving." Jaycen said dismally.

She turned to him, suddenly aware of his gaze.

"He's still alive," he said abruptly, saying those three words were as if they were the signature on his heart's death certificate.

She looked at him, confused for a moment before understanding lit her eyes. "Marcos?" she asked, needing to make sure. Jaycen nodded mutely. Relief and joy flooded her face. She looked around the empty sub. "Where is he?" she asked, rising unsteadily to her feet. Jaycen stood beside her.

"There are some bunks in the back. He's alive, but he's still not good. His dad is with him." She moved to the sleeping compartment, needing to see him for herself. Jaycen cleared his throat. He tore his eyes from her, trying to keep his voice even. "Gilbert wants us ready to leave as soon as possible."

She smiled over her shoulder at him and opened the heavy door. There was only a small electric lantern on a table next to the bunk that Marcos was laying on. His chest was bare; his midsection wrapped in thick white bandages.

Malcolm glanced at her as she walked in. "You're better?" he asked, standing up stiffly. He grabbed her in a rough embrace and said with a catch in his throat, "Thank you for saving my son." He stepped back, looking into her eyes with gratitude. She wondered guiltily if he knew she was the reason his son had been injured in the first place.

"Is he going to be okay?" she asked, kneeling down next to Marcos. She took hold of his hand, wishing she could talk to him; to thank him for what he did for her. And if he died—because of her—she shook her head as tears started to form.

"Time will tell, my dear. But if we don't have faith, there are no miracles, eh?" he said with a smile.

She glanced up to see Jaycen in the doorway, his face set in a grim mask. His eyes turned cold at the sight of Marin kneeling next to Marcos's form, holding his hand.

He was turning to leave when a boy came walking in.

"They got connection to the internet. Dr. Gilbert said you should come take a look."

Marin gave Marcos's hand a squeeze and followed Jaycen out onto the beach.

Twilight was stretching out along the horizon. White sand glistened before her, tinged with pink from the sun. The sub had its nose buried in the sand, thick ropes tied off to rocks on the beach holding it steady against the calm lapping waters. She stood on a wide stretch of shore ringed with coconut trees heavy with fruit. A small fire burned, and it looked like everyone was seated around it, watching a laptop computer. They looked like an oversized group of castaways, ragged and barefoot. The ones rescued from Leviathan were easy to pick out, their skin was still tough and leathery looking. She wondered if they would always look that way. Carefully she moved away from Jaycen to the outside of the ring and listened to the news, watching the scenes of destruction in what used to be her home. She thought of Paul fearfully. How could anybody survive that kind of devastation?

"Fires still rage over parts of California along the fallen San Andreas Fault. Geologists identified several fissures that opened, one of which is spilling lava down the streets of Santa Clarita. The flow is moving southwest and appears to be pooling in Pico Canyon. National guard troops are being sent in to help with the evacuation," the anchorman was saying.

People sat silently, transfixed, the remains of a meal sitting around them. Everyone had the same look on their faces, though nobody said it aloud—what have we done?

She felt someone approach her, but didn't turn to look, assuming it was Jaycen. He came to her side and put a hand on her shoulder, turning her to look into her face. "Are you doing okay, Marin?" he asked.

Marin's eyes widened and she threw her arms around Paul, crying out in joy. He swept her up in an embrace, rocking her back and forth as they stood in the sand.

"How did you get here?" she cried and laughed at the same time. Paul wiped his eyes and nodded toward Frank, standing in the shadows a few feet away, watching the reunion wistfully.

"He told me everything. I couldn't believe you were alive! I was there after your sub went down, I saw the explosion … I just can't believe it!" He gave her another bear hug, sniffing back tears of joy. After a few moments, he released her and glanced over at Frank. "I know who he is." He chucked Marin under the chin, grinning. "And all this time, I thought he was my friend because he liked me. Shoulda known it was all about *you*," he laughed.

Marin opened her arm and motioned to Frank. Hesitantly he walked forward and she pulled him into the shared embrace of the pieces of her family. They stood close together as the wind settled, leaving the air feeling cool and moist.

"Thank you," she said, looking up at Frank.

Frank shrugged. "I bet you have a lot of questions, don't you Marin?"

Paul nodded understandingly and moved back to the circle around the fire to give them time alone.

"Let's go for a walk, shall we?" he whispered. They strolled down to the beach and sat down on the damp sand. Frank reached down and picked up a tiny starfish stranded on the sand, showing it to Marin in the moonlight. He tossed it into the surf and sighed.

"You know your name was really supposed to be Amanda, don't you," he stated rather than asked. She nodded and he continued, "Funny, but you've been Marin so long that Amanda doesn't fit you at all."

"So, Emily was … mom's name?" she asked tentatively.

He shrugged. "Yes. I called her Emmie. She called me Douglas. She and her family were among the few to call me that."

"So, where did Marin come from? I saw it on the wreck of the houseboat."

Frank chuckled. "Our boat was called the Mariner. I suppose you don't remember, but you helped me paint it on the back of our boat. Well, as much as a toddler could be of help, anyway."

She smiled. "I think I sort of remember that."

He sighed. "That wasn't long before the accident. We were getting careless and slow. It was foolish of us to let our guard down."

"So, they named me after the boat?"

"I know. It was ironic. The last part was melted away, but what was left became a very appropriate name. Did you know Marin means 'from the water'?"

She nodded as he looked out to the sea, the wind pushing his hair back from his forehead.

"Do you want to know why you are different than the rest of us, Marin?" he asked quietly.

She looked at him and nodded.

"Starfish."

"Huh?" she asked.

Frank stretched his arms and put them behind him to prop himself up. "It has puzzled me for years, but I didn't put it together until I saw the last sample of your blood. Your cells regenerate spontaneously." He listened to the waves for a moment before continuing.

"You were never given an injection of Arydia, but your mother and I both were, so you were born with the ability to breathe underwater." He smiled, lost in memories. "Anyway, your mother took these supplements she developed using starfish DNA before she got pregnant with you."

Marin wrinkled her nose. "Ew."

"Yeah, that's what I thought. I never took it. I'm not one hundred percent sure she knew Arydia was going to go wrong at some point, but

I think she was starting to suspect and was working on some way to counteract it. You see, she was the first to take Arydia and she was already starting to change before any of us even suspected there was a problem. Her hands were starting to get rough and her eyesight was changing fast. She was afraid it would happen to all of us eventually." He sat silently for a moment, watching the last rays of the sun stretching peacefully across the darkness.

"Starfish can regenerate, did you know that? Cut off one arm and another one grows right back. What your mother did was infuse you with DNA that regenerates. Then everything was destroyed. Like Leviathan, I thought the secret was in the Arydia treatment and bent all my research into trying to find out how to unlock what we had done to ourselves to find a way to reverse or change it." He picked up a rock and skipped it into the waves.

"When I finally put the starfish into the puzzle, it all came together. You see, Arydia changes your cells drastically, but your body wants to remain constant. After a while your body tends to want to stay in one form and you lose the flexibility to change back and forth. But you, my dear, are in a constant flux of healing. So in essence, Arydia is killing your cells, but your other DNA is healing them. Dying and being born simultaneously. That's quite a feat. Your mother was ... is ... brilliant."

Marin listened quietly to the waves for a moment then sat up in shock. "Is?"

Frank sighed and leaned back onto the sand, staring out at the stars blooming in the darkening sky.

"I'm sorry, does talking about her upset you?" she asked.

"Leviathan took her. The night of the accident. They knew she was the mind behind the drug Arydia. They used us against each other, promising to let the other go if we would cooperate." He let out a long breath. "I used to hear her. Crying, talking in nonsense, calling to me when I was underwater." He wiped his eyes gruffly. "I think she's, you know, gone now. I can't hear her anymore. I haven't for a long, long time."

Marin was silent for a moment, thinking of the torture it must've been for both of them, and mourning for a mother she never knew, and would never know. She put an arm around Frank and he hugged her back. A thought suddenly occurred to her.

"Wait. You were a prisoner? So how did you escape?"

"I didn't. I was sent back to COAST to further their development of the AQUA program. They sent me on a short leash, hoping that I would eventually lead them back to the rest of the Arydians even if I didn't find a formula to replicate Arydia. They had time on their side, and they knew I wouldn't go anywhere with Emily in their hands as leverage." He looked over to her. "And with me in their pocket, they had complete access to COAST and all its resources, which they wanted.

"Did you know COAST belonged to your grandfather? I was raised there. It was our family business, though at the time, it was more of a fish hatchery," he said with a wistful smile.

"What happened to him?" she asked.

He shrugged. "They killed him."

She shuddered. "So, what do we do now?"

He smiled, his teeth bright in the fading light. "We go to our new home. Arydia. You know, like Europeans live in Europe, we thought Arydians should live in Arydia. We've been working on this project for a very long time." He sighed. "It makes Portus look like the foul rock it was. We've known for years that we would have to relocate. Portus was just meant to be a jumping off point anyway."

Someone approached from behind them. Frank sat up, alert, but it was only Jaycen.

"Can I join you?" he asked, sitting down next to Marin when Frank nodded.

"What's on your mind?" Frank asked.

Jaycen sighed, unsure of how to begin. "I have to go back," he said, avoiding eye contact with them both. Marin stopped breathing.

Frank didn't say anything for a moment. The cool air pushed gentle waves up against the sand. "I don't think you realize the danger of going back, Jaycen," he finally said.

"It doesn't matter the danger of it, Dr. Gilbert. All my mom has is me. If she's hurt or anything has happened to her, she's got nobody to take care of her. You people destroyed her world. I have to go help."

Frank sighed. "Jaycen, we did not mean for this to happen. It was never our intention to do any damage other than to cover our tracks. There was no way to know it could trigger something like this! Nobody wanted this to happen!"

"Still, this is the world we have now, isn't it," he said bitterly. "I can't turn my back and run like your people can. I have to find my mom and help her. "

Frank tried to keep his voice calm. "Jaycen, Leviathan isn't going away. It's like a cancer, growing deep inside many different countries, with resources you can't imagine. We have only bloodied their nose at best. They will hunt down anyone that had anything to do with us. And now we may have a hope that they think we are dead. At the very least, we know they don't know where to find us. If you go back, you will be endangering all of us."

Jaycen spoke, his voice cracking with strain. "Nobody could find me in the mess California has become. I can get in there and get her out before they can find her."

Frank turned to him slowly, his eyes sad. "You can't help her," he said. "I know what I'm talking about, trust me. If she is alive, they will find her. Then they will keep her as bait. They *want* you to come. You can't go back!"

"I can't just leave her! She has *no one*! Don't you understand that?" he cried furiously.

"I understand better than you know. But what will happen to us, to Marin," he said pointedly, "when you get captured? You know too much." Frank stood and brushed the sand from his legs and started back to camp. He paused for a moment and looked over his shoulder. "I'm sorry, Jaycen. I really am."

TWENTY-NINE

Jaycen sat on the sand next to Marin, staring at the sapphire waves caressing the beach and retreating. He was quiet, his thoughts lost in fires, earthquakes, pain and loss, all so far away from the gentle peace of the here and now.

He couldn't tell if he was lost in a dream or a nightmare. Somewhere out there, his mom was suffering, and he knew he had to help. Yet here he sat on the shores of paradise with the girl of his dreams, but nothing could make it perfect.

He turned to watch Marin, her face bathed in moonlight, staring up at the stars, worried, just as he was, but more complete with her father, Paul, and even Marcos. She turned to him, looking in his eyes. Something she saw in them changed her expression to dread. "What are you thinking about?" she whispered.

"I'm leaving," he said quietly, searching her eyes for the love he wanted so badly to see, to take with him.

"No, Jaycen." Her face filled with fear. She shook her head. "No. Didn't you listen to anything he just said?"

"I have to, Marin. I can't leave her alone in all that." He gestured to the east.

Her voice tightened and he could see her mind racing through all the reasons she could think of to stop him. It wouldn't make a difference. He had been through them all himself and always came up with the same conclusion. She got to her feet. "They'll catch you, Jaycen. Don't go!" she pleaded frantically.

"How can I stay?" he asked, rising to stand by her side, wishing she could supply the answer. Knowing it wouldn't matter if she did. He shook his head. "What kind of man would I be if I just left her alone? My own mother!" he demanded, suddenly angry. Angry at himself, angry at her, angry at a world that wouldn't give him a chance to ever attain the love of his life. "What would *you* do if Paul was left behind, huh? Just swim away to your new place and forget about him?" He gestured to the dark waves. "The person that raised you and sacrificed so you could have a good life, just forget about that and walk away? Is that what you want *me* to do?"

Marin's face went white. She shook her head vehemently. "No, Jaycen. But, it's not the same! You can't go! Can't you see it won't do any good?"

"How do you know that?" he challenged. "I can get to her before they do. I have to at least try!"

"And then what?" she asked. "Where will you go? Do you have the resources to hide from Leviathan for the rest of your life? They will find you!"

He reached into his pocket and pulled something out. A small, capped silver hypodermic needle rested in his open palm. "I'll change her."

"Where did you get that?" she gasped. "If you are caught with that, Leviathan has everything it needs!"

He looked down for a moment then caught her eye, defiant. "I stole it from Gilbert. After he changed Paul," he said pointedly. She stared at him then closed her mouth, her argument fading on her lips.

The wind kicked up swirls of sand around their bare feet, crying through the palm trees mournfully. "I don't want you to go," she said quietly, looking down at his suntanned feet dusted with white.

He stepped closer, placing his hand on her shoulder. "I don't either. But it doesn't change the fact that I have to." His voice caught, close to tears. "I have no choice."

He could see her eyes let go of hope as the reality of his situation sunk in with the knowledge that nothing she said could stop him. Her last argument was the worst and she said it softly, as if not trusting herself to look at him.

"You'll never find us again." As she said it, the truthfulness settled like darkness around him. Whether he succeeded or not, the moment he left it would be as if he had died. The ocean was immense, filled with unknown dangers and huge carnivorous creatures. Nobody but Noburu and Malcolm had the exact coordinates to where they were going, and they certainly wouldn't give that information out, especially to someone who very well could be walking into Leviathan's arms. If they had any idea he was thinking of striking out on his own they would probably disable him immediately to protect themselves. He could tell part of her was thinking of yelling to them just so they would stop him, but he put a pleading hand on her arm to stop her.

"No, Marin." She dropped her gaze to the sand and swallowed hard.

"You will never find us again," she repeated, breathing it out, as if hating every word. Hot tears spilled out of her eyes.

Jaycen had nothing to say. He knew what she said was true. There would be no coming back. The thought made his blood run cold. *Never.* What a terrible word. A closed door, a cliff wall, a tomb. Never. It didn't change anything. He still had to go. But now he knew there would be no return. He pulled her into an embrace, hating the world for destroying whatever chance they may have had together.

She folded into his arms, tears soaking into his shirt. "Please, no, Jaycen," she cried. "Wait until we get to Arydia. Then you can find your way back to me."

"Marin, if she is in trouble, she needs me now. I can't afford to wait."

He held her tightly, feeling her close against him, smelling her hair against his cheek. Her heart was pounding hard against his chest, and he smiled to himself sadly, knowing, at last, that she cared. It was almost enough to stop him from going, or to make her come with him instead of leaving her behind to be with Marcos. But he knew he would be haunted all his days if he didn't go back, and he had no right to take her from her family into the danger and horrors of the Armageddon that California had become.

Staying wasn't an option, either. Whatever life they had would be tainted, poisoned by the knowledge that he didn't try. It would destroy him, and he knew it. He leaned in closer, willing his heart to merge with hers, to join together and never part.

Movement caught his eye as the fire was scattered. People were destroying all evidence of their stay, preparing to leave.

"I have to go. Now. It's my only option," he said, his voice cracking, forcing his arms to release her. He leaned down and tilted up her chin with his hands, kissing her softly and pulling her away. "Marin, I will always love you."

He walked into the water backwards, watching her standing on the moonlit beach, silver tears tracing down her cheeks, her hands covering her mouth. She took a step forward as if to follow him, but he shook his head, paused, drinking her in with his eyes for one last time, then turned and dove into the waves. She stood there staring out into the empty sea, eyes blurred with tears, and he was gone.

ACKNOWLEDGEMENTS

Just as it takes a village to raise a child, it takes many people to create a story. Books are like a painting; a result of a palette of ideas, experiences, personalities and feelings an author gathers throughout life. Each person who touches them leaves a little imprint of color behind that can change the hue of the entire story. I'd like to thank everyone who added shades to my life's story, and particularly those whose brush marks are on this book you see before you. My sweet husband, Kelly, and my boys, who have been my life and joy and support while I lived underwater writing this book, adding ideas and thoughts along the way; my lifelong friend Karen Gruszkiewicz, who has been listening to AQUA since it was just a dream and is an amazing writer herself; Polly Lore and Vicky Despain who have always been anchors in my storm; Carol Barratt, who hammered out plot points with me on bike rides; my beta test subjects; Erika and Josh Brotherton, Natalee Bernardo, Lyndell Laherty, Jenny Parkinson, Cleoh Moses, Cheryl Reeves, Debra and Holly Thompson, Geri Anne and Jake Larimer, Paige Dunleavy, Alyson Johnson, Crystal and Jenny Fisher, Rebekah and Katie Williams, and Sarah Parkinson, who read the first drafts and shared their ideas, edits, and enthusiasm with me; Anna who is living Marin's life and Allie who has the soul of a scientist; Kirk and Jana Tryon and Nan Gardner for letting me bounce ideas off them; Mark Barratt, for his excellent advice; Lynne Hepler, who has helped me take this book from concept to print with her years of writing experience and encouragement; the youth I've taught over the years whose excitement for life was so contagious; Jake Vasquez from Dallas LDS Books who asked the right question that set me on this path; the team from Snowy Peaks—Kirk Edwards for seeing potential in this motley collection of words, and Heather Godfrey who helped me tie those words together correctly. Mostly, I have to acknowledge the people who had the longest time to color my world; my big, wonderful family of brothers and sisters, in-laws, cousins, nieces, nephews, uncles and aunts … but particularly my parents. To my Mom, who taught me to work hard and move forward without fear; and my fisher-Daddy, who taught me to love the water: This book is for you.

**Stay tuned for book two in The Arydian Chronicles, *Aura*
Released Fall 2017**

Mr. Hahn loved the color white. Every article of furniture in his opulent penthouse in the heart of Washington D.C. was white. The walls were white. The bedding. Even the appliances. The only color to offset the starkness of his home was the glassy black floor, black rugs, and black drawers in his bedroom. The effect made the room seem taller than it really was; the walls and ceiling having an ethereal feel, while the floor felt dark and foreboding. A heaven and hell as it were.

As Nate Greer walked for the first time into his boss's sanctuary he felt an odd sense of vertigo, as if the floor was a dark pit he was about to fall into. He did not relish his new assignment as Mr. Hahn's personal assistant and bodyguard, especially since it had been rumored that the position had only become free after the last assistant had been drowned.

Walking through the halls, he heard a strange gurgling coming from what looked like a bedroom. Could Mr. Hahn be in trouble? He stepped quickly into the room and stopped short in surprise. A massive tank lined a bank of windows against the far wall. Colorful fish darted though forests of kelp over six feet tall. Larger fish prowled along the rocky depths. It was easily the largest and most magnificent fish tank he had ever seen.

The light coming through the window cast the room in a greenish blue haze, beautiful and otherworldly. Movement caught his eye at the base of the kelp, and his eyes were drawn to a dark shape lurking on the bottom. He stepped forward, mesmerized by the size of the crea-ture at the bottom of the tank. He crouched, squinting to get a better look at the monstrosity when a webbed hand snapped out of the kelp and crushed a passing fish against the glass. Greer stumbled backward, overturning a chair in his haste. The fingers splayed against the glass had thin, yellowish membranes connecting them together.

As he watched, the fingers closed around the struggling fish and brought it to a face like nothing Greer had ever seen. Large eyes pro-truded from its head like ping pong balls. Wispy hair lifted from the scalp like black seaweed, swaying in the current. The hand moved closer to the creature's mouth, which opened to reveal unnaturally sharp, jagged teeth, which ripped the head off the fish, leaving tendrils of fish guts floating out of its severed body.

The eyes of the creature met Greer's, sending chills down his spine. The horrible mouth moved into a wicked smile, and the hand beckoned him closer. Was this thing trying to communicate with him? What kind of crazy monstrosity was Hahn keeping in here?

Greer crept closer to the glass. The creature gestured to the side of the room where a Plexiglas stepladder led to a platform at the top of the tank. Hesitantly, Greer stepped up the ladder, keeping his eyes trained on the creature. As he reached the top, the creature kicked its powerful legs and shot to the top of the water, breaking through with a splash and landing on the platform. Water cascaded down the side of the tank and into a drain concealed in the floor. Greer held tightly to the railing to keep from running from the room screaming.

"My appearance repulses you," the creature said flatly, reaching for a towel. "Good. That means you were not told about me. Above all, I admire the ability to keep secrets." Greer swallowed hard. This wasn't Hahn's exotic pet-it was Hahn himself! He realized Hahn was waiting for him to speak. He forced his throat to move past the lump in it.

"Thank you, Mr. Hahn. You can trust me to keep your secret."

"No. I won't. You will keep my secrets because you know I will kill you if you don't. That is where I lay my trust." He moved further onto the platform, forcing Greer to move down two steps. "I require my treatment before we speak further. Please bring me the syringe on the counter there."

Greer cursed his hands for trembling as he reached for a large hypodermic needle filled with green liquid.

"You have medical training?" Hahn asked, though Greer suspected he already knew the answer.

"Yes, sir. I am …was …a surgeon."

Hahn's bulbous eyes appraised him and he felt every word he said betrayed the terror and regret he was feeling. "Good. Inject me in the brachial artery of my left arm. It is quicker that way." He offered Greer his cold, damp, green-tinged arm.

Greer found the artery and made the injection. Immediately, Hahn began thrashing, moaning in agony. He pushed off the platform and fell back into the water, churning bubbles with his violent spasms. Alarmed, Greer ran to the top of the platform, debating whether or not to jump in and rescue his new employer. Before he could act, the movement slowed and Hahn resurfaced, looking completely different. His face was swollen and puffy, and his eyes were extremely red but no longer protruding. Reaching out a hand to the edge, Greer noticed the webbing between fingers, while still there, was less pronounced. Hahn reached out his hand and Greer bent down to drag him up to the Plexiglas platform. Hahn wrapped a towel around his thin, naked body.

"Fetch me my clothes and then we will talk."

* * *

The tank bubbled weirdly in the darkened room. Greer's heart was pounding, but he didn't know why. His employer would be back soon, his serum wearing off, and Greer was preparing his medications. The serum that changed Hahn was kept under lock and key. Nobody had access to it but Hahn himself.

The hairs on the back of his neck began to rise as his unease heightened. Of course every move Greer made was watched; crime lords are not known for their trust. This wasn't cameras or microphones, it felt like someone or something was in the room with him. Movement caught his eye in the tank, and he stopped what he was doing, walking closer.

The seaweed was so thick it was hard to see anything in the glass enclosure. There! There it was again! A tail so long …how did he miss it before? What kind of fish did Hahn have in this thing?

In a flash, the creature darted out from the weeds and Greer stumbled back in astonishment. It was a woman! Long hair flowed behind her, greyish green. She rushed to the glass, pressing webbed hands to it. Golden scales covered most of her body from the neck down to her streaming twin tail. He got to his knees, mesmerized. The woman looked behind him, her glance darting around the room, nervously. Hesitantly he touched the glass where her hand was, half expecting her to turn and race to the safety of her seaweed forest. Instead she drew herself closer to the glass, eyes pleading with him. She mouthed two words soundlessly to him.

"Help me!"

ABOUT THE AUTHOR

Katherine Armstrong Walters has been making up stories since she was old enough to talk. She was born and raised in Salt Lake City, Utah, but moved to Texas where she and her husband, Kelly, have enjoyed living in the country and raising their five fabulous sons, two cats, one snake and a small herd of chickens. When she's not writing she loves sketching, editing, painting, reading, being outdoors, remodeling, and travelling with her family. Her favorite hobbies include boating and Star Wars.

Made in the USA
San Bernardino, CA
08 October 2016